PANHANDLE DREAMS

Gwen Parker Ames

Writer's Showcase
San Jose New York Lincoln Shanghai

Panhandle Dreams

Writer's Showcase
an imprint of iUniverse, Inc.

For information address:
iUniverse, Inc.
5220 S. 16th St., Suite 200
Lincoln, NE 68512
www.iuniverse.com

ISBN: 0-595-23473-9

Printed in the United States of America

For my son, Alexander Ames and Cushites Kyle Borel, Quincy Ewell, Leneice Flowers, Darren Harris, Femi Lovelle, Michael Manns, Daniel McGregor, and Sommer Wynn

Contents

Acknowledgments

Writing is a singular triumphant journey crossing many paths until one leads home. On the paths I crossed to "Panhandle Dreams" there were people and places that guided me. I owe them a debt of gratitude:

The Fresh Air Fund for giving me the impetus to discover my gift.

The OBC Chicks, Anita Atkinson, Gale Britton, Carla Fallen, Joyce Hobbs, the "Lindas" Hope, Walker and Wise, Jill Lewis, Michelle Murchinson, and Janice Phillips (you were always so wonderful, providing voices for the Panhandle Dream characters when I needed you to) All of you listened and offered support when the chips were up, down or unexpectedly turned around. You all are the greatest!

Writer's Relief (Ronnie, Barbara and the gang) for providing the kind of excellent professional support services every aspiring writer should have.

Rachael Lovett and Marie St.Louis for being my first readers/supporters.

Christine Brown for coaching me through blocks, bullies, and ballyhoo

Martin Luther King for giving his life to so many and leaving a legacy that continues to inspire

My husband Donald and son Alex the loves of my life who allowed me the space to develop that part of me that must be shared.

St. Paul Baptist Church for its "Joy in the Morning" early service and beautiful stain-glass window that served as my muse for two chapters.

Dr. Gail Tate for being a friend, scholar, inspiration and all around cut up, attributes which are all absolutely necessary throughout this process.

My friend Gilbert Walker who is playing the piano in heaven now but left me with fond memories of times we laughed until we cried and he played the piano until the spirit enveloped us both.

Professor Shira Birnbaum, Harriet Epstein, Lori Seader, and Jodee Yablon for generously sharing your Jewish history, rituals and family triumphs.

Brooke Campbell, Christina Sweeting and Jerry Speier for helping re-create the photo of dreams.

Sally Wecksler my agent for stretching right along side me.

Momnie, Jean, Trisha, Burt Jr. Kenneth and Aunt Beckie for being my family and inspiration.

A portion of the proceeds from the sale of "Panhandle Dreams" support the "Lending Library Project"

CHAPTER 1

"Like anybody I want to live a long life"

"The King is Dead" was scrawled in chalk on the asphalt of Campbell Street across from Bond School and the fish market. Magnolia and Indigo hardly talked as they walked the usually short distance to Nims Junior High School. Last night their world had changed.

The silence that kept Magnolia and Indigo from their usual chatter had begun yesterday without warning.

When they got home from school and put their books down, Madear had given them marching orders to go to the bread house on Monroe Street. Every Thursday they would pick up the family's supply of ten loaves of white Sunbeam bread. Thursday was discount day at the bread house. The bread house did not give out bags to customers on discount day. People would come into the bread house with big boxes and crumpled-up brown bags to carry the loaves of bread they purchased. The "no bags on Thursday" store policy did not make sense to Indigo. The bread house seemed to be making a lot of money on Thursdays. She was sure they could afford to give bags to all the people coming to take advantage of their "five loaves for a dollar" sale. If they did give bags on Thursday, it would sure ease some of her and Magnolia's embarrassing troubles. They had to walk through the college campus full of college students carrying empty brown paper bags one way and brown paper bags full to the brim with red-and-blue Sunbeam bread plastic wrapping sticking out on the way back. Indigo was convinced that all the college students they passed on their trips to and from the bread house knew they didn't belong there. She and Magnolia would practice various postures to blend in the college scene. The brown bags with Sunbeam bread sticking out at the top made it hard for them to keep their business to themselves. Mr. Avery, a painter on the campus, for sure knew their business. He was Indigo and Magnolia's biggest teaser. He always rode on the back of a truck with a group of other painters, who waved and yelled at the traffic going by. Indigo and Magnolia would be just about to cross the street of the "set" where all the students hung out, to get to their duplex down the hill with the Douglases' bread supply, when that truck and Mr. Avery would appear. A short stump of a man would pop up, with piercing eyes aimed in their direction and butter-colored teeth shining in a mouth that always looked ready to whoop and holler to let all in earshot know Daddy Douglas's seed had spawned.

Indigo and Magnolia would run the rest of the way home, embarrassed by the attention drawn to them while they carried those ten loaves of white Sunbeam bread. It was then Indigo started her litany of promises never to eat white Sunbeam bread when she was able to buy it.

The evening had begun with the usual Douglas family after-dinner script. Indigo had played tag outside with Davis Jr. and Blueberry until the lightning bugs and mosquitoes came out. She watched her Aunt Sadie get off the bus and wave to her in front of the rooming house across the street before going inside for dinner. She remembered looking at herself in the mirror as she came in the living room door. Aunt Sadie had given the big mirror as a Christmas present. She said every house needed a mirror at the front door.

According to Aunt Sadie, a mirror had boomerang powers to force any negative spirits coming in the door back out the door.

"You got to be careful about the kind of spirits you let in your house," she would warn.

Aunt Sadie always had a funny saying about what something or someone needed or did not need and why things were the way they were.

It was Magnolia's turn to wash dishes and Indigo was glad because they had ox-tail stew for dinner. She hated when dinner was over and the scrapings stuck to the pots. You would have to soak the pots and even after you finished washing the dishes, you would be facing another night of washing pots. And in Indigo Hyacinth Douglas's mind, double work was never necessary.

The Douglases congregated around the television set in the living room to watch "I Love Lucy" and "The Andy Griffith Show" after dinner. Indigo had taken her place next to Magnolia on the big green rug underneath the mahogany coffee table with the ceramic figurines of dogs and cats sitting decoratively next to the latest issue of *Life* magazine. She took a quick glance at the figurine of the Irish setter to make sure the glue was still holding after the last " knock-down drag-out" with Magnolia. She could not remember what their fight had been about because they were always fighting about something or another. Being eleven months apart, they just naturally got on each other's nerves was what Madear would say. Madear offered this explanation when she was about to soften a restriction Daddy Douglas would have imposed for fighting. This was the order of things in the Douglas household. Daddy Douglas had an orchard of hickory switches he would threaten you with and use if you stepped out of line while Madear presented, pleaded or pardoned your case.

Indigo's thoughts about the broken figurine and the possible punishment that was sure to follow were interrupted when her Daddy came in the living room. He took his place on the gold brocade sofa that maintained the outline of the shape of his slightly round body regardless of how much you fluffed the pillows. She fixed her eyes on the television set to avoid his eyesight. If you got in his eyesight once he got on the sofa, you would become the "go get me this child of the evening." The "go get me this child of the evening" would have to go and get everything from a pillow to make him more comfortable, a glass of ice water to cool his thirst, to whatever he thought he wanted that evening. The casting of the "go get me this child" was a sort of comedy routine that Daddy Douglas did every night. All four Douglas children would sit arch-backed, trying to keep all eyes glued on the television set to avoid his glances until he chose the "go get me this child of the evening." One night, Indigo was trying not to grin at Davis Jr. and Blueberry hurrying to position themselves on the green rug without looking at Daddy Douglas. They were trying hard to freeze the expressions on their faces fast to look like they were totally caught up in the television show. Indigo's face began to break up into a smile when she heard Magnolia mumble under her breath, "Go get it yourself." This made Indigo want to let out a belly laugh. The thought of her Daddy hearing what Magnolia was mumbling under her breath made Indigo's face contort with restrained laughter. He would be on Magnolia like white on rice if he heard her. They all knew Daddy was capable of getting whatever he needed. He permitted questions when he was in a good mood. Sometimes they questioned him about having to go and get him things. The answers would come in a voice that permitted the questioner to proceed with caution.

"A man just ought to rule his house," he would say repeatedly.

Nobody had to do much speculating to know that Daddy Douglas believed he had a right to rule his four children.

"These children got my mark," he would say to Madear when he was particularly proud of something his four children had done.

To add to Daddy Douglas's pride, it didn't matter where the Douglas children went, from Ash service station to the bread house on Monroe Street, everybody talked about how much the Douglas children looked alike. Blueberry was chosen the "go get me this child of the evening." She had playfully pouted while doing Daddy's chores and fallen asleep by the couch before the end of "The Andy Griffith Show." Davis Jr. tried to figure out a way to get out of washing off, even though he smelled like sweat and the green grass he played tag on earlier in the evening. Daddy Douglas had gotten up somewhere near the end of "The Andy Griffith Show" and went to his bedroom. Magnolia had gone to the bedroom and become lost in one of her Nancy Drew mysteries.

Since Magnolia had washed the dishes, Indigo had to sweep the kitchen floor. She was trying to stay on the green rug as quietly as possible, hoping Madear would forget about the last chore of the evening. Madear had a mind like a steel trap. No tricks went past her. If she told you something to do when you got home from school, you could count on her checking if you did it at the crack of dawn when she woke you up in the morning. Indigo was hoping the kitchen floor chore would slip Madear's mind. No sooner than the thought came into Indigo's mind, Madear appeared in the living room door.

"Indigo, the kitchen needs sweeping," she reminded with one hand on her hip.

Indigo clicked the dial of the radio to find a tune to dance and sweep to. Sweeping the kitchen was her chance to practice the latest dance step. She loved to dance but dancing with boys made her nervous. When she swept the kitchen floor, she forgot about being nervous. The black-and-white linoleum in the kitchen became her private ballroom. She could practice her moves or slow drag with the broom without worrying about stepping on a boy's foot or looking silly. That night Madear started yelling for Indigo to turn the radio down before she could even hear the name of the record Cousin the disc jockey was playing. Cousin was WTAL's colored disc jockey. WTAL played colored music between eight and eleven at night. Aretha Franklin was wailing "Chain of Fools" when Madear stood in the kitchen door with her hands on her hips, nonverbally demanding the radio be turned down. Indigo's hand went to the right of the dial instead of the left and Aretha went up at least three octaves belting out, "When I found out, yeah, I was a link in your chain." Madear's eyes got big and her body started moving in Indigo's direction when Cousin abruptly interrupted Aretha telling her man he treated her bad.

"Radio listeners, this important announcement just in...

"Radio listeners, Martin Luther King, the civil rights leader for freedom, has been shot."

Madear seemed to switch her big eyes from glaring to a look of shock and sorrow while motioning toward the radio.

"Lord Jesus," she whispered, crouching nearer to the radio.

Suddenly Cousin became the bearer of bad news instead of soulful tunes. The more he spoke of the shooting details, the closer Madear got the radio.

She kept asking Cousin through the radio, "They killed the man?"

The way she clutched her chest and moved closer to the radio made you think she wanted Cousin's 10,000 watts to blare an explanation to relieve the grief-stricken frown that had come upon her face.

Daddy Douglas got up from his snoreful sleep sometime during the announcement and stood next to Madear. You could hear the voices of unrecognizable wails outside in the night. Daddy thought he heard the pops of gunshots. The evening had turned eerie just as Aretha moaned she found out she was just a link in her man's chain. Indigo's mind flashed to the mirror in the living room across from the door. She remembered her Aunt Sadie's words about being careful of the kind of spirits you let in your house. Cousin's 10,000 watts had bypassed the mirror. Just the thought of his announcement and Aunt Sadie's sayings made Indigo forget about dancing altogether.

Through the curtains in her kitchen, Indigo could see the kitchen of the Benjamins' duplex next door. Peering out her window, she wondered if Cousin's 10,000 watts had vibrated the news of Martin Luther King's death in the Benjamins' house. Mr. Benjamin was pacing back and forth in front of the television set. Mrs. Benjamin was watching him pace back and forth while alternating holding her face in her hands. This scene in the Benjamins' house could have easily been the prelude to one of their nightly brawls. Everyone on the 400 block of Osceola Street knew of the Benjamins' nightly fussing and cussing sprees. They would settle down around the time of the eleven o'clock news. Madear said that was about the time that six-pack of Budweiser would catch up with Mr. Benjamin. The word around the 400 block of Osceola Street was Mr. Benjamin drank to cover up his sadness. Daddy said he had gone to the best colored schools in the country but he could not pass the state architectural test to get the license he needed to make him an architect.

Clyde Benjamin worked as an architectural apprentice for fifteen years, creating the designs for most of the buildings downtown. But he never got credit for them. That honor would go to the partners of Whittier, Krass and Pepper.

"He does the work and the whites get the credit" is the way Daddy Douglas would tell the story to Madear. Benjamin is a genius, I tell you! He can recite poems like he is on a record playing on the stereo." he would continue telling Madear Mr. Benjamin's story in a speech laced with annoyance.

"Benjamin always telling them where and how to build. They listen when they want to and take all the credit when they do. They going ahead and building that Meyer's building downtown, when Benjamin says the survey ain't right. It is worrying him. I told him why should you worry? You told them and they won't listen because they don't think you know as much as they do. If the building ain't right, it ain't his problem. If it is right, he doesn't get the credit, so why should he worry?"

Mrs. Benjamin would talk to Madear about her husband's bad luck at the clothesline in the back of the duplex.

"He didn't always used to drink so much," Magnolia had heard her say one day. "He thought his degrees were going to do so much for us. A house, fine car and all that went with a good job like that. It just wasn't meant to be. It's not his fault."

She and Madear would shake their heads, agreeing Whittier, Krass and Pepper should just go on and pay Mr. Benjamin as an architect with all the fine work he did for them. The fact that they wouldn't just made Mr. Benjamin drown himself in Budweiser every night. Even though Mrs. Benjamin told Madear her private business, Madear did not tell hers. She did part with her strict rule of "keep your business in your own house" to tell Mrs. Benjamin Aunt Sadie's husband had left her just after they moved to Tallahassee to get a fresh start. Madear made a point of saying Aunt Sadie needed a job to pay her rent at the rooming house or she'd be thrown out. Mrs. Benjamin passed the word on to Mr. Whittier's wife, Trin, at the architectural firm's Labor Day barbecue. Aunt Sadie started working for the Whittiers right away, cleaning their house and taking care of their daughter, Bethann, after she got home from school. By Christmas, Aunt Sadie had enough money to pay the rent and buy presents.

Indigo could not tell if the Benjamins' usual was unusual from her view of their duplex in her kitchen. Madear and Daddy's reaction to Cousin's radio announcement was strange. She didn't believe they knew him personally or were related to him. She went over it in her mind and ruled out ever seeing Martin Luther King come to her house or church or the family reunions in the country. To make sure, she went to her bedroom to ask Magnolia about him. Magnolia seemed equally bewildered but always pretended to know the answer even when she didn't.

"He's a civil rights leader," Magnolia explained in a 'it's a too grown-up thing for you to understand' tone.

"She makes me sick," thought Indigo. Magnolia would pull one of those 'I'm older so I know things that you don't know' tricks. Usually when she used this kind of tone it meant something big! And big, Indigo knew, could be bad. Indigo remembered the last time Magnolia used the "grown-up" tone. She had nagged her and paid her the dollar she had been saving for a month to tell her the "Santa Claus secret." Magnolia had not only told her Santa Claus wasn't real, she had proved it. She showed Indigo where Daddy and Madear hide the Christmas presents. The joy of knowing had not been joy at all. Indigo had to pretend to be surprised on Christmas morning when she opened her presents, even though she had already seen them. Christmas was never the same after knowing. The memory of the Santa Claus secret was like one of Aunt Sadie's sayings. Knowing the secret had taken the "J" out of joy. Indigo stood contemplating if she wanted to press Magnolia for the Martin Luther King information. She knew Magnolia's response could change a part of her world.

Dying or being killed was not something Indigo thought much about. Grandaddy Nate was the only death in the family she knew about. When the news came about Grandaddy Nate, Madear cried and cried. She worried herself sick thinking about Grandma Dovie being alone. Grandma Dovie's voice had pretty much died when she came out of the woods. She only talked to Grandaddy Nate. Madear was convinced the grief of being without Grandaddy Nate would cause the rest of Grandma Dovie to die too. Aunt Sadie told her, "Everybody gotta die." The only solution Madear could find was to move the mute Grandma Dovie from Port St. Joe to the 400 block of Osceola Street. When she came to live in the bedroom next to Indigo and Magnolia, sadness filled the air for a long time. Madear's tales of her mother's vivaciousness to Mrs. Benjamin at the clothesline did not match the vacant stare Grandma Dovie wore. Indigo was so afraid of her and of dying, it prompted her to speak to God directly after her nightly prayer recitation.

"God, Aunt Sadie say, everybody got to die, but I'm not like everybody...and I'm gonna use my mouth to say so...Grandma Dovie probably would too if she wasn't so sad...I like it here...Aunt Sadie said it's like going to sleep and never waking up...but if you never wake up how you know if dying is good or not? Everybody saying it's good Grandaddy Nate is finally resting.... I don't want to be like everybody...I'm like anybody who is thinking straight...It ain't good he's resting cause his resting caused everything to change...nobody wanted that. Anybody that's a Douglas wanted things to stay the same...And like anybody, I want to live a long life...Amen."

The sound of the radio and television going distracted her from propositioning Magnolia. Madear and Daddy hadn't made moves to close their bedroom or to put their nightclothes on. Grandma Dovie's room door was cracked and you could see her sitting on the side of the bed, staring aimlessly at the wall. Daddy Douglas was sitting out on the front porch in the rocking chair, holding the rusty rifle that had belonged to his grandfather and sat hidden in the back of the big closet covered up with blankets. He just sat rubbing the rifle propped across his shoulder with an old red bandana, muttering something about "colored being natural." The rhythm of the rocking chair marked time and prevented Indigo from drifting immediately off to sleep. She glanced over at the set of Dick and Jane reading primers her Grandma had given her when she first started to read. She considered losing herself in the adventures of Dick and Jane until she fell asleep. Their world always seemed so perfect and faraway from whatever troubles were brewing on the 400 block of Osceola Street, but tonight an adventure was not enticing. Her mind languished in and out of conscious thought as she wondered with the depth of her twelve years who was Martin Luther King and what spirit had his shooting brought inside her house.

Indigo's sleep was interrupted by the sound of the television and the radio blaring at the same time. A practice not usually permitted by Madear. She groggily sat on the side of the iron spring bed that frequently fell off the slants during one of her and Magnolia's pillow fights. She could tell the uneasiness that filled the air after Cousin's announcement had not gone away. Looking across the empty bed,

Indigo knew she could find Magnolia in the bathroom fixing her hair. Magnolia would comb then brush her hair and pull it through a rubber band until her ponytail was tight enough that her fine edges were laid flat and a snarled nappy kitchen of hair was hidden under her bushy mane. Magnolia did not offer her usual demand for privacy when Indigo knocked and entered simultaneously. She just moved from the mirror above the sink and sat on the toilet while asking Indigo matter-of-factly if she had seen Madear and Daddy. Indigo started doing the "pee dance," causing Magnolia to roll her eyes and quickly move from the toilet seat so that she could relieve herself. Before Indigo could answer her, Magnolia began reporting how Madear and Daddy, the Benjamins and most everybody on the 400 block of Osceola had stayed up all night talking about Martin Luther King being killed. Indigo couldn't imagine Mr. Benjamin talking straight about much of anything without his Budweiser in his hand. When he had that Budweiser in his hand, he spoke loud and pushed his chest out. When he didn't have it, he'd nod his head when you greeted him and continue a one-sided conversation with nobody and everybody, sporadically shouting "All hail, All hail thou shalt be King in the hereafter!"

Magnolia said there had been gunshots in the night and Daddy had gone outside with his old rifle and stayed a long time. Mr. Benjamin had gone with him. Madear and Aunt Sadie had prayed on their knees in the living room, calling Jesus like they were in church to come see about Martin Luther King's killing.

"And how you know all this, Magnolia?" Indigo demanded.

"Cause I got up last night when Aunt Sadie came over, knocking loud enough to wake up the dead. Everybody wasn't sleeping like a baby. Madear was so into Martin Luther King's killing she didn't even notice me. She told Aunt Sadie things gonna git harder for colored now that Martin Luther King was gone. I stayed up long enough to get the news," Magnolia smugly reported.

Magnolia's commentary combined with Indigo's uneasy feelings from the night before. Without warning, a gripping memory surfaced in her mind. Indigo's mind flashed back to when she walked along the edge of Osceola Street one day, kicking the russet-colored leaves of autumn, when a bright tomato-colored convertible Impala with a white top eased up beside her. She could still see the reddish pigment of the man with hair the color of the dolls in J.M. Fields department store, massaging what looked like the fleshy color of a pig's snout between his legs. The tone of his voice, emphasizing the word "colored" with nasty words she had only seen written on the walls behind the bleachers of the Nims Junior High School gymnasium, caused her face to flush with shame. His piercing eyes examining the budding contours of her deep-chocolate body and the subsequent thought of his invitation to come take a ride with him made her quiver. The memory of this day was a secret that only Indigo knew and involuntarily revisited when the well of her emotions overflowed.

The sound of Madear's voice summoning the younger Douglas children to hurry for school suppressed Indigo's memories and snapped her attention back to Magnolia and the bathroom discussions. Indigo knew she had to be careful because she was having a moment with Magnolia that could go either way. Magnolia was so proud of getting the lowdown news on Martin Luther King's shooting she would probably share it without cost if Indigo played her cards right.

"What was everybody doing outside?" Indigo slowly questioned.

"Talking...about how things might get real bad for colored people," began Magnolia. "Daddy said, 'King's gone now. Colored people gotta watch their backs and stand up for their rights.'"

"What rights?" Indigo wanted to know.

"Rights like..." Magnolia started to say before Madear came to the door, ordering them out of the bathroom.

Madear was offering more precautions over their grits and eggs for traveling to school than usual. Mr. Benjamin was getting in his car to go somewhere and Daddy was going with him. Aunt Sadie called on the phone to say she couldn't ride the bus to work with Madear cause Mr. Whittier was gonna come pick her up. Finally Indigo would get to see that big fine gray car with the seats that felt like cotton Aunt Sadie talked about. But everything seemed mixed up. Daddy hardly ever went anywhere with Mr. Benjamin. Madear and Aunt Sadie always got the bus going downtown together. Aunt Sadie was Madear's baby sister and she always looked out for her. Madear would go the county clerk's office where she was a clerk typist and Aunt Sadie would get the bus out to Killearn Estates, where the Whittiers lived. But today was different. The only resemblance of the ordinary was Captain Kangaroo looking for Mr. Green Jeans on the television set.

"Don't talk to strangers. If someone tries to talk to or follow you, run!" Madear instructed as they gathered their books to go out the door.

"Who's gonna follow us?" Davis Jr. wanted to know.

"Nobody...just make sure you listen and do what I tell you if someone does follow you," snapped Madear.

"Why we gotta run, Madear?" Davis Jr. persisted.

"Cause the world done changed overnight, Davis Jr...The King is dead."

CHAPTER 2

"Their destiny is tied up with our destiny"

As Indigo and Magnolia walked their familiar path home from school they shared moments of their school day, pointing out ways the news of Martin Luther King had been a part of each activity. They both remembered the crackle of Mrs. Boone, the choral instructor, her voice sobbing through her usually crisply enunciated recitation of the Pledge of Allegiance. Mr. Stone, the band teacher and patrol squad leader, had joined the patrol squad as they assembled for the daily ritual of raising the flag in the courtyard of the school.

The school was designed so that all the classrooms could see the flag ceremony that started each day at Nims Junior High School. Mr. Tucker, the principal had told Daddy Douglas and Madear during the school's orientation meeting for new students, the rising of the American flag was a symbol of pride and hope for tomorrow. Indigo and Magnolia vividly remembered the "pride and hope for tomorrow" speech they had gotten from Daddy and Madear on the ride home from the orientation meeting in the family's baby-blue Ford Fairlaine. Daddy and Madear had big dreams for their children. Magnolia was going to be a lawyer and Indigo was going to be a doctor. Davis Jr. and Blueberry were still too young to be talking about what they were going to be. But the dream work for Magnolia and Indigo would be reported at every family introduction, reunion and church gathering.

The Superintendent of all the schools in Tallahassee had come to be a part of the flag ceremony. Magnolia and Indigo both agreed the presence of Mr. Forbes, the superintendent, at the all-colored Nims Junior High School must have been because of the news of Martin Luther King. Mr. Tucker announced Martin Luther King was shot and killed last night before the flag ceremony began. He had everyone to bow their heads in silence.

Indigo never liked to close her eyes when someone said bow your heads because she wanted see how everyone looked and what their faces told about what they were feeling. She could see her substitute teacher had that same grief-stricken frown Madear had on her face last night. Minutes after Mr. Tucker declared the moment of silence was over, the flag ceremony began. Mr. Stone's eyes had stayed fixed on the diamond-folded flag during Mr. Tucker's announcement. When the patrol squad positioned themselves to begin unfolding the flag to raise it, Mr. Stone grabbed it, threw it on the grassy mound and jumped up and down on it. The hours of poised pride that the patrol squad practiced had not prepared them for this sight of their patrol leader's act of protest. They were dumbstruck.

The sighs and gasps of astonishment echoed throughout all the classrooms. Mr. Stone offered no explanation after his dance of rage and Mr. Tucker, the principal, attempted to offer an explanation in rambling sentences to satisfy the curiosity of the school children, but he too was at a loss for words. Magnolia said she thought Mr. Tucker was trying to lighten up the tomato-red color that had suddenly come over Mr. Forbes's face. No one could offer an explanation for Mr. Stone defiantly turning 180 degrees, balling his hand into a fist, raising it in the air and deliberately walking out of the school. He walked past the patrol squad of dismayed boys and girls, wearing starched white shirts tucked inside navy-blue pants and skirts, with orange patrol belts fashioned in a perpendicular configuration across their chests. His walk picked up a stride as he came near the cafeteria staff of onlookers, whose eyes seemed to dance with excitement but whose feet remained planted at their post of employment.

Time seemed to stand still as Mr. Stone turned the corner, in search of his next brave steps before the class bell rang and the day started again. All of the teachers included in their lessons a discussion of Martin Luther King's greatness. Indigo remembered how none of her teachers could finish their sentences without tears swelling in their eyes and anger rising in their voices as she and her mates sat not knowing what exactly to do or say.

Magnolia softened the heaviness of their walk by jokingly comparing the shooting of Martin Luther King to the hully-gully dance that their parents talked about when they put their 45s on the record player. Magnolia described how Daddy would jump to his feet and stand in a semi-crouched position when he heard a song by Bobby Blue Bland. He would throw his hands in the air and clap them real fast while yelling, "It's hully-gully time now!" Indigo's thoughts reflected back upon her father looking at his audience of four children.

"You children don't know nothing about the hully-gully...Now that's something."

He would tease all of them, grinning until his jaws were stretched tight across his face. Then his eyes fell on Madear with a look that made her giggle. The longer the music of Bobby Blue Bland played, the more Daddy and Madear seemed to be caught in some sort of hot trance that could make you dizzy if you looked too hard at them turning and swirling. Sometimes they would do that hully-gully dance, reach out and hold each other so tight that you could see salty beads of sweat running down their faces. They would act like they were in another world, with their eyes closed tight enough you could see thin lines of veins on top of their eyelids. They would stay embraced like that long after the needle had worked its way across the 45. Indigo compared being in the room with Daddy and Madear when they were in their hully-gully trance but not feeling what they felt to the unknown uneasiness that had surrounded and remained with them since the news of Martin Luther King.

As Magnolia and Indigo continued their walk home through the bamboo bushes of the path leading to Palm Beach Street, Indigo contemplated cutting across the parking lot of the Shriner Club. On the other side of the Shriner Club parking lot was the 600 block of Osceola Street. Magnolia and Indigo could get home faster if they went through the bushes next to the Shriner Club parking lot. Once she and Magnolia cut through the bushes next to the Shriner Club parking lot and saw Grandma Dovie standing near the bushes watching the Shriners line up in formation, wearing their burgundy hats that looked like upside-down flower pots. Indigo and Magnolia were too nervous to walk through the Shriner Club parking lot when they were wearing their burgundy hats. The looks on their faces said outsiders and children were not welcome. Grandma Dovie had wandered nearly two blocks from home. Magnolia tried to take her by the arm but she wouldn't come. She had that blank stare on her face. She didn't offer any words but there was nothing wrong with the strength in her arms. She let them know she wasn't going with them and they left her alone. When they ran all the way home to tell Madear, she didn't seemed worried.

She said, "Grandma Dovie just got it in her to wander. She knows how to find her way home."

Daddy said the Shriner Club was where men gathered to play checkers, signify and tell lies. The afternoon after Martin Luther King was killed, the checkers rested in a tin cup while men gathered around the front page of the Tallahassee *Democrat* lying on top of a checkerboard. The Shriners were absorbed in the headlines that announced "Drum Major for Justice Slain." Just beneath the headlines was a picture of a black man that Indigo was sure was Martin

Luther King. She and Magnolia walked briskly through the gravel parking lot amid the musings of Martin Luther King's killing. Near the bushes, a sweaty-faced man sat in the propped-open door of a green Cadillac, drinking from a pint-sized bottle. He startled Magnolia and Indigo when he unexpectedly stood up. Then he turned and looked them right in the face, bellowing words at first they didn't understand.

"It's a crying shame, white folks killed King!" they finally understood him to say.

"Did white folks kill Martin Luther King?" Indigo questioned.

"I don't know…probably…" Magnolia replied.

"Why?" Indigo insisted.

"Cause white people don't like black people," Magnolia suggested.

"Why?" Indigo continued.

"Because they don't!"

"Magnolia, how do you know this…you always know everything!" Indigo declared.

"Yeah, Miss Perry Mason, I do and I'll prove it to you. The light doesn't like darkness…when the sun goes down it gets dark…no matter how bright the moon is…that's the way it is," Magnolia persisted.

"What?" shrieked Indigo. "What kind of sense does that make, Magnolia?"

"It's true…just think about it," snapped Magnolia.

"I can think about it but I don't know what you talking about," Indigo continued as she glanced at the city bus coming up the hill of Osceola Street. It reminded her that Aunt Sadie would be coming home on the bus soon. She knew Aunt Sadie could make sense of Magnolia's commentary and give her the straight and narrow on Martin Luther King.

Indigo was so puzzled after her conversation with Magnolia that she quickly did her chores and went outside to sit on the steps of her duplex. She wanted to meet Aunt Sadie when she got off the bus.

Aunt Sadie could always make sense out of nonsense. If she stood on the bricks surrounding the flower bed of azaleas, she could see the blue-and-white Taltran No. 6 bus making its way up the hill of Osceola Street. Indigo anticipated the bus shifting gears and the gushing sound of the bus driver putting on his brakes midway up the hill across from the agricultural college's poultry farm.

The early evening cooing of the chickens in the rows of white clapboard houses would cause the passengers to turn their heads if the windows of the bus were open. Aunt Sadie said the sea of white feathers and melodic cooing sound of the chickens nestled and perched for the going down of the sun put her mind on what the way station for heaven was probably like…soft music…people dressed in white as far as the eye could see…eyes closed in a trance waiting to be called to sanctuary.

"Everybody won't get the same call," Aunt Sadie would say. "Some people going to get the call that many of the chickens in the college poultry farm got."

"What call is that?" Indigo had asked Aunt Sadie one day.

"The call of hot grease burning their chicken butts," Aunt Sadie answered with a big grin.

Aunt Sadie's comments made Indigo think of Madear's fried chicken. She loved fried chicken but somehow she knew the call Aunt Sadie was talking about did not give the same pleasure Madear's fried chicken did. The bus whizzing by the 400 block of Osceola Street startled Indigo from her thoughts of Aunt Sadie's description of the way station for heaven and fried chicken.

As she jumped down from the bricks surrounding the bed of azaleas, a white man in a sleek gray Mercury drove up across the street from Indigo's duplex in front of Miss James's rooming house. Indigo could see Aunt Sadie sitting in the back seat of the car talking with a white girl who had the sandy-beige color hair of the girl on the Sunbeam bread bag. Indigo sensed the man driving the car was "Mr. Whittier," Aunt Sadie's boss, and the girl had to be "Bethann," his daughter and Aunt Sadie's charge. Indigo imagined Bethann to be much smaller. Bethann was as big as Indigo.

"Go-Go, come help me with my bags," Aunt Sadie yelled across the street while getting out of the back seat of the big gray car.

Bethann jumped out of the car too. Mr. Whittier sat inside the car with his hands gripped to the steering wheel and his eyes fixed straight ahead. Glancing at him out of the corner of her eye, Indigo mused on the accusation of the drinking man in the Shriner Club parking lot.

"Was Mr. Whittier the kind of white man who would kill Martin Luther King?" she contemplated without certainty.

Abraham Whittier rarely took the trip from Killearn to the south end of town to carry Sadie home, but today was an exception. The news of Martin Luther King being killed had turned the town upside down.

"The Negroes are behaving foolishly, probably half of them didn't even know him," he thought to himself.

Deep in his bones Abraham Whittier wrestled with the relevance of Martin Luther King's notoriety and the injustices he fought against. During childhood, his parents secretly compared King's injustices to the ones they suffered and eventually escaped in their old country. Squeezing the steering wheel, he raised his voice silently to contradict the stirring in his soul that wanted to mourn the news of Martin Luther King. Distracted by the scenery of the 400 block of Osceola Street, he frowned and dismissed the death of Martin Luther King as not his problem. But the clamor of his parents' previous comment about Martin Luther King and the Negroes was ever-present in his mind and whispering in his ear.

"Their destiny is tied to our destiny."

Breathing a sigh of impatience with the invasion of Martin Luther King in his thoughts, his eyes met the stare of Indigo's contemplation.

"Get in the front, Bethann, your father wants to get back to Killearn,"Aunt Sadie prodded.

Bethann walked up to the side of the car where Indigo stood peering at Mr. Whittier in the front seat and tapped her on the shoulder.

"Hello, are you Go-Go? Sadie's told me all about you. I'm Bethann." Indigo turned toward her with a startled look on her face, nodded and scurried to pick up Aunt Sadie's bags. Mr. Whittier motioned for Bethann to get in the car and turned the key in the ignition.

Indigo had never heard a child call her Aunt Sadie, "Sadie." Her Madear didn't even call her just "Sadie." She called her "Baby Sister" or "Sadie Weatherstone" when she was angry.

"I don't want her calling me 'Go-Go,' she don't know me," Indigo protested to Aunt Sadie as they climbed the staircase to the rooming house.

"She can get to know you. People got to get to know people to keep the world going round, child," Aunt Sadie dead-panned.

"The world is going around enough already for me right now," Indigo thought silently, struggling to carry her aunt's bags of Whittier leftovers and hand-me-downs up the stairs. Usually Indigo loved to carry Aunt Sadie's "Whittier bags" in anticipation of all sorts of treasures. That day, anticipation had given away to speculation. The bag of "Whittier treasures" had faces. Faces that Indigo could not stop associating with the words of Magnolia and the drinking man in the Shriner Club parking lot.

CHAPTER 3

"We are not satisfied"

Walter Cronkite began the seven o'clock news reciting the "King is Dead" discourses that seemed to permeate everything and everywhere. News reporters on every channel mouthed the gloomy announcement and talked of the retaliation of enraged Negroes. Daddy Douglas and Madear sat with their eyes glued to the television set as Walter Cronkite upgraded Martin Luther King's killing to an "assassination." Indigo and Magnolia argued over the correct spelling of the word. They wrote "assassination" out phonetically and looked it up in the big *Webster's Dictionary* that Madear ordered from the white man selling *World Book Encyclopedias* and globes door to door last winter.

Madear had sworn to Aunt Sadie, "I'd buy the rattles off a rattlesnake if I thought it was gonna help my children learn a little more."

"Book sense don't make common sense," Aunt Sadie had warned her.

Didn't matter Madear bought three boxes of those burgundy books explaining everything from A to Z. They sat in the boxes in the hall closet for three months until she could get the glass bookcase off lay-away from the furniture store across town for them to go in.

Magnolia read the definition out loud.

"To kill suddenly or by secret attack."

Daddy Douglas and Madear looked at each other and shook their heads as Magnolia read the definition. Daddy Douglas had insisted the kitchen be cleaned up after Walter Cronkite's news report.

"Shoot!" Indigo protested to Magnolia. "I wanted to get the dishes out of my way before 'Wild Wild West' came on. I know Madear is gonna be complaining about that smell of fish grease in the kitchen and that grits pot is gonna take forever to clean," Indigo complained.

"You never clean them good anyway," Magnolia said smugly. "Anyway, Daddy Douglas said tonight news was gonna make history. We probably gonna have to do a report on it for school. We might as well watch it now and get it over with."

"You think so, Magnolia?" Indigo pondered. "I bet old Mr. McDaniel in Social Studies will make us do one too. He likes reports better than tests. He says writing lets you look in a person's mind."

"Be quiet!" Daddy Douglas bellowed.

"Magnolia, you and Indigo ought to set an example for your brother and your sister. You two need to be listening to this," Madear added, looking up from her quilting pieces.

"The sniper is believed to be a white man registered under the name John Willard in a flophouse adjacent to the Lorraine Motel. He is being vigorously hunted by law enforcement as Negro protestors hurl Molotov cocktails and burn cities to the ground," Walter Cronkite told America.

"Good!" Indigo spontaneously proclaimed, looking around the room at the Douglas audience. "Maybe things can get back to normal," she added.

"Normal?" Daddy Douglas replied in a throaty voice laced with hostility while rising up from his reclined position on the brocade sofa. "Things ain't never gonna be near normal again, little girl, and you better know that now!"

Daddy Douglas's voice began to elevate and anger seemed to come up from his belly to his face. His feet began to pick up a thudding step back and forth across the hardwood floor of the living room, knocking over anything in his path.

"Negroes ain't been able to have a normal chance. Just a normal chance will satisfy us! Just a chance to be men and we would be satisfied! King gave his life trying to get us that chance! They got tired of him so they kilt him! Trying to finding out who kilt King won't change nothing! Negroes will not be satisfied with just knowing the name of the one who took our only chance to stand up! We are not satisfied! We will not be satisfied until they give us a chance to be men! We gotta make 'em treat us like sump'em if we want to be sump'em! King died for that!"

Indigo wanted to grab her comments and stuff them back down her mouth. Daddy Douglas was beginning to sweat. His body had gone berserk. Fight was in his hands. Fury was in his eyes. In the lines of his face were a worry giving way to an unfamiliar shame that looked out of place in her Daddy's demeanor. The worry lines increased with the intensity of his stupor. His spew of emotions seemed to have come without warning from a place far removed from what was happening at that moment. The "Negro rage" the reporter spoke of on Walter Cronkite's broadcast had touched down in the Douglas's living room.

Madear quietly put down her quilting and walked toward Daddy Douglas's pathway of protest that now included a broken lamp reserved for the coffee table. At first, she spoke to him in the tone of a disapproving wife admonishing her husband to straighten up and fly right. When she could no longer keep up with the rhythm of his feet or recognize the rancor in his rambling, she switched to a 'Lord, come by here cause all hell done broke loose' tone.

Daddy Douglas had become so enthralled in his loud diatribe that white foam was oozing out of the corners of his mouth along with words of ire, giving no indication that Madear's petition for peace in any tone was penetrating. The front screen door slammed and Blueberry's eyes let go swollen tears that emerged when Daddy Douglas's riot of rage began. Davis Jr. sat on the floor with his head down and arms folded across his bent knees, peeking out occasionally to survey the eruption in the living room. Magnolia sat perched on the green vinyl stool, looking straight ahead at Daddy Douglas.

Just when Indigo thought she could not bear the drama ignited by her words any longer, Aunt Sadie entered the front door. She did a quick study of Madear's face and began ushering Davis Jr. and Blueberry to the back rooms.

As soon as their backs faced the threshold of the living room door, Madear jumped on Daddy Douglas's back, and started kissing, cooing and wrestling him and his mantras of pain and protest to the floor. Magnolia and Indigo sat bug-eyed, watching their mother give solace to their father in a way that Magnolia would later insist was reserved for when their parents locked their bedroom door. Grandma Dovie had been sitting in the rocking chair in the corner of the living room. When Madear tackled Daddy Douglas, she stood up. For a moment, there seemed to be a glimmer in her eyes as she walked silently down the hallway to the back porch. Indigo stood shaking, praying her nightmare in the twilight zone would soon be over. She didn't know Martin Luther King any better than she had the night before, but she had just learned speaking ill of him could turn things wrong side out. She wanted to go up to Daddy Douglas and hug him to let him know she wanted to take her words back. She wanted to make him stop being so mad. She wanted to let him know he was as normal as all the white daddies she saw on television. Most of all, she wanted to disconnect his display of feelings from Martin Luther King, which seemed to be at the center of all the commotion he unleashed in the living room.

Aunt Sadie yanked Indigo and Magnolia with a 'don't give me no resistance' armhold and led them out of the living room to clean the kitchen. Indigo followed as she watched Madear and Daddy Douglas lying in a heap on the living room floor. The Zenith floor-model television played to an empty audience on the big green rug as a reporter spoke about Martin Luther King in retrospect. There he stood in a dark suit wearing a fedora, speaking in a resounding voice that made you listen.

"And we just went on before the dogs and we would look at them; and we'd go on before the water hoses and we would look at it, and we'd just go on singing, 'Over my head, I see freedom in the air.'"

Magnolia and Indigo cleaned the kitchen in silence. Aunt Sadie busied herself in the kitchen straightening whatever there was to straighten. While the television set flashed a glimpse of Molotov cocktails made with gasoline rags hurling in the air, the eloquent sound of Martin Luther King's words floated beyond the television set and saturated the air of the Douglas duplex.

CHAPTER 4

"The cry is still the same..."

It was Saturday. Two days after the assassination, and the haze surrounding the news of Martin Luther King had not dissipated. Mrs. Whittier telephoned Madear to send word she needed Sadie to come help with preparations for their holy days. She could've called Aunt Sadie at the rooming house but the line stayed busy most of the time. When Sadie suggested Indigo come along to keep Bethann company, Madear hesitated at first but on second thought accepted the offer.

Friday night's ill will still had a residue in the Douglas household. Madear's relenting had more to do with her anticipation of the air space one less child in the house created than supplying a playmate for Bethann. Any other time she probably would have nixed the idea altogether. Her Momma didn't cotton to the idea of taking care of white people's children and she didn't either. Sadie, on the other hand, did whatever she wanted to do or had to do.

Indigo skipped through her chores when Madear came to tell her about going with Aunt Sadie. Her mind was racing. She welcomed the opportunity to get out of the house and go as far away from the 400 block of Osceola Street as she could to avoid hearing or saying anything else about Martin Luther King. The Springtime Tallahassee parade was going to start up Monroe Street at ten o'clock. She calculated if she and her Aunt Sadie hurried, they might be able to see part of the parade from their seats on the Taltran bus.

They stood silently waiting and watching for the Taltran bus to come up the hill. It was full of South side folks going downtown to spend their Friday paychecks. Aunt Sadie got on the bus first and tossed six dimes in the fare collector. She knew the bus driver wouldn't let Indigo pay the child fare. A quick eyeball of Go-Go's body pointed out she was too tall and the pimples on her protruding chest had started to swell. Cree said Go-Go got the high chest from her father's side. "I power" in her chest, she said they called it. "I power" nothing, the child was becoming a woman, Sadie snorted to herself. Watching Indigo run to get a window seat, Sadie smiled as she also noticed her butt was starting to spread. A trait she felt crowned the Weatherstone women: the men pet and women regret.

As the Taltran bus whined its way up Adams Street, Indigo could see some of the department stores had broken windows and paper was scattered on the commonly clean sidewalks. "No Justice No Peace" scribbled in black spray paint on the McCory's department store door window blocked a clear view of the lunch counter. For a moment, she thought she saw Grandma Dovie's lean frame and empty face standing at the McCory's store window. She tried to show her Aunt Sadie where she thought she saw her Grandma Dovie but the bus was moving too fast. Sadie minimized Indigo's sighting, waving her hand, saying, "Grandma Dovie is going to put herself anywhere a parade is scheduled to be. Your Grandma Dovie loves a parade. They remind her of when she was younger and her Momma and Daddy paraded around the river in Port St. Joe."

The colored women rushing in McCory's to do their Saturday shopping made it even more difficult to spot Grandma Dovie.

"What would Grandma Dovie be doing at McCory's? Could she be waiting for the parade?" she questioned herself. The parade hadn't started yet and Grandma Dovie didn't shop. "Maybe she's been thinking about what I've been dreaming," she considered.

Indigo had often dreamed of eating lunch and sitting on one of those shiny chrome red-vinyl-topped stools. She could almost smell the pile of Vidalia onions frying in grease next to the juicy red hot dogs on the griddle. At the end of summer, when she and Magnolia went with Madear to put their school things on lay-away, those smells would tantalize her nostrils to the point of making her mouth water. Madear must have realized her torment because she would always begin chattering about what she planned to cook for dinner. It wasn't just the aroma of the food from the lunch counter Indigo salivated over. When the waitresses in their crisp white dresses with black aprons scurried toward a customer approaching the lunch counter to offer the daily lunch specials, the ambiance delighted Indigo's eye. Eating at the McCory's lunch counter window with all the world on display was what she thought it would be like to be queen for a day.

"Grandma Dovie didn't even know what day it was," she decided.

The bus passing the window of the McCory's lunch counter offered only a quick look, but it was enough for Indigo to realize even her dreams had been touched by the omnipresent news of Martin Luther King.

Attempting to ignore her growing agitation with the Martin Luther King news invasion, she began to occupy herself by surveying the changing landscape outside the bus window. The more she looked out the window of the bus, the more she could feel her Aunt Sadie's eyes watching her. Sadie had knowing eyes. The kind of eyes that could draw out answers or silence questions. Answers were what Indigo wanted.

The bus route crossed over Tennessee Street and Indigo caught a quick glimpse of the colorful Springtime Tallahassee floats parked in rows waiting for the parade to begin. The tailpipe of the bus chugged and blew out black smoke as the driver made his way past the magnolia trees alongside the antebellum houses on Thomasville Road headed to Killearn Estates, where the Whittiers and most well-to-do white folks lived. The blooming dogwood trees sprinkled pollen alongside the road, reminding Indigo of Dorothy and the yellow brick road in the land of Oz. "The Wizard of Oz" came on television during the Easter season. Dorothy trying to get home to Kansas made Easter complete for Indigo and her siblings. She was thinking about Dorothy as the bus continued to make its way to the gates of Killearn. Dorothy wanted to get home and Indigo wanted home to be the same again. She wanted things to go back to being the way they were. It seemed like everybody had two feelings since Martin Luther King died. Either they were mad or sad. She was sick of both.

"Aunt Sadie, when is 'The Wizard of Oz' coming on television?" Indigo asked as she continued to look out the window.

"Well, we sho'll could use some of them little happy munchkins round here now, can't we?" Sadie teased while fussing with the plaits on Indigo's head. "Yeah, some of them little roly-poly munchkins could make us all feel better. Right?" she continued.

Indigo looked around to smile in agreement with Aunt Sadie when their eyes met, creating an opportunity for clarity.

"Your Daddy ain't mad at you, Go-Go," Aunt Sadie began softly. "His mad is hurt. Hurt he can't help. Hurt that happened long time ago. Hurt that ain't fresh but the cry is still the same. It keeps hurting cause it ain't healed. The madder he gets, the more he hurts. And the hurt just bleeds through everything."

"How he got hurt, Aunt Sadie, and why talking about Martin Luther King makes him so mad? What he got to do with Daddy Douglas hurting?"

"One question at a time, child," Sadie playfully snapped as she leaned back against the dark green naugahyde bus seat cover, closing her eyes, preparing to tell what Indigo knew was the untold.

As Aunt Sadie leaned her head back on the headrest, she blinked her eyes rapidly and the nasal lull in her voice pulled everyone in earshot closer to hear more. The warm rays of the sun beaming through the bus window were causing her to begin to sweat on her arms. The moist sweat mixed with the scent of the Jergen's cherry-almond lotion that she generously lathered on her body each morning just because she was a "woman" began to perfume the air. The way her body twitched in the bus seat and her foot tapped to the beat of the bus engine chugging along were sure signs of the "tell-it mood."

"Child, you old enough to begin to know something about life. People are like clay pots. Your Daddy, your Momma and me, we're human but we made of clay. When the currents of life bear down on us, we get fragile and almost get to the point of breaking." Passengers on the bus greeted Aunt Sadie's words with nods and uhmms. Some turned around and looked in her mouth as she began to spin a familiar story of brokenness.

Indigo remembered tidbits of her Aunt Sadie's "brokenness story" when she made a double discovery in the back of the cedar closet in her bedroom. She had just found the clothing she handmade for her doll when the enchanting sound of Aunt Sadie's voice spinning a story with Madear came inside her closet. The cedar closet shared a wall with the closet in Madear and Daddy Douglas's bedroom. The natural crack in the cedar wood gave a skewed view and moderate volume to what went on in Madear and Daddy Douglas's bedroom when their closet door was open. The crack in the cedar wall became the conduit for deciphering the perplexities in and outside of the Douglas household.

Sadie was full of stories of the past that shined light on the present. A lot of the stories were shared in Madear's bedroom and vibrated through the crack in the cedar wall. Born with a veil over her face, she was the baby of the family. Grandma Dovie said that veil gave her powers to see beyond the human eye. She could draw the likeness of anything and make it look real by the time she was old enough to walk. She made sense out of nonsense when most girls her age were still playing with rag dolls. But wise beyond her years did not extend to matters of the heart.

Sadie Weatherstone could catch the eye of a man and the scorn of a woman. She got most any man she wanted but didn't keep him long. The romance would start out hot like a fire created by two explosives but it would end quickly, simmering like wet coals. Her answer to trouble in paradise was, "Men are just like Taltran buses: if you miss one, another will be coming soon." For as much as this answer provided her with variety, she remained in a state of constantly starting over.

"Fortifying the soul," she called it. "If your soul ain't fortified, you'll be mortified when trouble come."

Through the crack in the cedar closet, Indigo learned how Sadie told her compact mirror those very words after she collected herself to walk out the door as one of her paramours lay sleeping off a Saturday night of liquor, licks and loving. Her walks had taken her from the deep south to the wide-open west and back again. And she had seen plenty. Her small hometown of Port St. Joe taught her fear of whites, but her travels away from Port St. Joe whispered fear was kin to fascination. Fear and fascination teetering with each other in a tango of love on the verge of hate and vice versa.

When Sadie returned to the sands of Port St. Joe, she was adorned in all that her sojourn had bought and taught her. She used every opportunity to flaunt her dignified sophistication. The kind of flaunting that made you sit up and take notice.

"Just cause we had the same taste in dresses was no reason for her to put her hands on me. Wasn't my fault her man's eyes said he favored the dress on me. I've been called a nigger woman before; that don't bother me none. Just fear talking. Fear I looked better in the dress than she did. Fear her man thought so too. It wasn't her business how I got the dress. I earned it and I had a right to wear it. The truth be told, your honor, I'da served two attempted murder sentences if I had to before I'd be broken down to wear someone else's fear. You have a lot of time to think about silk dresses when you marking time in a dim-lit room with three concrete walls and iron bars for a door," Aunt Sadie confessed to Madear when she came with her suitcase and twenty-seven dollars in her hand to start over in Tallahassee.

"Was it worth it?" Madear questioned.

"You oughta know better than most ain't no price on dignity, Cree, no matter who's buying," Aunt Sadie retorted.

"What do you mean, better than most? Sadie, if you got something to say, just come on out and say it. Don't beat around the bush."

"Funny you should say bush, since it was what your man stayed glued to when he needed to stand up like somebody."

"Sadie Weatherstone, I'll be doggone if I let you talk about my man like that in his house."

"Cree, don't go gitting your panties in a wad, just a point I'm making. Nobody expected Hiram to fight a whole group of white men in sheets. But he could've stood up to them instead of letting them break him down."

"He was trying to save his life, Sadie!"

"Save his life! What about your Momma and your Daddy's life, and your life, Cree? What about three years of my life, was he trying to save that too?"

"You're going too far, Sadie! We ain't done nothing but try to help you and you come in here talking about Hiram like dirty dishwater."

"Cree, I thank ya'll for everything you tried to do for me but it don't change the fact that if Hiram would have stood up, things wouldn't turned out the way they did."

"You don't know that!" Madear almost shouted.

"I know that fear can take a hold of you so strong it can make you do things you thought you never would or could."

"And Hiram had more fear than a bull in a butcher shop that night. He was so scared he forgot about everything and everyone but his self." Aunt Sadie's voice trailed off, then Indigo heard a loud smack.

At first Indigo through something had fallen over. She reflected on when she first heard the news of Aunt Sadie having been in jail before she came to Tallahassee. Daddy and Madear had spoken about it in the kitchen. But Madear had told a different story to Mrs. Benjamin. Now Indigo realized her Aunt Sadie hadn't "been kicked to the curb by her husband" the way Madear had sadly told Mrs. Benjamin that day at the clothesline at all. She was a jailbird locked up with hardened criminals. "She could have been friends with killers, thieves, and God knows what else," Indigo whispered out loud to herself, searching for validity in the closet airspace. "This is better than Magnolia's Santa Claus secret," she thought. But if she taunted Magnolia with this news, she knew she would eventually have to tell of her secret hiding place. The cedar closet was something that she wanted to keep for herself for more reasons than one. It was where she learned to piece together her family history. "Perhaps, she pondered it would also be where she would find the clues to understanding the impact of Martin Luther King's death on her family."

The red light turned green and the Taltran bus neared a shady knoll, passing the entrance to McClay Gardens. The smell of magnolias abundant in the gardens permeated the air. Aunt Sadie's percussory moans had expanded as other passengers on the bus supplied their tales of brokenness. Indigo had grown weary of listening, trying to piece together secrets from the cedar closet wall and the Taltran bus's audience of call and response. Looking out the bus window at the gardens, she admired the beauty of the white magnolia flowers against the backdrop of trees with bark so dark they looked blue-black. She closed her eyes, desperately wanting this vision of lush gardens to pale her thoughts. The more she admired their beauty, the more they piqued thoughts of her father's rage and Martin Luther King being assassinated. When the bus neared the grove end of magnolias, a wave of disillusion tinged with an unexpected sadness began to rise in her chest, and the sun rays created a glistening reflection of the garden's image that seeped through the window and rested on her lap.

CHAPTER 5

"Only when it is dark enough, you can see the stars..."

The paternal Douglases were a family of fishers who migrated to the Florida peninsula for the autonomy of its waters. Whites owned the land but nature governed the waters. Nature was part of their being. Their seed sprouted when runaway slaves from the cotton fields of Georgia sought refuge in the company of Choctaw Indians living near the Georgia and Florida line. The fellowship bore a circle of proud reddish-onyx-color people with physical features of pecan-shaped eyes, full lips, high-bridged wide noses and coal-colored coarse hair. Generations of Douglases melded together fragments of African and Indian traditions to withstand the atrocities of a people enslaved.

The Douglas circle openly referred to these fragments as their "Iko."

Early in their lineage, under the autumn moons in the bush near the swamp, celebratory chants and dances of "Iko" gave off a radiance that kept even the meanest of white folks at a distance. Amazement and annoyance aside, white lore credited colored people living in the Florida peninsula "Iko" for the bountiful harvest of the Gulf Coast waters each year. "Iko" for this tribe was more than the presence of strength to bring forth bounty or the endurance to find the path to equality. It was a powerful whisper within the circle audible only to a few. Those lucky enough to have possession were conduits for the rest. It was a natural assumption that the leaders of this colored community had the "I" gift, or at least the knowledge of it.

The "I" people offered visceral insight into the unsettling complexities of existence. Their words and wisdom coupled to fuel strength and was seen as the lucky charm that kept the circle of community intact. Over time the Douglases and their kin were so widely known for their two days of "Iko raising" on autumn nights that white folks gave up counting on their help with the shrimp and oyster boats on those days altogether. The moonlit autumn ritual of loud chanting and elaborate dancing added to speculations about the "Iko" power. White and colored people outside the "Iko" community engaged in heated conversations about what they knew about "Iko." The truth was no outsider had proof to back up suspicions. The "Iko" community was entrenched in the Apalachicola surroundings but the intricacies of their legendary "Iko" power were not an area of public consumption. Only the "Iko" community circle knew "Iko" was a gift that could skip or lie dormant in generations. The circuit knew its "I" people by the way they walked with their chests held high, balancing the power they carried inside and radiated on the outside. Luna Douglas was one of the "I" people.

Hiram Davis Douglas and Hale Dennis Douglas were the seventh and eighth children of Luna and Hyacinth Douglas. They were a twin birth. In the "Iko" community twins were a rare blessing and two chances for "Iko" possession. The birth of the twins was difficult. Momma Lit's, the colored midwife's, rheumatism was acting up and she could not get to Hyacinth for the birthing. Luna was left to make use of what little he learned from the birthing of his other six children. He hadn't learned too much because Momma Lit only let him stay in the room until he could see the baby's head coming out. By that time, he was ready to drink the whole jug of corn liquor he saved for special situations. His rough and limited assistance nearly took the life of Hyacinth, and Hale was born slow. Nevertheless, Luna's gratitude for his double portion of prosperity was not diminished. He eagerly waited for the slightest signs of "Iko" to appear. He began providing manhood training as soon as the boys could walk. Every development was prefaced by a discussion of how "Iko" men develop. At first, the community marveled at what seemed to be Luna's double inheritance of high-chest-housed power. As time passed, the watch for "Iko" shifted exclusively to Hiram.

Luna and his boys often fished in the swampy bush yielding large supplies of fish, crab and oysters. Luna was gifted in his knowledge of the Gulf Coast waters. He would run his left hand along the bank of the bay to determine the best place to fish. He told his sons if the veins in his hands turned blue, that meant the fish were plentiful farther north closer to warmer waters. He traveled the roads selling wheelbarrows of fish and other seafood. Often travel was prolonged because Hale was slow and easily distracted by shiny things that gave off a reflection. The fishing waters distracted him. Glass buttons in the general store distracted him. Windows distracted him. Eyeglasses distracted him. Luna encouraged Hiram to be his brother's keeper. They were inseparable and spoke a language of their own. When Luna's twins were thirteen and the annual autumn "Iko" raising ritual was approaching, Hale's fascination for shining things changed the Douglases forever.

Luna was carrying a wheelbarrow of blue crabs with his two sons in tow. Hale wanted to steer the wheelbarrow. They had taken a short cut through the bushes away from the banks of the bay and no one was in sight. Luna gave the handles of the wheelbarrow to Hale and admonished Hiram to keep up with him. Hale raced through the tall thick bushes with Hiram directly behind him. The rustling sound from the breeze generated by the passing wheelbarrow blowing against the tall hollow blades of grass startled a white couple in a conjugal embrace. The young white man, fearing the approach of his lover's domineering father, jumped up and scampered to hide in the bush blades. Hale and Hiram stood awestruck. When Luna walked up, he cast his eyes down, motioning to Hiram and his brother to move swiftly. The abrupt change in their walking pattern tipped the balance of wheelbarrow, causing their crab supply to fall to the ground. Luna and Hiram scrambled to gather their blue crabs. Hale bent down to help, but his eye caught sight of a glass locket tangling in between the cream-colored breasts of the young white woman searching for her clothing.

It took minutes for Luna and Hiram to collect the blue crabs that had spilled out of the wheelbarrow. It took just as much time for Hale, enthralled with curiosity for shiny things, to wander closer to the young white woman. He came upon her half-dressed and groping inside the tall grass, searching desperately for her clothing. The glistening of the locket mesmerized him just as the young woman's domineering father parted the tall blades of grass, carrying his shotgun. The departed white lover, standing in partial view of Hale, quickly capitalized on the unpredictable casting of circumstances. He brazenly summoned the shotgun-carrying father to what appeared to be a physical threat to his daughter's chasteness.

"NIGGER!!!" the gun-toting father called out when he got sight of Hale. The barrel of the silver six-shooter glistened in the sunlight. Hale turned, startled by the loud voice of hostility and a glistening shiny gun pointed at him. One shot and he fell to the ground. Hiram leaped to avenge his brother's assailant but Luna knocked him to the ground despite his pleas and urgings. Luna struggled with Hiram and with himself. His "I" factor surfaced to save one son at the sacrifice of another. He trembled, holding Hiram until the domineering father and his daughter were out of sight and "Iko" asleep deep within his chest.

From Hiram's perspective, his "Iko" was stunted at the fall of his brother. By the time he reached manhood, his inability to save his brother had become a contradiction to his heritage that plagued him every day of his life.

Hiram was among the first generation of the Douglas clan to venture outside of the cycle of nature for economic survival. He left the fishing town of Apalachicola right after high school to find his fortune eighty miles away in the capital of the state. When hired as a flagman for Wilson's gas company, Hiram's jubilation deflated only when his father's consternation over the putting aside the family trade surfaced. Deep within, the family ways remained an important part of Hiram's life, even though his toils at Wilson Gas Company were followed with frequent promotions. He would return weekly to his family grounds to cast his net upon the waters that sustained his ancestors and savor the sounds of the down-home blues. The part-time earnings from the family trade were a symbol of his loyalty to tradition and preparation for marriage. By the time a man reached the age of twenty-one, he was married or in the process of becoming married. Hiram Douglas was twenty-one when he met and married Cree Weatherspoon.

Madear's cultural lineage was a merger of the Florida slaves and Cherokee Indians. The family tree branches extended out from to a small fishing town called Port St. Joe north of Apalachicola. Commerce was divided between harvesting the peninsula, and the sale of crafts to the rich passengers on the steam boats traveling through the panhandle. Entire families participated in the making of crafts and their sales. Nate and Dovie Weatherstone had two beautiful daughters. Each daughter had different and extraordinary talents. Cree Weatherstone, the oldest of the two daughters, was fair-skinned, unlike the light-brown color of her sibling. She was a natural salesperson with the customers at her parents' thriving craft stand on the side of Joe's Oyster Bar and Grill. Her Momma told her she passed on to her the knack for making jewelry out of the simplest form of nature. Dovie held nature close to her heart. It was a symbol of her Indian ways. When she saw her genes of nature in Cree, she convinced Nate to turn a deaf ear to her referring to Cree as Weatherstone instead of his name Weatherspoon. Nate didn't really care much about Dovie's name switching except on official occasions when he wanted Cree to be known as a Weatherspoon. He loved Dovie so much he would do almost anything to please her. Besides, everybody in Port St. Joe knew his name was Nate Weatherspoon. Nonetheless they called him Nate Weatherstone most of the time because he was Dovie's man. Sadie, the youngest daughter drew pictures and looked like Nate spit her out. She was Weatherspoon from day one. But as she grew older, she used both names to suit her mood or circumstances. She left Apalachicola at age sixteen when she won a scholarship to study art at a school for blacks in Chicago. Her father didn't want her to go but her mother said "Sadie" had the wit to get her through anything.

Joe's Oyster Bar and Grill was the finest restaurant in Port St. Joe. When the tourists stepped off the steamboat to fancy local cuisine, Joe Claxton's Oyster Bar and Grill was their first stop. As they walked by the side of the restaurant, Grandaddy Nate and Grandma Dovie's craft table of local artifacts would catch their eye and invariably the coins from their purses. No matter how full Grandaddy Weatherstone's moneybag was or how much bulge was in Grandma Dovie's bosom, they would minimize their profits. On Saturday evenings when Mr. Joe came to collect the $20 stand fee, they insisted they were barely making enough to feed their family.

White supremacy reigned in Port St. Joe and Old Joe Claxton was not going to stand for a colored man to prosper more than him. Even if he could stand it, his greedy wife Heloise couldn't. She had to have the best of the best always. She didn't much care how he got it for her. He had to get it. If that meant taking a little more from the coloreds to satisfy Heloise, he didn't hesitate.

Grandaddy Weatherstone and Grandma Dovie earned a good living at the craft stand, despite having to pay the stand fee every week. When they crossed the road and headed home, where all the colored people lived, the arch in their backs seemed to straighten up, the closer they walked toward a community that revered their prosperity. It didn't matter to Grandaddy Nate that Mr. Joe thought he was just a poor nigger selling wooden junk for a few pennies on the side of his restaurant. The heaviness of his moneybag on Saturday nights outweighed what any white person thought. When the news of the Southern Christian Leadership Conference voter's registration came to colored folks across the road in Port St. Joe, Grandaddy Nate began to think differently.

The SCLC held tent meetings all up and down the panhandle, looking for canvassers to encourage colored folks to register to vote. Hiram Douglas was one of the first to volunteer in Apalachicola. The deputized canvassers would work at their day jobs during the week and travel to the neighboring towns on the weekends. When Grandaddy Nate heard the message of the SCLC, he knew that their words of change echoed the struggles of his ancestors. Although he and Grandma Dovie kept $6,000 of their earnings in their mattress as a symbol of their secret independence, he knew freedom was not free for a colored man. Grandaddy Nate knew also from his African and Indian ways that the sun would not set long for him. In his heart he agonized over the possibility of his daughters suffering because of their skin color. He knew he would not always be around to protect them. His discontent caused him to long for the seed of a son to carry on the heritage that his ancestors began. But Grandaddy Nate knew Grandma Dovie was past child-bearing years.

When Grandaddy Nate sat down at the SCLC meeting and listened to the promise of the vote for colored folks, something stirred his soul. When he saw the pride of African heritage shine through on the face of Hiram Douglas from Apalachicola, something stirred in his heart. Grandaddy Weatherstone took pleasure and delight in listening to the weekend travels of Hiram, the SCLC canvasser. He could see the emergence of power in Hiram's chest when he talked about the work of the SCLC. He especially gleamed when Cree would sit in and listen to the important work of the SCLC. It wasn't long before Hiram and Cree began discussions of their own.

Hiram would make his way to Port St. Joe on Friday evenings and sometime help close down the craft stand. When Cree turned nineteen, Hiram asked Nate Weatherstone for her hand in marriage. Just as Grandaddy Nate set his mind on hosting the biggest spread colored folks in Port St. Joe ever knew about, for Cree and Hiram, the white folks began to get concerned about the voter's registration drive. Mr. Joe began to act mean when he came for his stand money and would ask Grandaddy Nate if he was holding back part of his earnings. Granddaddy Nate always denied his prosperity. Sometimes he had to find a secret place in the ground to bury his earnings until it was convenient to take it home.

One Saturday evening in early spring, Grandaddy Nate and Grandma Dovie's sales at the craft table were unusually good. They had earned so much that they had to find secret hiding places on their persons. There had been a steady stream of passengers coming from the steamships and they had delighted themselves in watching old peg-leg Smithee hobble up and down the pier carrying the belongings of the white well-to-do. The sight of Smithee bowing and scraping for people of his own kind signified the unspoken difference between being colored and being poor, white and of disrespected heritage. Being colored had expected indignities but being poor and of disrespected heritage was an atrocity intolerable for the more affluent white sons of Port St. Joe.

There were the rich white ship owners, the fish marketeers, the oyster restaurants and commodity shop owners. The coloreds worked for the white businesses as well as poor whites whose fathers settled in Port St. Joe when they could no longer ride the waves of the Gulf. The poor whites lived adjacent to the colored section of town separated by a small canal.

Just above the canal lived a white store owner that both blacks and whites called "Stud." Even though he tried hard to speak clearly, he spoke with a heavy accent that made it seem as if he was stuttering. Nobody ever bothered saying what his real name was. He had a wife and a son. Everybody greeted them as Stud's wife and Stud's son when they came in the store to buy or get credit. Sometimes his wife would spend the evening down at the canal mourning and singing something that sounded like the choral version of Stud's talking. She sang it repeatedly, kneeling down at the tip of the canal leading into St. Joseph Bay.

At the beginning of nightfall from the colored side of Port St. Joe, you would see her singing and bending over with the handle of a rake in her hand. She moved in a back-and-forth motion, raking empty oyster shells to the surface and placing ones that struck her fancy alongside the bank of the canal. After she finished her evening collection, the singing would begin again as she bowed down on her knees.

"Hevenu shalom alechem" were the words that she chanted.

The sound of her repeating these words became so common in the evening you expected to hear them right alongside the sound of the crickets singing at night.

When nightfall was completed, the singing stopped. She walked away from the canal dressed in black from head wrap to shoes, leaving her altar of shells behind. The daily currents from St. Joseph Bay would flow into the canal and wash the altar of shells away. Folks say she sang in tongues because she suffered with sickness. They believed she was searching for her healing, moaning out there in the night air of the canal.

Communal talk among the neighbors surrounding the river was limited to grunts from the poor whites, met with rapid bows of pleasantries from the coloreds. Colored people feared the poor whites most of all, because their hate was deep down for the coloreds. The colored people believed the poor whites were the most dangerous because they lived among them. Some even shared crops together. The division of the crops was not even. The poor whites got the larger proportion, as their ancestors had before, but the coloreds still managed to make a meager living somehow.

Despite this neighborly bond, some of the white men who lived among the coloreds across the canal just beyond the railroad tracks adorned themselves with the white hoods of the Klan at night. Smithee was a poor white living among the coloreds. He also frequently took nocturnal rides clad in white. A colored person could never live neighborly as long as the Knights in white rode the winds.

The Weatherstones had waited until dusk for Mr. Joe to come for his stand money, but he never showed up. Grandma Dovie wanted to get home to finish the planning for Cree and Hiram's spread. Grandaddy Nate reluctantly decided to go to the back door of the restaurant to leave the stand fee after contemplating the tone of Mr. Joe's changeable moods and the outcome if he didn't go. Grandaddy Nate hated going to the back door of the restaurant because Mr. Joe always tried to get extra from him for the stand fee. When Grandaddy Nate said he couldn't pay more, Mr. Joe would suggest having his way with Grandma Dovie as a means of payment. Then Grandaddy Nate would have to interest Mr. Joe in having a drink of his special brew of corn liquor. Mr. Joe would drink too much and reminisce about when his Daddy was alive and other days gone by. Grandaddy Nate would sometime have to drink more than he wanted and the night would slip away. When this drinking spree would get started, Grandma Dovie would slip away and go home alone.

Smithee would watch the drinking spree between Grandaddy Nate and Mr. Joe with a fixed stare. The anger in his eyes had flashes of envy that mirrored his longing to cozy up to Mr. Joe and elevate his status in Port St. Joe It was a longing shared with his older brother that began years before the moment of the anger in his eyes. Smithee's burning anger was the end result of eager anticipation of ill-gotten gains. The bounty ultimately cost his brother his life and relegated him to be looked down upon.

Grandaddy Nate did have something in common with Smithee. They shared the feeling that they were due far more respect than they received from the sons and daughters of Port St. Joe. As a colored man, Grandaddy Nate came to know his plight early in his life. He was a master at going along to get along. Smithee, being a white man, wasn't taught to hide his pride. He did know he needed to hide it. Pride brought him years of rejection by the well-to-do whites of Port St. Joe and a residence alongside the canal in the neck of the woods where the coloreds lived. Grandaddy Nate knew he was viewed as worthless in the eyes of the whites, but among those who looked like him he was revered. Smithee was practically useless to the whites of Port St. Joe except for when they would ask him to join them on the nights that the Klan rode. His value among the coloreds was also not very high since he scratched the same dirt that they did to eat. A fact that generated a surge of anger and power destined to destroy when he adorned his mask of white.

Grandaddy Nate dreaded the day when he would be unable to sidetrack Mr. Joe's passion for Grandma Dovie. Dovie's beauty made you stop dead in your tracks and not want to move. To watch her creamy carmel-colored body move could stir an exotically ethereal longing for passion. The greenish hue of her pupils framed by her silky blue-black wavy mane adorning her head was captivating. Men throughout Port St. Joe appreciated Dovie's beauty. Rumor had it during Dovie's courting days that she was once scorned by a handsome lover named Hank, who counted himself a ladies' man. The word was after agreeing to go their separate ways, Dovie asked Hank for a good-bye kiss. Hank, the consummate lover, complied, giving the kiss all the passion he could muster. The next time Hank was seen, his mouth was twisted and the only sounds that could come out of his mouth were similar to the barks of a dog. A few say he had a stroke, some say he just plain went fool. Some of the Colored sages across the canal in the neck of the woods speculated, "Crazy fool can run in your family and just come out when it's got a mind to." Most of the women said Grandma Dovie rooted him with her kiss. Grandma Dovie would only say, "Every dog got his day and some dogs got a longer day."

For all the beauty Dovie possessed, it took second place to her keen intuition. A character trait viewed as odd within the colored women's circles. She had few if any women friends, but the few she had, if asked, said there was something different about her. Dovie's African and Cherokee Indian heritage combined in equal strength, creating an aura around her at birth that affected her physically as well as mentally. Often when Dovie talked about her Indian heritage, she spoke of the moon festivals that her family attended. She told stories of tall proud men and regally beautiful women dressed in vibrant colors of nature chanting and dancing around the bay. Pride and amusement came across her face when she recalled how whites and colored people peeked at the festivals wide-eyed behind the bushes of the bay.

The plan was to hand Mr. Joe the stand money quickly and get home to the "spread" preparations. Grandaddy Nate knocked on the back door and asked for Mr. Joe. Smithee, the old sailor with the peg-leg, grunted from behind the door. Granddaddy knew it would not be a good idea to give the stand fee to Smithee and run the risk of having to pay double stand fee on the next Saturday night. He turned before answering Smithee, deciding rather to come over to Mr. Joe's restaurant first thing on Sunday morning to pay the stand fee. He knew Mr. Joe came to the restaurant at dawn every morning and he planned to meet him. The more Grandaddy Nate thought about it, the more he wagered Mr. Joe would be in a somber mood after a night of drinking corn liquor and gambling. Granddaddy Nate hoped his faculties would be so impaired he would skip the speculations about the stand fee.

Just as they stepped across the road leading to their neck of the woods, Grandaddy Nate and Grandma Dovie came face to face with a group of white men dressed in white sheets. One of the Klansmen viciously grabbed Grandma Dovie. She began yelling and screaming desperately for Grandaddy Nate to rescue her. Recognizing his prize, the renegade Klansman dragged Grandma Dovie off from the commotion of whites encircling Grandaddy Nate to a path leading to the canal. He tussled with her, falling to the ground and getting back up again because she had strength in her limbs. She fought him with all her strength because she knew her life depended on it. She broke free. He chased after her. She ran as fast as she could toward the canal at the mouth of St. Joseph Bay, diving into its muddy waters, hoping her attacker couldn't swim.

The sound of Stud's wife moaning "Heavnu shalom alechem" echoed the in the dark starless night. The Klansman let out a wicked laugh and dived in after her. The adrenaline inside him pumped an uncontrollable desire for the hunter to capture his game. Frightened, and fired up to fight back, she flapped aimlessly around in the muddy waters trying to escape. The sounds of Stud's wife moaning "Heavnu shalom alechem" beat in sync with her racing heart and beaconed her home. But he dashed her hopes and pulled her twisting arms until they yielded under his power. Using his weight as an anchor, he yanked her up over his shoulders from the water. Satisfied with his victory, he threw her to the ground.

Overcome by the struggle, she was breathless and dizzy. She could no longer hear the familiarity of Stud's wife moaning from somewhere in the canal. He stood over her, breathing hard, with bright eyes shining from behind the slits in the dingy white hood. He contemplated her fate. He shuffled between the idea of squeezing the breath out of her with his bare hands or releasing himself inside of the cavern of her butterscotch-colored body violently and brutally. When he realized he could do both, his excitement surged. He smugly warned her, he would gauge the order of his attack by the amount of resistance she gave him.

In a desperate effort to get away from her attacker, she closed her eyes and clutched her nails in the earth. She felt the hardness of something long move briskly against the side of her body with force. He screamed at the top of his voice, grabbing his groin, falling to the side of her. A long hard narrow piece of wood rake lay on the ground with bloodstains covering the tip of its protruding iron spokes. A slender hand pulled her and a voice said, "Run!"

She ran hand in hand in the dark with the voice, not knowing exactly who it belonged to. The path of their run led them to unfamiliar surroundings. Suddenly, the grip of the slender hand belonging to the voice loosened and the body of a woman fell to the ground. Dizzy and disoriented, Grandma Dovie gazed in the starlight upon the face of Stud's wife.

"You saved my life…it was so dark I didn't see you," Grandma Dovie gasped.

"Only when it's dark enough can you see the stars," Stud's wife answered in the choppy dialect that Stud usually spoke in.

The two women rested underneath the starlight, exchanging stories of escape. Thin lines emerged around the lips of the mouth of Stud's wife as she desperately tried to stammer out words to convey the terror of her journey in the starlight waters of Europe escaping the Nazis. The memories and the wounds of starlight water runs returned when she saw Grandma Dovie with the Klansman. Her nightly moanings at the canal were petitions of peace for those too weak to endure the runs. Some died in their footsteps. Others became the camels of the river, loading themselves with family treasures only to sink to their deaths. She raked the canal for shells to use as markers to grant the peace that escaped them. She shared stories of her family and of other Jews who were tormented and forced to concealed their true identities in Europe.

Grandma Dovie matched those stories with the atrocities her family and other coloreds faced against the Klan. They sobbed in each other's arms throughout the night for her being Jewish and Grandma Dovie being colored, grasping the striking irony of their acquaintance.

As morning approached, Stud's wife became Anacostia Whittnauer, whose choppy dialect had become as familiar to Grandma Dovie as a conversation with a colored woman from her neck of the woods. When they began to prepare to return to their separate yet similar lives, the fear of the previous night returned. Mapping out their steps, the possibility of not making it home again became real. The dread of their identities being exposed as they returned together intensified their fear and sorrow.

"My home is in a faraway country that I will never see again," Anacostia spoke choppily with tears running down her face.

"Your home is out here near this bay somewhere...with your husband and your son...we just got to find is all," Grandma Dovie replied, trying to focus Anacostia on the journey before them.

"But I cannot go. What if someone recognizes us? I do not have the strength to go unnoticed past by their eyes anymore. I am too weak. You must go," pleaded Anacostia.

"I am not leaving you out here for God's knows what to happen to you. Tangling up with the Klan is one thing, but causing harm to a white woman is a whole different matter. No sir, I'm not leaving you!" insisted Grandma Dovie.

"Dovie, you must go. We cannot go together. The minute I open my mouth to speak and try to tell our story, they will know that I am not from the South. They will know I am not one of them. I am different. They will know. I cannot pass through their eyes without my husband. They will kill us both. I will stay here and Seth will come look for me. He will think I lost my way. He will come look for me," Anacostia pleaded.

"I can't find the way by myself. God help me!" protested Grandma Dovie.

"You will find your way home, take this with you," Anacostia said, handing Grandma Dovie a small wooden box.

"It is a mezuzah. In my country we Jews kept the mezuzah on the doorpost as a sign and reminder of our faith. When our friends visited our home, they knew they were passing through a place that shared a bond with them. It is one of the few possessions I took with me when we ran from the Nazis. I hoped it would take us home again. We have shared a bond. Take it with you. It is a symbol of our acquaintance."

Grandma Dovie took the mezuzah, looking at it and then at Anacostia. "It has Whittnauer, your real last name, scribbled on the side. I will take it to your husband and he will come and find you," Grandma Dovie promised.

She knew it was not wise for them to go back together but she had found kinship in Anacostia and did not want to leave her. She would be able to use the woods to protect her. The woods were part of nature. Nature was part of her heritage. She slowly started her journey to find her way home. Each time she looked back, Anacostia waved her onward. Each step toward home triggered thoughts of the Klan that sent her racing aimlessly into the starless night. A night that could have been the end of her life had ended in bringing two unsuspecting lives together and apart.

CHAPTER 6

"I didn't sneeze..."

Hiram and Cree started a brisk walk in the dusk to the craft stand to help Grandaddy Nate and Grandma Dovie's close down. Hiram was just about to start a conversation with Cree about the green satin belt in his pocket when he gazed upon a vicious vision in white. His body twitched with the urge to strike out and somehow rescue his future in-laws from a legendary encounter with a fatalistic ending. As he hid himself and urged Cree to do the same, he thought of the portion of his manhood that was evaporating with each bludgeoning sound of fists and objects resounding against the physique of Grandaddy Nate. He thought of his brother Hale. He thought of the mighty efforts of the SCLC and their tent meetings as the pounding against Granddaddy Nate grew louder and his protestations grew fainter. From his thoughts emerged a conviction to hate harder these pale-hued men whose licks pressed the flesh of Grandaddy Nate and stole his earnings along with his dignity. He waited for the power of "Iko" to jump into his chest and give him a defiant strategy for rescue. He wanted it to jump into his hands, giving him the might to fight. But his rage blinded him from revelation.

Cree, nestled in the pollen-filled thicket, entered into a sanctified prayer she often heard her mother say in times of trouble with white folks. She dug deep down, trying to stir up prayer power she knew she needed to come up against the vision of rage before her. She called on the Lord, all his angels and bore witness to the name of prophets she could remember for an escape. She knew there was no escape. She also knew they had only two choices: hide or prepare to die. They were in a situation they could not control. The pollen in the thicket made her want to sneeze. The slightest movement, a cough or a sneeze would send disaster in their direction. Disaster was not included in her evening plans with Hiram. But things hadn't exactly gone as planned.

She began to recount the steps to her current demise. Mr. Joe always gave her things when Grandaddy Nate and Grandma Dovie left the craft stand for lunch or to run an errand. He called her his "private treat." He gave her hairpins and perfume. She let him nuzzle and kiss her on the neck. He gave her his single dollar bills and loose change. He kept giving gifts to her and she kept taking them and keeping it a secret. The steamboats would bring in all sorts of boxes with the finest stuff you ever did see. He had a habit of asking Granddaddy Nate to let her help him open up the boxes in exchange for goods that arrived damaged. Grandma Dovie protested but Granddaddy Nate said things white folks threw away brought a profit in the colored community. Mr. Joe provided Cree with a private firsthand view of the beautiful things "white women" wore. Sometimes to both their delight she modeled them for him.

"I saw a side of white people in Mr. Joe that Daddy and Momma didn't see. He didn't look at me and hate me cause I was colored. He said I was a goddess. I had no reason to be afraid of him. When he told me how pretty I was to him, I felt different. He made me feel like I never felt before. Why should I be scared anyway? Even Momma said being scared don't git nowhere," Cree justified to herself.

"I know Mr. Joe has one thing in mind when he gives me those presents with all that heavy breathing he does. That doesn't mean I have that on my mind and even if I did, no one has to know about it," she'd insisted to herself. "I give him a little kiss and let him feel me up sometimes. He gets excited sometimes and leaks on my legs and thighs. It doesn't mean anything. Sometimes I like what he's doing. When the colored women are whispering about how light my skin is or saying I'm not colored, I hold onto Mr. Joe's words and the way he made me feel. Those little gifts are insurance payments to keep Hiram on his toes. Just because Daddy liked Hiram didn't mean he was getting this 'milk' for free. There wasn't any harm in letting him think somebody else thought the milk was valuable," she conspired to herself. Even though Hiram had promised to marry her, she knew anything could happen between the thirty-five miles between Tallahassee and Port St. Joe. She wasn't about to let it be said Hiram Douglas "didn't need to buy the cow because he was getting the milk for free."

There wasn't any harm until Mr. Joe tempted her with that green satin dress with rhinestones sewed across the front. The dress was the most beautiful dress she'd ever seen in catalog books or anywhere else. Just looking at it, she knew it would fit every curve the good Lord gave her. Unfortunately, Mr. Joe didn't let go of the dress easily. He showed it to her and suggested she come to the back of the restaurant one evening to get it. She wanted it. Usually she didn't travel up by Mr. Joe's at night. It wasn't safe. The Klan wandered around at night and Miss Heloise, Mr. Joe's wife, was more likely to be around. Her parents' cautionary tales of whites' mistreatment of coloreds in Port St. Joe and the flash of Hiram at the soul-stirring meetings of the SCLC danced in her head. She recounted experiences with vicious white people and equally vicious colored people in Port St. Joe. She struggled to persuade herself that the secret gifts from Mr. Joe had nothing to do with the racial distress between the whites and coloreds in Port St. Joe. Changing the channels in her mind, she tried to focus on how much Hiram would desire her in the dress and resolved she would take it for love.

She went to the back of the restaurant one Friday afternoon. Grandaddy Nate and Grandma Dovie thought she was going across the river to the house to spend time with her sister. They didn't expect her back anytime soon. Hiram was coming that evening and she could just see herself wearing that dress at Smiling Willie's Juke Joint. She visualized heads turning as she came in the door. A Bobby Blue Bland tune would be playing on the jukebox. Hiram would place his hand at the small of her waist. Their pelvises would move in time with each other. She even toyed with the idea of letting him taste the "milk." After all, they were going to be married before long.

She knocked three times, just the way Mr. Joe told her. She pushed the screen door open just enough to look to see if anybody was stirring in the kitchen. Pots were simmering on low heat. The men from the oyster and shrimp boats had eaten and gone. Hattie Mae, the colored restaurant cook, had probably turned the fire down low to run back across the river to give her hungry children the leftover supper scraps. It wouldn't be long before she'd come back to finish cleaning up the kitchen. She eased into the stockroom where Mr. Joe kept his office. The dress, draped like an inviting temptress on a wire hanger, hung from the window latch. The sun shining up against it made the rhinestones sparkle and the green color look even more emerald. She slipped the dress off the hanger and folded it under her arm inside her writing tablet. The dress made the tablet look bulky.

She'd keep it pressed down underneath her arm, she thought to herself. Mr. Joe had really given it to her and it wasn't like she was stealing it, she quickly cross-examined herself.

Just a few steps and she would be out of the restaurant and on her way across the road to the river. Opening the screen door and looking from side to side, she started the walk home. The dress was hers. She had avoided Mr. Joe and his heavy breathing, saved the "milk" for Hiram and got the dress. Feeling confident, she had made her way cross the road leading to the river when she met Trina, one of ole Smithee's kinfolks. "Spoongal! Whey you going this nice evening?"

Trina questioned Cree with the authority of a white woman even though she was about Cree's age and poor white trash.

Cree thought of saying something sassy but she just wanted to get home with her dress without any trouble. "Ain't feeling good, going home," Cree answered, not breaking stride. She looked back and Trina was still looking at her. "She can kiss my foot, ain't none of her business no way," Cree cursed her in her mind. Suddenly the encounter with Trina made her think about what she was going to say when someone asked her where she got the dress. There wasn't a dressmaker in Port St. Joe who could claim the glory of sewing the dress. Even if it was, no colored person could knowingly afford to buy it.

With each step she took, her dilemma grew more daunting. Then the idea of hiding it in her trunk occurred to her. She raced in the house and found her sister Sadie sleeping, even though the sun had just gone down. She was lying on the sofa in a sheer robe with rows of feathered trim covering a short nightgown. Her face and hair were all made up like she was going somewhere. Cree's first inclination was to scold her for sleeping on the sofa, but she needed to hide the dress. She pulled the trunk out from under the bed and opened it quickly. Sadie's fancy dresses were packed inside the trunk. "Bad enough she comes back from Chicago with all these fancy clothes and ideas, she has her things all over the room and in my trunk too," Cree fussed to herself. Before she put the dress in between two of Sadie's fancy dresses, she noticed her green dress had belt loops but no belt. She hadn't remembered seeing a belt when she slipped the dress off the hanger and folded it under her arm. "Maybe it didn't have one or Mr. Joe lost it," she tried to reassure herself. She closed the trunk, relieved her secret was safe, and returned to the living room to deal with Sadie.

"Sadie, what are you doing with your things inside my trunk?" Cree asked, startling her from her nap.

"Girl, I got so many dresses and things I ain't got no place to put them…you weren't really using that trunk anyway," Sadie answered, stretching her eyes from her nap.

"How are you going to tell me what I'm doing with my stuff," Cree shot back.

"Well, there is room in there for your things. I don't really have anywhere around here to wear those dresses," Sadie responded, trying to avoid an argument.

Satisfied that Sadie wouldn't be going in the trunk for a while, Cree relented. But trouble was on the horizon. Hiram caught a ride and got to Port St. Joe earlier than usual that Friday. He went by the craft stand looking for Cree. Grandaddy Nate told him she had gone to spend time with Sadie, who just come back home from Chicago. Hiram had just begun his walk up the road going past Mr. Joe's restaurant and oyster grill when he spotted Trina sitting on the wharf. Everybody knew she waited on the oyster and shrimp boats to come in on Friday nights. She'd try to interest one or two of the men in a drink or whatever was his pleasure in exchange for cash. Hiram knew trouble when he saw it. Trina was trouble with a capital "T." He didn't want any parts of her but he had to pass her and give her the respect due a white woman in Port St. Joe.

Trina spotted him too. She quickly calculated the value of seizing the opportunity to engage in a little game of aggravation that could very well lead to cash. "Hey!" she called to Hiram. "Saw your 'Spoongal' on the road by the river in a mighty big hurry this afternoon."

"Afternoon, Madam…Miss," Hiram said, not really knowing which title was appropriate.

"Wonder why she was in such a big hurry," Trina persisted, getting up from the wharf, coming in the direction of Hiram's steps.

"I don't know, Miss Trina," Hiram said, trying to respond more respectfully in hopes she would leave him be. Trina was coming a little too close for comfort, but Hiram knew she had a point to prove.

"I bet Miss Heloise would want to know where 'Spoongal' was off to in such a hurry," Trina wheezed, blowing her tobacco-chewing breath in Hiram's face. "She'd be tickled pink to know why 'Spoongal' dropped this green belt with these shiny little stones on the buckle here, down by the river. Now Hiram, do you know any coloreds cross the river can afford a dress with a belt that has sparklers like this?"

Trina was on the prowl now. She thought she had a lead on something and she wasn't going quit until she got a piece of it. Hiram had a feeling where this was leading, but he just had to let Trina bring it to a stop.

"Miss Heloise was madder than a wet hen because somebody took her green satin dress with the rhinestones sewn across the front," Trina continued, making a circle around Hiram. "She said someone took it in broad daylight. She knew Hattie Mae didn't take it. It would take three of them dresses sewn together to fit Hattie Mae. But 'Spoongal,' now maybe that dress would fit her pretty good."

"I don't know what to say, Miss Trina," Hiram offered, knowing Trina wanted money for her information.

"Say how much it's worth to you to keep me from telling Miss Heloise bout this little belt," Trina glared. She was between a rock and a hard place. She knew if she went to Miss Heloise she would become a suspect. Her Uncle Smithee would have a crazy fit. He hated anything that drew attention to his low status in Port St. Joe.

Seeing no way to avoid Trina's demand, Hiram dug in his pocket and pulled out a handful of bills. After all, Cree was the woman he loved. She was worth paying money to avoid the kind of trouble that Trina was stirring up. Besides, most of his week's earning was in his shoe. Trina looped the green satin belt with the rhinestone buckle around his neck and walked back to her seat on the wharf, counting her cash. Hiram quickly removed the belt and stuffed it in his pants pocket. He shuffled along inwardly annoyed about being shaken down by down by the likes of Trina. He quickened his pace going to

Cree's house, feeling certain he'd be provided some sort of explanation.

He approached the screen door and Cree's head popped out just as he started to knock. "Hey, Hiram," she said, stretching out his name with sweetness in her voice.

"Well, well, Mr. Hiram," Sadie yelled, getting up from the couch to get a better look. "Come a-courting early this evening?" Sadie chided.

"How you, Sadie?" Hiram called back, smiling at Sadie's flirtatious tone.

"Fine as you," she added, looking him up and down.

"Hiram couldn't wait to come and see his sugar," Cree interjected to remind Sadie Hiram was taken.

"Pardon me," Sadie offered, blinking her eyes and fanning the air while remaining behind the screen door.

"You're excused," Cree acknowledged, letting Sadie know she could go away from the screen door.

She and Hiram laughed and embraced. "What you wanta do tonight, baby," Hiram whispered in her ear, kissing her on the jaw.

"Let's go to the juke joint and dance," Cree squealed.

"Okay, but I want to go for a walk so we can talk first," Hiram smiled, remembering the green belt in his pocket.

"I'll just go in and change and we'll go. We just have to stop by the craft stand and help Daddy and Momma close up," Cree said, giving him a squeeze.

Cree went inside and Hiram sat on the porch. It wasn't long before Sadie came out of the house and asked Hiram for a match to smoke a cigarette. Hiram always had matches in his pocket because he worked at the gas company in Tallahassee and they gave them away. When he went into his pocket for the matches, he pulled out the green satin belt with the rhinestones on it. "Oooh, what's that pretty thing, Hiram?" Sadie cooed, lifting the belt out of his hand.

"Nothing for you to worry about," Hiram answered, taking the belt out of her hand and putting it back in his pocket.

"But I'd like to worry about that, Hiram," Sadie whined.

"Worry about what?" Cree asked, coming out the door putting on her sweater.

"Now don't you look sweet, y'all going somewhere special tonight, Cree?"

"Just to Smiling Willie's," Cree answered with excitement. "You want to come?"

"It's been a while since I shook a leg," Sadie reflected, getting excited about the possibility. "Maybe I will come," she said.

"We'll see you there." Hiram stood, offering the greeting and leading Cree off the porch to the road.

Sadie went inside to the bedroom, tossing the idea of dancing at Smiling Willie's Juke Joint in her mind. The more she thought about it, the more the idea of getting dressed up for a night of dancing and dilly-dallying with the devilish side of men appealed to her. She flipped through the dresses in her bulging closet. She had so many dresses from suitors who tried to segue their attributes into her passions, she hardly had a chance to wear any of them twice. That night she wanted to wear something that would cause the joint to jump up and take notice.

Dissatisfied with the assortment in her closet, she reached underneath the bed and pulled out the trunk. She flipped the first two dresses back and there it was! "Ah yeah!" she thought to herself. "Go to the well and get the water cause Sadie setting the place on fire tonight," she teased, holding the dress up against her body in the mirror. For a moment it struck her odd she couldn't remember the suitor who gave her the green satin dress with rhinestones sewn across the front. Usually she associated the suitor with the dress but this one was escaping her memory. "Just as well," she thought, "I'll wear it and make new memories."

She swayed back and forth in the mirror, holding the dress up against her. The screen door slammed and Cree walked back to the door of the bedroom.

"What you doing with that?" Cree gasped.

"Fixing to wear it, girl. I thought you and Hiram were gone," Sadie exclaimed while still admiring the dress up against her.

"I came back to get a flashlight, you know how hard it is to see at night when the fog rolls in." Cree swallowed hard. Cree quickly began to assess how she was going to let Sadie know that the green dress belonged to her.

"Where did you get that from? It's pretty." Cree began walking closer as if admiring it for the first time.

"Some man or another. I can't remember who but I like his style," Sadie snickered while laying the dress out flat on the bed.

"You wearing it tonight?" Cree carefully questioned.

"Yeah, I think so, then I probably won't wear it again in who knows when," Sadie answered, looking the dress over.

"Well, give it to me after you finish," Cree blurted out, privately conceding to Sadie debuting the dress but relishing in the victory of it's ultimate possession.

"Be my guest after tonight," Sadie added, going to bathroom to draw her bath.

Cree left, nearly skipping, to get Hiram and leave. She had found a way to keep Mr. Joe's latest present without anyone being the wiser. The scene re-played in between her faint prayers petitioning rescue from her current circumstances of hiding in the bush.

Just as the corn-liquored white-sheet colored attackers grew weary of their actions, a shrill yell of pain and agony distracted them. When the group of Klansmen turned to see the origin of the yell, Hiram stretched to see if there was any sign of life in Granddaddy Nate. His body was crumpled, turned face-down in the sandy dirt of Port St. Joe. The dust from the beige sand mixed with Granddaddy Nate's blood made him look a shade darker. When the group of Klansmen realized the cry of pain was from one of their own, they all ran in the direction of the sound. Hiram seized the opportunity and sprinted across the road to Grandaddy Nate. When the Klansmen approached their member, a loud insurrection erupted as Hiram struggled to drag Grandaddy Nate across the road before the Klan returned. The crowd of Klansmen expanded across the width of the road. Hiram and Cree could see them carrying one of their members whose waist was covered in blood. They threw him on the back of the pick-up truck with screams that vented hatred for "niggers" followed by jokes laced with corn liquor and laughter about "loving brown betty."

Hiram helped a dazed and beaten Grandaddy Nate begin the walk to the road to cross the river. When they came near the road next to the wharf, they could see Sadie in a cat fight with Mr. Joe's wife. Miss Heloise was screaming that Sadie was wearing her new green dress. Sadie stood with one hand on her hip and the other resting on the rail of the wharf, insisting the dress belonged to her. Mr. Joe stood motionless with a bewildered look on his face. Trina sat on a rail just beyond the commotion, laughing to herself. Miss Heloise walked over to the rail, spoke while pointing her hand in Sadie's face. Sets of hands started flying in the air. Five minutes after Cree and Hiram spotted Sadie on the wharf, Miss Heloise was in the water screaming Sadie tried to kill her.

A good plan had gone bad. Sadie ended up in the jailhouse in that green satin dress. Cree didn't know whether to sneeze or go blind when she saw her sitting there. She tried to avert Sadie's attention by telling her about what happened to Grandaddy Nate. She described how she and Hiram had to hide from the Klan in a pollen-filled thicket that bothered her hay-fever.

"I didn't sneeze but I wanted to," she told Sadie.

"Maybe you should've and that dog, Hiram, would have remembered he had the belt to Miss Heloise's dress in his pocket and I wouldn't be sitting here," Sadie countered, looking Cree straight in the eye.

"I don't know what you're talking about," Cree answered, remembering the empty belt loops on the green satin dress.

"That trashy Trina told me when the sheriff were hauling my butt off to jail, Hiram paid her good money for the belt to this dress earlier this evening," Sadie sneered at her sister.

Suddenly fear seeped in Cree's heart and she recognized the power of her secret for the first time. But she could not help herself. She had to continue the lie to keep the secret.

She had to, she pressured herself in her thoughts.

"Port St. Joe don't send colored woman away to prison...none that came to mind anyway...they weren't...couldn't start with Sadie," she tried to rationalize.

"A few days in jail and Miss Heloise will cool off. Daddy will plead with Mr. Joe and everything will be fine. Sadie would be brought down a peg...no harm done," her thoughts continued.

Granddaddy Weatherstone's beating left him in a coma for four weeks. Colored search parties looked everywhere for Grandma Dovie but figured her for dead. The colored people in Port St. Joe talked quietly about the Klansman whose waist was covered with blood the night they came after Granddaddy Weatherstone and Grandma Dovie. They talked even more about Sadie sitting in jail in Miss Heloise's green satin dress. Some of the colored people thought the Klan tried to kill Grandaddy Weatherstone because he and his children acted like they were better than the other coloreds. Grandaddy Weatherstone was famous in the neck of the woods where the colored people lived for his stories about the prominence of his ancestors. A group of speculators were convinced the prize of the Klansmen's rage that night was Grandma Dovie. They all agreed what the Klansmen did to Grandaddy Weatherstone wasn't nearly as powerful as what Grandma Dovie must have done to the Klansman bloodied at the waist. Sadie's circumstances, on the other hand, were viewed as a situation brought on by her "wild and wanton ways."

Somewhere amidst all the colored people gossiping about the Klansmen's prowl with the Weatherstones and the mishap with Sadie and Miss Heloise's dress, the truth escalated and evaporated. Supernatural powers were bestowed upon Grandma Dovie and the devil proclaimed in Sadie. Four weeks after the Klan's stomping, Grandaddy Nate came out of the coma and Grandma Dovie came home as if time had stopped and started again. Dressed in torn, dirty clothing, she was still carrying her money bag with the stand earnings strapped to her body. Before she came home she had found her way to Mr. Stud's store in hopes of returning the small wooden box with "Whittnauer" scribbled on the side to her friend Anacostia. When she pushed open the store's creaking half-door, the familiarity of the many times she had shopped flooded her memory. She visualized Anacostia sitting idly, dressed in her black garments, assisting her husband with the food and houseware sales of poor whites and coloreds. When Grandma Dovie watched Stud's son serving whites before coloreds, she let it pass through her stream of consciousness as part of the standard business practices of white folks in Port St. Joe. After being in the woods with Stud's wife, those common standard business practices for Grandma Dovie seemed uncommon.

Stud's son stood and approached her with a greeting that included soliciting her needs. Grandma Dovie tried to speak but trembling overcame her.

"You want to buy something?" Stud's son asked annoyed at her indecisiveness.

Grandma Dovie managed to step to the counter. She stood tapping her chipped dirty fingernails on the wooden counter. She was tapping to draw the words. She needed the words to come forth and say what she wanted. The words had to come to her to say who she was looking for.

"Your mother...I am looking for your mother and my friend, Anacostia," she practiced saying in her throat.

Her dry mouth opened and tears flowed for a friendship that crossed lines of division. Stud's son watched her curiously, not sure of what to say or do. She wanted to know where her friend was but she knew her place. Hattie Mae bustled in the door holding a young'un on her hip and two by the hand about the same time as a skinny white woman smelling of moonshine carrying a small purse with $1 bills sticking out the top. Stud's son's compassion gave way to his sense of commerce. He looked hard at the dirty trembling colored woman and the skinny white woman smelling of moonshine. The skinny white woman was beginning to holler for Stud's son to get the groceries she needed. He knew the standard business practice but the colored woman's trembling softened him.

"Are you gonna buy something? If you don't buy you have to leave," he insisted.

Grandma Dovie bristled with frustration. Beyond trying to get the children to mind and Stud's son to take her order, Hattie was stretching her neck trying to get a good look at Grandma Dovie. Grandma Dovie, always a proud woman, made a wobbly turn in her dirty torn clothes and walked out the screen door to the porch, clutching the small wooden box. She wanted to keep walking but the trembling spell was too powerful. Hattie Mae followed her and began dragging her young'uns by their arms. She made haste getting back to her neck of the woods to tell the news. She sent one of her kinfolk to tell the Weatherstones about Grandma Dovie having a spell up at Stud's store. Hattie Mae's kinfolk and Hiram went up to Stud's store to help bring Grandma Dovie back. The sight of Grandaddy Weatherstone and the comfort of familiar surroundings helped the tremblings to stop but Grandma Dovie barely uttered a word otherwise.

On the day Sadie was sentenced to do five years for trying to kill Miss Heloise, Grandma Dovie wrote a note telling Cree to take the wooden box to Mr. Stud's store and leave it on the counter. Nobody had seen Stud's wife for more than a month. Mr. Stud was a fair man to the coloreds but he kept his personal business private. Grandma Dovie believed the box helped her find her way home. She wanted to find a way to give it back to Anacostia.

"Just leave it on the counter," the note instructed Cree.

Cree figured she'd use the trip to Stud's store to buy something for Sadie and a little something for herself. Rumors aside, Cree wanted Stud's wife to be the one who waited on her when she went to the store. Stud and his son made her uncomfortable. Once Stud's son came to Mr. Joe's office for a delivery and interrupted one of their box-opening interludes. From that point on, she thought he looked at her funny. She wanted to quiet the storm of deceit that thundered in her head. Sadie was going to jail. As much as she wanted to change that fact, she couldn't. If Stud's wife could just sell her the quinine she needed to make sure Mr. Joe's panting and leaking had not gone too far, maybe all would not be lost.

The Klan prowl, Grandma Dovie and Sadie's green satin dress became well known folklore among the people of Port St. Joe. The most Grandma Dovie would say through her written notes about the Klansmen's prowl was, "Every dog got his day and some dogs got a longer day." Sadie served her time in prison, waiting for a dog to come forward. Hiram and Cree, along with her secret, were married and left for Tallahassee on the last day of that year.

CHAPTER 7

"We cannot walk alone..."

The Taltran bus pulled up to the corner near the wrought-iron gates connected to huge red brick pillars on each side. The bus jolted when it stopped causing Indigo to quickly shut down the review of her family history. The iron pattern inside the gate looked like black lace. Its design was melded so tightly it distorted the view of the houses that were three times the size of the houses on the 400 block of Osceola Street.

Once inside the gate, Aunt Sadie strutted toward the sleek gray Mercury parked under a tree. Sitting behind the steering wheel was a white woman with brash beige sandy-color hair in a perfect french roll with a swirl coming to the front of her head. You could see her glossy red fingernail polish twinkling in the sunlight when she held her hand up to her matching red lips to smoke a cigarette. Aunt Sadie hopped in the front seat, offering Mrs. Whittier the time of day while changing her disposition from the Taltran bus sage to the housekeeper for the white well-to-do.

"Morning, Sadie," Mrs.Whittier nodded back, pulling smoke from the short cigarette and thumping the ashes through the crack in the window.

"Glad you could bring Cree's gal to occupy Bethann, she's been underfoot this morning and there is so much to be done."

Mrs. Whittier talked so fast she seemed to hardly take a breath between sentences. Aunt Sadie followed the rhythm of her talking pattern, nodding when she wheezed between sentences and offering a response when it was required.

"Indigo and Bethann 'bout the same age. I 'spect they'll find something to get into," Aunt Sadie offered between Mrs. Whittier's going on about her husband's high holy days and the upcoming recruitment for new members at the Killearn Country Club.

"High holy," Indigo thought to herself, sitting in the back seat of the Mercury and remembering Madear telling Aunt Sadie, "Mrs. Whittier wasn't even low holy."

After Aunt Sadie came home from her first day of working at the Whittiers', Aunt Sadie had noticed something hauntingly familiar about Mrs. Trin Whittier and mentioned it to Madear.

"Mrs. Trin Whittier was poor white trash who married up. She used to be Trina back in Port St. Joe," Madear had said, sitting on the foot of her bed within Indigo's cedar-closet earshot. "She was one of ole' Smithee's kin in Port St. Joe. Grew up scratching the sand for a living along the shacks by the railroad tracks right cross the way from us," Madear continued, trying to jostle Aunt Sadie's memory.

"Which one was she? There were so many of them mean little crumbstashers living around there," Aunt Sadie teased.

"Trina made it her business for you to know her. She was the fast-talking dark-haired one, always wheezing and hanging on to anything and anyone that looked at her for half a second. She used to steal loose cigarettes from ole man Stud. She left Port St. Joe with some trucker in a convoy carrying bottle glass out west. Nobody knew where she was or whether she'd come back. Smithee didn't much care. He'd gotten his use out of her. Folks figured if the wheezing didn't kill her, somebody she hitched up to would."

"How'd you find her here in Tallahassee, Cree?"

"I wasn't looking for her, I tell you that much," Madear continued. "But a leopard can't hide its spots. She married Stud's son, only he doesn't call himself that now. He went and got himself some fancy degrees and he's Mr. Whittier now. Money can work wonders."

"So Trin Whittier is a leopard?" Aunt Sadie said through a grin.

"She bears watching," Madear emphatically advised.

"And watch her I will," Aunt Sadie pledged, still talking through a grin. "'Cause I'm many things but I ain't nobody's leopard meat."

The ride in the big sleek gray Mercury passed manicured lawns and gigantic brick houses with black shutters. Indigo took notice of how much the houses looked exactly like the ones in her Dick and Jane first grade reading book and nothing like the house she lived in. They were big and inviting with the sunshine casting a shadow just enough to show how wonderful it was to be on a reading adventure with Dick and Jane. She could even see dogs that reminded her of Dick's dog Spot, playing on the lawn with children in their red wagons. In the window of one house she saw a cat that looked just like Jane's tabby Puff, lazily watching children play from the window sill. Indigo remembered imagining how much fun it would be to go to Dick and Jane's house. She wasn't just reading about this adventure. It was real. The neighborhood sites eased her mind of her troubles. With each passing house and lawn, she could feel herself becoming lost in the magic of visiting Dick and Jane's world.

When Mrs. Whittier turned into a circular driveway, Bethann came barreling out of the double front doors yelling Aunt Sadie's name, waving her arms in the air.

"Morning, child, morning, Bethann," Aunt Sadie said in a voice both cheerful and admonishing her to calm down. "Brought Indigo here so ya'll could play together. I got a lot of work to do so ya'll go run and play," Aunt Sadie said, nudging Indigo toward Bethann.

"Do you want to go up to my room?" Bethann turned and asked Indigo.

"I don't care," Indigo answered reluctantly.

Bethann's room was a fantasy in pink. The cover on the bed was pink. The matching pillows, fluffy curtains, rugs, everything was pink. Bethann flitted around the room like lightning, pulling out baby dolls, toys and games for Indigo to play with. Indigo stood mesmerized by the opulence of it all. She didn't know where to start first. She wanted to run around as fast as Bethann and touch everything.

Just as she was about to give in, one of Madear 's rules popped in her head: "Act like you got some home training. Don't be touching everything."

Indigo walked around the room, taking it in slowly. When Bethann took a breath, she turned and Indigo reached in her pocket and pulled out a small bag of jacks. Bethann, eager to do anything Indigo wanted, offered to play before Indigo could get the words out of her mouth.

"We need to play on the floor so the ball can bounce," Indigo directed Bethann.

"We can go downstairs in the kitchen," Bethann said gleefully.

"Naw, Aunt Sadie said we got to stay out of the way," Indigo replied, looking around the room, rubbing the base of a huge dollhouse.

"I know, we can go upstairs to the attic…the floor is wood there and the ball will bounce," Bethann quickly resolved. "Come on," she yelled, running out of the bedroom door.

Indigo picked up three baby dolls before hurrying out the door. One had a bottle with milk that disappeared when you turned it upside down. One cried when you squeezed her stomach. She sounded just like a real baby. And the last one had hair that grew when you brushed it. Indigo wanted to just stay in that pink room, play dolls and not ever think of Madear's rules. She imagined she was a movie camera, walking slowly, capturing every nuance of the room. She would re-play it that night in her mind before she went to sleep.

"Go-Go," she could hear Bethann calling, interrupting her pink fantasy. After a quick mental note to stop Bethann from calling her "Go-Go," she started toward the bedroom door.

When she passed a white table and chairs with pink tea cups set for two, she knew she had to sit down. A life-sized Winnie the Pooh bear was waiting to have tea with her. Bethann could wait for a few minutes.

After a few swallows of tea with Winnie the Pooh, she climbed the stairs to what Bethann called the attic. To Indigo, the attic was the size of Aunt Sadie's whole living space. Bethann sat cross-legged on the floor, eager for a jack stone lesson. Indigo circled the dusty room, peering inside of open boxes and gazing at discarded furniture. Even the Whittiers' packed-away items looked fascinating.

"Who lives up here?" she asked, plopping down in front of Bethann.

"Nobody, we just keep old things that we don't use anymore up here," Bethann reported. "Sometimes I come up here looking for treasure on rainy days," she added.

"Treasure!" Indigo mused to herself. "The Whittiers' house is a treasure in itself."

She slowly bent her knees and eased to the floor crossed-legged and bounced the red rubber ball against the hardwood floor. She began showing Bethann how to pick up jacks one by one and continued on to twosies, then threes until they reached tens. They played jacks until Bethann became masterful and Indigo became comfortable enough to begin hunting for treasure separated by wax paper in the dusty cardboard boxes that surrounded them. A few old hats, dresses and a couple of shawls provided the perfect backdrop for Indigo's imagination to fully absorb the Whittiers' house as that of Dick and Jane from her first grade reading primer. Bethann became Dick and Jane's Mother. Indigo became the affluent neighbor who lived in front of Dick and Jane's house. They pretended their children played together as they drank tea and shared their lives. The afternoon slipped away as they busied themselves in fantasy and fun.

"Bethann! Bethann! You and Indigo come down here and get something to eat," Aunt Sadie shouted from the second-floor landing.

Bethann and Indigo continued their play as if they had not heard Aunt Sadie's command. Swept up in a world of make-believe, they had blocked out the sights and sounds associated with their reality. The sound of Aunt Sadie's hard breathing and heavy steps trudging up the narrow attic stairs did not distract them.

"Did ya'll hear me calling ya'll?" Aunt Sadie exhaled, standing on the threshold of the attic door. "Now put all this stuff away and come on downstairs," she admonished, helping to gather items from their fantasyland.

Indigo hesitated, then stood, carrying the hats, dresses and shawls back to the cardboard boxes they came from. She folded each piece of clothing and separated it by wax paper just the way she found them. In the bottom of one of the dusty cardboard boxes she noticed a small wooden box with a word written on the side in cursive writing.

After pulling back the wax paper, she turned to Bethann and asked her, "What's this?"

"What's what?" Aunt Sadie turned and asked. "Now Go-Go, you know better than to be prying in people's stuff. That stuff ain't none of your business, put it back!" Aunt Sadie demanded.

"Sadie, she can have that old stuff!" Mrs. Whittier wheezed and whined, appearing in the doorway.

"I need you to finish this cleaning before Mr. Whittier gets home, he gets himself in an awful stew if this place ain't cleaned the way he likes it for his high holy days."

"Don't you fuss none, Mrs. Whittier, everything gonna be just fine before Mr. Whittier gets home," Sadie assured Mrs. Whittier while moving in her direction and rolling her eyes at Indigo.

Mrs. Whittier held onto the wall going down the stairs, sucking in hard breaths of air. By the time they reached the first landing, she needed to sit down in the Queen Anne chair in the living room to rest. Aunt Sadie studied her fair-skinned face tinged with blue intently and made herself busy close by. Mrs. Whittier clutched her chest for a while before she started breathing normal again. Aunt Sadie gave Indigo and Bethann five more minutes to come down from the attic before she would go up again.

"And Go-Go, you are not going to like it if I do have to come up there," she threatened. The phone rang while Aunt Sadie threatened mostly Indigo to come down from the attic. Mrs. Whittier was almost too weak to move after her hard breathing spell. She struggled to lift herself from the Queen Anne chair and reached for the phone.

"Hello," she wheezed. "Yes, Albert. Yes, I know. Yes, I will. Yes, this evening, yes," she could be heard speaking into the phone.

"I don't know what he thinks I'm afraid of! I grew up living among nig...Negroes. He must be getting himself all stirred up like everybody else in this town," Mrs. Whittier exclaimed, trying to restore herself to a comfortable breathing pattern while hanging up the phone.

"Albert wants me to drive you to his office downtown and he will take you home, cause it might be some trouble over your way," she reported, shifting to the rest of Mr. Whittier's conversation.

"I been married to him twelve years and every year this time, something gets him bent out of shape. Just once, I would like for spring to come without his high holy days driving me crazy. I wished he just let bygones be bygones," she heaved, clutching her chest.

Straightening the *National Geographic* magazines on the coffee table, Sadie turned to Mrs. Whittier's distress in a cavalier posture. Standing back on her heels with her hands resting on her hips, she quickly espoused, "Trouble is bygones are tied to the here and now."

Almost as quickly, she turned and continued straightening up, washing down and giving the house the thorough cleaning that Mrs. Whittier insisted Mr. Whittier required. She pursed her lips, frowning and tossing around in her head the sensibility of cleaning a house that was perfectly clean. As she splashed the lemon oil on the dust rag, she watched Mrs. Whittier move her lips, but she was not listening to what she was saying. The wheels of her mind were busy confirming she was duplicating her efforts. Suddenly the redundancy of cleaning overruled her better judgement. She turned to Mrs. Whittier, holding the dust rag, and point-blank asked for an explanation of Mr. Whittier's "high holy days."

Mrs. Whittier's agitation with her husband must have caused her to excuse Sadie's boldness. Usually she was a stickler for "help" knowing their place. She off-handedly remarked, "It's just a part of Albert's family's doings."

"The man has nothing to do with his family. He never speaks of them outside of this house. Every spring he picks out these days to go back to his family ways. He makes the house feel so morbid. He throws out all the bread and drinks cheap wine for a week. A morbid but clean house," Sadie blurted out.

"He gets over it after awhile." Mrs. Whittier shrugged her shoulders, demonstrating her reluctant toleration of the whole matter. Sadie continued cleaning but was perplexed at Mrs. Whittier's indifference toward her husband's family ways. Her first mind was to attribute it to the peculiarities of white folks and continue cleaning, but it was obvious Mrs. Whittier needed to unload some things off her chest.

Trin Whittier, by appearances, was the epitome of a fine Tallahassee white woman. The neatly coiffured hair, manicured red nails, town and shirtwaist dresses all accessorized with a minimum amount of gold jewelry and pearls to complete the "look." The traditional but tasteful cherrywood furnishings matched the floral window treatments in her home and connected the "home look" to a lifestyle. Her impenetrable veneer, coupled with her husband's success, was both a mystery and a magnet within the Killearn circles. It was a known fact the money of Killearn families came from generations of tobacco and seafood. Mr. Whittier was successful in his architectural firm, but that didn't guarantee him a place in the Killearn circle. You couldn't work your way into the circle. The circle embraced you.

Sadie often heard the Killearn ladies at Mrs. Whittier's luncheons whisper about her family background when she left the room. Trin Whittier didn't care what the Killearn ladies said behind her back. She even delighted in Sadie reporting their snide remarks to her. She counted the remarks as a measure of their jealousy. For Trin Whittier it felt good to be envied instead of the one full of envy. What did hurt was in her heart, she knew they thought she was an imposter. And in many ways she knew she was.

She had grown up Trina Smith, relative of "Ole Smithee," and feeling like an outcast in Port St. Joe every day of her life. She loathed the well-to-do for their lifestyle of luxury and opportunities. She constantly listened to them talk openly about her lack of proper training and upbringing, as if she was some sort of good-for-nothing. She swore in her heart that she would use every opportunity to change her station in life, no matter what she had to do or who she had to do it to, to make it happen.

One day everyone was going to know that she was somebody, she promised herself.

Her day of reckoning came closer when she stumbled across Stud's son washing dishes at the Waukulla Lodge.

Stud's son left Port St. Joe and parted ways with his father after his mother died. Practically penniless, he traveled north, taking odd jobs to earn him enough money to get to Tallahassee and study at the university. While working at the Waukulla Lodge one night, he stepped out the back door to pour out the dishwater when he noticed a shingle hanging from the crevice of the roofline. He reached to pull it down and a large piece of woodwork came crashing down. The sound of the crash startled a truck driver who was busy pummeling Trina into oblivion for stealing his wallet.

"That good-for-nothing truck driver stopped beating me when he saw Stud's son," she recounted. "He ripped my blouse and bra open and his wallet fell to the ground. He grabbed it and shoved me to the ground. I laid there eating dirt with my blouse open and bra ripped in two pieces. My bruised breasts were hanging in the air like overripe fruit. Stud's son rushed over to help me up but when I recognized him, I pushed his hand away.

"'I can walk by my doggone self,' I screamed at him. If I could walk by myself it would have been my pride that would have carried me, cause that truck driver had beaten me good. Stud's son kept looking me in the face and wouldn't walk away. 'Come,' he said, taking a strong hold of my arm, 'we cannot walk alone.'"

"Our walk together grew steady and singular as he shared his dreams for success and I tried to convince him to join me in leaving the past behind. We worked long hours at the lodge, trying to save our money to create a new life. The owner of the lodge was a bitter old man named Ira with a penchant for hard work. He took a special liking to Stud's son. At first, he guarded his conversation, only giving orders and the time of day. He never did talk much around me. I don't think he liked me too much. The closer he got to Stud's son, he'd make a point of reminding him of the condition he met me in. It didn't bother me one bit. I had Stud's son head over heels in love with me by the time that 'ole man' thought he should influence him otherwise. They'd talk out back of the lodge for hours about money business and all sorts of things. I remember the first time Stud's son told 'ole man Ira' about his parents being Jews. His face went blank and hard like stone. Ira waited a long time before he spoke. When he did speak it was stern.

"'Your dreams of success cannot include your parents' ways,' he warned him.

"You would have thought Stud's son had been hit with a hammer. He just stood there glaring at 'ole Ira.' Finally he softened and tried to persuade Ira to understand his parents' Jewish ways were a part of him. But Ira was indignant.

"'In this country it is the color of your skin that brings success, not what is in your heart,' he insisted to Stud's son.

"Stud's son grieved for his parents. He desperately wanted the life that his parents used to have before they came to Port St. Joe. It was a good life. Regensburg, Germany was a beautiful place even through his stories he shared with me," Trina recalled.

"He told of sepia-toned photographs of happy gatherings in the family garden. His memories of these photographs spoke of a time of safety and serenity that were left behind when the Nazis came and changed everything. What was once a place where he had the freedom to run and play without worry during his childhood was now either decimated or exiled to whatever safe havens families could find. He cried through tales of his family and neighbors being forced to go to far-away places like Argentina, Israel, England, New York and even small towns like Port St. Joe so that their lives could be spared. His father had chosen New York to live out the rest of his days in a place that had more Jews after his mother died.

"'It will be like the old days in Regensburg and I will not have to pretend not to know,' the father tried to persuade his son.

"Stud's son had lost hope of ever having the joy of his days in Germany. Now he was going to seek his fortune the American way, despite his father's warnings that some of the American ways they had come to know in Port St. Joe were similiar to the ways of the Nazis in Germany.

"Stud's son continued for a long while to disagree with Ira about concealing his 'Jewishness.' One night the Ku Klux Klan was holding a prowl meeting down near the swamps of the Waukulla River. After their meeting, two Klansmen feeling they were in 'common territory,' came in the lodge carrying their hoods in their hands and walking in their white gowns with red swastika crests on their chests. They wanted two cigars. Ira looked like he had seen a ghost. He was trembling and sweating buckets. They laughed at him. 'What's the matter, Ira?' they teased. 'You look like a nigger who just saw the Klan.' I laughed too, cause Ira looked mighty scared," Mrs. Whittier chuckled, lapsing back in time as she told the story. "Stud's son saw the Klan when they came in the door. He made a beeline to hide between the barrels of flour in the pantry. I never saw anything like it in my life," she continued, thumping a cigarette on the table that she pulled from the pack.

"You would have thought they were both nig…Negroes, not white men," she smirked.

After that night Stud's son began to see Ira's point of view more and more. With Ira's coaching, he began to forsake his parents' Jewish ways to travel the road of success in the Florida panhandle. His birth name was Albertus Whittnauer. He became Albert Whittier. Ira wasn't fond of me but I had the advantage of being pure white, and that was what was acceptable in the Florida panhandle.

"Blemishes withstanding, he told Albert I could help him become successful. Albert took a wife who became Trin instead of Trina. I was betting the arrangement would pay off with dividends one day. What did I have to lose? Albert Whittier knew little about women. And what he did know didn't apply to the kind of woman he married. I had a ticket to respectability, and he had a clear path to a white man's success," she reflected, squinting her eyes as if to underscore the bargain she had struck.

"'If you are going to meet success, you must start walking towards it,' Ira told Albert. 'But I don't have enough money saved,' Albert contended. 'I will give you a gift,' Ira spoke softly.

"'We have a responsibility to repair the world, it is our way,' he continued, looking at Albert.

"'We?' Albert answered in a distrustful tone.

"'Yes, we,' Ira answered back, wiping the moisture from his face.

"'I am a Jew and an old man. I am too tired and too afraid to long for the past. I must live in the present. When you first told me that you were a Jew like me, I thought that you were trying to trick me, to bring harm to me and the family that I have long ago lost track of. That night when the Klan came into the lodge, our fear was the same,' Ira confessed. 'You must go and seek your fortune. I have lost everything meaningful. Life will never be the same as it was in Germany ever again, but we must keep the memories,' he warned Albert, walking him to the office of the lodge.

"When they got inside the office, Ira gave Albert a suitcase with eighteen stacks of hundred-dollar bills.

"I had never seen so much money in my life," Mrs. Whittier exclaimed, stretching her eyes as if she was seeing the money for the first time. "I never made a practice of rolling dice often but my number came up that day. Each stack had eighteen hundred-dollar bills and there were eighteen stacks. When I asked Ira why he had the money packed the way he did, he was disgusted with my forwardness but explained Jews believed blessings came with the number eighteen.

"I didn't know or care much about Jews since I started to walk with Albert Whittier that night in back of that lodge. I still don't know that much about them and it doesn't matter.

"So you see, Sadie, Mr. Whittier's little snit about high holy days doesn't bother me much in the scheme of things," Mrs. Whittier smiled, picking up another cigarette.

"It's just nerve-wracking. Now, he's concerned with all these precautions since that nig...Negro King got shot. I don't know why he's so concerned about them colored people getting mad," she said as if Sadie wasn't colored.

Then, as if she suddenly remembered a rule that Killearn women made it a practice to be gracious at all times, even with their colored maids, she corrected herself.

"I mean, there is nothing to be afraid of…they'd better be afraid of…" she stumbled, not finishing her sentence.

Sadie stood amazed at how Mrs. Whittier could slip from the grace of Killearn-speak into Port St. Joe talk without even realizing it.

"Maybe the real point was the Killearn ladies realized it," Sadie pointed out to herself.

"Get the girls, Albert wants me to come to his office before dark," she demanded as she stood and walked to the credenza to get her purse. "I don't want to be late."

CHAPTER 8

"The issue is injustice"

"Hello, Cree, this Sadie. Mrs. Whittier is gonna to take us to Mr. Whittier's office and then he's gonna bring us home. We might not get home before it gets dark, okay? I will talk to you about it when we get home. Yeah, Indigo did fine playing with Bethann. She is a child, ain't no problem with children. Adults the ones with the problem. Okay, I'll talk to you when I get home."

Aunt Sadie hung up the receiver and began rushing around, making sure everything was spic and span before she left.

"Did you put everything back the way you found it up there?" she questioned Indigo and Bethann as they entered the kitchen.

"Yessa'm," Indigo started to answer.

"But I told her she could have this little wooden box that we found in the attic and Mother said it was okay too," Bethann chimed in.

"I said what was okay?" Mrs. Whittier asked, lightly patting her french roll, making sure every strand was in place while coming in the kitchen.

"This little box is okay for Go-Go to have," Bethann pressed.

"Oh yes, she can have it. It belongs to your father but he doesn't need it. He probably has forgotten he has it. Sadie, are we ready to go?" Mrs Whittier asked, changing the subject and reaching for her purse.

"Ready when you are," Sadie answered, shaking her head disapprovingly of Mrs. Whittier's disregard for Mr. Whittier's possessions.

"That was Sadie on the phone," Madear announced to Daddy Douglas, who was engrossed in the *Tallahassee Democrat*'s Saturday edition. She walked to the sink to start cleaning the mullet fish she ordered from Langston's Fish Market and began relaying portions of her conversation with Sadie. "Mr. Whittier doesn't want his wife over this side of town after dark, so she is dropping Sadie and Indigo off at his office downtown. Trina Smith ain't hardly scared to be around Negroes after dark. She grew up living with them in the dark every day of her life in Port St. Joe. They both did. Her husband's family wouldn't have a business if wasn't for the Negroes going to his store. Now Trina has changed her name to Trin, married, got access to some money and a Negro maid and she's fragile. She could be the talk of Port St. Joe for sure now!"

"She ain't nothing for me to talk about," Daddy Douglas added without looking up from his newspaper. "Just another white person starting over when Negroes can't even get past the starting line," he continued.

Recognizing she could be igniting the rage that had consumed her living room last night, Madear quickly tried to change the subject. "How do you want your fish, fried or broiled?" she asked gently.

"That's the very reason I'm going with Benjamin over to Frenchtown to the meeting tonight. Negro men are getting together to stand up and fight if they have to for justice. We ain't never gonna have to hide in the bushes again cause we afraid to take care of our own," he announced, trying to temper his rage.

Rolling her eyes and throwing the knife in the sink after nearly cutting her finger, Madear knew this conversation with Daddy Douglas contained a pieced-together anger from last night and a night fifteen years ago. She had tried to be supportive last night and other nights when he revisited being helpless against the Klan. Those thoughts were just too close to other secrets she wanted to stay hidden, but he just would not let it go.

"That Klan business was a long time ago. We were different people back then just, like Trina and Stud's son," she reflected. The more she thought about it, the more anxious she became.

"What you and Benjamin going to do over in Frenchtown, Hiram?" she asked him without trying to hide her growing annoyance.

"You gonna build some of those Molotov cocktails to burn down everything like those niggers doing on television? Do you think that's going to do any good, Hiram? Well, it ain't! It's just going to get you and drunken Benjamin in a whole lotta trouble!" She could hear herself yelling but she couldn't stop herself.

"Negroes been in trouble, ain't nothing new," he retorted, continuing his stare at the newspaper.

Beginning to get downright mad, Madear slung the frying pan on top of the stove, turned on the gas and continued to argue.

"You have a family to think of, Hiram!"she admonished.

He slammed the paper down on the kitchen table hard, taking a deep breath through his nose. "I *am* thinking about my family. I'm thinking about how I'm going to be the man I need to be for my son to grow up to be the man he needs to be, if I continue to be powerless."

"You been a man all this time, what has changed now?" she scoffed at him while putting the creamy Crisco oil in the skillet to melt. Refusing to let him answer, she continued her point. "Some Negro freedom fighter always up in the white people's faces about this, that and the other, and who probably was never at home taking care of his own family the way he should have been, gets killed and you lose your mind! Well, I am not having it, Hiram! Do you hear me? I am not having it!"

Rising up from his chair, as if he had been called to attention, he stood facing the direction of his wife, making gestures with his hands.

"That's just it, Cree, you never had it. You never had the eye to see that what happens to one of us happens to all us. You were too busy thinking about your pretty fair skin being an exception to the whites' hatred for Negroes rule. There is no exception. Colored is colored."

Startled but infuriated, she turned away from the stove and approached him. "Did I say I was an exception to the rule? Is that the impression you got because I want something out of life? The things I never had or never will get at the rate I'm going."

"You didn't say it out loud, Cree, you said it with the frown on your face when I left to go to an SCLC meeting or talked with your father about an SCLC meeting. No matter what horrible injustice happened to the Negroes, you always blamed the Negro for not going along. You can't see the injustice in whites," he pointed out, his voice lowering as if he was realizing the magnitude of his point as he made it.

"And all you see in white people is injustice. Maybe I can understand things are not always the way they look. Maybe I know when things ain't none of my business, and just maybe I got the good sense to walk away from trouble," she shouted, turning back to tend to the fish that was beginning to cook too fast.

"Trouble," he mumbled at first. "The issue is injustice. They start the trouble when they treat us unjustly. When we have to ride in the back of the bus and there are empty seats in the front, that's unjust. When we can't get what's due us as human beings, that's trouble they bring, Cree. When they treat Negro men like animals, to be feared, and our women like their greatest fantasy to have for their pleasure in secret, that's trouble. But the ultimate injustice is when their evil ways divide us. Do you know what I mean, Cree?" he ended, seeking understanding but consumed with disgust at his wife's lack of understanding.

"All I know is this is a bunch of foolishness. If you just tend to your business, right will come to you, Negro or white, it does not matter. Just tend to your business," she reiterated.

"First you need to know as a Negro you don't have no business, that's the problem," he said, walking in her direction. "You are just selfish to the point of being blind so you can't realize it! Has tending to your business brought what was right to you? Did your white special treatment and little gifts get you your right? Did it help get Sadie hers when she sat in that prison for five years?" He spoke the accusatory words standing right at her ear.

The sound of his words was like a piercing shot in the dark, causing her to shove the frying pan from the gas burner so fast the hot grease splashed on her arm, causing it to blister.

"I swear to God, Hiram, you have gone fool," she hissed, turning to face him. "What on earth are you talking about?" She tried to dissuade the direction of his conversation.

"I'm talking about you, Cree. I'm talking about what I should have talked about a long time ago. You think you can be colored when it's convenient! You can't have secret relationships with whites and it not bother me. It does! It doesn't matter how many gifts you get, secrets you keep or how many times you turn your eyes from the injustices done to Negroes, you are still a Negro and right now the Negro is powerless," he tongue-lashed her, standing so close a bead of his perspiration dropped in the hot fish oil and sizzled.

"How dare you speak to me that way, Hiram Douglas," she demanded, stunned by his bold references to the past. "You have no right to say those things to me," she continued, cautious her denial could make matters worse but desperate to keep the past in the past.

"I have every right," he growled. "You think I don't know. You think I don't see or didn't see."

Before he could finish his sentence, Benjamin knocked on the back door and yelled, "Hiram! All Hail! Thou shalt be king hereafter! Are you coming my good man?"

He turned on his heels, raising his hands in dismay, and announced, "I'm going to Frenchtown with Benjamin," as he walked out the back door.

Cree was so angry and shocked by her conversation with Hiram it took her a minute to get her thoughts together. When she did, she went to the back screen door and yelled his name at the top of her voice. She knew she couldn't stop him because she heard the wheels of Benjamin's car spinning in the mud before she got to the door. She just yelled his name hoping to thwart the impact of the conversation they just shared. Even though she was sure it would be re-visited again. She was mad enough to spit. She wanted to spit on somebody and that somebody was Hiram, but writing in her writing tablet had to suffice.

"Why was he was dragging up mess from the past?" she contemplated. "Could he really think I'm selfish?" she wondered. She began to finish the conversation with herself. "What was wrong with taking gifts from someone who thinks you're pretty? What does it matter if they are white? Why should I get caught up in all that Martin Luther King mess if I'm not having the kind of problems he's always preaching about? I'm just trying to make it doing the best I can do. When we couldn't make the rent and his pride wouldn't let me ask Momma and Daddy, where'd he think the money came from? It's a poor rat that ain't got but one hole. If somebody can help me along the way, what does the color of my skin have to do with anything? Hiram is wrong and pig-headed. I can't help if white men appreciate me. I can help if their appreciation gets out of hand sometimes. I can control that. Just a few gifts and a little credit here and there."

She kept examining her conscience, trying to pinpoint why Hiram couldn't see her point of view. Even though her gut told her exactly why he couldn't. She refused to give in to the bad feelings that surrounded that night the Klan came and Sadie went to jail. She had buried Mr. Joe's gifts and what she did to get them in the crevices of her mind. She had even ignored tongue-wagging speculation when she and Hiram were blessed with Magnolia seven-and-a-half months after wedded bliss. That part of her life had worn a "do not disturb sign" for years. That sign was not about to come off now. She was a young woman when Mr. Joe had given her secret gifts that were his pleasure to give and no Negro she knew could ever afford. "I ain't ashamed of nothing. Magnolia was premature and that all there was to it," she rationalized before abruptly jumping up to scrape the cornmealed mullet droppings from the burned fish grease.

"Hiram was just making things bigger than they were because he was all caught up in the shooting of Martin Luther King," she assured herself. She felt bad King was killed but that wasn't a reason to throw caution to the wind, she satisfied herself, poking the over-cooked mullet until the grease bubbled through the forked holes. "He and Benjamin will come to their senses after having one too many beers. Then he'll come home wanting my attention." She smiled at her thoughts, flipping the fish on a paper napkin to soak up the grease. The thoughts of Hiram's adoration calmed her. She wanted him to know she was serious about him joining up with them Negroes over in Frenchtown. There was not going to be any confusion in her house if she could help it. She outlined all the ways she would make Hiram sorry for the things he said to her. Then she turned off the gas on the stove and covered up the hard fried fish.

To expend some of her nervous energy, she decided to go and meet Sadie and Indigo downtown at Whittier's office. Magnolia and the young ones had gone skating with the Wallace children down the street and would not be back until late. Hiram coming home to an empty house would serve him just right, she sneered to herself.

"I feel a tremendous weight of grief, Hiram my good fellow. I am burden as if someone in my family has died" Benjamin said, breaking the silence while clutching the steering wheel with one hand and chug-a-lugging a Budweiser with the other.

"I know what you mean, man, I feel the same way," Hiram said, staring in the direction of Frenchtown just below the trailers in Polkinghorne village, still feeling the sting of his fight with Cree.

"You ever wonder why they called it Frenchtown?" he asked Benjamin, trying to change the subject and his mood. "Nothing but poor Negroes living there and none of them I know can speak French, but then Negroes can do a whole lotta of things that people don't know about," he said, amused by the possibilities of his statement.

"The Negro has expertise that exceeds the thinking of many," Benjamin added, providing segue into discussion about his job at Whittier, Krass and Pepper.

"It has been my recommendation that the Meyers site is not suitable for construction," he started. "I am certain there is a gas tank buried there. " he predicted. "Bob Pepper and I read the geological reports together. He thinks the geologist found sedimentary rocks because the land was once a marine basin. I have found no evidence to support his marine basin theory. The types of sedimentary rocks described in the report are usually present in erosion leaks from a gas tank. The rocks form because of a mixture of soil, gravel and gas. If the firm goes forward with their plans to dig without proper precautions there could be an explosion."

"Well, you told them the tank was buried there. They didn't listen. You did your part!" Hiram tried to reassure him.

" Mr.Whittier is a pretty fair gentleman, especially when the other two are not around. We talk architect to architect. He listens to me. However when it requires supporting my position in front of Krass and Pepper he abandons logic. They insist their professional experience out weighs my educational training despite my advanced academic training. If one of my ideas succeeds, they wear the credit like armor. It's enough to make you choose intoxication as a constant state of mind," he said, reaching down to the floor for another can of the six-pack of Budweiser in a cooler.

"Well, you do enough of that already," Hiram slipped in, causing them both to laugh.

"Why is it that we Negroes got to prove everything that we know to be true? We can't just be right. We don't have that kind of power Absolute unquestionable power the way white people have. Our lives, our families, our jobs, everything we need to change that died with King. He died, man! Died! Dead! Gone!" Hiram bellowed, beginning to let his emotions get the best of him again. He didn't care that he was too loud and Benjamin didn't seem to mind either. He needed to be heard the way Benjamin needed to prove that he was right about that gas tank. King had given his life so the Negro could gain power as human beings. He once heard his pastor say Negroes gaining power over their lives had to start small, like a ripple in water flowing, then flooding until it became a wave strong enough to change the shoreline. He figured getting Benjamin to point out where he thought that gas tank was, was as good a "ripple" as he could think of to start with. Convincing Benjamin took a while but he finally agreed.

They stopped at the Gulf Service Station on Railroad Avenue so Benjamin could call his office. Before Benjamin got the courage to make the call, he got out of the car to get five dollars worth of gas.

"It's illogical to make the telephone call to Mr. Whittier, if the car does not have the petroleum to travel," he protested. The Budweiser he guzzled down had given him a slight buzz and his eye-hand coordination was slightly off. He had some trouble putting the gas nozzle in the gas tank. He pumped a good portion of that five dollars worth of gas on his hands, the front of his pants and on his shoes and socks. Anxious to make a good impression in front of his boss, he took some old rags from the trunk of his car to soak up some of the gasoline he spilled. He threw the rags in the back seat and the gasoline smell filled the car space. Hiram tossed him a dime to make the telephone call to Mr.Whittier and assured him the gasoline smell would be long gone by the time they reached the Whittier, Krass and Pepper building, even though he wasn't sure it would.

Hiram knew Mr. Whittier was at the office because of Sadie's call earlier. If Mr. Whittier was still there, somehow he was going to coax Benjamin, despite him having drunk two cans of beer, into proving his point about the gas tank being on the construction site. If they could prove it to Whittier, he would have to halt construction and Benjamin would have a sense of satisfaction. Satisfaction, he felt, preceded power. He wasn't sure if his plan was going to work or prove anything, but it felt like they were about to gain some satisfaction and they both needed to think power was not far behind.

Whittier answered the phone on the second ring. Somehow Benjamin managed not to let the buzz of the Budweiser cause him to blubber his sentences. Hiram could see his head bobbing up and down the way a man bobs his head when his number comes in. He opened the car door and started the ignition with a smile. " Mr.Whittier said he'd listen."

Albert Whittier stood with the telephone receiver in his hand. Why, he questioned himself, had he agreed to spend time on a Saturday afternoon talking with Benjamin about some gas tank he believed was on the construction site? The contractors were going to start digging on Monday. Krass and Pepper had made it clear they thought Benjamin was a good copy and errand boy but had little expertise in architecture. Thousands of dollars were tied up in the project. They were not about to rely on the hunches of their colored help, who spent far too much time in the cabinet where they kept their good Scotch. Clyde Benjamin was a knowledgeable man well into his forties and Albert Whittier knew his hunches had proven right on other projects. He praised Benjamin for his skills openly when they were alone in the draft room, but he felt cowardly for not speaking up when his colleagues frequently claimed Benjamin's suggestions as their own. The firm viewed Benjamin's infrequent brilliance as an added advantage afforded them for their forward thinking to hire a Negro as part of their team.

"Perhaps I owe him," he thought to himself, reflecting for a moment on the words of Ira to "repair the world." "I'll give him a half-hour and promise to pass the information along, that should pacify him and allow me to get back to work."

"Hi, Daddy," Bethann squealed, interrupting his reflective thoughts.

"Hello, pumpkin!" Mr. Whittier responded with the reddish color of joy spreading from the corner of his month to cover his whole face. "What did you do today?" he asked.

"Indigo and I played up in the attic. We found a lot of treasure."

"Treasure in the attic?" he mused.

"I let them go through some of those old boxes in the attic," Mrs. Whittier interjected into the conversation as she came into the door, putting her purse on a desk.

"Mother said I could give Indigo a gift from the treasure."

"That's nice," Mr. Whittier answered, preoccupied with the drawings on his draft board.

Sensing her husband's preoccupation with his work, Mrs. Whittier informed him, "Sadie is sitting out in the car waiting for you to take her home. You aren't going to be long, are you? You promised we would go to the Springtime Tallahassee reception at the country club tonight. I looked all over Thomasville to find my gown for the Spanish Krewe and I picked up your tuxedo. The Spanish Krewe is the first level for provisional members. Bill and Bob are in the War and Reconstruction Krewe but they are old-time Tallahassee. One of them are sure to be voted to lead the parade as Andrew Jackson in a couple of years. The membership committee will be at the reception. They may announce that we are provisional members tonight. We must be there. It is all arranged. Bethann is having a sleep-over at the Daleys."

"I know I promised, dear, but this topographical survey is needed for the contractors on Monday and it just isn't ready. I'm afraid we're not going to make it."

"Albert, I've been waiting for this opportunity for a long time and we're not going to make it because of a survey? Why can't you finish the survey on Sunday?"

"I will probably have to work Sunday as well to finish it. I'm really sorry but I must have it completed by Monday."

"You're not really sorry. You don't care about what this means to me! We are going to be presented as provisional members. I can feel it. We are shoo-ins and you are going to let our chance slip out the window?"

Indigo knew when grown-ups were about to get into a fight and it sounded like Mr. and Mrs. Whittier were about to get into one. She wanted to leave the room but Bethann was busy touching things in her father's office. She could hear one of Madear's rules coming in her head: "Don't mind grown folks' business." Then another rule, "If your company stays put, you stay put," popped up behind that one. Her instincts told her if she busied herself by playing with the wooden box Bethann had given her earlier, she would satisfy both Madear's rules.

Mr. Whittier signaled his wife to table their discussion for later and walked over to the charts on the wall next to where Indigo was sitting playing with the little wooden box. Mrs. Whittier, obviously annoyed, pulled out her cigarette case and lit up a cigarette, even though there was a sign that said "no smoking." He took off his glasses, wiped his furrowed brow and sighed at the sight of his wife smoking for a moment. Resuming his composure, he forced a smile as he approached Indigo, glancing down at the little wooden box she played with in her hands.

"What do you have there?" he said, reaching slowly for the box. Upon closer examination of the box, his face contorted, turning a slow red. He swallowed hard before he spoke.

"How did you get this?" he demanded to Indigo.

Bethann, startled by her father's tone, rushed toward him. "Daddy, I gave it to Indigo, Mother said I could."

"This is not a toy! It is personal! It belongs to me." Mr. Whittier spoke with anger and a deep conviction.

With a sullen look on her face, Bethann protested, almost in tears, "But Daddy, I can't take it back. I gave it to Indigo."

Mrs. Whittier had purposefully allowed her thoughts to drift out the window along with her cigarette smoke, wandering the seven miles down Monroe Street toward the McClay Gardens Country Club. She was contemplating how she could finagle Killearn membership without going to the obligatory cocktail party. Bethann's pleadings interrupted her thoughts and she raced over to the middle of the office with her cigarette perched between her fingers.

Mr. Whittier turned towards his wife and shouted, "You had no right to give away my personal belongings."

Bethann began to cry. Indigo wanted to leave the room, with or without Bethann.

"What personal belongings?" Mrs. Whittier mocked.

"This personal belonging," he rebuffed, holding the little wooden box in his hand close to her face.

"Bethann, you and Indigo go outside and play or something, your father and I need to talk privately," Mrs. Whittier dictated, trying to hide her anger.

"Can Indigo keep the box, Daddy?" Bethann whimpered.

"NO!" he shouted, causing Indigo to reach for Bethann's hand and lead her out of the room.

"Damn it! Albert Whittier, don't you ever use that tone of voice with my child again." Trin Whittier threw her partial cigarette on the floor and ground it with the sole of her shoe, and readied herself for battle with her husband.

"All this hoopla about that little wooden box! You had forgotten all about it."

"This wooden box is Jewish! It represents who I am and what I must pass on to our child!" he shouted back, rubbing the name "Whittnauer" printed on the side.

"It's who you *were*, because now you are a fool who can't let go of the past," she belittled him.

"I am a fool, a fool to let go of who I am and what I believe in?" his voice escalated.

"You are a fool to think you are passing this garbage on to Bethann! Have you gone crazy? Albert, look around you! Do you think for one minute you could have achieved all of this, if you really were what that little box represents? No, you couldn't! Jews are not welcome in Killearn. Get ahold of yourself, this little wooden box means nothing!"

"It means nothing to you. It means everything to me!" he roared with a sadness in his eyes.

"Albert, for God's sakes, stop this!" she pleaded with contempt.

"You will never understand," he began to say just as Benjamin and Hiram walked in the door.

"Mr. Whittier, I came over to have that talk. We spoke on the phone, sir?" Benjamin began.

"I'm sorry, Benjamin, I can't talk about that right now, something has come up," he said, shaking his head, looking flustered.

"But sir, I brought my friend, Hiram Douglas. We came over to have that discussion regarding the Meyers project. It'll only take a few minutes and if we can walk out to the construction site, I can make my point more clearly." Benjamin insisted.

Hiram looked like he was about to become sick to his stomach. It was the kind of sudden sickness that erupts when dignity is derailed by disgust. Disgust was part of the expression on all their faces. It was deeply etched on Mrs. Whittier's face as she fidgeted just beyond the conversation. Hiram watched Benjamin plead to share his knowledge and skills, hoping Mr.Whittier would listen to give Benjamin some satisfaction, but he didn't.

"Is that gasoline that I smell? I just can't take the time right now, Benjamin. Perhaps some other time," Whittier insisted, walking around in circles, removing his glasses and putting them on again.

"But Mr. Whittier, I'll just..."

"Nigger! He said he didn't have time today, did you hear him?" Trin Whittier let the words come rushing out of her mouth like a flash of sharp lightning in the summertime.

Benjamin's chance at satisfaction was gone. The voices in the room suddenly stopped as her words ripped through the room, imposing a shocked silence. The eyes of the men gazed at Trin Whittier. The hardness in her face reverberated, transcending the moment in which they stood.

CHAPTER 9

"A certain kind of fire no water could put out"

The late-afternoon sun descended in the sky, casting a rust-colored hue over the construction site behind the Whittier, Krass and Pepper's office building. Hiram and Benjamin stood silently on the threshold of the rear exit, watching the daylight turn into dusk. Benjamin pulled out a Budweiser from the lining inside his jacket and held it in his hand. The sound of Albert and Trin Whittier's muffled voices vibrated the air space outside the building. Even though Hiram knew his legs had carried him out of the room when Mrs. Whittier issued the order to leave, the sequence of his departure was not clear. In southern nomenclature, the tone she used to mouth the word "nigger" meant move quickly. But it wasn't her tone that trivialized his discontent. It was her timing. She torpedoed the target at a time when there should have been a truce. After all, the King was dead.

Hiram looked somber-faced beyond the parking lot at the construction site in the distance. He spotted Indigo and Bethann playing a pat-a-cake game just beyond a contractor's rig parked in the parking lot. He threw up his hand and waved, remembering for a moment the look on Indigo's face last night when his expression of grief over Martin Luther King's death erupted. Indigo quickly returned his wave while trying to keep up with the fast version of the "Miss Mary Mack All Dressed in Black" song with Bethann.

"Is that your Daddy?" Bethann gasped between lyrics.

"Yeah, he's the one without the hat. That's my neighbor Mr. Benjamin with him," Indigo answered, trying to keep Bethann focused on the rhythm of the game. Bethann dropped her hands to her sides and stared in the direction of Hiram and Benjamin. Indigo turned and followed her stare.

"He doesn't look so angry," she posed to Indigo.

"Well, he was last night. Just like your Daddy was today."

"Why you think they got so angry?"

"Your Daddy got mad because you gave me his personal stuff. My Daddy got mad because Martin Luther King was killed."

"My Daddy and I watched the news reporter talk about Martin Luther King's killing on the television last night. The reporter said the colored people were making cocktails and starting fires."

"Yeah, they were making Molotov cocktails with bottles of gasoline and old rags they lit with matches to start a fire," Indigo added proudly. Suddenly she was glad Daddy Douglas had insisted she watch the news.

"My Momma said that would never happen in Killearn."

"Probably not," Indigo added, thinking of the afternoon she had just spent in Bethann's resplendent neighborhood.

"What's that in your neighbor's hand?"

The loud tinging sound of metal hitting against metal interrupted their conversation and Indigo's relishing thoughts of playing at Bethann's house. She could see her father and Mr. Benjamin pointing in the direction of the construction site where the loud tinging noise was coming from. She could also see Mr. Benjamin holding something in his hand. She knew from the many times she'd watched him through her kitchen window he was probably holding a Budweiser can. Indigo had enjoyed her afternoon of mutual sharing with

Bethann but providing an explanation of Mr. Benjamin's Budweiser can felt like a part of the Madear's "keep your family business in your own house" rule. The tinging sound reminded her of the school bell at Nims Junior High and instantly she realized how much time had passed since she left her Aunt Sadie sitting in the Whittier's car.

"Let's go see if Aunt Sadie is ready to go!"

"O.K., let's race. "

Bethann squatted near the ground in position to bolt while tying her pink sneakers.

Indigo hesitated. "Maybe I should go see if my Daddy is gonna take me home."

"Nooo! They look like they're leaving. Let's just race to Sadie sitting in the car."

Hiram and Mr. Benjamin were waving their hands in a loud discussion that floated monosyllables in the direction of Indigo and Bethann. Squinting at them in the distance and listening even harder, she thought she detected her father yelling. The faint sounds reminded her of his yelling the night before. Spontaneously she discounted going closer to him. In a pirouette motion, she faced Bethann, pumping her arms in preparation to race to the finish line.

"One, two, readeee…Go!" she shouted, running ahead of Bethann toward the front of the building, making a path diagonally across from her father and Benjamin.

"No fair! Cheater! I wasn't ready!" Bethann jetted behind Indigo with Hiram and Benjamin in her distant peripheral vision.

Hiram and Benjamin had heard the tinging sound also. It had momentarily distracted Benjamin from the Budweiser in his hand. His eyes darted in the direction of the construction site trying to locate the origin of the sound. Hiram turned to follow his gaze. Benjamin spotted a man in a hard hat hammering metal stakes in the ground. He glanced at the Budweiser he was holding and then looked back at the man hammering stakes.

"Hiram, my good fellow let's just get out of here." He held his Budweiser high up over his head, pointing it to the sky in a frail attempt to justify his urge to drink. "It's enough to make you drink, I tell you."

The dejected look Hiram saw on Benjamin's face in Mr. Whittier's office was back again. Hiram intuitively knew just by watching Benjamin that the tinging sound and the man hitting the sledgehammer deepened the lines of dejection on his face by the minute. He contemplated encouraging him to tell the man at the construction site about the gas tank. If he could convince him, they could still salvage some satisfaction and gain some power out of this day. He wanted to try. He needed to try as much for Benjamin as for himself.

"Man, you could tell that man out there with that sledgehammer about the gas tank."

"No I shall not try to convince any more Caucasians today! Often these ministers of darkness, tell us truths in little things to betray us into deeds of greatest consequences", he replied using a Shakespearian verse.

Benjamin waved his left hand in the air, holding tightly to the Budweiser with his right. He had an aching for the beer now. It didn't matter that it had begun to get warm from being in the inside of his jacket lining. The buzz of the earlier Budweisers had long worn off. He needed to feel the liquid in his mouth washing over the place his pitiful pleas had come tumbling out. He visualized the foam rising up in his throat so high he would need to swallow hard to keep from strangling. His throat ached with thirst to drink it down fast. He wanted to feel the alcohol rush to his brain and create a fog in his mind. The gastric juices in his stomach churned in anticipation of the explosion with the Budweiser. The Budweiser was his prescription for demoralizing episodes at Whittier, Krass and Pepper.

"When inspired by brilliance at work, drink Budweiser after work," he sneered to himself. "If symptoms continue, drink as often as necessary until symptoms subside or you die inside, whichever comes first," he confirmed, squeezing the beer can without realizing it. "This can is all the power I need," he nodded to himself. "The gentleman, out there is setting up the four survey markers. They are going to break ground on Monday," he conceded to Hiram.

"Don't you get tired of drowning yourself in that Budweiser?"

Hiram lunged forward, determined to grab the beer can out of his hand, but Benjamin held it up high out of his reach. With disdain in his eyes, Benjamin flicked his thumb underneath the tab of the beer can and white foam oozed out.

"If you want somebody to listen to you, throw that can down. Nobody can help a drowning man who wants to drown. You're trying to drown out what you know. You can't do it, even if you stayed drunk twenty-four hours, seven days a week. You would still be a college-trained architect, and no Budweiser can take that away. It is one thing for them to not believe in you, but you don't believe in yourself. It's you holding you back! Not them! YOU! That makes you good for nothing. You got a chance here to talk and prove what you talking about." Exasperated and sweating, Hiram stood staring Benjamin in the eye. Benjamin stood looking past him, gripping the beer can of oozing white foam.

"What you got to lose, man? King already lost everything," Hiram asked in a last-ditch effort.

Benjamin began walking dropped-shouldered toward his car, looking at the white foam starting to saturate the sleeve of his jacket.

"The King is dead, man!" Hiram yelled.

Albert Whittier emerged outside the building just as Hiram's admonishment of Benjamin hit the airwaves. He saw the man hammering in the construction site. He heard the tinging sound in syncopation with the screeching of Cree Douglas driving her Ford Fairlane's rubber-burning tires into a tight parallel parking space. He watched her bring the car to an abrupt stop and get out. She walked up to him mouthing words, but he could not concentrate on what she was saying. She stretched her big eyes at him in speculation and continued inside the building. He didn't respond to her abrupt walking pattern because his mind was on Benjamin standing near his car by the construction site. He had promised to listen to Benjamin. It was his intention to listen. But his daughter's genuine attempt to boost a budding friendship had awakened silent voices from his past. The voice of his mother Anacostia, the voice of his father Abraham, the voice of Ira, and the voice of Trin whom he realized he knew least of all, sang in unison in his head.

The trepidation of his mother's "The Jewish tradition must not be broken" repeated in rounds with his father's "It is up to you, my son, to repair the world." The concerto continued with Ira's cautionary phrase, "It is the color of your skin that brings success not what is in your heart," and ended with Trin's bitter words of hate. "Nigger, did you hear him? Did you hear him, nigger?" Did you hear him! Did you hear him! Did you hear him! JEW, did you hear him? JEW! JEW! JEW!

Cree entered the Whittier, Krass and Pepper office building slightly put off by Mr. Whittier not answering her when she asked if Sadie was inside. "Everybody is acting crazy, white folks included, since King got killed," she thought to herself. She walked into the receptionist area and met Trin Whittier coming out of the back offices.

"Well, well, well, if it ain't Spoongal?" she purred to Cree with fire in her eyes. The blaze in the irises of her pupils was ignited long before meeting Cree in her husband's office or on that sandy road in Port St. Joe fifteen years ago. That inferno was a certain kind of fire that no water could put out. Its fumes were perpetually fueled by a deep fear and instinct to survive by any means necessary.

Cree stood facing Trin Whittier, puffing a cigarette, decked out in her Killearn finery. The venom in her voice contradicted the virtues represented in her attire. From her tone, Cree knew she was about to have her past excavated piece by piece for the second time in what was becoming a long day. She watched closely the way Trin Whittier scrounged the cigarette between her lips before she exhaled. Her mannerisms paled in comparison to the first time their eyes met in a Tallahassee encounter. Trin Whittier had been anxiously trying to make a good impression at the Ladies of Killearn annual dogwood tree planting tea at the county office. Cree had been a waitress in the county cafeteria then. Her boss had given her the opportunity to serve at the tea as a commendation for the pleasant personality she always had for the white bosses who ate in the cafeteria.

Trin Whittier and Cree Douglas became two actresses playing opposite each other vying for reviews that could lead to stardom. The dogwood tree planting tea audience looked upon them both as amateurs. Trin Whittier's performance as a lady of Killearn wasn't flawless but it was good enough to get her another invitation when she asked to be invited.In accordance with Southern protocol, Trin Whittier upstaged Cree Douglas's performance and from that point on, they were typecast in a long running predictable saga.

"Good afternoon, Mrs. Whittier, is Sadie done yet? I came to pick her up before it gets too dark if you don't mind. I'm sorry to disturb you, Mrs. Whittier. If I can just get Sadie and Indigo, I'll be gone."

"I know you're sorry; a nigger is always sorry," Mrs. Whittier said, blowing the cigarette smoke out hard and coughed harder, standing by the window. A loud tinging noise outside the window caught her attention. She looked outside the window, turning away from Cree for a minute to determine where the noise was coming from.

The tinging sound became louder. Bethann approached the corner of where her father was standing, and the figures of Benjamin and Hiram stood in the distant background. She was racing to join Indigo at her family's car in front of the building. She kept her stride while peering to see her father's face from a distance, hoping his anger had subsided. Albert Whittier noticed her but could not find the words to address her.

Hiram's words rang in Benjamin's ears. "It's you holding you back!" Benjamin raised the oozing beer can over his head and threw it toward the construction site with all his strength. Trin spotted the man with the sledgehammer. He raised the sledgehammer high above his head and brought it down, making the tinging sound even louder. The remainder of the Budweiser spilled over the ground of the construction site. Bethann caught a glimpse of Benjamin reaching back and throwing the can up in the air. Trin Whittier cursed her husband as she caught a glimpse of him facing the parking lot perpendicular to the two Negro men standing in conversation. Cree looked around the room to see if there was any sign of Sadie and Indigo. The sledgehammer came down on the fourth marker once with another loud forceful ting. Albert Whittier saw Benjamin turn his body when he flung the Budweiser in the air. He began to walk towards him without knowing what he should say. Hiram saw power emerging in Benjamin's pitch and sighed a breath of satisfaction. The Budweiser can hit one of the red-tagged survey markers with a clunk. Indigo jogged back around the corner to see what was keeping Bethann. Mr. Whittier came closer to Benjamin's car. Hiram came closer to them both. Trin raised her fist to knock on the window to get her husband's attention. Indigo and Bethann began running hand in hand to the car where Sadie was sitting. Cree walked over to ask Mrs. Whittier once more if Sadie and Indigo were ready. After the sledgehammer hit the marker the fourth time, the tinging sound became prolonged and deafening. Within minutes the construction site and the utility poles connected to the Whittier, Krass and Pepper building erupted into a thunderous inferno knocking Benjamin, Hiram, and Mr. Whittier to the ground. Gasoline filled the air. The part of the Whittier, Krass and Pepper building that was not engulfed in flames shook from the force of the explosion, causing windows to crash and walls to crumble. Suddenly fire was everywhere.

Benjamin slowly pushed his upper body up from the ground using his forearms. The reflection of the blistering rays of heat danced in his eyes. "Fire!" he mumbled to himself, rising slowly, nodding and cracking a smile.

"Fire! Fire! Fire!" he burst in a giggle, rising to his feet. A jubilant dance took possession of his feet and through a peal of laughter he raised his arms in the air, screaming to the top of his voice, "All Hail thou shalt be King hereafter"

CHAPTER 10

"We've got to see it through"

The vibrations from the explosion cracked the windshield of the Whittiers' big Mercury sedan and jostled Sadie from napping in the back seat of the car. Orange flames fanned the wind just beyond Mr. Whittier's office building smoldering in black smoke. A wave of worry began to creep into Sadie's mind as she remembered watching Indigo and Bethann skipping in the direction of the office building earlier that afternoon. The black smoke from the flames made the sky so dark it was hard for her to determine the time of day. She was sure she had not been dozing in the afternoon sunlight for more than forty-five minutes, but everything around her suggested day had turned into night. She shoved her shoulder against the car door and pulled the latch. The acrid smell of smoke filtered through her nose and burned her throat when she stepped outside.

The power of the explosion knocked Indigo and Bethann into the hedges surrounded by crape myrtle bushes just as they turned the far end corner of the building. They hung onto each other tightly, stretching their eyes in amazement at the panorama of smoke and flames.

"I want to go home," Bethann pouted, breaking their silence.

A red blush in the milk-color skin tone of her cheeks began to stretch across the fine, blond, short hairs all over her face. Tears were trapped in her eyelashes. Indigo thought of how much fun she had playing in Bethann's attic that afternoon. She had taken a trip inside the perfect world of Dick and Jane. She did not want it to end, even though she knew it was time to go home. The sky was getting darker by the minute from all the smoke and fire. It had been more than an hour since she and Bethann left Mr. Whittier's office. The uneasy feeling she had about Martin Luther King and the trouble that followed since the news of his killing was broadcast over the radio had returned, more powerful than ever. She felt the joy of her visit to the perfect world of Dick and Jane slipping away. She gripped Bethann's hand tightly, hoping to regain the warmth they shared throughout the afternoon.

"We are going home. We have to find my Aunt Sadie and your Daddy. Then he will take me home and then you…"

"I don't want to go with you to your 'nigger' house! I want to go with my Momma to my house."

Indigo had heard the phrase before. She had even heard her father exclaim it to Mr. Benjamin during some jovial neighborly discussion.

"Go to your house, nigger, or come to my house, nigger."

But the way Bethann said the words "your nigger house" made Indigo's face feel warm. She felt the grip of their hands together loosen along with their budding friendship. She wanted to believe the slippery sweat of their palms caused the separation, but the stiffness in Bethann's body said otherwise.

"SADIEEE!" Bethann yelled with hysteria building in her voice.

"Aunt Sadieee! Over here," Indigo shouted, determined to regain solidarity with Bethann.

Sadie's eyes followed the sound of Indigo and Bethann's voices through the pastel flowers of the crape myrtle bushes adorning the landscape of the building adjacent to Mr. Whittier's. She raced to the bushes clutching her chest, feeling her heart pounding in her palm. The closer she came to the girls, the more the bittersweet aroma of the crape myrtle flowers mixed with black smoke filled her nostrils. Sadie looked back at the building, and huge clouds of black smoke jutted out of the windows and swept up to the sky. The puffs of black smoke against the backdrop of the sun setting in the sky cast an onerous shadow on her path. The weight of her deliberate steps sunk deep into the soft earth. She came within arm's length of the crape myrtle bushes surrounded by cedar mulch and evergreen hedges when Bethann jumped out and tugged vigorously at her arms.

"Where is my Momma, Sadie? Where is Momma?"

Indigo eased from crouching beside the bushes and stood next to Bethann, who was beginning to have an urgency in her whining to match the water swelling in her eyes.

"She is with your father, they must have..."

"No, they were in the office, and my father got angry at me, so my mother told us to go outside. Then I saw my father outside walking near the parking lot. He wasn't far from Indigo's Daddy and her neighbor with the 'cocktail' in his hand," Bethann blurted out without stopping for a breath.

"Slow down, Bethann, what neighbor? What cocktail?"

"Mr. Benjamin," Indigo answered with a look of surprise and sadness on her face, slowly turning in Bethann's direction.

"The cocktail the news reporter was talking about on television last night," Bethann continued.

"Mr. Benjamin and Daddy were in the parking lot and Mr. Benjamin was..." Indigo tried to explain but Bethann cut her off.

"I saw Indigo's neighbor throw a cocktail like the Negroes on the news and start the fire."

"No, you didn't! You did not see that! Aunt Sadie, she did not see that! It is not true!" Indigo protested, looking at Bethann with an expression of shocked disbelief.

"I *did* see him throw that '*cocktail*'! I saw him! You saw him too! You know you did! I asked you what was in his hand and then he threw it and fire and smoke started coming from everywhere!" Bethann began to whimper, returning the stare of disbelief Indigo sent in her direction.

"Aunt Sadie, that's a lie!" Indigo was forbidden to say the word *lie.* She also knew her words needed to be forceful to refute what Bethann was saying. If using a word forbidden by Madear was what she had to do to convince her aunt Bethann was not speaking the truth, she was willing to risk the consequences of Madear's switch.

"It didn't happen that way. Mr. Benjamin didn't…" Indigo tried to continue.

"Where is my Momma?" Bethann demanded in distress, almost collapsing in Sadie's arms. "I do not see her out here. Where is she, Sadie? Where is my Momma?"

Sadie looked in the direction of the Whittier building, and a swirl of black smoke hovered near the front of the building and floated out in the parking lot. The sirens of the county's four fire trucks were blaring. People were beginning to gather and gaze. She knew Mrs. Whittier hadn't come back to the car because she would have awakened her, dispensing closing orders for the day. She could feel trouble of giant proportions brewing within the smoke she inhaled. Over the past two weeks every other night she had dreamed of a young girl running down the street, taking her clothes off as she ran. Last night she dreamed it was scorching hot as the young girl ran down the street. The first thing she did when she got up was thumb through the Oracle dream book she bought from Economy Drugstore in Frenchtown. She discovered "running and taking off clothes" meant "something someone wants to remain hidden was going to be revealed." She had a sinking feeling. A feeling she had not had since she ended up in a jail cell for five years. She never forgave Hiram for keeping quiet about the dress buckle in his pocket. She began to converse half-aloud with herself, weighing her speculations.

"Maybe he had taken it for Cree and was too shamed to admit it. If the sheriff knew it was a 'nigger man' who took the dress, the consequences would have been swift and severe. It still doesn't justify me having to pay the price for Hiram's fool's love," she grunted. In her gut she knew Cree was somewhere in the middle of Hiram's involvement with that belt buckle, regardless of the number of times she denied it. "He never stopped trying to please her, even though no man could," she continued to analyze. She and Cree were sisters, she equated in her thoughts. "But Cree had needs that went too deep for satisfaction. Being as light as she was and Daddy giving her everything she whimpered for did not help. When she got older, she just looked for men like Daddy that she could whimper and get what she wanted. That was the problem. Cree wanted everything including the best of both worlds and not caring to belong to either."

Reminiscing made the hairs on Sadie's neck rise up. But the thought of Mrs. Whittier in that office building filled with smoke and Benjamin having something to do with it rattled her even more.

"Come on, child, we will go to the car and your Momma will come before long," she tried to soothe Bethann.

"No, she won't because she's inside, Sadie. I did not see her come out. She's inside and there is smoke coming out of the windows. I want my Momma," Bethann pleaded.

"Hush now, child! We are going to find her! You are getting yourself all upset. Everything is going to be all right." Sadie spoke forthrightly, cuddling Bethann in her arms while leading her in the direction of the car. Indigo stood motionless, breathing the smoke fumes and replaying Bethann's words.

"Your nigger house…I saw Indigo's neighbor throw a cocktail like the one on the news."

Her words cut with the surprise of a concealed knife among friends. It sliced her apart from Bethann when they had been so close in Dick and Jane's world. Then with the swiftness of an assailant, it cut away at Indigo's familiarity with the 400 block of Osceola Street.

She had not realized when her visit with Bethann veered into the realm of her emotions. She stood there not sure of whether to follow Sadie and Bethann or run to find her father and Mr. Benjamin to try and hold on to the comfort of a world only days ago she had been sure of. Standing still, breathing in the putrid smell of black smoke and replaying the sound of Bethann's vista for "her house" and the "cocktail" put Indigo on the verge of tears.

For nearly two days now, she wrestled with the news of Martin Luther King and his invasion in her life. The vigor of his name and the reaction of those hearing of his killing had created an aura that was both unstoppable and overwhelming. The water from her eyes began to flow freely, calling forth a wailing cry deep within her chest that bore pain and confusion. A warm radiating pain consumed her in the squall of black smoke. It heated the warm water gushing from her eyes. Pain resonated from her insides where assurance and familiarity mapped out the boundaries of her existence only two days ago. Her confusion expanded to a world in flux without map or boundaries. Everything had changed and was changing.

Martin Luther King's name laced the conversation and actions of all the people around her. She did not know him, but she felt him under her skin. She had not heard his voice before last night, but now it rang in her ears. Talk swarmed around about him in proportion to the tale of "the vampire" fifth grade boys at Bond School swore stalked the path cutting across Palm Beach and Saxon Street. When the "vampire tales" were at the peak of schoolyard discussion, she had dreamed each night of walking through the path alone. Her heart would race as hard as her legs would carry her, trying to escape the faceless vampire. The dreams would wake her exhausted and sitting on the side of the bed. She would slide down on her knees and head for the kitchen, careful not to wake Magnolia, who had little indulgence for the vampire tales. The creaky sound of the refrigerator door would summon Madear to meet her in the kitchen. They would share a glass of ice water, talk about how much she was growing, and eventually meander into a discussion of what the dreams meant. The conversation always ended with Madear standing, offering a reassuring touch and nudge to return to bed. Indigo knew the nudge was a signal to stand and start in the direction of the bedroom. On cue, Madear would offer a one-armed hug and say, "We've got to see it through, Indigo." Madear's response offered understanding of Indigo's fear of the faceless vampire but offered no clear antidote for escape. Walking arm in arm down the short hallway from the kitchen to their separate bedrooms, Indigo knew the "we" in her mother's soothing maternal good-night greeting really meant she had to see it through. Nevertheless, her mother's words were comforting. When she closed her eyes, the drowsiness would come quickly, leading her to the path of dreamless sleep.

The circumstances of the day and the two days previous were the centerpiece of a teary reflection pool with currents too strong to soothe with maternal Band-Aids. Taking in everything in her reflection caused an awareness to swell up in her blossoming chest like a new vest. She cried aloud, making her chest heave up and down like a water pump with its handle stuck. Finally, she deciphered her mother's words had not been antidotal at all but preparation for the days and nights that followed her hearing the news of Martin Luther King. Timidly, she pressed her hands across her chest for calm, cupping her sore protruding nipples. With the expansion of each of her fingertips, she took stock of the place her anticipated bosom would be. Her mother's words describing the high-chest "I" people on her father's side now floated from the crack in her secret cedar closet and embraced her. She contemplated trying on the double "A" training bra Madear bought as part of her school clothes. "Why did you buy this for me? I don't need it," she whined when her mother pulled it out of the Lerner's shopping bag.

"Yes, you do! You got titties coming," Madear insisted.

"I don't want them," Indigo protested.

"You're getting them whether you want them or not. It's nature's gift to you," Madear advised.

"Child, titties are a treasure the Lord gave women as a way get a man's undivided attention," Aunt Sadie teased, adding to Madear's advisement.

"Sadie, you ought to stop!" Madear giggled.

"It's true, Cree. The Lord knew that apple trick was a good one. You know a man always looking for a chance to get even. The good Lord let some man come up with the idea of these bras just so they could get even," Aunt Sadie vamped, pulling her blouse down, disclosing the purple lace of a "D" cup to Madear.

She knew she could find treasure in her mother and aunt's conversations, especially the ones she heard in secret. Strings of conversations replaying in her head were beginning to sound like a message that you find in a connect-the-dot activity book. Just knowing there was a possible remedy for the madness she was experiencing made the flow of warm waters from her eyes decrease. Her head felt clearer. "See it through," she repeated, abbreviating her mother's words, searching for their comforting power.

She could see her Aunt Sadie and Bethann walking in the direction of the growing crowd of people assembling beside the fire truck parked next to the Whittier building. The deputy sheriffs dressed in green and white uniforms restrained German shepherd dogs in midair, using leather leashes. When an eager spectator got too close, the sheriff allowed the teeth of the dogs to graze the skin on his arm just enough to draw blood and respect. A chorus of "The King is Dead!" "Black Power!" "Power to the People!" rang out. The crowd seemed bigger and louder than what Indigo had seen in the news reports on television. Indigo started to run to catch up with her Aunt Sadie and Bethann. Then she just walked, looking straight ahead, listening to the refrain, holding her chest up high.

CHAPTER 11

"Non-violence or non-existence"

The power of the explosion from the parking lot knocked Trin Whittier and Cree to the floor, followed by an avalanche of books and furniture. Smoke was beginning to seep in. A concrete beam had fallen from the ceiling and blocked the door. Cree opened her eyes and strained to touch her brow. It was bloody. Underneath the blood was a swollen spot pulsating a dull pain. She heard Trin Whittier strain the walls of her chest to cough. The cough triggered Cree's memory before the explosion. Then she remembered she had come to meet Sadie and Indigo to give them a ride home when she encountered Trin Whittier with her teeth on edge. It was all coming back to her. The fight she had with Hiram was the catalyst that brought her to Mr. Whittier's office in the first place. Now she would make him double sorry for the way he had spoken to her that afternoon. She would not have to say a mumbling word. The guilt he was going to feel for the part he played in her lying with a gash on her head in Mr. Whittier's office would be compensation enough for his carrying on and digging up the past. Things could not have worked out better if she had planned it. He had made her so mad she had to go and get Sadie, her baby sister, to console herself, she mused. He would hate hearing that. She had come face to face with the "nigger hate" of Trina Smith dressed up as Trin Whittier. She anticipated he would feel intense guilt for not being able to protect her. Her thoughts pondered if his chest would throb against some of that "Iko strength" he always talked about ran in his family. This explosion just sweetened the pot, she contemplated. He would be so beat down with guilt she was convinced he would not want to talk about Port St. Joe and the past for a long time. She relished having this advantage over him. The advantage would be useful later. Now she was lying on the floor of a smoky room with a gash on her head.

"Help me. Somebody help me. Spoongal!"

Cree stiffened with silence when she heard the voice.

"Why didn't she just die?" Cree thought to herself. "She is a miserable white woman. The good Lord cursed all women with a few days of misery each month, but Trina Smith's misery is above any woman I know," she analyzed further. She had determined Hiram was due a comeuppance, but being trapped with Trina's venom was not part of the bargain.

"Spoongal!" Trina's breathing was heavy, followed by a soft whistle. Cree remembered what the Negroes from her neck of the woods in Port St. Joe used to say about Trina's wheezing. "The wheezing will kill Trina if a man didn't do it first."

"I'm over here, Mrs. Whittier," Cree finally answered, hoping the circumstances that surrounded them would dilute the acrimony between them.

"Well, come over here and help me. I can barely breathe and I want to get out of here."

Even though she was blowing like a train locomotive about to come to an unplanned stop, Trina continued to barrel out orders, Cree thought to herself. Instinctively, she used an overturned chair on the floor to pull herself up. She stood steadying herself, looking around the smoky room with furniture sprawled all over it. It was almost completely dark from the haze of black smoke with just a small stream of white light peeking through the metal vents high above where the tall bookshelves had stood before the explosion. A pungent odor laced the black smoke, and Cree was beginning to taste bitterness in her mouth. The taste of bitterness and the confinement of the room made her feel light-headed. The price of teaching Hiram a lesson was getting expensive. She needed help. No one knew she was inside the Whittier building except Mr. Whittier, and he had looked right past her when she approached him. She could not count on him to help her. After all, he was married to Trina, and she would be his first priority. When she looked over at the metal vent with the light streaming through it, the glare it cast in her eye made her head hurt worse. It was becoming obvious she could no more help Trina than she could help herself.

"Spoongal, for God's sakes, get over here and help me get out of here," Trina spoke laboriously.

"We're both trapped in here. I cannot help you and help me, too," Cree spoke, surprised at her own words. She was breaching the relationship rules between Negroes and whites and did not care. What good was behaving the way it was expected for Negroes to act around whites if she and Trina were going to die? she thought to herself.

Trina forced a dry laugh. Cree could see her body clad in a red dress struggling to pull up from among the disarray of furniture.

"But if you don't help me, Spooongal, you die whether you get out of here or not," Trina spoke stretching out her words because it hurt her lungs to speak.

Cree started to give a pugnacious reply but looked up at the dark smoke coming in from the vent overhead. She dragged her body near the debris away from the vent. Just as she leaned onto a rail to assure her footing, Trina crawled up to her feet, limp from wheezing so hard. Cree, half-standing and half-near collapsing, looked down at her. The tables had turned but the circumstances were too grave to fully enjoy the power of the change.

"Help me," Trina whispered through a wheeze.

"You can help yourself if you cover your mouth to keep from breathing the smoke," Cree snapped.

Trina tried to cover her mouth with her hands but began to choke and cough.

"I can't. I can't breathe. I am going to die. Help me," she pleaded

"How can I help her? She just as soon spit on a colored person than help them, and she wants me to help her. She has been the source of nothing but pain and trouble for me, and now she wants me to help her. If it wasn't for her, Hiram would have never gotten that green belt and maybe I wouldn't be in this smoky room," Cree thought to herself. Suddenly Hiram's unbridled anger for white folks began to make sense. "It would suit me just fine if Trina Smith, all dressed up as Trin Whittier, would just die in the thickness of all this smoke."

"You are on a high horse, aren't you, Spoongal," Trina wheezed, managing a grin. "You think you are just as much woman as me. Your bright near-white skin is what got you fooled. You think you got a license to be treated like a white woman. I know what it's like to want something you cannot have, Spoongal. I lived it every day of my life in Port St. Joe, but then I am white and you never will be. You want all that comes with being white so bad you would do anything. Including letting your sister go to jail and watching me die here in this smoke. You might not kill me outright, but you would watch me die. If you had a chance, you would flash those big hazel eyes and wiggle that big butt in front of my husband to get everything I own. Of course, you would do it in secret."

"And if your husband wasn't taking a look at this big colored butt in the first place, I wouldn't be able to get a thing," Cree snapped back. The snide response was all she could muster after having her coloredness challenged for the second time that day. The attack unleashed thoughts she had gathered for years.

"It wasn't my fault I was born a fairer shade of brown, but it's been my burden," she sighed in the recesses of her mind. She was the runt coloring of her parents' otherwise deep-brown litter. A coveted bright curiosity everywhere she went. Her mind raced with reflection of the agony she suffered because of her skin color. Among coloreds, she was the measure of good hair and skin. Among whites, she was the desirable selection. But when she tried to benefit from any of the praise extended her, she was restricted and rejected. She used to love to listen to Hiram talk about the better days King and SCLC were bringing for colored folks. His non-stop talk of freedom would go on for hours, and you could see his enthusiasm swelling up in his chest. He really believed they had some kind of power to change things. "I was captivated by the gleam in his eyes," she remembered. Too bad that gleam in his eyes could not charm all Negroes into believing. You got as many shades of Negroes as you got colors in the rainbow. Everybody knows a rainbow comes from the power of light, and the light is white. Somewhere, way back down the line, somebody figured out the closer the shade was to white was where the real power was. Negroes cannot expect white folks to treat them equal when they're fighting each other for lightness like crabs in a barrel. "Some are born with it like me, and some are spending every nickel they can trying to get it from a bottle in the drugstore," she surmised.

"You barely colored and sure not wanting to be colored," Trina shot at Cree, disturbing her introspection. "You are the worse kind of nigger, Spoongal. You are a pretender. You act colored among your kind, but the minute you are out of sight you'd do a nigger in as quick as I would to get ahead."

"Wrong! I wouldn't do anybody in to get ahead. You should save your breath. You would not want to die at the hands of a nigger," Cree taunted. She could not restrain her uncensored anger and frustration. She did not care. The possibility of dying was real. If she was going to meet her Maker, it was going to be with a clear conscience.

"You should hope I don't die. If I die, your whole family is going to suffer. The suffering will start with that weasel of a husband of yours and his friend who works for Albert. They were in here worrying my husband before I threw them out, and I saw them in the parking lot right before this building blew apart, and, Spoongal, you Know once the police comes, all niggas's any where near here are going down, including you."

Trina heaved her chest hard as if it took every ounce of her strength to relay what Cree knew was the bitter truth. Her thoughts were racing like the engine of a speed car in a derby at the fair-grounds. Trina's words stung the same way Hiram's did earlier that afternoon. Cree's own words of indifference were the ones that had her hands trembling.

"I am not any nigger. I am a slightly-white-colored nigger. I cannot do anything about it, and I am not sure I would if I could. What in the hell was so wrong with it anyway? If 'green-colored' people had a better life, I would roll around in the grass until grass stains became a part of my skin," she admitted partially to herself and Trina. "Skin color has caused me nothing but hurt in my life. I can admit that. Poor Sadie, my own sister, sat in jail for five years. It just 'bout killed me every time I thought about it. Things just got out of hand. My husband Hiram is a good colored man. But you gave him that doggone belt and put a wedge of doubt between us that has lasted for years."

"Trying to make peace with your Maker, Spoongal? Touching, but I need you to get me out of here more than I need or care about ole Miss Heloise's dress you stole a lifetime ago. And you need to try and get out to help your old man and his friend come up with the bond money they are going need to get out of jail. I can hardly breathe in here."

"What in the world was Hiram and Benjamin doing at Mr. Whittier's office? They were supposed to be going to Frenchtown for the Martin Luther King rally," she thought to herself. As much as she did not want to admit it, Trina was right. Just as sure as Hiram and Benjamin were in that parking lot where the explosion came from, they were going be in a world of trouble when came time for 'fending and proving. She knew Hiram had gone overboard with all this business about Martin Luther King being killed, but now things had gone too far. She frantically began to pull at some of the fallen furniture and debris, trying to remove it from the entranceway. The gash on her head was beginning to hurt again. She dropped to her knees from the strong smell of smoke and sought refuge underneath an open-backed desk. Trina lay gasping on the floor just on the other side. The smoke was making her wheeze more than Cree had ever seen before. She was having trouble keeping her eyes open. The smoke was burning Cree's eyes too. Cree knew they could not inhale the smoke much longer, or it would kill them both. Trina looked at her with desperateness, wheezing for help.

Cree thought about the rainbow and shades of Negroes. She had never been closer to white and the light than she was right then. She had power. Her lungs were stronger than Trina's. Death would come quickly. All she had to do was sit and do nothing, using the best of the non-violence Hiram said King promoted. "Hiram and his Martin Luther King would be proud," she smirked. She did not have to deliberate between non-violence and non-existence. She had not lifted a finger, and non-violence was in full operation as Trina Smith drifted off into a non-existence. The sirens blared outside. She hoped rescue would come before her lungs gave out. She had to stop breathing so much smoke if she was going to survive. Her mind raced to find something to filter the smoke and save her lungs. The hooks in the back of her form-fitting bra were digging in her skin.

Sadie would often tease her about "trying to fit a melon in the space of a lemon." "Girl, you need a larger bra," she would chastise. Whenever those hooks started to wear deep into her skin, the larger size would become an option. Despite Sadie's words the dividends she received from the cleavage a 38D gave her made the discomfort seemed worthwhile. She reached under her knit blouse and used two fingers to unsnap the cotton vise. When she exhaled, the elastic band sewn around the edge of the bra relaxed, leaving imprints of the pressure that had been encasing her torso. The bra straps slipped down her shoulders, leaving welts of relief. In a callisthenic motion she took the bra off completely without removing her knit blouse, the way she did every evening the minute she got home from work. She placed one of the bra cups over her mouth and recognized a new value in a size 38D.

The smoke was lulling Trina into sleepy unconsciousness. The soot from the smoke darkened her skin to the shade of a light-colored Negro. Cree watched her struggling to breathe while fighting the drowsy pull of the smoke. Trina could hear the faint sounds of voices and sirens outside the building. She caught flashes of Cree pulling her bra out of her sleeve. She felt as if she was being levitated in a cloud of the black smoke engulfing the room. Through the blink of her lashes, she saw Cree put the bra cup over her mouth. She wanted to yell and demand help, but her voice was lost in smoke. Mentally she girded herself to fight against the urge to float. Her lungs were getting tired contracting to breathe. She felt herself drifting toward a light beyond the smoke back to Port St. Joe.

She felt like her brain was splitting. One half wanted to yell with all the hatred she had inside for Spoongal to come and help her. The other half could not pinpoint the place or the time her disregard for the coloreds began or why it was important. The brightness of the light suspended the drifting when she reached the memories of Port St. Joe. She stood in midair looking back as the brilliance of the light seemed to demand accountability. She anticipated questions from the light and answered in detail.

"Ma and her Pa said the coloreds were shiftless and lazy and needed the rod of correction from a white person before they would do right. They never explained why. When Ma died of fever and Pa drank himself to death, I went to live with Uncle Smithee. He did not care much for the coloreds either but he hated the well-to-do whites in Port St. Joe more.

"'They treat me like they better than me when their white skin ain't no whiter than mine.'

"The only difference I could tell in the way whites treated him and the way they treated the coloreds was in the eyes. The coloreds could not look a white in the eye. It was not allowed. Smithee looked them in the eye and it was as if they did not even see him. I don't know which made him madder: the fact that they looked right through him or that he was powerless to do anything about it. I just know his hurt hardened to a hateful disposition and handicapped him and everyone in his presence. I was a part of that presence. I could not escape the wrath that came with it. I shared what Uncle Smithee felt but weighed it differently. I didn't like the way they treated me too, but I loved the power they had. I studied them very closely. I put together what I knew with what I saw to master the power they had.

"Uncle Smithee colleted the rent from coloreds sharecropping on the north property deep in the woods of Port St. Joe. The Kirklands, a rich white family owned the land but rich white families seldom bothered to collect money from coloreds. They hire whites like Uncle Smithee to do it. Mr. Kirkland was not regular in picking up his rent money from Uncle Smithee but Uncle Smithee regularly used it to buy corn liquor. Mr. Kirkland would get mad as a firecracker when Uncle Smithee did not have his money. He would threaten to fire him and put us out of his house. After coming to get his money and getting mad enough to do harm a few times, he offered Uncle Smithee a technique to collecting rent from "coloreds."

Mr. Kirkland told Uncle Smithee, "colored people will pay whatever you say if you say it right. It's the way you say it!" Even if they do not owe they will pay. They keep their extra money in a white handkerchief tied in a knot. Look for a bulge in their pocket, the extra money will be there, Mr. Kirkland insisted waving his index finger to make his point.

Uncle Smithee relied on Luke, one of the colored sharecroppers to round up all the others for rent collection. Once when Luke came to the house to let Uncle Smithee know the other sharecroppers were ready for rent collection, the technique was put to the test. The effects of corn liquor and the need to replace Mr. Kirkland's money pushed Uncle Smithee to demand double rent. Luke's eyes stretched with surprise but remained cast down. Uncle Smithee grasped the doorknob, to steady his gait and a glare to force down his sense that blood did not come from a turnip and Luke did not have the money. Luke shuffled his feet while sweating up a storm trying to make Uncle Smithee understand his demand was unreasonable He pulled a dirty white handkerchief from his pocket and wiped his face repeatedly. Sometimes he just held the dingy white handkerchief to his mouth as Uncle Smithee repeated his demands for double rent. Between Luke's 'well, sirs' and 'no disrespect, sirs' was a discerning look. Maybe he was trying to see if the corn liquor was just getting the best of Uncle Smithee's judgment. Each time he lifted his eyes up to examine the power behind Pa's words, his eyes would retreat downward. Luke put the handkerchief back in his pocket. Up and down their eyes went like a tug-a-war. Uncle Smithee came closer and spoke firmly, bearing his eyes down on Luke. Luke surrendered, pulling dollar bills and the handkerchief out of his pocket."

Floating in an abyss of smoke and darkness she relived her memories. She recounted the triumphs in her life beyond Port St. Joe against a screen of bright white light. She had risen from poor white trash to become a white woman of Killearn. Only Luke's handkerchief streaked with darkness eluded her, dangling just before her eyes in the light.

CHAPTER 12

"The content of their character"

The sirens were blaring. The sound came within earshot of the thirty or forty colored families living in the rundown wooden houses high up in the ridge beside the railroad track. The neighborhood overlooked the Whittier office building on Gaines Street. Gus Manning, a shoeshine man in the Whittier building, and a group of men were getting ready to set up for their Saturday evening crap game that would continue well into the night. Women were sitting on their front porches marking time, getting a head start on Sunday dinner. Some sat in pairs sharing tales of their work week and catching up on their soap operas on the edge of the front porch. They picked collard greens, laying the leaves for cooking on yesterday's newspaper and throwing the leaves with wormholes in them in a brown paper bag. Others rocked back and forth in wooden rocking chairs, shelling peas in silver tin pans or pots with blackened bottoms sitting in their laps. The children playing in the front yards scampered underneath the front porches when the explosion from the Whittier building filled the sky. The women nervously gathered the children and ushered them inside. Gus and a small delegation of the men and a few of the women decided to cross the railroad tracks and get a closer look.

Everyone had been on alert since the news of Martin Luther King's death hit the airwaves.

The neighborhood heard the shooting and rancorous chants of "Black Power" from the students up on the hill at Florida A&M that night. For seven hours, the students armed themselves with rounds of ammunition including guns, rocks and bottles bombarding the police and any strange cars that came within the vicinity of the campus. The folks in the neighborhood on the ridge heard the revolt and some were motivated to join in. Other residents weighed their losses and waited. When the explosion of the Whittier building lit up the sky over Gaines Street, it was another call to arms. Many of them had jobs in the office-building cafeteria or as janitors or like Gus they worked together at the shoeshine stand in the Whittier building. The thought of their loss of income drew them to the parking lot of Mr. Whittier's building.

Gaines Street sat on the periphery of Florida A&M. The university sat on one of the seven hills in Tallahassee. The boulevard or the "set" as the college students called it was the heart of the university. When the explosion from the Whittier building filled the sky, it beaconed the already agitated students hanging out on the set. When the folks from the ridge reached the parking lot, the students had already arrived. The ridge folks took one look at the smoking building and huddled together in prayer. The students began to organize their protest. Gus, the cafeteria workers and the janitors began to moan in unison, anticipating the sting of harder times. Before Gus could raise the raspy crackle in his voice to get the first "Father God" out of his mouth, the white deputy sheriffs and police officers arrived, jumping out of their squad cars swirling nightsticks in air. They penetrated the crowd of ridge folks and students within minutes, swarming around them like flies on rotten meat. The design of executed maneuvers anticipated trouble far worse than the police experienced Thursday night on the set. Yellow tape marked a line between the colored crowd and a distance beyond the smoldering building. The police used their nightsticks to enforce the line and thwarted the bravado of any colored person considering a challenge.

Sadie saw the crowd gathering from a distance and made Bethann and Indigo get in the back seat of Whittier's car as soon as they reached it. The car was parked directly in front of the crowd and the police officers' boundary line. When Bethann and Indigo got on their knees and looked out of the back window, they were in full view of the chaos erupting. An ambulance with *Tallahassee Memorial Hospital* written on its side was parked near the front entrance of the Whittier building. Sadie kept her eyes fixed on the ambulance. The thick-pane glass door that had led to Mr. Whittier's office was off the hinges. Fragments of broken glass jutted out of the frame. Two white medics bustled out of the entranceway, carrying a woman on a stretcher with a plastic apparatus over her mouth. Sadie sat up straight and peered over the front seat. She strained to see through the front window of the car, then abruptly decided to take the girls and walk over to the ambulance.

"Come on, girls! Come now!" she ordered Indigo and Bethann.

Indigo and Bethann were still wide-eyed from watching the crowd of coloreds being held at bay by Tallahassee's officers. They followed Sadie out of the back seat of the car without questioning. When Bethann saw two medics coming out of the building with the woman lying on a stretcher, she screamed to the top of her voice.

"Momma! Momma!" she shrieked, running to the side of the stretcher.

Sadie and Indigo ran with her but they could not keep up with her. Bethann reached the medics carrying the stretcher and flung herself on top of the woman they were carrying. Sadie and Indigo reached the stretcher and looked at the woman lying on it. It was hard to tell if the woman on the stretcher was a white woman at first. Her blond hair streaked with soot still resembled the Breck brand of strawberry-blond number #27 that Mrs. Whittier bought from Sullivan's Drugstore. The black soot darkened some of the whiteness in her face. The red dress sticking out from under the white sheet and those sparkling red fingernails were the dead give-away. It was Mrs. Whittier lying on that stretcher. The white medics kept trying to push Bethann away but she kept calling her Momma, trying to shake her and wake her. Sadie tried to pull her back but Bethann's grip was firm. Indigo tried to tell her friend everything would be all right, but Bethann never took her eyes off her Momma lying on that stretcher. Sadie and Indigo had lumps the size of a quarter in their throats and water welling up in their eyes. They both shook their heads, trying to imagine how the day could have gotten so out of hand.

Mr. Whittier walked up with a deputy sheriff at his side. He gulped at the sight of the woman lying on the stretcher covered in a white sheet. His face tightened and grew red when he recognized the woman was his wife. Mechanically, he reached to pull his daughter away from the stretcher. Bethann whimpered like a baby and cried out for the maternal assurance a child needs when the world becomes too cruel. She clung onto the stretcher with all her might, trying to arouse her mother from a smoke-induced sleep. Mr. Whittier cupped her face in his hands and spoke softly to soothe her. She looked over to Sadie and reluctantly let go her grip on the stretcher.

As soon as she steadied herself, she began to spit out to her father the account of the colored man with Indigo's daddy throwing a Molotov cocktail and starting the fire. The deputy sheriff watched the interaction between Mr. Whittier and Bethann closely. The two medics looked on somberly, shaking their heads. Mr. Whittier looked bewildered but the deputy sheriff looked interested.

"Daddy! I saw him throw the cocktail in the air. I saw him do it. He threw it in the air and then the explosion and fire started. I saw him, Daddy. I was walking with Indigo and I saw him."

"No, you didn't! You are a liar. You did not see that happen. You know you did not!" Indigo had leaped from Sadie's side and stood in front of Bethann, Mr. Whittier and the deputy sheriff.

"I did see it and you know I did. He threw a cocktail just the way the colored people did on the news last night. All those colored people were mad about that man King so they made Molotov cocktails and burned everything down. I saw him throw it. I saw him. He threw it at my father's building and started this fire. Now my mother is hurt," Bethann screamed at Indigo.

Indigo glared at Bethann, trembling with anger. The deputy ignored Indigo and began to ask Bethann where did she see the men last. Bethann raised her hand to point in the direction of the parking lot. Indigo knew she had to protect her daddy and Mr. Benjamin from a lie. Her Aunt Sadie always said, "Lies have the power to hurt people." Now right before her eyes Bethann's lie was about to hurt people she cared about if she did not do something to make the truth come forward. She wanted to just shake Bethann and make her realize the Molotov cocktail she thought she saw Benjamin throwing was nothing more than his daily portion of Budweiser.

When Bethann pointed toward the parking lot, describing Benjamin and Daddy Douglas, Indigo could not contain herself. She ran to the deputy, grabbed his arm, and began to yell.

"You've got to listen to me. It didn't happen that way at all. She just *thinks* she saw him throw the cocktail. He threw something but it was not a cocktail. We were a good distance away from Daddy Douglas and Mr. Benjamin and she could not see, but I see him every day and I know he did not do it. I know him. I know them both…" Her voice trailed off as the deputy pushed her to the ground. He put his hand on the gun in his holster and snarled at Sadie.

"You better get a hold of your 'nigger child.'"

Indigo lay whimpering face-down in the grass in front of the Whittier building.

"Wait a minute, Officer. She's just a child. I did meet with Benjamin and the child's father earlier this afternoon in my office. Benjamin is a colored apprentice in my architectural firm. He came to see me about some plans earlier. I did see them standing in the parking lot."

"That's where I saw him throw the Molotov cocktail," Bethann chimed in.

"Did you see him throw anything? Niggers everywhere have been rioting since this King nigger was killed the other night. Could he have been a member of one of those nigger riot parties?" the deputy interrogated, staring at Mr. Whittier.

"Well, I saw them but I can't say, I mean what I'm trying to say is, I've known Benjamin a long time, he's not the kind of guy that would be a part of a riot or throw something like that."

"When did you last see them?" the deputy questioned irritably.

"Earlier, it was almost dusk but I saw them right before the explosion."

"Can you show me where they were when you last saw them?" the deputy asked, motioning Mr. Whittier and Bethann to come with him.

Sadie pulled Indigo up by her arm. The weight of the day's happenings was bearing down on Indigo's legs. She felt weak. Sadie grabbed her by her waist and helped her to stand.

Sadie hugged Indigo's waist tightly, cast her eyes in the direction of the Whittier car and began to step. Indigo lifted her head up to force her body to follow the direction of her Aunt Sadie. Another pair of ambulance medics carrying a body on a stretcher out of the Whittier building distracted her. She focused on the medics carrying the body on the stretcher. As they got closer, Indigo could see the body was not covered the way Mrs. Whittier was.

The nipples on the woman's breasts were pointing up at the sky in full view, bouncing in the cool spring breeze to the rhythm of the wheels that carried her on the stretcher. Sadie recognized the woman first.

"Cree!" she screamed, dropping her hold on Indigo's waist. Indigo nearly stumbled. She could not move. Her eyes were having trouble focusing on the woman lying motionless on a stretcher. She heard what her Aunt Sadie had called the woman but she did not want to hear.

Sadie ran to the stretcher and tried to cover up her sister's chest.

"We found her with a half of a bra covering her nose and mouth, lying across the white woman we took out earlier. The other half of the bra was in her hand. Too bad, the white woman could have used it. Is she kin to you?"

"She's my sister. Is she all right? What was she doing in there?"

"We just try to save them, we don't try to figure out how their situation came to be. She is in better shape than the white woman is, though. She used that big bra to cover her mouth and that probably saved her life. A few more minutes and the white woman would have been dead. We are taking her to A&M hospital. That is the teaching hospital and where most colored people go. They are probably going to keep her overnight."

"Can't you cover her up better than that? There was a sheet over the white woman," Sadie demanded, pointing out the difference in the way they were transporting Cree.

"Did you hear what that nigger said?" one of the white medics retorted.

"Well, you know their King went and got himself killed the other night and niggers are going crazy all over everywhere," the other medics joked.

"As long as they understand that kind of craziness in Tallahassee will cause them to end up like their King," one of them said as their backs faced Sadie and Indigo.

Indigo felt like someone had socked her in the stomach. Martin Luther King was making things go from bad to worse again, she thought to herself. It was bad enough her mother was lying on that stretcher, but what she wondered most about was if she was going to die. She had never even known her mother to be sick. Now she was lying on a stretcher with her eyes and ears closed to the world. She was bypassing the duration of a prolonged sickness or the spontaneity of an unforeseen car accident, the way people rode in the back of ambulances on television. Indigo felt her legs fighting against collapsing to the ground of a world pulsating with the aura of Martin Luther King's death. She wanted to vomit. Her head was spinning. She wanted it to spin until she could not hear or feel the effects of his name. She wanted to be dizzy until her eyes blurred. She wanted to block out all the chaos he was causing. If the hands of time could go back she would have skipped the Thursday evening he died altogether, she vowed to herself.

The deputy shined his flashlight on two figures casting a dark shadow off the curb of the sidewalk.

"Yes, that's Benjamin and his friend," Albert Whittier pointed out to the deputy. "They came to see me a little after four this afternoon. We did not talk long. My wife became impatient with Benjamin's talk and asked them to leave," Albert Whittier explained. Bethann squirmed, holding her father's hand.

"What they want to talk to you about?" the deputy queried.

"Benjamin was worried about the plans for the construction out here. He didn't think we should break ground."

"Did they get mad when your wife asked them to leave?" the deputy inquired.

"Well no, not really. Benjamin is an agreeable kind of guy, he just…" Albert Whittier's voice trailed off because the officer interrupted him.

"What about the other one, was he mad?"

"I didn't notice," Albert Whittier answered, beginning to get annoyed.

The burly deputy wore a short reddish-blond crewcut and chewed a cigar between the gaps of his tobacco-stained front teeth even when he spoke. His broad chest with a badge on the flap of the shirt pocket demanded authority and respect. His manner made Albert Whittier uncomfortable. He felt the urge to choose his words carefully. The deputy shined his flashlight directly in the face of Hiram and Benjamin. Hiram raised his hand just above his head to shield the glare of the flashlight from his eyes.

"Is anything wrong, Officer?" Hiram asked, careful to downplay his indignation.

"Get on your feet and put your hands in the air so that I can see them," the deputy shouted.

"Officer, is that really necessary? I told you I know these men. Benjamin has been with my firm for several years. He and his friend came to see me. I do not believe they came to hurt anyone. I can vouch for the contents of their character. I mean I can vouch for the contents of Benjamin's character."

Bethann tugged hard on her father's hand and started to plead. "They hurt Momma, Daddy. I saw one of them throw that cocktail and start the fire."

The weight of her words and the deputy's insinuations confused him.

"Let me do my job, Mr. Whittier! On your feet, niggers."

The deputy pulled his gun to emphasize his directive, shifting his weight to one leg. His eyes twitched as he stared down at his perpetrators with small beads of sweat beginning to saturate the band of his regulation Stetson hat. His hands had never killed before. His heart had sworn to protect and serve. Physically his world had never been within ten miles of a colored person. He had never even had a conversation with a colored person, with the exception of dialogue exchanged in some act of servitude. His training reinforced "niggers" were about to commit a crime or running away from one. It had been the first "point to remember" the day he began the academy. Now it was his guide for action in the line of duty.

Hiram and Benjamin jumped to their feet and raised their hands in the air. They looked at each other and then at the deputy shining the flashlight in their eyes. Hiram swallowed and took a deep breath, bracing himself for an encounter every colored man anticipated and most feared. The transformer in the streetlights hummed. The tall chrome poles beamed light across the parking lot. A streak of the light glistened off the barrel of the deputy's gun. Hiram thought of when his brother Hale had looked down the barrel of a glistening gun. Hale was not afraid. His passion had been shiny things that were a distraction and annoyance to those who watched over him. The flicker of reflective light consumed his small ability to focus. Laughter spread across his face when he captured mirrored images offering meaning to the complex world living around him. Death claimed him carrying a look of child-like exuberance, having delighted in reaching for the brilliance just beyond him.

In the midst of deadly chaos, Hiram was having an epiphany about his brother. Maybe the "Iko" he had thought skipped Hale's simple life had actually guided him fearlessly through it, Hiram concluded to himself. He had dismissed any reverence for "Iko" the night Hale died. Breathing through his nostrils, biting his lips to keep them from quivering, he challenged family lore to bring forth "Iko" if it was coming.

Benjamin was still giddy from the explosion. He had not grasped the full meaning of the deputy's order.

"I can explain the particulars of what happen here, Deputy." Benjamin was talking fast, spouting out words in the early-evening air, turning around to face the deputy. "We were walking to my vehicle over there when—"

"Turn around and keep your hands in the air," the deputy growled, interrupting him.

"Benjamin man, do like he says. Don't say nothing," Hiram warned, turning his back to the deputy and extending his hands higher. The deputy put his gun back in his holster and pulled out his nightstick. He tapped Benjamin's arms with the nightstick, indicating he could bring them down from the air.

"I came to see my employer over there, Mr. Whittier, and my friend Hiram accompanied me," Benjamin explained.

"You always come to see your boss man on a Saturday afternoon?"

"No, sir. This is the first time."

The deputy walked closer to Benjamin, looking up and down. He breathed deeply and leaned in close.

"What did you come to see him about?"

"I wanted to discuss a potential problem with some construction plans we've been working on."

Albert Whittier seemed as nervous as Benjamin and Hiram. He wiped his brow and removed his glasses repeatedly.

"Is that right? What's that smell?" the deputy continued to question Benjamin.

"Lots of smells out here tonight, Deputy. Which smell do you mean?" Hiram offered, trying to stop Benjamin from talking too much.

"A smart nigger, huh? A man was killed out here tonight, boy! I want to know about the smell of a dead white man and the smell of rags soaked in gasoline used to kill him," the deputy roared, walking closer to Hiram and then back to Benjamin.

"I am not sure what you mean by that statement, sir. We came to talk to my employer over there and—" Benjamin tried to explain between the deputy's interruptions.

"And then you made some explosive cocktails to get your boss man to realize your point of view?" the deputy queried, sniffing and rubbing his nose.

"No, sir! The very idea is absurd!" Benjamin insisted.

"Officer, I told you I know this man, he wouldn't have anything to do with anything like that," Mr. Whittier pleaded.

"What's that I keep smelling," the officer demanded, ignoring Mr. Whittier. He moved closer to Benjamin and bent down near his waist. "Put your hands in the air." He began patting Benjamin down on his chest, back pockets, front pockets and ankles. "You wouldn't be carrying a weapon out here, would you, boy? Since that nigger King got himself killed, you cannot be too careful."

"No, sir," Benjamin answered.

"It's gasoline I'm smelling. You are reeking with gasoline. It's all over your pants," the deputy announced.

The deputy put his nightstick away and pulled his gun. He moved swiftly to examine Hiram for the smell of gasoline and stepped back, satisfied. "You are both under arrest for murder, arson and conspiracy."

He spit out the charges in rapid succession before he pulled his walkie-talkie from his left hip pocket and radioed for back-up. More than thirty deputies were on the scene in less than five minutes. They combed Benjamin's car until they found the rag he used to wipe up the gasoline he spilled at the gas station.

After Benjamin and Hiram were handcuffed and shackled, the deputy turned to Albert Whittier, who looked dejected. "What were you saying about the contents of those niggers' character?" he smirked.

CHAPTER 13

"When will you be satisfied?"

Albert Whittier could not remember the words he said to the deputy walking through the front parking lot of his office building. He was looking for Sadie and the Mercury sedan his wife drove to the office. The red Scooter Baker he had driven and parked behind the office building was destroyed in the explosion. He held Bethann's hand tight. He could feel the sadness on her face spread to his hands, covering his arms and extending to his chest the way bleach stains dark clothes.

He reflected how misery entered his life that afternoon like a volcano. Trin had spewed the warning ashes of disaster when she demanded Benjamin and his friend leave. The explosion, Frank Malloy getting killed, Bethann accusing Benjamin of throwing the cocktail that created all this damage, and watching Trin roll out on a stretcher was like standing at the bottom of the volcano watching the hot lava bubble down with nowhere to go.

Bill Krass and Bob Pepper were standing just beyond the crowd with two deputies in the front parking lot. Albert Whittier could read the frozen worried faces from a distance.

"Albert, over here!" Bill yelled, waving his hand.

Albert walked up slowly, greeting his partners somberly.

"What the hell happened here? Frank Malloy from the construction company is dead," Bob blurted out.

"I know." Albert spoke just above a whisper.

"Well, what do you know about it?" the voice of one of his partners asked.

Albert Whittier was having trouble focusing his eyes on which mouth the words came from in the dim streetlight. Bill and Bob had known each other since grade school, played football together at Florida State and attended graduate school together. Their families were a part of a group of Tallahassee families that plotted their children's path to success from the moment of conception. Albert met the twosome in his first year of college and played a big role in tutoring them toward an advanced degree. Albert had the brains and they had the brawn to make just about anything go their way. They were both big and muscular with large hands that gripped tightly in a handshake. They both walked with a strut and swaggered, periodically grabbing their crotches to let you know they were in charge. They were good company to have around if you were an unknown trying to fit in. Sandwiched between the two of them, Albert was instantly welcomed in any circle.

Bob's strut had a limp because of a bad fall he had taken on the gridiron doing his college years. Other than that, they were inseparable in their demeanor. They could finish the other's sentences in business discussions. Bob was cool as a cucumber, but Bill was the one with the temper. Over the years, he had managed to suppress his tongue in genteel business conversations. Nevertheless, when something got in his craw and angered him, his eyes would flash red and his voice would waver between booming and yelling until Bob took the lead. Albert could not see the pupils of Bill's eyes. He had heard so much and seen so much already, who was asking the questions hardly seemed important.

"There was an explosion is all I know," Albert sighed.

"The deputies here say Benjamin did it with one of those 'cocktails' they reported on the news the other night. They say gasoline was all over him and on rags in his car. They say he had someone with him," a partner's voice added.

"Benjamin came to see me earlier this afternoon. He wanted to talk about the construction plans. He thought something was wrong with them. My wife was with me. It was not a good time. They left and the explosion happened."

"Did you see it happen? It has destroyed the whole office building. The rest of the tenants in the building will be looking to us to take care of this, Albert. This could blow our contract with the State. Benjamin's place needed to have been made public a long time ago. He is just an errand boy. What does he know about building plans?"

"I can't believe he did this crime. He just doesn't seem like the sort of guy that would," Albert Whittier tried to interject.

"He doesn't seem like the kind of guy that would do what, Albert? Bite the hand that feeds him, burn down the business he worked for even though we gave him a chance when no one else would! Albert man, Benjamin is a nigger and there is no telling what a nigger will do. Those people do not care. They are unpredictable and cannot be trusted. We trusted him and look what it brought us."

"Benjamin has been a satisfactory and loyal employee to us. I am sure there is some reasonable explanation for this. If we put our heads together we could probably work this mess out," Albert pleaded.

"Enough is enough. There is nothing to work out for Benjamin. The nigger has to face the music. We will probably be sued, Albert, and lose everything, all because of our generosity. Is that what you want? When will you be satisfied then?" The partner's voice seethed with anger.

Albert nervously reached inside the pocket of his pants, trying to deflect the sting of his partner's wrath. He disliked it when they spoke so crassly but he accepted their dispositions as the bitter part of success. He touched the wooden box inscribed with the name "Whittnauer." He remembered his reaction to Bethann giving away the wooden box. That reaction started the flow of discord leading him to where he stood. He stroked the box with his index finger and let it rest inside his pocket. The feel of the wood sent him to faint memories of his family's happiness. The memories were so much a part of him that he had long forgotten whether he had experienced them himself or lived them through his parents' stories. He thought of his mother and her wanderings in the night to the Port St. Joe waters. He longed for the comforting sound of her voice wailing as she completed her nightly ritual of placing stones along the bank. Then he thought of Ira and his warnings about success. "Success in this part of the world cannot include what you know to be true in your heart."

On occasions when he had passing thoughts of his mother or Ira, their mere memories brought comfort to the sullen spaces of his emotions. Now as his life unraveled, he grappled with the fading memories of his loved ones.

His mind shifted to the tenants who rented space from Whittier, Krass and Pepper in the smoldering office building. The upper-level floors were rented out to the State of Florida. It had been Bill's mastermind idea to rent space to the State of Florida in a long-term lease agreement immediately after they pooled their credit for a bank loan to purchase the building. Albert remembered being afraid of such a large investment responsibility. Nevertheless, both Bill and Bob assured him property ownership was the American way for successful white men. After the sale was final, Albert felt more like an American than he ever had before. He knew the government would have insurance to cover any losses or repairs caused by the explosion. He tried to contemplate the financial solvency of the other tenants. The firm of Whittier, Krass and Pepper had established a solid reputation around Tallahassee. They had earned a good reputation even though some of their practices were not always honorable. Sometimes this fact created a troubling thought for Albert Whittier, especially when he remembered his father's words: "to repair the world." The firm was successful. This explosion could not ruin their success. Bill and Bob would see to that.

Thinking of the tenants on the first floor troubled Albert Whittier. The round colored face of Gus, who shined shoes in the lobby, flashed before his eyes. His stand was probably ruined but he could shine shoes in any office building in town. He would have to replace his polishes. He probably would not have the money. Albert knew Gus had four mouths to feed up on that ridge. Making colored folks' business his business was a practice he learned from his father. Knowing how many children were in the house, when a child was born or someone in the family died helped his father project his profits. Albert calculated the cost of replacing shoe polishes. Gerard Construction took up the three offices on the right. Their company was the first tenant of Whittier, Krass and Pepper. Frank Malloy had been a good construction supervisor. He was top notch and careful. He always checked the work site out a couple days before the work crew came. He had even placed the survey stakes himself. He had been on nearly every job Whittier, Krass and Pepper did with the Gerard Construction Company. Now he was dead.

Then there was the odd short fellow, Berns, who owned Berns Title Company at the far end of the hall. Bob and Bill made jokes about him paying his rent each month in cash and change. They said he did not believe in banks and kept all his money locked up in a safe in his office. They would watch him drive up every day in his 1950 blue Edsel bearing Levy County license plates with black smoke coming out of the tailpipe. He walked briskly with his eyes cast down, swinging his brown paper bag lunch in one hand and a mason jar in the other. When he noticed Bill or Bob looking at him from the window, he would swing his hand up in the air just above his forehead as if he was saluting, pause and call out, "Morning," before continuing his pace. He was pleasant but not overly friendly. His conversations never extended beyond general pleasantries. He always ended his days at noon on Fridays. His noon Friday workday ended even if it was during Bill and Bob's obligatory once-a-month on Friday tenant meetings. He would quietly stand and excuse himself, to the irritation of Bill, who ran the meetings. Bill saw the monthly afternoon tenant meetings as a gathering of the good ole white boys who were movers and shakers in Tallahassee.

The meetings were a forum to discuss building operations as well as an opportunity to make sideline deals. Bill and Bob both vehemently agreed and brought it to Albert's awareness that leaving the meeting before it ended was a breach of Southern gentlemen protocol. Albert always looked for an opportunity to prove he not only understood the protocol but also ascribed to it. Bill and Bob designated Albert as the peacemaker in the partnership. This role lent itself to persuading others to ascribe to whatever position Bill and Bob felt important.

One afternoon while Albert was in the men's bathroom, Berns joined him. Albert seized the opportunity to correct Berns's bad manners. He was at the urinal when Berns came and stood one urinal over from him. Assuming the cocky self-assured posture of his partners, Albert swaggered a couple of steps back from the urinal, shaking his penis like a power rod.

"Berns, how's it going?" Albert greeted him, continuing the penis bravado.

"Very well, Whittier," Berns answered, enunciating the "er" on the end of Albert's last name and looking over at him with a pause longer than Albert thought was necessary.

Using his best sales pitch to point out the merits of staying to the end of the monthly Friday-afternoon tenant meeting, Albert quickly adjusted himself. Berns stared at him, arching his bushy eyebrows, and walked to the sink to wash his hands. He continued to stare at Albert. The more he stared, the more Albert felt his confidence slipping. Berns's silence punctuated the end of the conversation. Albert remembered walking away from Berns, perplexed by his snub of silence.

Days later when Albert was posting a notice of the next tenants' meeting on the bulletin board by the water fountain, Berns walked up carrying the mason jar he used to drink his daily supply of water. You could find him at the water fountain with his mason jar at least three times a day. A ritual that further fueled Bill and Bob's position on Berns's odd ways was his disregard for Southern graces. Oddity notwithstanding, they all agreed, "He was the best Title man this side of the Florida panhandle, even if he was from Levy County." Albert started his pitch for Berns to make an effort to stay to the end of the tenants' meeting. Berns filled his mason jar with water and began to drink. As Albert talked of the merits of the tenants' meeting, Berns came and stood beside him.

"What is your birth name?" He asked the question referring to nothing and everything. Berns again invoked silence to punctuate his question, just as he had done in their previous conversation. Then Gus Manning's booming voice announced a vacant seat for a shoeshine, signaling a potential customer was entering the lobby. The announcement broke the silent interlude and Berns walked away. It had been nearly four months since the encounter but Berns's question still lingered in Albert's mind, rendering him incapable of predicting what Berns would want or need.

"The way I see it, Albert, it's our civic duty to let these deputies here know the real Benjamin. He got himself caught in this King mess they keep showing on the television. We knew he had a drinking problem because he drank on the job. We would dock his pay and he would straighten up. But lately he's been on some sort of binge, mouthing off about King getting hisself killed."

Albert gulped at how easily Bill concocted the tale of Benjamin's tenure with their firm.

"Albert, we know you are a bit more tolerant with niggers than we are here in Tallahassee," he continued, gesturing to Albert for emphasis. “Benjamin has taken your kindness for a weakness. We have heard him speaking out of turn. He has just gotten too big for his own good, if you ask me. This week he started leaving flyers around that he made at this office with our supplies. The flyers said something about niggers for justice organizing over in Frenchtown. The same kind of justice-seeking groups that set our nation’s capital on fire the other night. I heard it is a bunch of Jesus-hating Jews backing this nigger organizing. Of course, we knew the colored people been upset about this King fellow and we’ve been very concerned. That, however, does not give Benjamin and that nigger friend of his the right to start this fire! We just cannot stand for this. Wouldn’t you agree, Albert?” Bill glared at Albert with the weight of their partnership in his eyes.

“Mr. Whittier, a man came looking for you. Berns, he said his name was. He said he recognized your car. He wanted to talk to you about the fire and I want you to know me and Indigo will be going on home now,” Sadie scooted near the yellow line and yelled to Albert Whittier before his partners could respond.

Sadie had pushed through the crowd of colored people and stood near enough to the meeting of Mr. Whittier, his partners and the deputies to be within earshot of their verbal exchange. What she heard had made her blood boil. She knew she needed to get going in a hurry. Mr. Whittier’s conversation with his partners and the deputies reinforced her suspicions that she could not count on him. All she could think about was her sister was lying half-naked on a stretcher somewhere and Hiram and Benjamin about to go to jail. From the way Mr. Whittier’s partners were talking, she contemplated they were intent on having them in jail for a long time. She mentally thanked God and all his angels that she made Indigo stay behind and missed the partner’s conversation.

“With everything that went on out here this afternoon, if Go-Go had heard those crackers talk about Benjamin and her Daddy the way they did, the poor child would have lost her twelve-year-old mind," Sadie reasoned to herself.

She began to recount her steps in her mind. She was nervous about leaving Indigo back in the car at first because that white man, Berns, hung around. She had told him where to go and find Mr. Whittier, but he stood waiting. She made Indigo lock all the doors in the car just in case.

"Daddy, I want to go find Momma," Bethann whined. She had been quiet throughout her father's entire dialogue with his partners and the deputies. "Can Sadie go with us to help us find Momma?"

"No, Missy, I can't! My sister is hurt and I have to get away from here and go see about her. I do not have time to help you find your Momma."

Sadie tone's was curt. She only called Bethann "Missy" when wanted to let her know she was overstepping her boundaries. She could see Mr. Whittier's partners and the deputies out the corner of her eye. Trouble was already brewing and she did not need to stir the pot. Mr. Whittier had given her a good job. Good job notwithstanding, she was not about to be caught up into Mr. Whittier's troubles when she had big troubles of her own.

"Albert, we need to finish this!" Bill's eyes were flashing and his voice began to take on a demanding tone.

"We have enough to take them to jail with the evidence we've gathered. We can take a statement from your partner first thing in the morning," the deputy with the most stripes on his shirtsleeve announced.

"All three of us will come down to the jailhouse first thing in the morning, then this matter will be settled. I'll drive," Bill insisted and nodded in Albert's direction, indicating the matter was decided.

"I'll try to find Berns and talk to him, but I really must go and see about my wife. Sadie, I can take you home or to the nearest bus stop...This has been quite an afternoon," Albert rambled on, searching the faces of his partners, then Bethann and then Sadie.

"You're in no shape to talk to any of the tenants tonight. Tomorrow we will decide how we are going to handle things. Go see about your wife."

Albert Whittier nodded his head after Bill spoke. The gesture acknowledged his loyalty to Bill and Bob's leadership and welcomed a respite from an afternoon threatening to loosen his grip on the handles of his world.

CHAPTER 14

"*My four children*"

Gaines Street was nearly three miles from the 400 block of Osceola Street. It could have been three hundred miles. Sadie was determined to walk home that night. Indigo's feet and whole body were too numb to feel the steps it would take for her and Aunt Sadie to reach home. Mr. Whittier could not or did not do much to stop her. He had his own troubles.

The garbage men were cleaning up the horse manure left on the street from the Springtime Tallahassee parade earlier that day. The parade was the winning prize of a battle to get the Legislature to move the capital seat from Tallahassee last year. When the news report of the campaign to move the capital seat appeared in the town paper, the glove-wearing white daughters and cigar-smoking, power-packing sons of Tallahassee sprang into action. Pastel pamphlets with "Tallahassee, Where Spring Begins" were distributed all over town. At some point in the rallying to keep Tallahassee as the capital seat, the idea of a festival was born. The glove-wearing white daughters sipped tea and discussed how the festival would preserve and promote the heritage that belonged to all the citizens of Leon County. After Rev. Hester, the mouthpiece for the colored people in

Tallahassee, watched the parade last year, the floats became a part of his pulpit commentary.

"With all those white faces supposing to represent Florida's history up there on them floats, you'd think colored people were nothing more than the part of the scenery in this state," he bellowed and his congregation moaned.

The parade started in a big block formation stretching from just below the capital on Monroe Street to the beginning of Tennessee Street alongside the Greyhound and Trailways bus terminal. Hundreds of people lined the parade route. The colored people watched the parade in clusters along the designated route. Colored people stood three rows deep on each side of the street for nearly the six-block stretch between the Capital building and the Vogue Dress Shop on Monroe Street. The Capital Building and the Vogue Dress Shop were at the beginning of the parade route. It was also near the south end of town, the home of Florida A&M University and nearly five thousand colored people. The high school bands marched first in the parade. The white high school bands marched stoically by the colored clusters. When the colored bands came marching up Monroe Street, the colored clusters yelled and screamed with excitement. People within the colored clusters talked openly to each other as they stood along the parade route waiting for the opportunity to admire the uniforms paid for with profits from fried fish and chicken dinners. The colored bands stepped so high their knees and thighs flexed to make a perfect V coming down on the asphalt. Their line formations were so straight you could look down the line and watch the gold shiny buttons lined across the abdomens of the band members go up and down as they blew merriment from their used instruments. When the colored bands reached the end of the parade route at Frenchtown, the last cluster of colored people welcomed them. Frenchtown was where coloreds thrived and died. Lincoln High, the only black high school, was there. Colored dentists and doctors had offices there. Colored stores and stores that gave credit to coloreds were there. Good times rolled in Frenchtown. The minute the colored cheers escalated for the colored high school bands in Frenchtown and the marching band lines snapped into precision pomp and circumstance, the bars offered free watered-down drinks.

The university bands followed the high school bands. Florida State's marching band of Seminole Chiefs high-stepped to patriotic tunes of John Phillip Sousa in the spring sunshine as white people clapped their hands and waved American flags. Their garnet-and-gold, cream-color-inlaid uniforms highlighted the crown of feathers on their heads. The Florida A&M's Mighty Rattlers snaked-danced throughout the parade route in their orange-and-green uniforms with snake eyes and fangs glistening in the Florida sunshine. Their drum majors performed dancing routines that defied gravity. The colored crowd bobbed and rocked to the tune of a lively reconstructed Negro spiritual that boasted the pride of being associated with FAMU.

"I'm so glad, I'm from FAMU! I'm so glad, I'm from FAM-U! Singing Glory Hallelujah, I'm from FAM-U!!!"

A white beauty queen rode on a float for every blooming flower in Tallahassee. Azaleas, lilies, magnolias and dogwoods all had their queen. The parade culminated with the smell of fish frying and Southern Comfort barbecue on the grill for sale until dusk. Then white folks pretending to be founding aristocrats dressed up in vintage clothes roamed around the festival until it was time to go to the Springtime Tallahassee reception at the Country Club. Everybody who was white and considered somebody went to the Springtime Tallahassee reception.

Aunt Sadie scoffed at a white couple dressed in historical clothing posing on the steps of the Capital building for a photographer. The woman's pastel antebellum dress gently swayed back and forth in the night air. The confederate officer's brass buttons on his jacket glistened in the moonlight along with the mood they seemed to enjoy. Aunt Sadie's gait was so full of fury it left an imprint on the soft green spring grass and caught the attention of the springtime celebrants. Their eyes locked across the grounds that separated them. For a brief time they were aware of each other on that august April evening. In the annals of history, they would recollect the moment as a time having gone awry.

Magnolia was peeking out of the kitchen curtains when Sadie and Indigo came across the yard to the back porch. Magnolia wore her pride of being the oldest Douglas child like an invisible badge of power across her chest. Nevertheless, not knowing where her parents were or when they would be home on a Saturday night pushed the power of the invisible badge to its limits. She must have looked out the kitchen window fifty times, hoping that Madear and Daddy Douglas would drive up. It was after seven o'clock and Davis Jr. had eaten as many butter sandwiches as his stomach could hold. Blueberry had fallen asleep eating a moon pie. Grandma Dovie had just returned from a day of wandering. Rowell Watson, Indigo's pesky four-eyed friend who lived up on Adams Street, kept calling every half-hour to speak to her. Every day he found a reason to call or come down the hill to the 400 block of Osceola Street to show or tell her something. A perfectly smooth rock, a four-leaf clover that was really a three-leaf clover he managed to attach another leaf to, a small spinning top he said was really from Africa, were just a few of the treasures he'd bring to capture Indigo's affection. He was a regular annoyance to Magnolia. The missing leaders of the Douglas household on a Saturday and his telephone inquires about Go-Go were wearing Magnolia's nerves thin.

A plate of fried fish sat on the stove. Madear had not left a note telling her to open a can of creamed corn or to cook some grits to go with the fish on the stove, which would have been the limit of her cooking ability. She could tell something was wrong when she came home from the outing with the Wallaces. The house was completely empty on a Saturday evening. Daddy Douglas and Madear were not at home. She had called her Aunt Sadie at the boarding house and she was not at home either. Someone was always home on Saturdays.

Saturday afternoons at the Douglases' were reserved for reinforcing life lessons through chores. Madear washed and pressed her daughters' hair on the back porch. Daddy Douglas took Davis Jr. to get his hair cut and shined their shoes on the steps of the back porch. Grandma Dovie sat or stood by, providing assistance where it was needed. It was mostly needed helping hold Blueberry down to wash her hair. Blueberry was terrified of the shampoo getting in her eyes and burning. Once shampoo lather got in her eyes and she bolted out of the back screen door and down the steps. She did not see the rake that fell when she upset the hair-washing bowl on the back porch. She tripped and tumbled down the stairs with her clean hair rolling in the dirt. From then on Grandma Dovie gently held Blueberry with one hand and covered her eyes with the other as Madear washed her hair. Indigo knew from first-hand experience if she kept her eyes closed tight the green shampoo would not burn.

After the hair washing, Grandma Dovie held the wide-tooth and skinny combs in one hand and can of hair grease in the other while Madear straightened the heads. Back-porch hair straightening happened every two weeks. Blueberry had soft short hair that looked like clumps of cotton after the sun dried it. Magnolia's hair was silky smooth after washing. It was the same as Madear's. A pat of grease and a strong brushing was all it needed. Madear never had to use more than a warm comb to make Blueberry's soft knots unroll. Indigo had thick brittle hair that curled up like steel wool once the warm Florida sun rays dried it. Magnolia often teased Indigo that she was the one in the family with "can'tshedon'tshe" hair. When Indigo asked her what kind of hair that was, Magnolia would burst into a belly laugh explaining "you can't comb it and don't you try hair." Madear had to use a red-hot straightening comb to make Indigo's hair bouncing and behaving. Despite her warnings to sit still during the pressing, teeth marks of the straightening comb were usually emblazed somewhere on Indigo's neck or ear.

On the off weeks everyone got their hair greased by Madear. She used Royal Crown hair grease and bumped the knots out with a warm comb. Daddy Douglas said, "Royal Crown was strong enough to fry fish in." Madear said she had to use Royal Crown grease to handle the hair Indigo and Blueberry inherited from his side of the family. The "hair doing" would end with Madear brushing Magnolia's brownish-red mane, saying, "Your hair is your glory! You can have on the prettiest dress money could buy, but if your hair's not right then you are not right!"

One Saturday, Indigo went with them to collect dimes for a handicap children's drive. The child with the most dimes won a trip to the Capital building with the principal. Indigo wanted to win. Daddy Douglas and Davis Jr. went to the barbershop right after lunch on Saturdays. By the time they arrived a group of men would have a checker game going on in the corner of the room. Another group would be sitting in chairs lined against the wall "shooting the breeze," waiting to get their turn in the chair at the barber shop next to Ma Mary's Kitchen. Daddy Douglas was not sure of the real name of the barbershop. Everybody just called it the barbershop next to Ma Mary's Kitchen. Smiling Willie ran the barbershop. He did not seem to mind that people called it the barbershop next to Ma Mary's Kitchen. When someone asked him about it, he would just grin and say, "The way I see it things are working out for me and Ma Mary's Kitchen just the way it is."

Between "shooting the breeze" with the men in the barbershop and eating from Ma Mary's Kitchen, it took three hours for Daddy Douglas to get him and Davis Jr. a "low cut with a part on the side and fill up Indigo's dime collection card."

Daddy Douglas kept shoe-cleaning materials in an old silver paint bucket. The shoeshine bucket was full of rectangular and round brushes. Shine rags and tins of brown and black creamy polishes sat in a black leather case inside the bucket. Hours would pass as they sat on the back-porch steps and he showed Davis Jr. how to clean his Sunday shoes with a knife and brush before putting the polish on.

"A man's shoes can tell his whole life story. What your story is going to be starts right here in polishing these shoes," he would say to Davis Jr. as they brushed and scraped dirt off their Sunday best.

He showed Davis Jr. how to make a lather of the creamy polish, using enough to cover the tips of two fingers.

"Spread the good stuff around, then in bad times you'll have something to fall back on," he cautioned, stroking the polish on the shoe in a circular motion until it formed a waxy film. "Know the walk you walk!" he emphasized, snapping the shine rag across the leather shoe until he could see his reflection in the waxy polish.

"The condition of a man's shoes sums up his worth," he would say, standing up, motioning to Davis Jr. to gather the shoe-cleaning materials.

The next chore of Saturday was preparing for Sunday. Magnolia and Indigo helped shell peas, shuck corn or pick greens for Sunday dinner. Madear cooked beef or fried chicken. Grandma Dovie speechlessly baked something for dessert. By nightfall, the kitchen was full of aromas reserved for Sunday. The night ended with Madear insisting that all her children hang their Sunday clothes on the closet door before they went to sleep and Daddy Douglas sampling some of the Sunday fixings before he went to bed. The Douglas Saturday activities were off schedule and Magnolia was fretting.

When Magnolia saw her Aunt Sadie coming through the kitchen door she ran up and hugged her. Aunt Sadie started giving out directions the minute her feet hit the linoleum of the kitchen floor. She put a pot of grits on the stove to boil, roused Blueberry and told Davis Jr. to go wash up without skipping a beat. Grandma Dovie made a path back and forth from looking out the screen of the back porch to rocking in her rocking chair in her bedroom next to the kitchen. Magnolia placed six clear plastic glasses decorated with pink and yellow tulips and matching plates around the metal table. She grabbed a clump of forks in the dry cloth and placed them around the place settings. When she began scooping sugar from the sugar jar to mix with the packets of grape Kool-Aid drink mix on the counter, pure worry got the best of her. She stopped fixing the Kool-Aid drink and held onto the kitchen counter as if it was about to go somewhere. She called out to Indigo at the top of her voice.

"Indigo, where are Madear and Daddy Douglas?"

Grandma Dovie stopped rocking in her rocking chair and sat still for a minute.

"They were at Mr. Whittier's office," Indigo managed to get out. She wanted to blurt out everything she had seen and heard in the last three hours. The vision of what her eyes and ears had seen and felt were just too big for the words to come out of her mouth.

"What were Madear and Daddy Douglas doing there?"

"I don't know," Indigo started to say as her eyes turned watery.

Grandma Dovie walked quietly in the kitchen and stood by the dining room table.

"What are you about to cry for? What happened?" Magnolia insisted.

"Who's about to cry?" Aunt Sadie asked, walking in the kitchen, moving over to the stove to stir the pot of grits while looking over at Indigo.

"Aunt Sadie, where's Madear and Daddy Douglas?" Magnolia asked directly.

"You two come on over to this table. I want to talk to you," Aunt Sadie directed.

They both knew their Aunt Sadie had that "I want to talk serious" tone in her voice.

Magnolia stood for a minute next to the sink staring at Indigo, looking for an indication of what her Aunt Sadie was about to say. Indigo knew what her Aunt Sadie wanted to discuss. She knew she was going to fill in the gaps of an eventful day that had been a daydream and a nightmare all wrapped into one. She knew and she was tired. Tired of what her eyes had seen. Tired of what her brain was trying to understand. She could feel Grandma Dovie and Magnolia's eyes watching her. Their eyes were seeking to know what she knew and where she had been.

Just as they were about to sit down at the kitchen table the telephone rang. Magnolia jumped to answer it on the second ring.

"Hello, Daddy! Daddy, Madear is not here. I thought she was with you...Aunt Sadie is here. Just a minute."

Indigo sat down quietly. The more she listened, she sat up straight in the vinyl-back chair. She glued her eyes on Magnolia as she handed the telephone to her Aunt Sadie.

"Aunt Sadie, Daddy Douglas wants to speak to you. He said to hurry up because he doesn't have much time."

"Hiram, are you all right?" Aunt Sadie spoke in a low tone and moved closer to the phone on the wall.

"Sadie, where's Cree? I need to let her know what—"

"That you are in jail." Sadie finished his sentence and began her own. "Cree was hurt in the explosion at the Whittier building," Aunt Sadie said, turning around when she heard Magnolia gasp.

"How did that happen? What was she doing there?"

"I don't know, Hiram! What were you and Benjamin doing there is a better question. Mr. Whittier and his partners think you and Benjamin..."

"I know what they think and I do not care," he declared before asking about his wife. "Is Cree in the hospital?"

"You don't care what they think now because you are mad. Those crackers are mad as a wet hen about that fire and their building burning. There is no trouble worse than a bunch of mad..."

"Than a bunch of mad redneck crackers who hate niggers so much they could kill just to look at them, they could bomb a church and kill four little girls whose only crime was being colored and going to Sunday school. Now they have killed the one colored man who was brave enough to stand up and fight against all of them. I don't give a doggone how mad they are!"

Joe Wilson was the only colored to work at the jail. He knew Daddy Douglas and Mr. Benjamin from around town. His job was to pass out the jailhouse clothes and any other items that new prisoners needed. It was a good job and the sheriff trusted him. He worked the night shift alone. It was busy. His job was to move prisoners to their holding cells. After the Whittier building explosion the jail had more prisoners than usual.

"Douglas man, you got to hurry it up! That deputy will be back in here before long. I want to help you because I know you are a good man but I got a job I aim to keep!" he admonished Hiram, interrupting the conversation with Sadie.

Sadie used the duration of the interruption to think of a way to try to make Hiram understand the graveness of Saturday's events.

"Look Sadie, I can't talk long. Joe Wilson is a friend of mine. He let me use the phone. Tell Benjamin's wife where he is. Go see about Cree and take care of…"

"What's going on in here, Wilson? What's that nigger doing on the phone?"

Sadie heard another loud voice boom, followed by a rustling sound just before she heard Hiram yell, "My four children!" His voice trailed off and the phone made a clicking sound. Sadie looked at the receiver for a minute and then hung it back on the receiver on the wall.

"Why is my Daddy in jail? Where is Madear?" Magnolia demanded with blush marks in her face. She looked at her Aunt Sadie, then at Indigo. Her eyes were getting red. She squinted as if holding her eyes in a steady gaze would help her comprehend better.

"There was an explosion at Mr. Whittier's office. Your mother was hurt because she was inside the building when it happened. The medics think she is going be all right, though. Soon as I get things settled here I am going to walk up to FAMU hospital and see about her. The police think your Daddy and Mr. Benjamin caused the explosion."

"Why do they think my Daddy had something to do with it?" Magnolia continued, exasperated by all her Aunt Sadie had said.

"With everything that's been going on since Martin Luther King got killed, nobody been thinking straight, especially white people. They put your Daddy and Benjamin in jail because they colored and they were there. Only God knows why they were there. Right now, all they thinking about is every colored person they know is capable of doing something." Sadie was trying her best to tell what happen without making matters worse.

"Well, my Daddy didn't do anything like that!" Magnolia answered tearfully.

"We know that, baby. We all know that," Aunt Sadie said, consoling Magnolia and Indigo, who had put her head on the table and begun whimpering at the beginning of Sadie's version of what happened.

The telephone rang again and Grandma Dovie handed it to Aunt Sadie.

"Yes, this is the Douglas residence. Mr. Douglas is not here. I am his sister-in-law, though. I had planned to walk up there in a few minutes. We live just on the other side of FAMU campus, it would not take me more than fifteen minutes to get there. Thank you, Lord! Yes, yes, I will be there at visiting hours tomorrow. Thank you, Doctor. God bless you. Goodnight."

Grandma Dovie, Magnolia and Indigo hung onto every word Aunt Sadie spoke into the telephone. They all stood looking at her as she hung up the phone.

Aunt Sadie walked over to her audience and stretched her arms out like she wanted to continue where she left off with hugging before Grandma Dovie handed her the phone. Then she sat down in one of the chairs at the table as if the heavy weight of the day had taken a seat in her lap. She raised one of her hands upward to the ceiling and looked up before she spoke.

"Thank God for goodness! The doctor that took care of your Momma when they brought her into the hospital was on the phone. She's awake now. She swallowed too much smoke but not enough to do too much damage. She is going be all right in a couple days. I am going to go see 'bout her tomorrow at visiting hours. Visiting hours start at one o'clock, I believe. I can go right after church. Everything is going to work out just fine. Now get up and get this kitchen cleaned up. I think we're all too worn out to eat anyway."

Aunt Sadie got up and turned the fire off under the pot of grits. Magnolia began picking up the place settings from the table. Grandma Dovie walked out on the back porch. Indigo just sat at the table, so overcome with fatigue the two thick tight plaits holding her hair in place even seemed tired. She wanted to just put her head down on the table and sleep Saturday away. "Come on, Go-Go, get going and sweep this kitchen floor," Aunt Sadie instructed.

Indigo struggled to get up and walked out on the back porch to get the broom. Out of the corner of her eye she caught a glimpse of Grandma Dovie standing on the corner of the top back-porch step, raising both hands to the sky. For a second Indigo thought she saw Grandma Dovie's lips moving. Madear said Grandma Dovie had not moved her lips to speak since Granddaddy Nate died. But in the twilight Indigo saw Grandma Dovie's mouth opening and closing like she was in conversation with somebody. Indigo took a step to get a closer look but clumsily knocked over the mop bucket, causing Grandma Dovie to turn around. When she looked at Indigo, the blank speechless stare on her face was where it had always been. She slowly walked past Indigo, looking downward without explanation. Expressionless, she went to her room, closing the bedroom door behind her. Indigo took her broom and began sweeping the kitchen floor. "Madear put these plaits on my head so tight and I'm so tired maybe my eyes are crossed and I'm not seeing straight," she mused to herself. She concentrated on the whisking sound of the straw going across the linoleum as she swept the floor. The kitchen window was open and the crickets hiding in the damp muddy bamboo bushes behind her house were providing a back-up melody to her sweeping song. "The crickets hid their voices until evening. Maybe Grandma Dovie did too," she pondered.

"Go-Go, finish sweeping up that kitchen and get ready for bed," Aunt Sadie shouted.

Magnolia and Indigo got ready for bed in silence. Magnolia's silence included sharp glances in Indigo's direction. Indigo knew the unfolding of Madear and Daddy Douglas's whereabouts had not set well with her sister. There was an unspoken language between the Douglas sisters. If one sister had the inside track on what was going on, it was that sister's obligation to tell the untold. Magnolia was the oldest sister and she usually had the "untold" to tell. Indigo knew her hard glances were meant to underscore a change in the arrangement was not appreciated. Under ordinary circumstances, she would have enjoyed the bragging rights but she was not in a mood to celebrate. She just wanted to go to bed. She wanted to feel her head hitting the feather pillow on her bed. She could feel the beady nubbins of the chenille spread crawling up her body when she imagined pulling the covers over her head and drifting off to sleep. She longed for slumber that would wake up to a morning after a very long bad dream.

The sound of her Aunt Sadie's voice distracted her. She was yelling to Grandma Dovie as if she was hard of hearing. It was a one-sided conversation. "Doesn't Aunt Sadie know Grandma Dovie could hear, she could not or did not speak? It doesn't matter how loud she yells or what happens, Grandma Dovie is not going to speak about it," Indigo thought to herself, feeling anger growing within. Her anger was new and uncomfortable. Grandma Dovie's brooding silence and unpredictable walks had caused Indigo to be afraid of her. Madear and Aunt Sadie's commands to heap affection on Grandma Dovie eluded Indigo.

"Give your Grandma a hug," Madear would chide the Douglas children.

"She barely bends her arms to hug you back and she always looks right past you. She never says a word. It's scary," Indigo thought to herself. "Magnolia is afraid of her too," Indigo insisted in her thoughts. If Magnolia was afraid of something, she acted as if she did not care about it. Whenever Indigo tried to talk about Grandma Dovie in an inquiring sort of way, Magnolia acted like she didn't want to be bothered. It made Indigo even more uneasy and fearful. Now the fear had turned to anger. The flip happened because she wanted Grandma Dovie's blank face to turn into a smile. A smile that would spread her lips open and let out a warm voice like the grandma she imagined Dick and Jane would have. Her anger rose because she knew she saw Grandma Dovie's lips opened up in a conversation and closed when she came near.

Madear said, "Every closed eye was not asleep." Indigo added, "Every shut mouth might just speak if it's got a mind to. Grandma Dovie has a mind to speak, she just doesn't have a mind to speak to any of us," Indigo grunted to herself. Sadie's yelling in a one-way conversation interrupted Indigo's thoughts again.

"I'll be back over here early in the morning to get everybody up and ready for church. Lord knows we need to go to church with all the trouble we got going on round here," Sadie yelled, walking through the front door, her voice fading in the night air.

Indigo stepped out of her bedroom and saw her grandmother sitting in her rocking chair. She nodded her head up and down as Aunt Sadie spoke. Her eyelids were half-closed and one hand of her red fingernails tapped slowly on the arm of the rocker. Indigo knew she would probably be asleep by the time Aunt Sadie reached the door of her boarding room. Someone had to make sure the front door was locked to keep anything else from turning the Douglas household even more upside-down than it already was. The clicking sound of the front door lock turning was a nightly signal that all was safe and could be at rest in the Douglas house. She never knew which one of her parents locked the door each night. She had never even thought much about it before. Now neither of them was there to do it. Magnolia was mad and fast asleep. She could not count on Grandma Dovie. Grandma Dovie had started rocking back and forth but was beginning to drift off to sleep. She was part of the picture of regular routine after Madear's Saturday-night chores. Her legs would cramp up from sitting so long and Madear would have to rub them down with green alcohol. Madear was not home and Indigo did not know when she would be home. Daddy Douglas was in jail. She had seen her Grandma Dovie's lips move in a conversation with the night air and wanted that conversation to include her. She longed for the assurances of the Douglas nightly rituals. If the past two nights and three days of Martin Luther King were any indication, her family rituals could be outdated. She sighed deeply, realizing the high-chested "Iko" her family teased Daddy Douglas about could have passed on to her. "In the morning I'm going to talk to Magnolia about this," she decided. With that decision made, she turned the deadbolt lock on the front door until it clicked. Then she walked a few steps, turned and checked the lock again.

CHAPTER 15

"Guilty of wrongful deeds"

The clanking of pots and smell of bacon sizzling in a black iron skillet on the stove stirred Indigo and Magnolia from sleeping. They climbed out of bed and sat on opposite sides of their second-hand four-poster bed looking out at the day. Magnolia curiously called her Aunt Sadie's name and waited for a response.

"Ya'll get up in there and start getting ready for church. Breakfast will be ready in two shakes," Aunt Sadie yelled back.

Magnolia stood up and walked in front of the mirror attached to the bureau while untying the knot of the scarf tied on her head. The satin scarf slid down on her shoulders. She patted her wavy mane with admiration. When she looked at her reflection she saw Indigo sitting on the bed behind her.

"I don't know why you didn't tie up that wild bush on your head last night," she smirked and giggled.

"Excuse me, are you talking to me now?" Indigo commented, stroking her hair, trying to make it lie down.

"I am not thinking about you. That nappy head of yours looks a mess," Magnolia teased.

"So what!" Indigo exclaimed, suddenly aware of her hair challenge.

"So you are going to look a mess when we go to church because Madear is not here to fix that head." Magnolia's words confirmed the possibility of yesterday's mishaps spreading into a new day. She appeared uneasy in front of the mirror, abruptly announcing, "I'm going in the bathroom first."

As Magnolia made a beeline for the bathroom, Indigo got up to go see what her Aunt Sadie was doing in the kitchen. She hoped Aunt Sadie would recognize her hair dilemma and offer assistance. The telephone rang and Aunt Sadie hopped to answer it without ever noticing Indigo. Indigo dejectedly walked through the living room to get the newspaper off the front porch.

"Hello, Douglas residence," Sadie answered.

"Uhm, Sadie. This is Mr. Whittier…I. I aahm…"

"Yes, sir?

"Mrs. Whittier was hurt badly last night. The smoke and her asthmatic condition really damaged her lungs. She is going to be moved to Shands Hospital in Gainesville this afternoon. They're more equipped to handle her injury there."

"I'm sorry, sir."

"I was wondering if you could come over to be with Bethann. I will probably be gone a couple of days until she is settled. I know you don't normally sleep over but this is an emergency."

"Sir, I'm having an emergency of my own. My sister was hurt last night too…She is still in the hospital and you know her husband is in jail. I cannot come stay with Bethann. I have to take care of her children. We are getting ready to go to church right now. I am sorry but I—"

"Sadie, I really need you to help us out. I am willing to pay you extra."

"I appreciate the thought of the extra money, sir. God knows we're going to need it but I just do not see how I can help you and help my own. Can't she stay with one of your neighbors?"

"You know we are private people. We do not like to impose. Besides, Bethann is very upset about her mother. She did not get much sleep. The fire at the office building was very disturbing. She needs to be around someone familiar. Sadie, we need your help. We have been good to you. A good job like this one is hard to come by, with your past being what it is."

Indigo walked in the kitchen while her Aunt Sadie was still on the phone. The connection was so amplified her Aunt Sadie held the phone away from her ear. Indigo could hear her whole conversation. She put the rolled-up Sunday paper, held together with a green rubber band, on the table and listened.

"Sir, let me call you back later. I got things to do here. I will call you back later today when I can see my way clear." The skin on Sadie's dark-brown neck was developing a reddish hue, the way it did when somebody's talk was getting on the bad side of her nerves. She quickly ended the conversation before Mr. Whittier could plead for her assistance again. She shook her head as if the worry in her face would go away. "Go-Go, get dressed for church, child. The trouble of yesterday done walked right on into the Lord's day."

The phone rang again and Indigo answered. It was Rowell. Rowell was Indigo's boyfriend. She was his girl supreme. He provided the lens inside "boy world" and answered the questions she was too bashful to ask Magnolia about. She was the image of the girl in his imagination he bragged to his friends about. He was her comrade, confidante and competitor. She was his dearest darling and double dose of luck. She was blossoming in parts of her body that made her feel uncomfortable around most, except him. He wore thick glasses and had asthma. She could outrun him easily. She waited for him to catch up with her. He understood isosceles triangles, dangling participles and photosynthesis and she did not. He adored her so he acted as if his knowing about these things did not matter. They rallied for each other.

"Go! Whey you been? Did your sister tell you I called last night?" he blurted out in lightning speed.

"Yeah, she said you called," Indigo began while watching her Auntie move around the kitchen humming a song.

"Did you see your Daddy's picture in the paper?"

"What picture?" Indigo answered with surprise, hastening to grab the Sunday newspaper on the kitchen table.

"It's on the second page. It says he and your neighbor started that big fire last night."

Indigo did not finish her conversation with Rowell. She hung up the receiver while he was still talking. She stretched the green rubber band on the newspaper so far it popped. She flipped the front page to the second so fast part of it ripped. There it was. Daddy Douglas and Mr. Benjamin handcuffed together with the white deputy in the big Stetson hat standing beside them. The caption underneath the picture read: "Alleged Arsonists Captured."

Indigo could not move. She could not speak.

"Child, why are you looking at that paper? Go get dressed!" Aunt Sadie chastised.

Indigo just kept on looking down at the newspaper on the kitchen table. Magnolia walked in the kitchen with her floral housedress covering her slip, bra, and panties.

"Who was that on the telephone?" she asked.

"Just Mr. Whittier. He wants me to come over and take care of Bethann while he goes to see about his wife being moved to the hospital in Gainesville. He got trouble and I got my own trouble. Go-Go, get going, I told you!" Aunt Sadie rambled on.

Indigo could feel every syllable climbing up her throat struggling to alert the room their family business was outside the house.

"L-O-O-K!" she finally said.

"Look at what?" Magnolia asked, walking over to the kitchen table.

Aunt Sadie covered the scrambled eggs and walked over to the table too. Grandma Dovie came out of her room and stood at the kitchen door.

"Do Jesus!" Aunt Sadie gasped.

They all just stood at the kitchen table peering at the newspaper article with Daddy Douglas and Mr. Benjamin's picture above it. Magnolia quickly read the article silently. Then she summarized what it said. "They think Daddy Douglas and Mr. Benjamin started the fire with a Molotov cocktail because Martin Luther King was killed."

"It says they 'allegedly' started the fire. That means they are not sure…The police think they did it. They got to prove it." Aunt Sadie tried to de-emphasize the impact of the newspaper article.

Magnolia started to cry. "If I just looked at Daddy Douglas and Mr. Benjamin in this paper and I didn't know them, I'd believe they did it," she blubbered.

"Why, because they are colored? Oh, so you think because they are colored that makes them guilty of wrongful deeds. Not just colored people do stuff to get themselves in jail or in the newspaper. You know your Daddy and Benjamin. Your Daddy is not guilty of burning that building down. Mr. Benjamin is not either. Enough of this kind of talk! We need to get on up from here and get to church, because nobody can fix this mess but the Almighty. He works in odd and mysterious ways." Aunt Sadie spoke in a shaky voice.

Indigo started to cry too. She looked away from the newspaper to the set of dominoes on the windowsill. Through her warm salty tears and glassy eyes, she wondered, "If the Almighty can fix things, why hasn't he fixed it before now?" Her thoughts began to calculate all the bad things that had been happening since the news of Martin Luther King came through the radio last Thursday night. Bad things had happened one right after the other. She picked up pieces of the dominoes and looked at them.

Life on Osceola Street had been all the life she knew for twelve years. She had not needed to know anything more. Her mind flashed through the familiarities of Osceola Street. In a daze, she lined up the dominoes on the windowsill. She imagined Osceola Street was the black ends of dominoes lined up together. She picked up a domino piece with five white dots on one end and held it for a while. Whites had not been a part of the world she was familiar with on Osceola Street before Thursday night. She matched the domino with the five white dots up with a matching domino piece opposite a black. She touched the black space and rubbed it. Then she matched all the dominoes, the ones with white dots and the ones with black spaces together, stood them up in a perfectly straight line, and knocked them down.

When the news of Martin Luther King came through the radio on Thursday night, she knew trouble blew in on the radio airwaves. It was a strong wind that blew trouble causing everything sturdy in its path to tumble down like dominoes one right after the other. First, school was strange. Then Daddy Douglas went crazy, yelling and tearing up the house for no good reason. Now he was in jail and Madear was hurt. She had hoped the last domino of trouble had fallen when she closed her eyes to go to sleep last night. Looking at Daddy Douglas's picture in the Sunday paper, she knew another round of trouble dominoes were about to fall. She knew everybody else in the Douglas house knew it too.

The phone rang again. Magnolia answered it even though she was still whimpering a little about the picture of Daddy Douglas and Mr. Benjamin handcuffed together in the Sunday newspaper. After she said "hello," she shouted in the phone, "Don't you know she can't talk to you now!"

Indigo knew it was Rowell. She knew he would know to call back later. They understood the signals in each other's lives. Magnolia put the receiver on the Mylar-top table and Indigo picked it up to verify the dial tone. She took the receiver and hung it up. Then the phone rang again.

"Hello, Douglas residence," Indigo answered.

"Sadie?" the voice of a girl answered.

"No! This is Indigo. You want to speak to my Aunt Sadie, Bethann?" Indigo tried not let her rising anger flood the conversation.

"Indigo, I know you are mad at me. I am mad at you too. You know you saw that man with your Daddy throw that cocktail and start that fire! We saw it together."

"You are a story-telling liar! I did not see no such thing and your stories done caused a whole heap of trouble," Indigo swore at Bethann.

"I am not lying and you know it. My Momma got hurt, you know!"

"I don't care about your Momma. My whole family is hurt because of what you said." Indigo balled up her fist as she spoke and paced around, tangling up the telephone cord.

"Go-Go! Who are you talking to, child? Give me that phone right now!" Aunt Sadie demanded.

"Hello, Sadie speaking, who is this?"

"Sadie, this is Bethann. Are you coming to stay with me?" Bethann asked, nearly whimpering.

"Bethann, where is your Daddy, child? I told him I could not keep you today. I got too many things to do today, child. Go get your Daddy and put him on the phone. Lord have mercy," Aunt Sadie complained.

"Daddy is outside getting the car ready, Sadie. Why can't you come, Sadie?" Bethann whined.

"Because I cannot come! Go get your Daddy, Missy!" Bethann was beginning to get on Aunt Sadie's nerves and it showed.

"He said we're going to the lake at McClay Gardens, Sadie. I do not want to go to the lake. I do not want to pick up stones."

"Bethann, did you hear me tell you to go get your Daddy? Now I mean go!" Aunt Sadie talked to Bethann like she was one of the Douglas children. Indigo knew she was serious.

Aunt Sadie held the receiver without saying a word. It seemed like she was holding the receiver for a long time but Indigo knew it was only the length of time it took for toast to brown a dark-coffee color. Indigo had placed the toast in the toaster at the beginning of her tussle with Bethann. When the dark-coffee-color toast popped up, Aunt Sadie laid into Mr. Whittier.

"Mr. Whittier sir, I told you I would call you back later today. Having Bethann call is not going to help none. I got my sister and brother-in-law's children to care for. I do not see how I can help you too. I do not have time to come out to Killearn today. Can't you understand what I am saying to you, sir? I just do not see any other way."

"Bethann can come to stay with you, Sadie." The words came out of Albert Whittier's mouth without reference.

"Stay with me, sir?"

"Yes, it will solve everything. I will be gone a few days next week and then maybe two days every week until Mrs. Whittier gets better. This way things won't be so out of order." He spoke as he planned.

Aunt Sadie paused, grunted, ground her teeth, then with a bit of edge asked, "Who's going to take her to school in the mornings?"

"You can take her on the bus or I will leave money for taxi fare. It will only be for a few days each week," he insisted.

"You can leave taxi fare and it's going to cost you two days extra each week, sir. Bring her over on Monday afternoon sometime."

Aunt Sadie paused again. Then she held the receiver to her chest, shook her head and hung the phone up. Indigo walked over to the windowsill and rubbed her hand over the fallen dominoes. Another one had fallen before she had a chance to get the others up.

CHAPTER 16

"I can see God working"

Aunt Sadie led the stride of the Douglas clan down the hill to the steps of the First Baptist Church. The white concrete-block church was located in the 600 block of Osceola Street. The gruff voice of Sam Harvey, the oldest gray-haired deacon in the church, was leading the devotional singing. His voice resonated the words "Jesus on the Main Line" beyond the church walls and stained-glass windows paid for with the sale of fried chicken dinners and raffles. "Jesus on the main line, tell him what you want. Jesus on the main line now." An usher met them at the door of the church. She was a middle-aged woman dressed in a stark white plain dress so full of starch that it looked paper-thin. A gold medallion was pinned over a pocket near her chest. The medallion had satin ribbons attached and emblazoned with a picture of the First Baptist Church just above frayed gold fringe. "Usher" was imprinted in black letters on white cardstock encased in a small rectangle covered in plastic at the top of the medallion. A crown of circular white lace covered her head. Her white-gloved hands simultaneously held church bulletins and greeted parishioners.

"Morning, praise the Lord! Morning," she smiled and greeted people, flashing her white tooth with the gold star outline. When the stream of churchgoers got thicker, she struggled to keep up the pace of passing out the church bulletins, touching hands and flashing that gold-starred smile.

"Do you think the angels at the gate in heaven have a gold tooth with a star in it like that?" Magnolia, half-smiling, whispered to Indigo.

Indigo did not answer or smile. Her mind was on her Daddy Douglas's picture in the Sunday newspaper. Her frustration had risen about as tall as she was. She was fed up and being in church was not doing anything to help her mood. She wanted to do something to stop everything that was happening but she did not know what. If she knew the words to say, she would have shouted them out. If she just knew who to go to, she would have run there and been back by now. She did not know what to do or say or where to go. When Aunt Sadie demanded everyone put on their Sunday best to go to church, she complied out of sheer desperation and there seemed to be no other options. It also helped that she remembered her Aunt Sadie's penchant for knowing the right thing to do in confusion even if it did seem useless now. The Douglas household really was in a state of confusion, but the chances of Aunt Sadie's "Almighty" plan working seemed like a long shot. Daddy Douglas's picture in the Sunday newspaper did not help matters either.

Aunt Sadie was dressed in a form-fitting ruffled bodice dress with purple shoes and matching hat and gloves. She could feel the force of the Douglas eyes questioning her outfit when she strolled across the street to take the walk down the hill to the church. She quickly explained she was wearing her purple odyssey because she needed the glorious touch of the "Almighty." Swearing aloud with her hand held up to the sky, she declared, "The Almighty was drawn to shades of purple," until Grandma Dovie slapped at her hand. When she shimmed past with all the Douglases in tow to the mid-section of church, women sitting in the pews watched. She said she wanted to "sit right in front of the pulpit so the preacher's words could pour out a blessing." Magnolia nudged Indigo when they whisked by two of the churchwomen sitting on the end of a pew. They whispered about Aunt Sadie's big hips stretching the seams of that purple dress. They said it loud enough for Aunt Sadie to hear them. If she did hear them, she acted as if it did not matter to her. Her eyes faced straight ahead in a determined stare. When the Douglases reached their seats, Indigo looked around her. Women wearing hats in every color of the rainbow accessorized in feathers, lace, bows, buttons and beads fixed their eyes on the pulpit. Ebony-skinned men with deep lines on their faces and dirt under their fingernails clothed in starched white shirts and pressed suits also sat with fixed eyes. Everybody in the church seemed to have that same determined stare of anticipation focused on the pulpit.

Rev. Hester, a tall, heavy-built man with salt-and-pepper hair, stood before the pulpit in front of the choir stand. A large picture of the "Almighty" hung just above his head. Indigo averted her eyes from staring at the picture because Aunt Sadie once warned her, "The eyes of the 'Almighty' can look deep in your soul." "Humph," she thought to herself. "If he looked in my soul right now he'd know I don't know if being here is going to help anything."

In a husky booming voice, Rev. Hester announced, "The Lord is in his holy temple. Let all the earth keep silent." Indigo stood on cue with the rest of the colored congregation, looking forward. While everyone else focused on the pulpit, Indigo's eyes darted around the room. She was looking for evidence. Evidence to ensure everything was going to be all right, the way Aunt Sadie said it would be. The evidence would clue her in on what to do and how to act. Osceola Street and her whole life had been turned upside-down. It was going to take a whole lot of fixing to set things straight again. Eavesdropping at the crack in her cedar closet was where she got evidence going to church helped Aunt Sadie get her past troubles fixed. She did not know the full details of her aunt's troubles. They were whispered so low she could not hear them clearly. She did know her aunt swore the "spirit" fixed things in her life and kept on fixing them. Her testimony made for good listening at the crack in the cedar closet, but it was not enough proof for Indigo. Indigo wanted proof positive. The stakes were too high. Daddy Douglas was in jail when he should have been sitting in his black suit with the rest of the men in the deacon corner. Madear was in the hospital and Mrs. Jackson had to read the church news because Madear was not there to do it. Madear took pride in reading the church news each Sunday. As long as she could remember, she had never known her parents to miss going to church on Sunday. As far as she was concerned, things could not get any worse. She was willing to try almost anything to make things go back to the way they were. Even if "anything" included pretending to get "the spirit" in church, if she had to.

Church was both an amusement and oddity to Indigo. Sometimes she and Magnolia were able to get some good laughs. The memory of one good laugh popped in her mind. She could remember it like it was happening all over again. While the congregation exercised by standing and sitting to sing hymns, Indigo's mind drifted. She replayed a time when Mrs. Fitzgerald, the choir director, fell on Gilbert, the piano player, while he was playing. Gilbert played the piano keys with his eyes closed. From the moment he touched the ivory keys his eyes rolled back, his lids closed and by the time his lashes fluttered, you knew he was someplace playing way up high above the clouds. Within minutes, his gift of music passed through his fingers and captivated all who listened. Mrs. Fitzgerald was a narrow woman with a pointed chest that heaved when she belted out her soprano voice. She only wore her bra and panties underneath her robe. Her dress, hanging on the back door of the choir room on Sundays, drew even more attention to her neckline.

Madear said, "She was just plain nasty."

Aunt Sadie said, "Mrs. Fitzgerald took off her dress when she put on her choir robe so she could sing better. When you pass on your gift you got to be free," she tried to convince Madear.

Mrs. Fitzgerald usually sang a few bars of the gospel selection before the choir joined in as a cue for them to stand and get ready to sing. Once they stood, she walked up to the choir steps to the tune of the gospel they were about to sing. On the Sunday she took "the dive to glory," Gilbert was playing a fast version of "Glory, Glory, Hallelujah." Mrs. Fitzgerald sang out, "Gloree, Gloree, Gloree, Gloree," stirring the choir to their feet. Then she started her tiptoe march up the narrow steps that led up to the choir stand. Just as her soprano voiced was about to blend her "Gloree" in with the choir's "Glory, Glory," one of her three-inch-heeled shoes got caught on a protruding nail. When she tried to free herself from the nail, she stepped on the hem of her choir robe. Gilbert was already in a trance somewhere above the clouds. He was pounding the piano keys and pumping the pedals underneath his feet, so he did not see her stumble. Mrs. Fitzgerald did a half-turn, trying to pull the hem free. The turn caused her to lose her balance and sent her spiraling backward in a spread-eagle position. When her narrow body hit Gilbert's hands tickling the ivory keys, the zipper on her choir robe moved down, exposing the erectness of her chest. One of her rubber bra pads popped out and landed on D flat. The choir started singing "Hallelujah!" Gilbert opened his eyes and his crouched hands froze in midair. Mrs. Fitzgerald let out an embarrassed high-pitched "O Gloree!" and grabbed the rubber bra pad and stuffed it back inside her choir robe. She had to straddle her legs and wiggle her butt down the piano scale to regain her composure, but she made it to the choir stand before the choir stood to sing in unison.

The whole scenario generated a chorus of muffled laughter throughout the sanctuary. Indigo and Magnolia's giggles got the attention of Sister Valentine, sitting in the corner designated for the mothers of the church. She stretched her long neck and cast an evil eye in their direction. Her eye contact was enough to make them suppress their laughter deep inside their stomachs until church was over. Sister Valentine had chastising rights of all the parents in the church. If she caught you doing something wrong, she could and would chastise you with your parents' blessing. In the Douglas household if Sister Valentine or one of the other mothers had to chastise you, there would be trouble to pay.

It did not take long for Indigo's memory to fade back into the reality of the middle aisle she was sitting in. She sat motionless and agitated. How she yearned for trouble as simple as laughing at Mrs. Fitzgerald diving for glory and getting her evil eye and possible boxed ears from Sister Valentine. She knew the kind of work she would have to do to divert any trouble Sister Valentine could bring. The kind of trouble the Douglas family was facing was a completely new kind of trouble that she knew nothing about.

Rev. Hester started out slow and deliberate, speaking in a voice that sounded like it bounced off large silver bells.

"Trouble came our way this week. Colored people have been having trouble for a long time...This week trouble came and killed Martin Luther King!"

"My Lord," "Yes, it did!" "Lord have mercy," the people in the pews answered back.

"They killed him but they didn't silence him. I hear tell there is rioting in the streets all over this country, even right here in Tallahassee. They killed the messenger but they did not kill the message!"

"Amen! Praise the Lord! Hallelujah! Thank you, Lord!" came the thunderous reply.

People began jumping to their feet, clapping their hands and rocking from side to side. Indigo hoped the prelude to the evidence she sought was about to come forth. Rev. Hester surveyed the room and paused during the cheering to drink from his water glass next to his Bible. He took a big gulp of water and held it in his mouth for a few minutes, then he swallowed it slowly.

"This is Palm Sunday. The Bible tells us the Almighty walked the streets lined with people crying, 'Hosanna! Hosanna to the King!' Palm Sunday for Martin Luther King was four years ago. King was awarded the Nobel Peace Prize. He traveled all over Europe and other parts of the world where crowds cheered him and yelled his name. Our calendar tells us that it is Palm Sunday…When Martin Luther King fell dead to an assassin's bullet, our calendar fast-forwarded to the hope of Easter morning." People in the pews jumped to their feet. They were dancing, praying and shouting. The ushers were trying their best to revive the ones that got the spirit and maintain order. Gilbert was so far above the clouds he did not notice the stirring effects of his music. His music elevated the crowd while punctuating the preacher's words.

"The Almighty has a plan for black and white to walk together as brothers and sisters. This is the hope that Martin Luther King left for us. It is the hope of Easter. He alone will work it out. We are his children. He takes care of all his children. We shall overcome!" Rev. Hester bellowed to the church crowd.

"We shall overcome! We shall overcome!" they responded, bursting into song.

"Maybe somebody here is out of the ark of safety or needs prayer during this time of trouble. Come to the altar for a word of prayer. Prayer changes things," Rev. Hester pleaded, walking down from the pulpit to the altar, lowering his pitch to a more soothing tone.

The people flocked from the pews to the altar. They shifted their emotions but kept their eyes fixed straight. Indigo sat floating in an ocean of oddity, gazing at the churchgoers who "got the spirit" and the picture of the white "Almighty" hanging over the pulpit. She was anxious. Her anxiety heightened until she replayed the entire church service in her mind. Rev. Hester had preached until his white preaching robe was wringing wet. Several times the octaves of the people's voices in response to the sermon reached fever pitch. They trembled with tears, spun around with exhilaration and danced undauntedly in the aisle. The spirit-filled ones spoke in tongue-rolling eyeball-popping words that Indigo did not understand. The choir sang until their voices sounded hoarse. Sam Harvey, the gray-haired deacon, prayed himself happy. The words that had been the catalyst for the "spirit" flying around the room seemed false. Rev. Hester announced the "Almighty" wanted "blacks and whites to walk together." Something inside of her moved. Actually it jumped from her heart to her head and lodged itself behind her teeth. The whole pew heard her say No! after Rev. Hester's proclamation. Aunt Sadie and Grandma Dovie's necks jerked around in her direction as if the string of pearls around their necks had a loose spring. Rev. Hester's words were both maddening and confusing.

Hadn't they seen the newspaper that morning? she wondered. Didn't they realize next to the news of Martin Luther King being killed, whites had added to the Douglas family's trouble in great numbers? A white deputy had pushed her to the ground and arrested her Daddy. It was white Bethann who insisted she saw Mr. Benjamin start the fire! More and more she was beginning to believe Magnolia: "Light didn't like darkness thinking." To make matters worse, the "Almighty" that hung over Rev. Hester's pulpit was white! She gasped.

She was a prisoner in her mind. The whole world was changing and everyone in it. She had come for something to help stop the change. Aunt Sadie was convincing when she said the "Almighty" could fix things. According to Rev. Hester, the "Almighty's" prescription for fixing things was hope for something that never was and, judging from the past few days, never could be. She closed her eyes and leaned her head back against the pew while the church services ended. She drifted from Thursday to Sunday, replaying the moments that led her to the edge of anticipation directly in front of the pulpit. Her aunt nudged her to stand and join in singing the closing hymn, "Until We Meet Again."

"That preacher knows he preached today," someone exclaimed.

"God was working in this building this morning!" another parishioner added.

"Yes, sir, God was moving in this church this morning," Aunt Sadie exclaimed, hurrying to go over and greet one of the Killearn housekeepers she rode the Taltran bus with during the week.

Magnolia took Blueberry and Davis Jr. to the bathroom during the service and never returned. Grandma Dovie wandered out of the church immediately after Rev. Hester admonished the parishioners to "go in peace." The church emptied almost as fast as it filled up that morning. Indigo sat alone on the pew, watching the afternoon sun shining through the stained-glass windows. The glow of the sun beamed kaleidoscopic rays of light between the pews. The rays glistened against the church walls and on the looming picture of the white "Almighty." Indigo watched the multi-colored hues of reds, greens, blues, and yellows saturate the painted creamy skin of the "Almighty" until it appeared darker. "Maybe Magnolia doesn't know everything," she thought to herself. Awestruck with wonder leaping in her eyes, she focused her eyes above the pulpit.

"Did you need prayer, little sister Douglas?" Rev. Hester had eased up beside Indigo without her noticing him. He was still wearing his white preaching robe.

"No! I do not need, I mean, no thank you," Indigo quipped, rising from the pew with her eyes still on the picture of the "Almighty."

"The 'Almighty' has the power to change if you just trust him," Rev. Hester began. "I heard about your Momma and Daddy's troubles," he blurted out before Indigo had a chance to say anything.

"Yeah, can the 'Almighty' fix their kind of trouble?" Indigo asked eagerly.

Rev. Hester walked over to Indigo extending his big hands and placing one on her shoulder. "God can fix anything. He has all power," he insisted. Indigo felt her body began to turn toward Rev. Hester in anticipation of receiving some of the Easter hope that was the evidence she came for in the first place. For a moment, she turned her eyes and her attention to Rev. Hester.

"You have to let God work this out, child," he insisted in a pastoral tone. Then, just as unexpectedly as the rays beamed through the stained glass, a cloud passed in front of the sun. The streak of multicolored rays disappeared from the room and from the picture of the creamy-toned "Almighty" hanging over the pulpit.

The sudden darkness in the room distracted her from Rev. Hester's wealth of comfort. Indigo looked up at the picture of the Almighty. The creamy-toned skin of the "Almighty" was even more apparent than before.

"I can see God working," she sighed.

CHAPTER 17

"I may not get there with you"

Albert Whittier used both hands to steer his big Mercury to the right. He was trying to lean into the curve to avoid running off the road. The wind whipped across his face, making his eyes water.

He shook his head from side to side to suppress the effects of the whipping wind and maintain a clear view. The wind was an unavoidable hazard since the needle on his speedometer was approaching seventy when he met the curve. Bethann had noticed a road sign when her father approached the curve. She was sure it said a lower speed limit than her father was driving. His fast driving was making her nervous. She wanted to say something about the road sign but talking to her father had not been easy since yesterday. The wind blew her golden tresses in a rapid stinging motion across her face. Albert Whittier noticed his daughter's uneasiness but his own uneasiness was taking control.

His partner Bill had telephoned just as he grabbed his keys to leave and go pick up Sadie.

"Albert, we're looking at what is in the best interest of the partnership. We want you to join us at the county jail to give your statement about the fire at four this afternoon." He spoke in his formal cigar-chewing tone.

Albert Whittier knew the "we" in Bill's sentence was the result of a joint conversation with Bob, his other partner. He also knew he could not ignore this telephone call.

"This is an important matter, Albert, it affects all of us. Our company and our livelihoods are at stake here. We know you can see our point of view," Bill stressed, his voice ebbing and flowing in the juices of the cigar.

Sadie had insisted he take her to pick up her sister at the hospital and then drive them to the county jail when he telephoned her to say he was leaving the house to bring Bethann over.

"My sister will want to see about her husband when she gets out of the hospital. It's the least you can do, seeing how I'll be taking care of Bethann beyond what was I was hired for. I know these are my family problems. I am helping you with your family problems. The way I see it, one hand washes the other," Sadie interjected in a tone that let Albert Whittier know she would not bend easily.

Albert Whittier had arranged for an ambulance to transport Trin to Shands Hospital in Gainesville. He wanted to be there when it arrived with her. The last thing the charge nurse told him on the telephone last night was, "There will be paperwork to fill out when your wife arrives at Shands."

He felt the pull of obligation from all the requests made of him. He could feel the eyes of the pullers strengthening their chokehold, trying to press him into a submission of truth as they saw it. He had a commitment to his sick wife, regardless of the ambivalence stirring in his heart when he thought of their relationship. Bill and Bob were his partners in what had been a successful business. He could picture the stern looks on their faces, anticipating what they had worked hard for being in jeopardy. He knew Bill and Bob's demand for the presence of all the partners was a counter-attack strategy. He knew he needed Sadie's help and there was no way around it.

She wasn't really eager to help him but he was counting on her knowing she had to help him, he thought to himself.

Visions of Bill and Bob, Trin and her nurse and Sadie rolled around in his head. Benjamin's polite voice asking to speak with him echoed the loudest repeatedly in his ears.

"Mr. Whittier, sir…may I have a word with you, sir?" Benjamin asked repeatedly the Friday before Saturday's explosion. A word was all he wanted. Benjamin's words had always been true and important to the operations of the firm, even though no one ever told him, Albert Whittier thought to himself. Albert Whittier thought of the times he wanted to tell Benjamin how he valued his words, but he valued the favor of his partners more. They talked of "chastising Negroes like Benjamin and keeping them in their places." Albert Whittier tried to remember what he saw of Benjamin before the explosion. His head throbbed and his eyes blurred when he tried to visualize Benjamin throwing the Molotov cocktail.

"Where are we going, Daddy?" Bethann asked, interrupting his private visions and voices.

"We are going to pick up Sadie to take her to pick up her sister at the hospital and then we are going to the county jail and then—"

"The county jail? Why are we going there?" she asked.

"Because I'm doing a favor for Sadie and because I need to do some business there," he answered in a tone that suggested he was justifying his plans to himself as well as Bethann.

"I don't want to go to the county jail. Why do I have to go?" Bethann began to whine.

"I have much to get done this afternoon, daughter! I am being pulled like a rubber band. You know your mother is being moved to Gainesville and I am driving down to be with her tonight after I take care of Sadie and the business that I have to do at the county jail…I need cooperation…Do you understand?" he asked firmly.

"I understand but I don't see why I can't go to Gainesville with you. I want to be with my Momma."

Without prompting he began reciting a proverb aloud that his old friend Ira taught him years ago. "The eyes believe themselves; the ears believe other people."

"What are you talking about, Daddy? I'm talking about going to see Momma," Bethann insisted with a reddened face.

He had not fully understood Ira's proverb when he first heard it. Shaking his head from side to side, he navigated the big Mercury down Thomasville Road, and Ira's proverb seemed like a perfectly good answer to his daughter's inquiry and the circumstances before him. Bethann continued to question him but he said nothing as he slowed down the speed of the car and entered the city limits.

Sadie paced in front of the azalea bushes while looking down Osceola Street in anticipation of Mr. Whittier's big Mercury driving up. When she spotted him driving up Osceola Street, she yelled for her traveling entourage.

"Momma, Go-Go, y'all come on! Mr. Whittier is coming. Magnolia, you make sure Davis Jr. and Blueberry behave and do their homework. The Reverend is coming to get you at five. Make sure they look clean and presentable for when your Momma and Daddy see them," Sadie called out briskly making her way out of the screen door and down the front steps.

When Mr. Whittier drove up to the Douglas duplex at 424 Osceola Street, he could see Sadie coming across the grass to the curb and a group of Douglases standing in the threshold of the front porch screen door.

"Morning, Mr. Whittier," Sadie greeted, walking fast up to the driver's side of the car.

"Sadie," he nodded, looking quizzically at the Douglas group.

"My Momma and Indigo are going with me to pick up my sister from the hospital so the family can be together when we see my brother-in-law at the jail. The Reverend is coming by to pick up the other three children later...They're too little to go inside the hospital but the jail will let them in to see their Daddy."

"Very well, Sadie, please hurry and get in. I have to meet my partners at the jail."

Relieved by Mr. Whittier's cooperation, Sadie motioned for Grandma Dovie and Indigo to get in the back seat of the car.

FAMU hospital was just a short ride up Osceola Street. It sat on a hill diagonally across from Baker's Pharmacy. Mr. Baker, the pharmacist, was a keen businessperson from a generation of doctors and pill-pushers. When he built his pharmacy across from the hospital, he invested in the future of FAMU. When or if the sick got well enough to go home from the hospital, they usually needed a prescription filled and Baker's Pharmacy was there to fill it. Sadie politely made conversation by asking Mr. Whittier about his wife, even though it seemed like she was not interested in a reply. Bethann turned around from the front seat and caught a glimpse of Indigo. When Indigo saw Bethann looking in her direction, she pretended not to notice her. Grandma Dovie stared out the window of the back seat.

"She's being moved to Gainesville this afternoon and if I can get all these errands done, I plan to be there when she gets settled," he sighed.

"How are you, Miss Bethann?" Sadie moved on with her pleasantries, ignoring Mr. Whittier's resignation.

"Okay, but I want to see my Momma." Bethann began looking in her father's direction.

He cut his eyes in Bethann's direction, drove his big Mercury into the circle driveway of the hospital, and pulled up to the door of the entrance. Sadie didn't respond to Bethann's plea but got out of the car just as it came to a halt and motioned for Grandma Dovie and Indigo to follow.

"Bethann, we're staying in the car, Sadie won't be long," Mr. Whittier ordered, emphasizing "long" and looking in Sadie's direction.

Sadie hopped out of the car and was at the revolving door before Grandma Dovie and Indigo made it the short distance from the hospital driveway to the revolving door of the hospital entrance. She was through the spinning revolving door so fast Grandma Dovie and Indigo stood watching on the sidewalk as she strutted to the nurse's station.

"Cree Douglas. I'm here to pick up Cree Douglas, she's being released today," Sadie reported to the nurse.

"Cree Douglas has already been released and I've been waiting for forty-five minutes," a wispy voice crackled behind Sadie.

"Cree, girl, how are you feeling? Have you been waiting long? Mr. Whittier was late picking us up. You probably need to sit down. Come on, let's get you in the car." Sadie spoke nonstop.

Grandma Dovie and Indigo stepped out of the revolving door, rushing past Sadie to embrace the mother and daughter in a long hug who had troubled their hearts with her absence. Water from Indigo's eyes dripped onto her mother's dress. Grandma Dovie's long slender arms extending to petite manicured fingernails patted a rhythm on her daughter's back. Sadie smiled with fondness as her generations embraced. Her smile shrank when she looked through the pane of glass next to the revolving door and saw Mr. Whittier sitting in his car. He sat gripping the steering wheel of his big Mercury, looking straight ahead. He had not moved to a parking space. Bethann was stretching her neck, peering through the revolving door.

"Come on, ya'll, we better get going. Mr. Whittier is waiting for us. He didn't even park the car," Sadie directed, sensing Mr. Whittier's agitation.

"Madear, I was scared when I saw you coming out of that building. You looked like you were..." Indigo's voice cracked and her mother quickly took her face in her hands.

"I'm all right now and everything is going to be all right just as soon as we can get out of here and go and get your Daddy. Everything will be all right," Cree assured, arching her back as if preparing for the task ahead of her.

Grandma Dovie nodded and offered three quick pats of reassurance on her daughter's back. The four women began walking slowly out to the Whittiers' car. Indigo held the hand of her mother. Grandma Dovie touched the shoulder of her daughter between strides and Sadie gently nudged them along, keeping her eyes on the Whittiers' car. When Sadie opened the car door, Mr. Whittier turned and glared at her.

"Sadie, I must get going I have to meet Bill and Bob at the jail and I told you—"

"And we need to go to the jail, thanks to Bill and Bob," Sadie snapped back, forgetting her manners.

"I beg your pardon," he snapped right back at her, asserting the importance of remembering her manners.

"I'm sorry, sir. If we could just get to the jail it will be better for all of us," she softened, trying to smooth over her forwardness.

He mumbled to himself and started the engine of the Mercury.

"How is your wife, sir?" Cree spoke cautiously, waiting for a mention of her efforts to save his wife's life.

"She's being moved to Gainesville today. They have better facilities to treat the damage to her lungs. She is asthmatic and inhaled a lot of smoke. She is lucky to be alive." He spoke tentatively, as if realizing the magnitude of his wife's situation for the first time.

"Daddy," Bethann whined upon hearing her father's account of her mother's condition. He patted her leg to comfort her.

"Luck is just one of the things your wife has always had on her side, Mr. Whittier. She'll make out all right," Cree smirked to emphasize familiarity and ambivalence.

"This whole situation has just made you people take leave of decent and respectful conversation," Mr. Whittier spoke with obvious annoyance.

Sadie and Grandma Dovie lifted their heads and perked their ears, trying to anticipate the direction of Cree's nice/nasty tone with Mr. Whittier.

"No disrespect to you, Mr. Whittier, I'm just saying your wife always had a way of making things work her way, even if she is practically from the same place as colored people in Port St. Joe," Cree added unflinchingly.

"And I'm just saying I think Mr. Whittier has had just about enough of your pleasantries concerning his wife, Cree. Besides, you don't need to be tiring yourself out talking so much," Sadie jumped in, rolling her eyes in her sister's direction, trying to soften her words that consumed the airspace in the car.

"What do you mean by that?" Mr. Whittier demanded

Grandma Dovie began to fidget. She was growing increasingly nervous as she watched her daughters and Mr. Whittier in discussion. Indigo had not let go of her mother's hand since they embraced. She squeezed it tighter even though her mother stared blankly out of the car window. Bethann watched the faint color of veins pop up in her father's reddening neck. Indigo's and Bethann's eyes met. Indigo recognized a familiar helpless look in Bethann's eyes. It was the same helpless look she had worn when her Daddy had a yelling crying fit about Martin Luther King on Friday night. Indigo quickly studied all the faces in the Whittiers' Mercury and the pit of her stomach began to churn as if she was going to be sick. A car ride had never made her sick before. A car ride was always exhilarating to her. Daddy Douglas's Sunday car rides were a ritual she eagerly anticipated. It was one of her favorite adventures.

When Daddy Douglas drove the family to Key West to see his Uncle Junie, she had been so excited on the eve of the trip she could not sleep. The ride was more than eighteen hours. Everybody in the family was bored of riding but Indigo was not. She delighted in hours of passing scenery from the back seat car window. Flashes of dogwood trees and pecan trees melded into moving vignettes of palm trees alongside sandy beaches. When Magnolia and the other Douglas children did not complain about too much wind coming in on them, she would roll the car window down and smell the aromas of the scenery passing by. She would stick her head out the window, her plaits would swing back and forth, and her eyes would tear.

"Your eyes are tearing, Indigo, get your head back in that window before the wind cut your eyeballs," Madear would yell from the front seat.

"I need adventure goggles, Madear, like Amelia Earhart," Indigo would say.

"You're not Amelia Earhart, child. Get your head back inside before you ruin your eyes and your chance to see where we're going," Madear warned, chuckling.

"As much as that child loves to gaze and ride, she's not going to miss a thing," Daddy Douglas added to the amusement.

"I can see this is not going to be an adventure I'm going to like," Indigo thought to herself, sensing the tension in the car. It was a short ride to the county jail. It took about fifteen minutes to drive a short distance down Wahnish Way, then over to Pensacola Street near FSU football stadium and then on to Appleyard Drive. The county jail sat at the end of Appleyard Drive. Indigo expected Appleyard Drive would be a street full of apple trees. She had fantasized about the Douglas family stopping during one of their Sunday-afternoon rides to pick apples. The Douglas Sunday ride to Appleyard Drive turned out to be part of one of Daddy Douglas's "life lessons." He had talked nonstop for the entire Sunday afternoon drive about choices that lead people to jail. The irony of remembering Daddy Douglas' Appleyard Drive lesson on the way to visit him in the county jail jumbled the thoughts in her head.

"You didn't answer my question!" Mr. Whittier asserted, looking at Cree in his rearview mirror.

The car grew quiet. Sadie turned around, looking at Cree in a "don't start nothing and it won't be nothing" kind of way.

Cree started to blurt out something and decided to pause first. Then she started talking very slowly, choosing her words with caution. "No offense, Mr. Whittier, I was just commenting on your wife's way of getting people to give her what she wanted back in Port St. Joe. She got what she needed is all I'm saying."

"And you find fault with her for this?" he questioned.

"Well, her ways are where I find fault," Cree added.

"Port St. Joe was many years ago. People change to survive and to succeed. They cannot stay the same," he added reflectively.

"By people you mean white people, don't you, sir. Colored people do not have the chances you're talking about."

"You people had chances in Port St. Joe. Some more chances than others," Mr. Whittier declared, descending into a lengthy recount of his parents' toils as shopkeepers in Port St. Joe. Then he sighed and asked, "What did their favorableness cost them?"

"Now what do you mean, sir, when you say some colored had more chances than others?" Cree pressed.

"It cost them their very lives," he ranted, causing Bethann to jump, startled by his voice.

"My mother got pneumonia after she lost her way in the woods one night. She used to go down by the bay where the colored people lived to sing and place stones on the bank. It reminded her of the life we left behind. She must have become confused about which way to go home. My family helped colored people but they lumped us together in their fear of whites. They did not help us when we needed them. It was weeks before we found her. The August rains had been heavy and she had no means of shelter. Some colored men looking for a fishing hole found her but were too scared to bring her back to the store. They said the Klan was roaming. They insisted they feared for their life if caught with a white woman. They walked the twelve miles out of the woods to Poppa's store to tell us where she was. By the time we got there, she was so sick with fever she never recovered. Her last memories were of helping a colored woman. We showed you people kindness and look how you repaid us," he declared, banging the steering wheel.

Tears streaked Grandma Dovie's face as she listened to Mr. Whittier speak of his mother and her friend. Unspoken remorse remained trapped within her vocal cords.

"The Weatherspoons always paid because we had the money to pay. Your wife, on the other hand, was a horse of a different color. She always seemed to have other means of payment," Madear sneered.

"Cree, for the love of the Almighty, what has come over you? You must not be feeling well. Did the nurse give you some medicine? Maybe you need to take it now," Sadie pleaded, looking back and forth at Mr. Whittier and Madear.

Mr. Whittier pressed the brakes of the Mercury with force, causing the car to come to a screeching halt near the curve. "I will not allow you to disgrace my wife!" he bellowed, looking back at Cree.

"Nobody is disgracing nobody, Mr. Whittier. We all just plain worn out with everything that has happened is all. Everybody's nerves are on edge. Cree does not mean any harm. Let's just go on to the jailhouse, please!" Sadie jumped in nervously, trying to calm Mr. Whittier down.

"I will not drive this car another inch until I get an apology!" Mr. Whittier demanded.

"You want me to apologize for speaking the truth," Cree hissed.

"Cree, for goodness sakes, stop this!" Sadie insisted.

"Stop what? Stop reminding everybody Trina, or Trin Whittier she calls herself, was a conniving piece of trash from Port St. Joe before she came up to Tallahassee? Now she has turned herself into a Miss Killearn want-to-be. She has never done anything but make people's life miserable and the one time the tables turned on her, mercy stepped up to the plate. She has luck on her side all right."

Mr. Whittier jumped out of the front seat of the car, opened the back door and demanded Cree to get out of the car.

"Get out! Get out right now! What gives you the right to judge my wife? You were no different than she was. You are nearly the same—"

he started to say "color" and stopped as the rage surged like mercury in his face.

Memories of hush words from the hole of the cedar closet rushed around in Indigo's head.

"Mr. Whittier, sir, please! We need to get to the jailhouse and I got to take care of Bethann for you," Sadie begged.

Grandma Dovie's eyes darted from side to side. She balled her hands in a fist, opened them and closed them repeatedly. Then she elbowed Cree hard in her side. Cree sat still with a tornado of emotions swirling in her face.

Sadie's words fell on Mr. Whittier's ears and his eyes twitched the way they did when he suddenly remembered something. He looked decisively in his rearview mirror at the colored entourage he was chauffeuring. He blew a deep breath, shaking his head as if he was trying to level the elevating rage in his face. He stood breathing hard, gripping the back car door with white knuckles that had blotches of red between patches of hair. His eyes transfixed in Cree's direction. The traffic light changed and a police car cruised behind a mail truck about twenty feet away.

"I will not allow you to disrespect my wife and ride in this car," he spoke sternly, bending next to Cree's ear.

"Cree, cooperate, will you? Hiram is waiting on us to get to the jail…" Sadie pleaded.

Cree looked at Sadie, then at her mother and then back at Mr. Whittier. She wiped the sweat from her face with her hands and took a quick glance at herself in the mirror above the steering wheel. She could see the police car approaching the parked Mercury. She turned her body to the opened car door and extended her legs outward, returning the glare to Mr. Whittier.

"Cree, what are you doing? Where are you going?" Sadie shouted.

"Madear!" Indigo whined, pulling her mother's arm.

"Cree, we have to get to the jailhouse...Come on, Hiram's waiting for us." Sadie was trying her best to say something that would make Cree stop but she could not.

"I may not get there with you," Cree said over her shoulder as she stood to get out of the car.

The police officer slowed down when he approached the big Mercury and looked curiously at Mr. Whittier. A white man transporting colored help was just an ordinary occurrence. Nothing had been quite ordinary since the news of Martin Luther King being killed blared through the radio. Mr. Whittier offered a nod at the police officer to let him know he had things under control.

"Everything all right here?" the police officer yelled, pulling down his sunglasses, leaning over in the direction of Albert Whittier to extend his voice through the opened window on the passenger side. For a brief moment, Mr. Whittier and Cree stood face to face, suspended in the present by past circumstances.

"Everything's fine, Officer," Albert Whittier stammered, turning to face the police car.

The officer revved the engine of his patrol car, nodded, satisfied with the response he'd been given, and cruised past the Whittiers' Mercury. Albert Whittier watched him drive away, breathing a sigh of relief. When he turned back toward his car, it was just in time to catch the backside of Cree Douglas walking up the road toward Appleyard Drive.

CHAPTER 18

"The world is all messed up"

The lobby of the jail smelled like bleach mixed with pine. Sadie ushered Grandma Dovie and Indigo across a green-and-beige linoleum floor of squares to a worn green sofa. Indigo could see Magnolia, Davis Jr. and Blueberry down the hall at the vending machine. Magnolia was banging on the vending machine, trying to get salted peanuts for Davis Jr. and Blueberry.

"Magnolia!" Aunt Sadie spoke loudly, waving her hand, summoning the Douglas children in her direction.

It took less than ten minutes for Mr. Whittier to reach the jail. It was another thirty minutes before Cree Douglas walked into the lobby dripping with sweat from her brisk walk down Appleyard Drive.

"Cree, Mr. Whittier was just trying to help us. You just got out of the hospital, for goodness sakes. Look at you! You are wet with sweat. You should've stayed in the car!" Sadie pounced on Cree when she stepped into the lobby.

"Momma," the Douglas children cried in unison, rushing in her direction.

"Where's Rev. Hester?" Sadie inquired.

"He told us to sit out here and wait for you all. He went in the back offices," Magnolia reported, extending her arms around her mother's neck.

Albert Whittier, looking straight ahead, hustled Bethann up to the information desk. Bill and Bob spotted him immediately. So did Indigo.

"Albert, over here! Over here, Albert!" They waved their hands for Albert to come in their direction.

Albert Whittier, gripping Bethann's hand, hastened over to the corner of the room where Bill and Bob stood fidgeting. The Douglas family sat huddled in the opposite corner. Indigo moved toward an artificial plant sitting in front of a window that both divided and connected the room.

"Albert, we have a statement prepared for you to sign. As soon as you sign, we can get out of here...We have already arranged everything...We can get on with our business." Bill spoke authoritatively.

Albert quickly scanned the typed sheet of paper. His eyes widened and he looked from Bill's face to Bob's face.

"It says here that I smelled the kerosene on Benjamin when he came to the office. It says that I saw him throw the Molotov cocktail. I..." he spoke hesitantly.

"We're just saying what happened, aren't we, Albert," Bob asked suggestively.

"I saw him throw the cocktail," Bethann chimed in.

"So you're just supporting what your daughter saw," Bill insisted, handing Albert Whittier a pen.

"But she's just a child..." Albert countered.

"A child whose mother was nearly killed and father's business nearly ruined," Bob added, growing impatient with Albert's hesitation.

"Albert, be reasonable. Benjamin and his friend are guilty. There is no way they are going to get out of this with the evidence the police have and everything going on in this town, in this doggone country for that matter. Negroes are rioting and running rampage everywhere. It is up to the good law-abiding citizens like us in this town to help the sheriff to get things back in order. You can't help these Negroes now, Albert. Hell, even they are saying their King is dead," Bill explained with a wry smile.

Albert Whittier's hands quivered as the tip of his pen met the paper. Indigo bit her lip to keep it from quivering.

A tall deputy jingling a set of keys came over to the Douglas clan and announced visiting hours.

"Come this way," he said with a half-smile and eyes darting warmly in Davis Jr.'s direction.

Davis Jr. was carrying his rubber ball. The deputy looked at the ball in his hand and asked Davis Jr. if he liked to play ball. The deputy said Davis Jr. looked like baseball player. A smile spread across Davis Jr.'s face. He practiced throwing that rubber ball against the back steps and catching it every afternoon. On Saturdays, Davis Jr. shared his progress with Daddy Douglas. After their shoe-shining session, Davis Jr.'s rubber ball hitting Daddy Douglas's leather baseball glove made loud smacking sounds.

Davis Jr. beamingly told the deputy, "My daddy says I got a throwing arm like Satchel Paige."

"Then you must be a pretty good," the deputy added.

Indigo walked behind them, wondering if her father would ever say those words to Davis Jr. or catch his rubber ball again.

Daddy Douglas was dressed in a gray-and-white-striped jumpsuit sitting in a chair at a metal table, holding a small tablet of papers and a pencil. He had shackles on his feet and they made a clanging sound when he stood to greet his family. Blueberry nearly leaped in his arms. Davis Jr. and Magnolia followed with a tight embraces. Sadie and Grandma Dovie walked over and stood close. Indigo stood beside her mother next to the metal table.

"It is so good to see you all," Daddy Douglas said through a big grin and throaty voice.

"If it was so good to see us you would not be in here in the first place," Madear snapped.

Her words were like a shot from a starter pistol. It called everyone to attention. All eyes turned in her direction.

"I did what I had to do! What any colored man with any kind of pride would've done," Daddy Douglas roared.

"What any colored man would've done? That is the whole problem with you! You are hung up on color! You cannot think straight! A real man with a family would not have gotten involved in this mess," Madear spoke angrily.

"Maybe you should be more hung up on color then you would know your place," Daddy Douglas shot back.

"Will you both stop this? There are more important things to be discussed…For starters, how are we going to get you out of here, Hiram?" Aunt Sadie jumped in.

"He got himself in here, let him get hisself out," Madear sneered.

"I'm in here because of what we're talking about now. The conversation is long overdue." As Daddy Douglas spoke, he made the shackles around his ankles rattle.

"And what conversation is that, Hiram Douglas? What conversation could be more important to talk about than one about you sitting here in this damn jail not knowing when or if you are going to get out? Tell us! Tell us!" Madear insisted angrily.

"Cree, please," Sadie asked, trying to calm things down.

"He can't get out because Mr. Whittier and those men aren't letting him out," Indigo shouted before she realized it. "I heard them talking in the waiting room and they were saying Daddy and Mr. Benjamin are staying in jail for starting that fire. You didn't start that fire, did you, Daddy?" Indigo spoke, looking at her father, in a voice of a small child.

"What did you expect they would do, Hiram? Did you think they would join you and Benjamin over in Frenchtown? They are going to try to lock you all up for good. Where is this going to leave your family? Did you think about that when you went to stand up for your precious King, Hiram?" Madear yelled in Daddy Douglas's direction.

"I expect to be treated like a man given the benefit of the doubt by you and them. These white cracker police are looking for a nigger to blame. If standing up for King's dreams makes me that nigger then I'm it," Daddy Douglas declared.

"You are a big fool, Hiram Douglas! You and Benjamin made a bomb and set that building on fire. Thirteen years of marriage, you threw away when you threw that bomb. You risked it all for Martin Luther King's dreams. His dreams got him dead and left his four children without a daddy. You won the dream and the prize, Hiram!" Madear yelled, shaking her finger and standing in front of Daddy Douglas.

"I'm the same man that I was when you married me. You just never really noticed. I am sitting here with these shackles around my feet because of my convictions. I love my children and I am always going to take care of them, even if the world is all messed up now. Taking care of them is more than just making sure they eat and have a roof over their heads. I have to make sure they have justice. Colored people do not have justice in this country. Have you noticed? Of course not! That would mean you would have to believe you were colored." He spit the words out of his mouth as if they tasted bad.

At some point, the harsh words passing between Daddy Douglas and Madear drew tears from the eyes watching their interaction.

"I'm as colored as you are and I do not need to prove it to anybody!" Madear snarled.

"No, you do not have to prove it. Just live like the rest of us colored people. We cannot use powder on our faces like you, pretend to be white and sit at the McCrory's food counter and eat our lunch. Even if we could, we would not because we are not white or near white. We are colored, all different shades but we are colored and know it." Daddy Douglas spoke with the same wild look he had in his eyes when he watched Walter Cronkite's broadcast after Martin Luther King was assassinated.

Indigo's heart beat faster with each harsh word her mother and father spoke to each other. She could not cry anymore. She wanted to cry but the water just stopped when Daddy Douglas spoke about Madear putting powder on her face and eating at the McCrory's lunch counter. She remembered Madear telling her and Magnolia," McCrory's leftovers were more special than eating at the lunch counter."

"How did Madear come to know about those leftovers?" Indigo wondered to herself. "Did she talk about those leftovers because she had sat at the counter top on the red-covered stools? Had she tasted those Vidalia onions that tantalized the nostrils of all who smelled them? Madear never said she sat at the McCrory's counter but she never said she hadn't either." The questions raced through Indigo's mind so fast that she couldn't think to provide answers. All those times she watched longingly the white women and men eating at the lunch counter, she knew the colored people were not allowed to eat there because Magnolia had explained it to her. When Madear spoke about the McCrory's leftovers, Indigo thought she was just offering soothing words the way mothers did when children longed for something a parent couldn't possibly provide. The thought of Madear eating at the McCrory's lunch counter among the white women and men made Indigo take a hard look at her mother's skin. She knew her mother's complexion was fair but suddenly she became aware of just how fair it really was. Over the last four days, she had thought more about white people than she had in all her twelve years. Her new friendship with the only white girl she ever talked to ended when she told a lie and got Daddy Douglas and Mr. Benjamin put in jail. Colored people everywhere, even down at the Shriner's Club, were talking about how white people killed King. Now Daddy Douglas said Madear had pretended to be a white person.

"How much longer are you going to be, Sadie, I have to get going," Mr. Whittier asked nonchalantly, peeking his head in the visiting room.

"As long as it takes," Madear spoke sharply in Mr. Whittier's direction.

"Sadie..." Mr. Whittier spoke sternly.

"We'll be ready in a minute, sir," Sadie chirped.

"Do you see me standing here? I said we'll take as long as it takes," Madear shot at Mr. Whittier.

Mr. Whittier stepped inside the visiting room and deliberately closed the door.

"I have always seen you. I saw you on the ride over here making a horrible situation worse. I see you continuing to do the same in this visiting room...You have never been hard to see." He spoke to Madear in a tone that signaled he had unsuspected knowledge.

"So since you see me, hear me and get the hell out of here. We don't need you," Madear shouted.

"Settle down, Cree, you are talking to a white man...Haven't you noticed?" Daddy Douglas sneered at Madear, clasping his hands together on the table.

"And you think that matters to me?" she torpedoed back.

"It always has before, what's different now?" Daddy Douglas countered.

"The problem with you, Hiram, and this stupid white man here are that you live in the past. Come to this real world where you are sitting on your butt in jail and your trashy wife is in a hospital somewhere trying to breathe." Madear's eyes spoke as loudly as her mouth. Her eyes were wild and she was ready to attack.

"Would part of that real world be those occasions in Port St. Joe when I saw you armed with trinkets from the arms of Mr. Joe? On the other hand, maybe the real world might be when you returned my family's mezzuzah and you asked me to sell you quinine for your sickness. Would that be the real world you're talking about?" Mr. Whittier spoke venomously.

"Or maybe your real world would be letting your sister take the blame and going to jail for something you did. No! No, your real world has got to be letting a brother believe his love was so strong you got pregnant on the first night you were together. Better yet, the combination of your genes and my black almost blue genes created a light near-white baby. Then you insisted on giving the baby a name like Magnolia to point out the whiteness every time you looked at her. That's your real world, Cree, isn't it." Daddy Douglas choked on some of his words but the impact was like a ton of lead crashing down in the middle of the room, breaking everything in its path.

"I am not ashamed of anything I have ever done. Whatever I did, I did it because…" Madear's voice trailed off.

"Because you are selfish and always think of yourself, sister," Sadie responded with tears streaming down her face.

Facing Daddy Douglas and realizing the conversation was on the way to a place that her marriage had not been before, Madear bit her lip and spoke in a whine. "Hiram, I'm not the problem here. White men are not your problem. You are."

"A white man is your problem. Because a white man was your Daddy," a voice sounding like pipes rustling on a windy day answered, causing everyone to turn to look in the direction it came from.

Grandma Dovie stood up and walked over to her daughters, who stood and sat within two feet of each other. Looking from side to side at both of them, she talked slowly.

"Back in Port St. Joe when I was a young woman, a white man raped me before I married your father. Cree, Nate raised you like you was his own. Nobody never much questioned your skin color and sharp features. Except you! I have the same sharp features as you. When I tried to instill pride in you for your skin color, you were never satisfied. Did you want me to tell you I was raped? Your Daddy,

Nate, the one that raised you and gave you everything and more than you needed. He was proud to have you as his child. Very proud! We never told you because we figured it was no need. Now you need to know so maybe you'll stop all this hate inside of you."

Madear began to bend over as if some spicy food had decided to wage war on the lining of her stomach. Her face was a picture of contortions of hard-to-decipher emotions. Indigo's stomach churned. She couldn't be sure if it was what Grandma Dovie was saying or that she was saying anything at all that was causing her pain. Everyone in the room looked like they were about to be sick from the same spicy food. Rev. Hester looked hard-pressed to find a suitable religious phrase for the occasion.

Just when it seemed like there was nothing else to be said or nothing more shocking to be revealed, Indigo watched her grandmother turn to Mr. Whittier and continue her spell-binding speech.

"Stud, son, your Momma was one of the kindest women you ever want to meet. She saved my life one night out in the woods. She was tired of hate too. She wanted to go back to her old country and her old life. Being out in the woods reminded her of all the people she lost because of hate. At the bay every night she would remember. You should remember too."

Grandma Dovie's words moved Mr. Whittier in a physical way. His torso, arms and hands trembled. He looked like someone had turned up the radio full blast, shocking his eardrums, and he wanted to cover his ears. He turned around in a jerking motion toward the door and mumbled, "Sadie, I left Bethann at the information desk, I'll be in the car."

Indigo sat trying to avoid looking at Magnolia, who was weeping uncontrollably. She did not dare venture into the triangle of Grandma Dovie, Sadie and her mother. Daddy Douglas looked dejected, sitting at the metal table shaking his shackled feet. His eyes wandered around the room until they met Indigo's. She thought their eyes meeting signaled an option for solace. How she longed for a glimpse of the high-chested pride that Madear and her Aunt Sadie associated with Daddy Douglas's family. The few feet that separated them seemed foreign and far away. The four days since Martin Luther's King's death triggered changes all around Indigo, she had held her breath and tried to visualize her life returning to normal. The last forty minutes in the jailhouse visiting room made normal seem out of reach.

As soon as she walked over to Daddy Douglas, the jailer opened the door and announced visiting hours were over. He grabbed Daddy Douglas by the arm, nearly lifting him out of the seat. Davis Jr. and Blueberry ran over to their Daddy and locked their hands around him. Magnolia walked over too but stopped just short of the embrace.

"Daddy!" Indigo shouted. He did not answer but he shoved a writing tablet in her hand and tried to hug all his children at one time.

CHAPTER 19

"It really doesn't matter what happens now"

It was a silent ride from the jail to the 400 block of Osceola Street. No one said a word. The silence continued when the Douglas family got out of the car and Sadie and Bethann went across the street to the rooming house. Madear must have taken the bus or ridden with Rev. Hester because she left before everyone else could get outside to Mr. Whittier's car. She was not home when the Whittiers' Mercury drove up to the Douglas duplex.

Grandma Dovie's talking did not stop at the jail. When she got out of Mr. Whittier's Mercury she asked him to get out too. She ordered the Douglas children in the duplex. She and Mr. Whittier talked for a long time. From the window of the Douglas duplex, it looked like Mr. Whittier was assuming the position of the stomachache that whizzed around the jailhouse visiting room. Before he got back in his Mercury, he hugged Grandma Dovie with a hug like she was kin.

When she walked into the duplex, it was with an air of confidence and familiarity. She headed straight for the kitchen and started putting pots on the stove. Davis Jr. and Blueberry got busy on the back porch counting soda bottles in between asking about supper.

"Grandma, when are we going to eat?" they asked in unison as if they had been asking her all their days.

"In about two shakes. Ya'll get off that back porch and go wash up," she hollered over her shoulder as if she had been speaking every day of her life. "How could she just start talking without explanation? Maybe she has been talking all along. I could have sworn I saw her mouth moving on the back porch the other night. Why didn't she let us know she could talk? Why all of a sudden with everything else going on does she started talking now?" Indigo wondered with bewilderment and annoyance.

Indigo could not get her eyes off her grandmother and her newfound voice. She was not quite sure what to make of what her eyes told her and what the new voice told her ears. Whenever something shocking happened in the family or on the 400 block of Osceola Street, she could count on Daddy Douglas to put it in perspective at the supper table. She realized she was still holding the writing tablet that her father gave her at the jail. The reality of his absence and the awareness of what that absence would mean was beginning to set in. She visualized his cap hanging on the back of the chair at the dining room table. The cap hanging on the back of the chair at the head of the table signaled the Douglas clan, to dinner. She looked at the copy of the Tallahassee *Democrat* rolled up in a green rubber band on kitchen table. No one had bothered to open or read it. She hoped for a sign of pages turned back or the sports section lying on the floor as a symbol of his insatiable appetite for the outside world.

She sat down in his chair at the head of the table and held the writing tablet close to her face. It was comforting in the midst of the unsteady feeling that was consuming her. The unsteadiness left her not knowing what or how to feel. In addition to not knowing what to feel, she did not know what to believe.

"Should I believe my Momma was able to sit on the red top counter stool at McCrory's and taste those mouth-watering Vidalia onions sizzling on the grill with hot dogs by pretending to be a white woman. Is my Momma half-white? Is she half-colored or completely colored or just white? Which part is colored and which part is white? Was Momma the reason Aunt Sadie went to jail? Aunt Sadie did go to jail. I did hear right in the cedar closet. My sister Magnolia is half-white too, or since Madear is half-white and Daddy Douglas said on the sly, Magnolia's Daddy was white, is Magnolia completely white? Is my sister white?" She was so engrossed in her thoughts she dropped the writing tablet on the kitchen table. When it hit the table, it fell open to a short letter written in Daddy Douglas's handwriting.

"Dear Indigo (Go-Go)," the letter began.

She did not want to read any more. So much of the information that had come within her earshot that afternoon was spit out for all to hear, regardless of how much it shocked or pained the listener. She needed a place that was familiar and private to read what Daddy Douglas had written to her. She needed the sanctity of her cedar closet.

She raced to the cedar closet, passing Magnolia sitting on the bed, staring at the mirror attached to the bureau in front of her. She could feel Magnolia hurting but she could not bring herself to offer comfort. The tacit rules of their birth order did not lend themselves to the younger sibling comforting the older one. Indigo wished Daddy Douglas had sent a letter for Magnolia. She knew in her gut Magnolia was sitting in front of that mirror searching for some indication of who she really was in the Douglas family.

"If only she asked," Indigo continued to think to herself, "I would tell her proof of anything familiar is hard to find since Martin Luther King was killed four days ago."

Magnolia never even looked up. The knob to the cedar closet was on the floor underneath a chair. Davis Jr. liked to take the glass doorknobs out of the closet doors. The face of the glass knob was flat. When Davis Jr. put the knobs on the floor, he twirled the iron stem that stuck out of the knob like a spinning top. Several of the closets in the Douglas house had missing knobs because of his love for spinning tops. Indigo scooped the knob up and stuck its iron stem in the door shaft. She pulled the string to the light switch and closed the door tight. The dim light in the closet barely cast a shadow underneath the closet door. The light was dim but it was bright enough to read Daddy Douglas's letter in private.

~

Dear Indigo (Go-Go)

I want to talk to you so you will understand. There are things you have to understand and do for yourself. Everything is different now. You think Martin Luther King's death is the reason everything is so turned upside-down in the family. Well, you are only half right. His death rang a bell inside of all people, especially colored people. It rang and is still ringing, whether they are listening for it or not. This includes me. You must think it had to be a loud bell to reach so many people. It would take all the paper in this tablet to explain all that he did. Besides, it still would not mean anything to you. Your Momma and I have kept all of you inside of the 400 block of Osceola Street all your lives. You must get to know Martin Luther King's story and his dream for yourself. You might think this will be hard because he died four days ago. You will hear his message everywhere. I have heard you and Magnolia talking about "when you get grown" and the things you are going to do. Make this one of the things you do. Find out who you are. Then decide which way you must go. Search everywhere. Dream your own dream. Be brave. Hard times are coming. You have power inside you. Douglases got Iko power. It really doesn't matter what happens now. The rules have been thrown out. I love you.

Daddy

Daddy Douglas's letter had not given her the relief she hoped. She was not exactly sure what she was hoping for before she read it but now that she had read it she still wanted more. It was a surprise to her when he shoved the writing tablet to her at the jailhouse. Writing tablets were all over the house. Daddy Douglas and Madear wrote in them and on scraps of paper. Indigo tried to remember everything about Daddy Douglas's writings, hoping her memory would provide some explanation for his mumbled jumbled letter to her.

"Every night right before he got up from the supper table and went into the living room, he pushed his plate away at the dinner table and scribbled his writing on portions of the newspaper or scraps of paper. Sometimes when Magnolia and I cleaned up the kitchen after supper, his writings would be lying on the kitchen table. Once Magnolia picked up a scrap and read it while I acted as a look-out. I was watching the hallway to the kitchen, anticipating an adult intruder, but Daddy Douglas came into the kitchen from the back porch. He saw Magnolia reading the scrap of paper. He paused for a minute and then he walked over and took it out of her hand without saying a word. Magnolia never told me what she read. A few weeks after that happened I saw his scraps of paper on the kitchen table. When I picked them up I saw lines of sentences about the news in the Tallahassee *Democrat* or on the television, reactionary paragraphs to conversations with Mr. Benjamin when he talked about his job, love sonnets about Madear and pages and pages of plans for his children. Then there were equations using alphabets instead of numbers.

"This letter does not make sense. He does not have to tell me about hard times coming. They are already here. Aunt Sadie said a person dreams when they are sleeping peacefully. I will never dream a day in my life again, because I will never be at peace again. How can I? Everybody and everything is crazy and it is all on television and in the newspaper," she rebuffed Daddy Douglas's writings out loud.

The sound of voices coming through the cedar crack made her soften her rebuttal. The voices were spoken in rapid succession; Indigo had to put her ear right next to the crack to decipher what was being said. Even straining her ear, she could not be certain who was really speaking.

"Don't talk to me! You have not talked to me in years, why are you talking to me now?" Madear screamed.

"Cree, settle down. We're all hurting here! You are not the only one! Nothing has changed, we are still family," a voice that sounded like Aunt Sadie said.

"Everything has changed and you know it, Sadie! Can you tell me you are not mad at me for sending you to jail? Can you tell me that? I am not about to stand here and tell you it does not matter to me after all these years to learn my real Daddy was a white man. I had a right to know, Momma. You should have told me. You know you should have told me. You robbed me!"

"What good would it have done you? Half-white is not completely white. It wouldn't have changed anything."

"Do I look half-white to you? Take a good look, Momma. You do not know if it would have changed anything. You have no way of knowing that!"

"Don't swear at me. I'm your Momma!"

"A Momma who kept a secret about who I am and who my father was my whole damn life!"

"Cree, now if that's not the pot calling the kettle black. You have done the same thing to Magnolia! Momma did what she had to do. You did what you wanted to do!"

"You don't know what it was like. Besides, I am talking about me right now! Momma kept me from feeling comfortable in my own skin. You have no way of knowing how I have felt all these years. Nobody understands what I feel!"

"And no one gives a sh…" Aunt Sadie stopped short of saying.

"Don't use curse words in this house. I will not have it and the Lord is not pleased with it!"

"Ah, face the music for the first time in your life, Cree. You have a mess of your own doing and you know it. Who your Daddy was has nothing to do with why you took Mr. Joe's gifts and made a baby with him. It has nothing to do with your stealing that dress and letting me take the blame or pretending to be a white woman eating at McCrory's lunch counter. All those things are choices you made because you wanted to make them. How in the hell—sorry, Momma—can you expect sympathy from anybody when you hurt everybody!"

"Yeah, I wanted Mr. Joe's gifts! He looked at me like I was something rare and beautiful. He told me that. He said I was unlike any another nigger or white woman. A diamond beauty in a patch of rough, he called me. Colored people did not see me the way he saw me. If the men saw me at all, it was because I was the closest they could get to have a white woman for themselves. Colored woman just hated me in general. They treated me as if I was some sort of misfit."

"Shut up, Cree, shut up before I slap you silly,"Sadie threatened

"You can't stand to hear it but it's true. I do not look like you or Daddy. People whispered when I walked by. I guess they knew Momma's dirty little secret. It hurt me deep. I loved Hiram then and I love him now. I needed a baby to look like me. Mr. Joe loved me. I did not love him exactly. I loved the way he loved me. I wanted to reproduce that kind of love in a child that looked like me. I wanted her to be comfortable in her own skin, something I could not do. I could not make that kind of baby with Hiram. I never wanted him to know. I thought about getting rid of it. I just could not do it."

"Why are you telling all this? Why now?"

"Cleanse your soul, child," Grandma Dovie encouraged.

"I want to be free of this. If Momma can free herself to tell me my Daddy was white man, I free myself too."

"You should be ashamed!" Sadie admonished

"But I'm not! From this day forward, I am not going to be. I bought the quinine from Stud's son but I could not take it. I just could not. I had a chance to bring a baby into the world looking just like me and make it better for her. That is what Hiram's precious Martin Luther King would have wanted. Hiram and I were both in the struggle. We were just struggling different ways. I am deeply sorry, Sadie, for what happened to you. I did not mean for things to turn out that way. Once Ms. Heloise got involved things just spun out of control. There was nothing I could do. It would have messed up everything. I would have been pregnant in jail and Hiram would have never even touched me. It was not the best way but it was the only way. You do not know what it is like to be halfway in on one side and halfway out on the other. Everything would have been fine if Hiram would have just left his suspicions rest. Every night he scribbled, trying to figure out the probability of him producing a baby light as Magnolia. He would let it die down and then he would start up again. Since King died, he started with it again."

"I'm sorry for Hiram but I don't really care about all the rest of this, Cree, I don't really care."

"Hush that talk! We all care, everybody cares. We just do not care enough about the right things. If we cared enough about the right things, King would not be dead. Hiram and that neighbor Benjamin would not be sitting in jail now. Sadie, you would not have sat in jail all those years, and your sister Cree would know the love she wants so bad is right inside of her."

The conversations vibrating through the cedar crack exhausted Indigo. Gone were the joy and excitement of hearing family secrets firsthand. Besides, Indigo was sure Magnolia and anybody else who wanted to listen could hear the amplified bedroom conversations that blared through the walls between her grandmother, mother and aunt. All the details had left her weak. Her ears hurt from straining to listen. Her eyes burned from reading Daddy Douglas's words in the dim closet light. Her head throbbed from the overload of information flooding through her brain. Her feet twitched from the impulse to run as far away as she could from the 400 block of Osceola Street and all that had happened over the past four days.

"Indigo! Indigo, where are you?" Her Aunt Sadie was looking for her and calling at the same time.

There was an imprint of shoelaces across one side of her face. Salvia was dripping out the corner of her mouth. She did not know how long she had been sleeping. Her body felt heavy and her stomach was growling. She stumbled out of the closet holding onto the writing tablet.

"What were you doing in that closet, child?" Sadie demanded.

"Nothing, I mean I was sleeping."

"You don't sleep in the closet. Go in the kitchen and get yourself something to eat."

"Where's everybody?"

"Magnolia's in the kitchen eating, Davis Jr., Blueberry and Bethann are in the living room watching television."

"Bethann!"

"Yes, Bethann!"

"Where's Madear?"

"Your Momma went down to the Shriner Club."

"Madear doesn't go to the Shriner Club," Indigo responded indignantly. She had seen women sitting in parked cars with men outside the Shriner Club but it was unthinkable for Madear to be one of those women, despite all that had happened over the last four days.

"And who made you an expert on who goes to the Shriner Club? Your Momma certainly did go to the Shriner Club tonight," Sadie rattled off, then attempted to soften her tone after looking at Indigo's face. "Maybe she just needed to be someplace different for a while," she added, going out of the bedroom door.

"Maybe," Indigo answered, trying to swallow the possibility of her mother being inside the Shriner Club. Walking out of her bedroom into the hallway leading to the kitchen, she realized she did not have any idea what went on inside the Shriner Club. She only knew what she and Magnolia had seen going on outside the Shriner Club.

"Daddy Douglas said men went go to philosophize and tell lies," she told herself. "But what do women do?" she wonder silently.

She had seen groups of men standing outside the Shriner Club talk loudly and slur their words. What few women she did see in the parking lot sat in the front seats of parked cars so close to the men at the steering wheel, it was hard to see it was two people in the car until you walked right up on them. She knew the drinking started in the parking lot because of the many times she and Magnolia kicked empty beer and liquor bottles when they cut through the parking lot.

When she saw Magnolia sitting at the kitchen table, she jumped at the opportunity to get some clarity.

"Did you know Madear went to the Shriner Club?"

Magnolia did not look up or stop picking at the unrecognizable supper on her plate. She just nodded her head.

"Why did she go?"

"How am I supposed to know why she went there? I'm not a mind reader."

"I didn't say you were. I just thought you knew why she went there," Indigo spoke, acknowledging the unusual lack of confidence in Magnolia's reply. Magnolia kept her eyes downward in her supper plate in a distant mood.

"Well, do you know where Grandma Dovie is?" Indigo asked, knowing she was not ready to face a "talking" Grandma Dovie, but she just wanted to make sure every possible Douglas was accounted for.

"She's sitting on the steps of the back porch," Magnolia answered, scraping her plate of half-eaten supper in the garbage can.

Indigo peeked through the screen door and saw the top of Grandma Dovie's wavy-haired head. She started to go outside but decided to go in the living room instead. When she came to the doorway, she saw Davis Jr. and Blueberry asleep on opposite ends of the sofa. Their legs barely touched the sagging middle section that once outlined the shape of Daddy Douglas's body. Aunt Sadie sat in the matching chair to the sofa, rolling her hair on pink sponge rollers. Bethann sat on the green rug, turning the channels on the television set and adjusting the rabbit ears.

"We only watch channel six," Indigo said before she knew it.

"Why?" Bethann asked curiously.

"Because that's the television channel we watch!" Indigo answered, rolling her eyes and growing impatient. "Madear said we can't get any other channel on this hill," she added, convinced she had provided the information that would let Bethann know she was a visitor in the Douglas living room and should act like one.

"Let's see what we can get on this thing," Aunt Sadie jumped in, getting up from rolling her hair. Magnolia walked in and joined the circle of Indigo, her Aunt Sadie and Bethann around the television set.

"There's channel four. Look at how clear it is," Magnolia exclaimed.

Indigo did not want to look at the picture on the television set even though it was clear. She really wanted the television set to be turned off altogether. It was hard to watch what was going on in the living room. She wanted to see Daddy Douglas and Madear in their nightly positions. She had never realized how comforting it had been to see Daddy Douglas's big body stretched out on the sofa, floating somewhere between mashed-potato-and-gravy heaven and whatever was on the television set. Madear mending socks sitting in the chair next to him would have been the second half of the security equation she needed. Now everything was out of order. Davis Jr. and Blueberry were on the sofa asleep and not in their spots on the green rug. There wasn't a spot for Bethann, yet she had invaded the Douglas living room and created one for herself and no one seemed to care. The more she watched the scene in the living room, the more it seemed like big rules were being broken. Fear and agitation crept into her mind. She knew she needed to make them leave the channels on the television set alone.

"Daddy Douglas doesn't like for anyone to change the television channels. That is a rule he does not allow anyone to break. Magnolia knows better than that," she mused to herself. "When he comes home, Magnolia is going to get it," she sneered in her private thoughts.

Then she walked away, suddenly more aware of a sentence Daddy Douglas had written in the writing tablet.

"The rules have been thrown out."

CHAPTER 20

"Turn me round"

Dear Iko,

"AK" Magnolia puts her fine hair in perfect-sized braids all over her head. Then she puts lotion on the braids and rolls them on sponge rollers. The next morning she takes a fork from the kitchen and picks the braids loose. She makes her hair look crinkly and wild on purpose. She says it is an Afro and natural. I do not see anything natural about it. For something that is natural, it sure takes a lot of work. She is putting bronzed powder on her face too. It is too dark for her. Ever since that day Daddy Douglas announced Magnolia was given her name because of her whiteness, she's been on a mission to prove how colored she is. Rowell teased her about the face powder on the way from school one day. He told her, "Your color is coming off on your collar." Then he suggested Magnolia paint her face darker. At first, I started laughing with Rowell. Then I noticed Magnolia was not laughing. Rowell is my friend but Magnolia is my sister. Sisters do not go against each other. She took off after him like a bullet and I took off after her. She caught him on the hill near FAMU's band field. The tuba section was warming up, making oompah sounds in a circle formation. She hit him so hard I thought she had knocked the wind out of him. He was already breathing hard. Sometimes he had a hard time catching his breath when he ran or did something physical. If it wasn't for the group of painters riding with Mr. Avery on the back of a paint truck passing by and yelling for her to stop, she would have beaten him flatter than a pancake.

Rowell was laughing but I knew his feelings were hurt. I put my books down and sat on the grassy hill beside him. When Magnolia took her anger on up the hill to our duplex, Rowell and I lay back on the grass laughing. I rolled on my side because I thought I heard the drums of the FAMU Marching 100 doing their warm-up beats. The drums are my favorite part of the band. Before I realized what was happening, Rowell's hand was on my shoulder. I was so involved with the beat of the band I hardly noticed him. I thought he was trying to tell me something so I turned around. We were face to face. I could smell the mustard relish he used on his lunchtime hotdog. His bottom lip quivered a bit. Then all of a sudden, he kissed me. He kissed me hard. I opened my mouth to say something but he slid his tongue up against the smooth insides of my mouth and attached his tongue to mine. The sensation made me feel faint-like. My blouse was crawling up my back and I could feel his sweaty palms touch my 34B. I arched my back to distract him. I was not ready for a boy to touch my breasts, even if it was only Rowell. His touch made my skin tingle all over. I was having my first kiss and it was with Rowell. The sound of heavy footsteps scared us and we jumped back from each other, laughing. The rest of the band was coming to the band field to practice. They walked right by us. Rowell jumped up and said he had to get home. I wanted to talk about "our kiss" but he was in a hurry. He ran ahead of me and said he would call me later. I was disappointed. When I got home, Magnolia was in the bedroom with the bedroom door closed. When I went to open the door, I could hear her crying. She was telling Grandma Dovie what happened. I try hard not to talk to Grandma Dovie unless I am forced. I went into the kitchen. I just do not understand how she can just stop talking for years because she wanted to and start talking again after years because she wanted to. I think it is safer just not to talk to her at all. I will just wait to tell Magnolia when she feels better.

Indigo

"Mr. Benjamin and Daddy pleaded no contest to arson and second-degree murder." Indigo heard the words and hastily put down her pencil and writing tablet. Then she opened the tablet again and scribbled "no contest, arson and second-degree murder" in the corner margin. She stopped and waited, straining her ears for more news before returning to her nightly writings. For the past year, she had begun using the writing tablet to write letters and keep track of life since her father gave it to her. He told her she had power known to all Douglases, called Iko. She wondered for months where this "Iko power" had been when everything she knew to be true went crazy. "Aunt Sadie always says, 'Don't block your blessings,' and I am not about to start," she thought to herself. To be on the safe side, whenever she wrote her thoughts in the writing tablet she started with "Dear Iko." This way she was covered. Maybe Iko, or at least writing the word, would help straighten out the Douglas family mess.

She wrote in the writing tablet nearly every day. Sometimes just words she heard and did not understand or thoughts about things she did not understand or wanted to change. Sometimes she wrote twice a day if she went to the jailhouse to see Daddy Douglas or if Madear's outing to the Shriner Club extended to the whole weekend. To keep track of what she was writing, she often labeled entries "BK" and "AK." "BK" was short for life before King and "AK" was short for life after King. "BK" entries usually were her wishes for the life that she once knew and wanted to return to.

"There were fun times before Daddy Douglas went to jail," she reminisced often.

"AK" entries were pleadings, simply trying to cope with life she had come to know. Life times that she daily wished were gone. She was sitting at the kitchen table near an open window when Madear's privately spoken words to Mrs. Benjamin flowed through. The cool air of December in Florida blew in the window and made chill bumps rise up on her arms. Her body bristled. She was not clear whether she was chilly or the anticipation of more turns in her family life caused the physical reaction. The air was laced with the scent of trash burning. She opted to continue writing before the breeze of burning trash disturbed her mood for writing.

~

"BK"

Madear and Mrs. Benjamin used to hang clothes on the clothesline and exchange small talk about what was happening in each other's lives.

~

"AK"

Since Daddy Douglas and Mr. Benjamin went to jail, Mrs. Benjamin did not seem to have that much laundry to hang out. Aunt Sadie, with the help of Grandma Dovie, had taken Madear's place in doing the Douglas family laundry. The only time Madear went anywhere near the clothesline was to get to the trash pile behind the duplex. Magnolia said she saw her one night "turn a bottle of something up to her head until it was empty and then toss it on the trash pile."

Indigo looked up and stopped writing, refusing to allow her stream of consciousness to wander into what the "something" was that Magnolia saw Madear drinking at the trash pile. Looking through the kitchen curtains inside the Benjamins' duplex, she learned months ago that Mr. Benjamin was not the only one to enjoy a Budweiser at night. Even though Mr. Benjamin had been in jail a year, the brown paper trash bags were full of Budweiser cans when she tossed her garbage on the trash pile between the duplexes. In spite of everything Madear had stopped doing "AK," Indigo was glad she still talked with Mrs. Benjamin, even if burning trash had replaced hanging clothes out on the clothesline.

"Hiram is so into that Black Power stuff, he didn't even try to fight the charges," Indigo heard Madear say.

"And Benjamin's just fool enough to follow him," Mrs. Benjamin grunted.

"What are we supposed to be doing while they're fighting the revolution inside a jail cell? I will tell you what I am going to be doing! I am going on with living and you better do the same," Madear suggested to Mrs. Benjamin while stirring the burning trash with a broom handle.

Indigo peeked through the gingham curtains in the kitchen window just in time to see Mrs. Benjamin raise her eyebrows and crease her brow at Madear's suggestion.

"That's no secret," Indigo thought to herself. "She's been doing that since the day she came home from the hospital." Even saying the words in her mind were upsetting. Everybody on the 400 block of Osceola Street knew about Madear's "new living." At least that's what Rowell kept telling her. It was all her Aunt Sadie and Grandma Dovie ever talked about. She was sure Rowell would not lie to her. Rowell's Daddy was tapped into every social circle inside of the 400 and 800 blocks of Osceola Street. He was the mail carrier. Mail carriers knew everybody's business. People knowing or talking about the Douglas business was a part of everything "AK" that bothered her. Thinking about her life "AK" was too hard. Writing about it was easier and made her feel less.

"AK" contd.

Madear made it easy for people to know and talk about her business. The Shriner Club had become a part of her weekend pastime. When she went, her make-up looked like the Japanese satin dolls in J.M. Fields department store. You could signal a speeding train to stop with the red color of her lips. She wore coral lip color to work in the mornings with her strawberry-blond hair swept up in a French roll tucked back with a rhinestone barrette that I couldn't remember when she first saw it. When a box of strawberry-blond hair dye appeared in the bathroom, Aunt Sadie laughed at Madear.

Teasingly she asked her, "Do you believe blonds have more fun?"

Madear and Magnolia got very mad at Aunt Sadie for different reasons. Magnolia let loose one of her "natural hair was better than dyed or straightened hair" speeches. It did not do any good though. On Friday nights, Madear's fire-engine red, lips made her strawberry-blond hair stand out even more. Her long slender fingernails were also painted

> red and held cigarettes that I never noticed "BK." She looks beautiful, like the women I see on television or in one of my old Dick and Jane primary readers, but she looks nothing like Madear "BK."
>
> Indigo

"Magnolia, what does 'no contest' mean?" Indigo asked Magnolia as she hid the writing tablet in her drawer.

"It means Daddy Douglas and Mr. Benjamin are not going to fight against people saying they started that fire even though they didn't do it," Magnolia explained without looking up from the thick book she had her nose buried in.

Magnolia's explanation triggered Indigo to remember Daddy Douglas referring to fighting in one of their letter conversations. Then she began having a "BK" flashback of when all the Douglas family watched television together. She had hastily written back, pleading with Daddy Douglas to tell the judge how Mr. Benjamin could never hold his hand steady enough to throw a Molotov cocktail because his hands were too busy holding Budweiser up to his mouth. Daddy Douglas answered Indigo's plea in one of his irregular telephone calls.

"Did you get my letter, Daddy? Are you going to tell the judge about Mr. Benjamin?"

"Go-Go, sometimes you got to fight with all your might and sometimes you got to use your might not to fight with your hands. You just have to stand. This is one of those times. The colored people need to stand for something now!" He spoke fast, trying to make her understand and save enough time to talk to his younger children.

"Daddy Douglas got his mind fixed and firm on what's important to him, he isn't thinking about what's important to us," Indigo pouted, returning to her conversation with Magnolia.

"Madear is no different," Magnolia sneered, looking up at Indigo. "If you think about it, she's worse cause she's right here with us and it's like she isn't here," Magnolia continued to Indigo's surprise.

"What do you mean? She is here with us except for the weekends when she goes out," Indigo tried to justify her contradictions to Magnolia's observations.

"She isn't here when she's here. Indigo, stop thinking like a baby! When was the last time she ate dinner with us or sent us to the bread house? If it was not for Aunt Sadie being around sharing what little money she gets for keeping Bethann and Grandma Dovie living here, things would probably be more of a mess than they already are. Just the other day the man from Tallahassee Furniture Company came here about his money. Madear has not paid the bill in months!"

"Don't talk to me about Grandma Dovie! Bethann makes me sick!" Indigo snapped.

"Bethann's Daddy pays Aunt Sadie and maybe you have not noticed it, but Daddy Douglas is not around to bring in grocery bags on Friday night! You're just mad with Bethann cause you thought she was 'Miss It,' and then she showed her true colors and lied about Daddy Douglas and Mr. Benjamin throwing that cocktail. That's when you found out she wasn't 'sugar, honey, iced tea.'"

"Magnolia, you are cussing and I'm going to tell!" Indigo warned.

"Tell! Tell! I do not care...Who are you going to tell anyway? Grandma Dovie's out on the porch. I don't see you running to tell her anything. What are you so mad with her about anyway? She's hardly the reason everything is so turned upside-down."

"Yes, she is the reason for it! She kept Madear from knowing about her Daddy. If she hadn't done that, none of this would be happening."

"You really are a baby! What happened back when we were not born is not important! We cannot do anything about it. It is what is happening now that is important. Now Daddy Douglas is not really Daddy because he is in jail and Madear is not so dear. We're just like any other colored family that is the product of white people's imagination. Your Daddy is in jail and Momma's out selling tail."

The hostility in Magnolia's voice could reach out and cut you like a knife. Indigo knew she still hurt from the dreadful words everybody heard in the visiting room of the jailhouse that day, but she wasn't prepared for the upheaval of rage that Magnolia dished out.

"These are your parents you're talking about. You would never talk like this if they could hear you. Daddy Douglas is still your Daddy whether he's in jail or…"

"No, he's *your* Daddy!" Magnolia interrupted with pain in her eyes. "He writes you, not me! His skin is black like yours," she shouted venomously.

The impact of Magnolia's words struck Indigo in her chest and stuck there like sap on a pine tree. For a minute, she just stood there. Magnolia was jealous. The revelation came to her clearly.

Underneath all that anger, Magnolia was accusing her of stepping in her shoes and taking Daddy Douglas's affection. Affection she felt rightfully belonged to her since she was the oldest. Ordinarily, Indigo would have delighted in this change of circumstances but the look on Magnolia's face would not have welcomed her pleasure.

"There is enough of Daddy Douglas to go around, Magnolia," Indigo offered.

"I do not want him around. You are the one who needs him. Daddy Douglas has his black pride now. Not anybody who looks like me is black enough. That's why you're getting all the attention now, Miss Blackie."

Magnolia sat on the edge of the bed with two feet of space separating her from where Indigo stood. Indigo was prepared to honor Magnolia for being the oldest. This time she had gone too far. Indigo drew her left hand back swiftly, intending for it to land squarely on Magnolia's face. Magnolia anticipated Indigo's move and blocked her with a raised forearm. Then she kicked Indigo in the stomach, causing her to fall back against the bureau. Indigo garnered her strength and lunged forward, grabbing Magnolia by the braid in the back of her head. They tussled and rolled off the bed, hitting the hardwood floor with a loud thud! They snarled and pulled at each other, banging against the furniture in the bedroom. Punches flew and fingernails scratched, trying to force each other into surrender. The breaking of skin and smears of blood were not enough to stop the war that had erupted between them.

"Take it back, you heifer! Daddy Douglas is your Daddy too!" Indigo screamed, yanking Magnolia's ponytail, pulling her head to the hardwood floor.

"No, Blackie! He's your Daddy. Only the white Momma is mine," Magnolia growled, pushing Indigo off her with all the force inside her.

Indigo's head hit the base of the bedpost. She felt a searing pain. It was not just in her head. It swarmed over her body like locusts. Flashes of her sweeping the kitchen floor and hearing the news of Martin Luther King mixed with the sights and sounds of the days that followed. Daddy Douglas and Mr. Benjamin handcuffed merged with Madear donned with ruby lips and matching fingernails leaving for the Shriner Club. This picture was sandwiched between Grandma Dovie talking to Mr. Whittier and Bethann vigorously changing the channels on the television set. All the pictures came together in a black-and-white montage swirling around in her head. The pain turned up the volume of every family memory in her head "AK." She saw them. She heard them. "White instead of Colored! Colored instead of Black! Colored only! White only! White first! Colored second! Black never!"

"What's going in here?" Aunt Sadie shouted, coming in the door of the bedroom with Grandma Dovie standing behind her.

"Indigo started it. She hit me first," Magnolia answered somewhat timidly, looking down at Indigo.

"Doesn't matter who hit who first, you're the oldest. And you know better," Grandma Dovie chided.

"What were you fighting about?" Aunt Sadie asked, walking over to Indigo. "Are you all right, Go-Go? Your eyes look glassy. Did you hit your head?

"I said what were you fighting about in here, Magnolia?" Aunt Sadie demanded and Grandma Dovie sanctioned by putting her hands on her hips.

"Madear's white and she's white and I'm not even colored, I'm black," Indigo spoke with slurred speech.

"We better get her to a doctor, I think she's hit her head," Grandma Dovie spoke, reaching to lift Indigo to the side of the bed.

"Esther Wallace lives at Six Thirty-Four Osceola on the lower end of the block. She is a charge nurse at FAMU hospital. I starch and iron her uniforms every other week. She still owes me for the last time. I will send Magnolia over to get her. We don't have any extra money for this foolishness!" Aunt Sadie added quickly, reaching to help Grandma Dovie lift Indigo.

"Don't let her fall asleep. Help me turn her on her back. If the child falls asleep she could go into a coma," Grandma Dovie warned.

Indigo could hear snippets of conversation around her. Her thoughts were jumbled up inside her head. She felt woozy but her memories were clear as rainwater.

"Turn her over! Turn her over." She listened to the words repeat in her mind. She surrendered her body into Grandma Dovie's reach while her mind slipped into "BK" memories. There was a mental snapshot of playing with Magnolia in the sun on the front lawn. There were two sisters laughing, dancing, and showing off gymnastic abilities in a silly game of tag. Then she heard the voice of Madear coming through the screen door.

"Magnolia and Indigo, get out of that sun! That sun is going to turn you blacker than raisins. Go play in the shade."

They never talked about why she said such a funny thing. Magnolia knew and Indigo had come to understand Madear sometimes said and did funny things. They turned her funny sayings into a game.

"Turn around, Indigo, let me see if you're a raisin yet," Magnolia would tease and the game of tag would begin. They would run after each other, playing tag, laughing until their stomachs hurt in this game of raisin-turning.

Magnolia bolted out of the door, running down the hill to Esther Wallace's house in the 600 block of Osceola Street. It took two tries for Grandma Dovie and Aunt Sadie to grip Indigo's arms and legs so that her head was perfectly still. When they eased Indigo onto the lumpy bed, Grandma Dovie kept reminding Aunt Sadie to "turn her over."

"No! Turn me round...Turn me round...I'm not a raisin yet!" Indigo yelled, flapping her arms around on the bed.

CHAPTER 21

"Difficult days ahead"

The trip to Raeford Correctional Prison took a little more than four hours. It seemed like an eternity, Indigo thought to herself as she watched the passing foliage along the interstate. This road trip was different from the road trips the Douglas family took "BK." Now "AK," Madear fussed about having to drive to Raeford to visit Daddy Douglas. She would start fussing two weeks before she made up her mind to make the trip. By the time everyone got in the Ford Fairlane to go, her angry detailed mantra of "why Daddy Douglas was sent so far away in the first place" would have been repeated several times. After that she would fuss about how much money it was going to cost in gas to get to the prison. Then she would worry about what she would miss at the Shriner Club. If that did not satisfy her need to worry, she would try to anticipate if she could drive faster enough to get back from Raeford without being too tired to go out. Sometimes the fretting and worrying would lead her into cycles of screaming. She would scream about "having to put her good-for-nothing life on hold" because Daddy Douglas was locked up for five years. The only good thing about the screaming was Davis Jr. and Blueberry would start nagging her. They would ask her repeatedly whether she was going to take them to see their Daddy.

All she had to do was promise to take them and they would be satisfied for a while. Sometimes she gave in and sometimes she did not. The nagging and screaming commotion was nerve-wracking to be around, Indigo reflected to herself.

Aunt Sadie said Madear carried on that way "when her love fire came down on her and she couldn't find anybody to put it out." When Aunt Sadie really wanted to make a point, she'd add, "Cree, you know you are going to go, cause the coalition won't give you that su-su money if you don't go!"

After Martin Luther King was killed, many colored men went to jail. Colored men, husbands, brothers, uncles and friends, all claiming to have had a run-in with the law because they were standing up for the dream. Aunt Sadie said, "Probably most were really standing up for the dream but some were just using the dream as cream to cover up the larceny that was always a part of them." The standing up was so widespread it pinched the pocketbooks of the women and families of these men. Two sources of money coming in the family shrank to one. Men were sitting in jails who were accustomed to working.

One Sunday when the Douglas clan went to church, a boy about eight years old was standing and squirming beside them. Old Man Gus was standing next to the head usher greeting churchgoers. He was the head deacon. The head deacon was next to the preacher in power at the church. Often Old Man Gus stood in position on the top of the church stairs greeting everyone. That particular Sunday it was not too long before he caught sight of the boy standing near the Douglases, squirming around and making a fuss.

"Son, you need to be in the nursery with all that wiggling around you doing," Gus slightly chastised him.

"My feet hurt," the boy said, looking down.

"You too young for your feet to be hurting," Gus chuckled.

"He ain't too young for his shoes to be too little," a woman who must have been his mother answered.

"No disrespect, ma'am," Gus nodded sheepishly.

"None taken. My husband is in jail for standing up so colored people could have a future and I'm just trying to do the best I can for me and my children," the woman explained in detail like she wanted people to take note of her situation.

"Amen, ma'am, I can't fault you for that," Gus answered, turning to go inside the church.

Gus had been giving shoeshines in the state building for as long as he could remember. He was a steady hard-working man, slow to rouse. However, when he believed in something, he held onto it like a bulldog with a bone. Many of the older men like Gus talked about how bad it was that King was killed. They also talked about not wanting to risk spending their last days behind bars. They wanted to do something. Something to symbolize they were standing up as the younger men stood up. They started the Brothers United Coalition. Gus got it started that same Sunday he talked with the boy with the hurting feet. It was the Sunday after Daddy Douglas was sentenced.

After the church clerk read the sick and shut-in prayer list, she asked the congregation for any last-minute announcements. Gus raised his pointer finger to get the clerk's attention.

"Sister Clerk, ma'am, I have an announcement to make if you will. We all here are listening to the misfortune of our church families with their illnesses and what-have-you. It is good to pray for the downtrodden and sick. Praying is good but prayers need feet. We have to do something! It was all our dreams that they tried to kill on that balcony. Maybe our bodies are too old to bear jailhouse shackles but we can do something. We got some difficult days ahead before another one is going to stand up like King. We cannot just sit back and do nothing. That time is past. We can help take care of some of these families of the men who stood up and went to jail for King's dream. We might be too old to stand up but we ain't too old to help others grow up to stand. These men got children that need food, clothes and shoes. We got to stand up for them."

Shortly after Gus made his announcement in church, Madear started getting three hundred dollars every three months. He convinced twelve of the older men to get together and start a "su-su" for the families of all the men they knew were locked up. They each put in twenty-five dollars a month. The "su-su" would take turns giving money to the families of men locked up because of King's dream. When Gus prayed over the money he took in account that some of the money would be going to the families whose loved ones were in jail for reasons having nothing to do with King's dream. He asked the Lord to bless them too.

When it was Madear's time to get the "su-su," Gus brought the money to the house himself. Before he gave her the dollar bills wrapped up in a roll, he'd remind her to "make sure you tell brother Hiram when you see him about the work the coalition is doing for the families here." Madear would smile and nod as she walked him to the screen door. As soon as he turned the key in his truck ignition and Madear turned her back, she'd suck her teeth and push the money down inside her bosom.

"Yeah, I'll tell him all right, when I see him," she said through her teeth.

"I don't believe she ever did tell Daddy Douglas about the 'su-su,'" Indigo calculated.

In spite of the quarterly intervals of "su-su" money coming around and Madear fussing about going, by the time that blue Ford Fairlane got to the prison Daddy Douglas was eager to see his visitors. Indigo kept track of the time of arrival by watching the passing scenery. She knew when the blue Ford Fairlane passed the Winn-Dixie distribution plant it was just about an hour before they'd drive up to the prison gates. She could hardly contain her eagerness. She was eager to see him and talk about his last letter or her latest entries in the writing tablet. Everyone seemed eager or nervous about seeing Daddy Douglas. Madear and Magnolia seemed nervous. Davis Jr. was eager to tell new stories that demonstrated mastery of the manhood training Daddy Douglas provided before he went to prison. Blueberry was eager to add more memories to the fading ones she had of him as a young child. Aunt Sadie and Grandma Dovie were eager too. You could see it on their faces. When Grandma Dovie took the ride, she said the long ride gave her "the piles." "There is nothing worse than an old woman can't hardly go cause she got the piles," were her actual words.

Thinking about Grandma Dovie's sayings made Indigo glance over to the opposite side of the back seat of the Ford Fairlane where Magnolia sat. Davis Jr. and Blueberry always sat between Magnolia and Indigo.

"Things haven't been one hundred percent with Magnolia since she put that knot on the back of my head!" Indigo bemoaned in her thoughts. She and Magnolia could not resist rolling their eyes at each other when Grandma Dovie talked about her piles.

"I don't know what piles are but they sound nasty," she added to the memory, surmising that Magnolia would feel the same way if they still shared the way they used to. Indigo drifted off into a daydream, watching Magnolia.

"Magnolia always knew the right answers and the reasons why things happened the way they did, even if it was bothersome to hear," Indigo daydreamed.

Recently Magnolia had taken to wearing long printed skirts and sometimes a turban on her head. Aunt Sadie told her the turban made her look like the calypso woman on the hot sauce bottle on the shelf above the stove. Indigo agreed. She always carried a book with her to visit Daddy Douglas. She clutched it in her hand or alternated looking down at its pages throughout the entire trip to Raeford. You could not tell if she was deep into the words she was reading or just trying to hide inside her book. The books changed from Nancy Drew mysteries a couple years "AK," when she got her Afro to stop flopping. She started reading books on communism, African history, politics and race. She was spending most of her free time going to rallies or collecting things to send to the motherland. When she was not "working for the cause," as she called it, she was working part-time at the A&P grocery store to get money to go to the motherland. Sadness crept into Indigo's heart when she daydreamed about Magnolia. As time passed "AK", she had helplessly watched Magnolia turn into someone different. It was someone she did not like. It was someone she did not know. Someone who was distant and very different from the sister she had known and loved "BK." Life "AK" had forced a divide between the two of them that was as wide as the distance between the motherland that Magnolia was so mesmerized with and the 400 block of Osceola Street. Indigo smiled to herself as her thoughts drifted to a recent conversation with Magnolia about the motherland.

"Indigo, we're collecting school supplies to send to Liberia, Africa—the new nation in the motherland. Can you give me some of your used pens and pencils to send?" Magnolia asked with enthusiasm.

"Why are you bothering to send stuff all the way to Africa? Your motherland is in Port St. Joe," Indigo remembered teasing her.

"Just like I figured, you're not ready for the revolution!!! You need to wake up because it's not going to be televised," Magnolia quipped back.

Even their fights about one knowing more than the other were different. The "AK" fights were nothing like the "BK" ones. The "BK" fights about the value of information were part of quick-witted exchanges that bonded and protected them from the scrutiny of parents, friends or foes. The "AK" fights about information stretched the separation between them that began in the jailhouse visiting room five years ago.

The Ford Fairlane hit a speed bump when it turned off the interstate highway. The signal let Indigo know they were approaching the prison gate. She dismissed her daydreams of Magnolia and began mentally preparing for her visit with Daddy Douglas. The prison regulations stated in its visiting manual, "When a visitor drives up to the gate of the prison all passengers must get out of the vehicle to be searched." This infuriated Madear.

"The nerve of them, treating me like a common criminal," she would complain.

"You colored, aren't you...they think you a common criminal or least coming to see one," Aunt Sadie reminded her.

Magnolia said it was "just part of the black man's struggle." She stopped using the word "colored" about the same time she started wearing her turban and focusing her attention on the motherland.

Grandma Dovie said, "The way I see it, the sooner they search you and get it over with, the sooner you get to see your Daddy."

She made it seem like the big white hands of the guard patting you and looking in your personal belongings was as natural as breathing. It must have been natural only for colored folks because it was not natural for Bethann. For a white girl traveling with a colored family to Raeford to visit one of the men she thought nearly killed her Momma and destroyed her idyllic family life, nothing could seem natural.

This time before the Douglas clan took the road trip to Raeford, Madear had fussed night and day. Old Man Gus had come a week later than usual to bring her the "su-su" money. Mr. Whittier had dropped Bethann off at the boarding house but Aunt Sadie was not there. Bethann just walked across the street and came in to wait for her in the living room. As Bethann got older, she looked more like her mother, which made Madear even less tolerant of her presence. Soon as Aunt Sadie opened the screen door, Madear started fussing.

"Sadie, Bethann don't need to go with us to Raeford, bad enough she's here with us most of the time anyway," Madear started.

"She's here most of the time because I'm here most of the time trying to help run this house while you out doing whatever you feel like," Aunt Sadie went back at her.

"I'm grown and I can do whatever I want to do. I still say she does not have any business going!" Madear shot back.

"And where should she go while we gone, since Mr. Whittier is paying good money that is coming in this house for me to look after her."

Madear paced around for a while. After she realized she could not come up with anything to counteract the financial impact of what Aunt Sadie was saying, she added, "She doesn't need to go!"

Bethann did go. Aunt Sadie put all the Douglas children under strict orders not to mention to Bethann where the family was actually going on Saturday morning. She told Mr. Whittier they were all going to visit a sick relative right outside of Jacksonville. Aunt Sadie knew Bethann was nosey and happy to have any opportunity that put her closer to her private business, so she knew resistance would be minimal. Bethann slept the entire trip. Aunt Sadie spent the time rationalizing she was not lying. Raeford Correctional Prison was right outside of Jacksonville and Daddy Douglas was a relative. Madear always said, "He was sick in the head to have gotten himself put in prison."

At first when Madear stopped the car at the guardhouse, Bethann's eyes widened like an animal about to become prey. She stiffened her body in the middle of the front seat of the car, refusing to come out. Aunt Sadie pulled and yanked until she got her to get out of the car.

Madear got out first and walked up to be searched. Indigo bolted out of the back door behind her. After the searching formalities, the guard handed Madear the visitor's book.

"Who are you here to see?" the guard grunted at her, shoving an ink pen in her direction.

"Inmate number seven-nine-three-four-two-oh, Hiram Douglas, he's in for arson and attempted murder." She scribbled Daddy Douglas's name and inmate number and passed the book to Indigo. Indigo hastily signed her name, noticing that Daddy Douglas had an earlier visitor whose handwriting she could not read. She did make out the last letters of the name ended in "ur."

Bethann was standing a few feet from Madear when she announced whom she was visiting. She nearly lost her breakfast on Madear's shoes. She did not want to believe her lying eyes or, in this case, her swindling ears. The look on her face was gaunt. The blind trust she shared with Sadie showed in her face and cheeks. Suddenly trust evaporated along with the color in her face. Indigo watched her and for a moment she felt the urge to console her, but then the guard opened the chain-link gate to the prison entrance. Instead, she anticipated the familiarity of a world spinning out of control and walked forward.

When the guard tried to pat Bethann down, she grabbed his arm and told him, "I'm not with them. I'm not going to see him."

"You got to go with them or stay in the car," the guard said without the slightest empathy.

"I don't want to stay in the car…I am not going anywhere. I want to call my Daddy," she began to whine.

"Go or stay, it don't matter to me…the telephone booth is over there," the guard pointed between two spits of tobacco juice.

Aunt Sadie pleaded and coaxed Bethann for what seemed like an hour.

"Child, you need to go in there. If you do not go in, you are not ever going to get over this. It'll eat you up," Sadie warned her.

"I'm never going to get over people who I know tried to kill my Momma."

"You do not know what really happened! You will never know if you don't go in that prison and find out for yourself!" Aunt Sadie expensed her uneven logic.

It was the intensity of the Florida sun and various grouping of other colored people who chose to stay outside rather than inside that finally convinced Bethann to come in. Indigo watched as the guard searched her. She kept her face muscles tight and squinted her eyes like a fighter entering a boxing ring. She held her head up and looked straight ahead. The sight of her made Indigo giddy with anticipation. Her need for revenge for all situations "AK" seemed like it was finally going to be satisfied.

The months had turned into years since Daddy Douglas had been in prison. Time had made his face look ashen, like a fading picture. "He needs to get out more in the Florida sunshine instead of getting locked in solitary confinement for organizing the brothers," Indigo thought to herself.

"Daddy!" Davis Jr. yelled with Blueberry and Indigo joining in.

Normally Indigo would have walked up and said, "Hi Daddy!" but she wanted Bethann to be as uncomfortable as possible with the Douglas children's demonstration of exuberant affection for their father and her accused. What effect the demonstration did have was lost on Magnolia. She said a soft hello, retreated to the corner of the visiting room and opened her book. Bethann motioned to join her but Magnolia gave her a hard look and she walked behind her and sat a few feet away.

Indigo watched Bethann intensely as she sat a few feet away from her parents. The visiting area was jam-packed with prisoners and their families. Daddy Douglas spoke awkwardly, trying to make small talk with Madear.

"How you been? The children look good and growing by leaps and bounds too."

"Hiram, if you feed them they'll grow. That is, if you got the money to feed them," she said curtly, making a disgusted frown, fidgeting, avoiding his eyes. Then she handed him a brown paper bag with a magazine in it. He looked at it quickly and tucked it under the table on his lap. She continued to talk about bills and he talked about the struggle of the black man in and outside. They spoke two different languages sometimes, oblivious to each other's questions, until the wall of silence returned between them. He casually slipped in the possibility that he could face charges and possibly more time for a rally he staged with other inmates. She vaguely touched upon her growing disinterest in raising a family alone. After a long pause and empty words, they faced each other. Perhaps she anticipated what he was about to say. Because when he said the words, she had a reply.

"You don't have to come no more, Cree," he said.

"I can't, Hiram," she said.

For as much as she wanted Bethann to see the Douglas family as a family, she wished at that moment she would disappear. Her parents had just put a period behind the ultimate "AK" moment. She wanted her pain to be private from the masses and pieces of families gathered in the visiting room. Most of all, she wanted it to be private from Bethann.

"Just make sure my children get to see me is all I ask," he said, resolved.

"As much as they want to...just don't try to turn them against me," she added contemplatively.

After they spoke the ultimate "AK" words, they walked in separate directions across the visiting room. Madear, twisting the lower half of her body in a liberating womanly sort of way, retreated shamelessly over to a barred window full of the blistering Florida sunshine. He ambled over to Magnolia, looming over her and placing his hand in the middle of her book.

"Let me talk to you for a minute, Magnolia," he said gently.

"Yes," she said as if she was prepared for the interruption.

"Seems like a lot of news comes in the visiting room of a jailhouse," he began.

"That was a long time ago," she interrupted.

"I know, but there are things we need to talk about," he continued.

"It is not relevant now. I've changed, Father," she insisted.

"'Father'?" he questioned curiously.

"Yes, you are my father. You are the male being who raised me and sustained me with life. You are!" she spoke, looking directly into his eyes.

"But I did not give you life," he continued carefully.

"What does it matter now? You had the power to sustain my life and you did that. That is what matters now. The oppressor planted the seed but you made the fruit grow…I can embrace the scars of the oppressor…can you?" she spoke as if she had rehearsed the words a hundred times before that moment.

"I…I can't. It's not as simple as all that…there is so much you do not understand," he stammered at her in amazement. His face looked shiny like glass. He pressed his lips together but the words were stuck somewhere behind his tongue. He just looked and walked away to break the intensity of a moment he was not equipped to address. Magnolia retreated to her book. He walked in the direction of Bethann and their eyes met. She seized the opportunity to prove Aunt Sadie wrong.

"You tried to kill my Momma and I hope you stay in here and never get out," she hissed at him.

"And you're worried that I might try to kill you, white princess?" he toyed with her.

"I'm not worried about you. You're right where you belong," she continued.

"Not yet but I will be." He laughed wickedly, walking away from her, moving in Indigo's direction.

The range of Indigo's feelings fluttered back and forth, trying to find a resting point. She was sickened to the point of disgust at Daddy Douglas's rejection of Magnolia's whiteness. She found pleasure in his taunting of Bethann but to her surprise she also felt her pain. The contradiction struck her but the realization of the fleeting visiting hour did also. She decided to accept the pleasure and revisit her disgust later.

"Don't you hate her, Daddy?" Indigo asked when he walked over beside her.

"If I hated her I would be in real jail," he said, smiling.

"You are in real jail, Daddy," Indigo reminded him.

"Physically but not mentally. My mind is free. I have the power to keep my mind free," he insisted.

"I don't know what you're talking about."

"You will one day. There are different kinds of jails. You can choose your lock-up."

"Did you choose this jail?"

"Yeah, I did. I got freedom at the same time. I guess you can say it's kind of like the two-for-one special you get down at the bread house," he added, smiling now.

The crackling static of the intercom pierced their conversation. "Visiting hours are now over. All visitors please proceed to the check-out area," a heavy voice boomed over the intercom.

"I want you to write to me, Go-Go." Daddy Douglas stepped forward, reaching for Indigo to hug her and dropping the magazine out of the brown paper bag he had tucked in his pocket.

Magnolia heard the announcement and got up quickly, gathering her things. She walked over to Daddy Douglas and Indigo as Davis Jr. and Blueberry joined them. Stepping short from the reach of his embrace the gloss of a magazine on the floor near Daddy Douglas's foot caught her eye. She stooped to pick it up and nearly lost her balance. She grabbed the magazine by the front cover, causing it to open to a white woman lying spread-eagle on a couch, with tassels dangling from her breasts. Before she closed the magazine, curiosity got the best of her. She stood straight up, flipping pages of white women in various positions of nakedness. Just as Daddy Douglas noticed her, she closed it, jerking her head so hard her turban shifted. She closed the magazine and her eyes and swallowed hard. Then she stepped closer to Daddy Douglas.

"Father, I wanted to say good-bye. I do not know when I will see you again. I am going to the motherland in a couple of months. Be well," she said, handing him the magazine.

CHAPTER 22

"My eyes have seen"

Dear Iko (AK)

Magnolia's eyes were so red they looked like she washed them in Vidalia onion water when she left the prison. She did not say a word to anyone on the ride back to Tallahassee. I kept watching her. There was a story in her eyes. A story like the one the baby King girl had in her eyes the day they buried her Daddy. A story so big, only eyes opened so wide they looked like they could not shut told how big. That's how the baby King girl's eyes looked. They looked like she had stretched the muscles of her eye sockets so wide a glassy shield glossed over her eyeballs. You could tell she had been looking everywhere for her Daddy to come out from anywhere to put an end to all that sadness around her. The Daddy that bounced her in the air and told her how big she was getting. The Daddy that laughed belly laughs at her riddles when no one else would listen. That is the Daddy she was looking for. Not the one lying in that casket. Those eyes looked over the hundreds of people sitting for her Daddy to be buried and did not see them. Her eyes said those people did not know the Daddy she was looking for. The Daddy she stretched her eyes so big for was a Superman. He could do anything.

She could not have been much older than Blueberry "AK." She looked to be just past a baby but still babyish. The blank look in her eyes took your attention away from her shiny black pigtails tied in white ribbons dangling beside her black face. Baby King girl's face rested deep in the lap of her Momma's black dress. The crowd of reporters around her rattled off the names of the people in attendance and tried every way they could to report the details of a fallen leader. The baby King girl's eyes had the scoop. "Daddy wasn't going to be around to be Daddy no more." Magnolia was more than ten years older than the baby King girl was, but they had the same story in their eyes.

Indigo

Rowell was waiting on the front-porch steps when the Ford Fairlane pulled into the driveway. His big smile behind his thick glasses brought a smile to Indigo's face. She bounced out of the car and headed in his direction.

"Since he kissed me things were kind of sometimey. But if he ever tries it again or if I let him try it again, I'm ready," she thought to herself, quickly counting up the number of boys she'd kissed with her fingers on one hand.

"Where you been, Go?" Rowell asked, standing as she approached.

"We went to visit my Daddy," she answered without pretense.

"A little ride to see the jailbird in the family," Bethann chided as she hurriedly walked past them, heading curbside to cross the street to Aunt Sadie's boarding house.

"Watch your mouth, Bethann," Aunt Sadie warned, walking behind her to the boarding house.

"I could just beat that heifer to death if I had a mind to," Indigo hissed through her breath.

"Oh, if you had a mind to, huh? Well, your name is not Magnolia and you cannot just go around beating people up because you do not like what they are saying...at least not without back-up you can't," Rowell advised, half-joking and half-serious.

"I got back-up. I got you," Indigo teased, playfully pinching him on the arm.

"You got me now but not for long. I'm starting college at FAMU," he said, catching her hand and looking her in the eye.

"What are you talking about?" she asked with a stunned expression.

"There is this new program at FAMU that lets you go to college your junior year in high school. I signed up for it," he announced, half-smiling.

"Why? Why did you do that?" Indigo whined.

"Because I'm ready for something different, Go-Go! Colored people are not colored or Negroes no more. They are black. 'Say it loud,' James Brown says. 'We are Black and Proud.'" He did a little dance strut to emphasize his point.

"It's a whole black world out there and I'm ready to see it," he glistened.

"But you're leaving me!" she said softly, surprised by her emotions.

"Leaving you…I am never going to leave you, Go-Go! You talk like you my girl or something. You not my girl, are you?" His glance fell on her chest as he asked with a sly grin.

"No! I'm not your girl," she snapped, folding her arms to cover up her chest and to keep him from looking in that direction. "I just mean you're not going to be around like you are now. We will not be walking home from school and you will not be coming over because you are busy with college. Magnolia is going to Africa and now you're going to college early. I have to be going.. She stopped without finishing her sentence.

"You will be coming to college the next year. I am just checking it out before you get there so I can tell you what to do when you get there. You're going to be fine and we're always going to be fine because we're tight, Go-Go." He reached out for her like he was going to hug her, but he took her by the shoulders and turned her from side to side instead.

"Rowell Watson, let me go. I got to go inside." She squirmed, trying to get away from her feelings.

"What you got to go inside for?"

"I got things I got to see about. Things that are none of your business."

"What are you so mad about, Go?"

"I am not mad, I just have to go inside," she lied.

"You don't have to go inside. Why don't you stay out here for a while? We could walk up to the band field and listen to the band practice."

"No! I have to go inside. You got your business all straight. You are going to college. I am going inside to see about my business. I'll see you tomorrow if you're not too busy with college." She ran up the steps, doing half-turns as she spoke.

Rowell sat outside on the steps until it was dark. He just sat there, waiting. Indigo would peek through the curtains at him and he would turn around just in time for her to shove the curtains in the living room window shut again. This game went on until it was too dark to tell if he was still sitting there.

It was eight o'clock before Indigo swept the kitchen floor. Magnolia had washed the dishes in record speed after the potluck supper and retreated to the bedroom. Indigo swept the floor with brisk long hard stokes, making dust and dirt fly around the room. It was a chore she must have done more than a hundred times. Sometimes she swept begrudgingly and sometimes she swept to mark time. As the night breeze came into the open window, scattering the debris, she thought of sweeping to stop time. She was so into her sweeping she did not notice Madear come into the room until she was right beside her.

"What are you so mad about?" Madear asked matter-of-factly, wearing a skintight white skirt and off-the-shoulder black top.

"I am not mad," Indigo answered, looking at her mother and surmising that she was about to go out for the evening.

"You sure are sweeping like you are mad about something...I am going out for a while. Your Grandma Dovie is in the living room and

Sadie will be over as soon as she gets finished with Bethann and that mess," Madear spoke, going out the back door.

"Why can't you stay home with us sometimes? You are our Momma!" Indigo shouted, knowing the screen door had already slammed shut.

Disgusted and feeling the heat of annoyance, she went back to her sweeping. She glanced down and was just about to bring her arm up in a swinging motion when she saw Madear's feet standing on the straw of the broom.

"I believe you're getting too grown for your own good. Your titties might be big as mine, but you are not a woman yet and you sure are not grown. I'm your Momma and you will respect me," Madear hissed, still standing on the straw of the broom.

"I just meant..." Indigo stammered, trying to get her thoughts together.

"You meant what, Indigo Douglas?" Madear shouted, taking the broom from Indigo's hands.

"I meant everybody is leaving or gone already. We are not a family anymore. Nothing is the way it used to be. You dress up and go out and we never know when you are coming back. Mommas should be home, not at the Shriner Club."

Indigo did not see the slap coming but her eyes felt the sting. She was speaking from her heart and not paying attention to how her words sounded.

"How in the hell do you know where Mommas should be? Big high titties, fifteen and you think you can tell me what to do. I will beat your little grown behind if you ever speak to me like that again. Do you hear me?" She slapped Indigo again with the back of her hand.

"Pull up that bra strap! Your titties look like you nursing a newborn baby! You need to have some pride about yourself! When was the last time you ran a warm comb through your head? You old enough to do it yourself!" she demanded, half-condescending and half with maternal concern.

"This is the real world, not some fairy tale you living, Indigo. Where have you been for the last five years?" Madear spoke in an exasperated tone while Indigo closed her eyelids and cast them downward.

"You keep holding onto the past. The past is gone. It is never coming back again. You are not a baby anymore. You are a young woman, steps away from being a full woman. Hell, your titties look like you a woman now. Steps that are coming so fast they will be here before you realize it. Open your eyes!" she said, grabbing Indigo's face.

"Open your eyes, I said! Open them! There, they're open now!" she demanded, squeezing Indigo's face.

"Have your eyes seen we're not living happily ever after like Dick and Jane in those damn primary readers you're holding onto? You want to tell grown people what to do, then grow up! Grow up and stop living in make-believe. Colored people trying to get opportunities to be who they want to be since the Almighty King was killed. I was never a real fan but because of him I have a second chance to go out and get my happily-ever-after. Life is funny like that and I am taking it. I do not care if it is at the Shriner Club or wherever you think it is. I don't give a damn. I'm going to get it," She spoke the last sentence strongly and almost out of breath.

"Your Daddy got his getting locked up. Magnolia is all about getting hers with all that African mumbo-jumbo stuff she is talking and wearing. If she knew what I know, she wouldn't have to be bothered with any of that 'Back to Africa' stuff. She just needs to feel comfortable in her own skin. She has a right to! But she has to take the right." Her voice cracked for a moment and her eyes moistened.

"I knew with that skin color and them light eyes she'd be as pretty as a flower. The world got an open door for her. She has got her own ideas, though. Now, you are not like Magnolia! I named you Indigo because that is what color you were when you came out of me. Indigo, a blue-black baby. You were hollering your head off. You are going to have to work extra hard to make it. Your skin is going to be the first thing the world is going to notice. No matter how smart you are or what you can do or not do. There is no getting around it. You had better start focusing on yourself. Forget about your Daddy and me. We are history. History is the past. It is not doing you a bit of good. Your Daddy and I have already let go. It is time you know where you are going and how you plan to get there. You cannot get any more from your Daddy and me. Use what you got."

Madear threw the broom down on the floor just as abruptly as she had taken it from Indigo's sweeping hands and started her journey out into the night again. Indigo stood beside the broom lying on the floor, thinking about the rattlesnakes that sometime roamed in the backyard of the duplex. She had grown up fearing the rattlesnakes and the deadliness of their powerful bite. Right then, all she could think of was what it would be like to be one.

"Then I could shed this skin," she fantasized to herself.

She did not raise her eyes past Madear's beige-colored legs going out the door. She did not dare for fear Madear would find her indignant and another one-sided confrontation would ensue. Even though Madear's words cleared up all the hushed voices in the cedar closet and loud confrontations in the jailhouse waiting room, it did not cushion the shock of the intensity of the meaning of the sounds hitting Indigo's eardrums. They were like the poignant vibrations of a dog whistle. Rowell had given her one once as one of his many "treasure" gifts. Rowell said the whistle had power. One afternoon while they were watching a group of dogs trying to dig and scratch their way inside the poultry yard, he showed her. When Rowell blew the dog whistle, she heard a faint sound. The vibrations were so shrilling the dogs scampered and ran. Indigo wanted to scamper and run too. Instead, she scolded herself in her mind because a confrontation with Madear was not her intention.

"They were just words that have been sitting in the middle of my high chest for the past five years 'AK.' They came out because they couldn't stay in any longer," she rationalized.

Lately she noticed it had become difficult to hold back words that voiced the anger and frustration inside of her. Especially words that generally rested within her chest or writing tablet. Words and sometimes surprising feelings presented themselves when she least expected them. Words laced with deep anger and a heaping amount of aniexty for what could come next. The words surfaced and demanded freedom when she talked with Daddy Douglas, Madear, Magnolia and Rowell.

"Rowell!" she sighed with dismay.

Suddenly she found herself alone in a frustrated conversation, speaking partially aloud with the broom and kitchen as an audience.

"They all talk about the world. The world was changing. King dying brought about a change. They needed to find their place in the world. What about this place right here on the four hundred block of Osceola Street? What about keeping up with the people in this world? This is the world where family and close friends should count for something. Mothers love their daughters no matter what! Daddies choose to be home with their families. Friends stick by friends. Can't they see what is important? Where are their eyes? Can't they see?"

Brushing tears to the side of her face, she thought aloud, "My eyes have seen what is important! It is not Martin Luther King and his dying! If I had a wish to be granted, I would erase the name King from the universe. Then maybe everyone would not be leaving and I would not have to watch," she contemplated in her mind, responding to the surge of water in her eyes that was now beginning to make her chest heave.

Even though her collage of emotions cross-examined her thoughts, the results did not provide answers. Trying to shake off the impulse to cry harder, she unconsciously went to the back porch. She began to take her bicycle down the steps without giving thought to the time. The sky was pitch-black except for the quarter-moon hanging over the rooftop of the duplex. The lush pecan trees cast dark ominous shadows against the side of her white-painted duplex.

If Madear knew she was even thinking about riding her bicycle this time of night, she would start a fussing spree that would last long after the Douglas house went to bed, Indigo recollected. The reality was Madear was not there and had not been there for more nights than she cared to remember "AK." Madear would not know if she rode her bicycle or not. Grandma Dovie was asleep in her rocking chair and Aunt Sadie had not come across the street from the boarding house. She usually came over from the boarding house around ten o'clock to make sure everything was safe and in order when Madear went out for the evening. She would go in the living room and fall asleep during the eleven o'clock news, intending to watch the late show. Madear would find her sleeping on the couch in the early hours of the morning when she came home. Most times Aunt Sadie just spent the night on the couch and walked back over to her boarding house when the sun came up. When Bethann was staying with her, they would both sleep on the couch. The sight of them sleeping on the couch emphasized the change in the Douglas family and infuriated Indigo.

The red-apple clock over the stove said it was twenty minutes before nine o'clock. It would be more than an hour before Aunt Sadie came across the street. Indigo knew she could ride her bicycle for a while and be back before her Aunt Sadie ever crossed the street in front of the duplex. She rode her bicycle when she wanted to get somewhere faster than her legs would carry her. Now that Magnolia was so busy with her work for the motherland, she and Indigo rarely went to the bread house together. When Madear called on Indigo to fill the family breadbox, she rode her bicycle down the hill through FAMU's campus to the bread house. One of the few chores she did "BK" that she could still do "AK." When she climbed up on the black seat of her Schwinn Flyer bicycle, her mind was set free. She forgot about her family life in disarray. She did not think of life "BK" or "AK." She did not worry about covering up or keeping her arms folded across her chest. In the night air, she wanted to forget about the words Madear used her hands to reinforce. The words that framed an image of her existence were slapped across her face and in her mind. She just wanted to throw caution to the wind, hold onto the handlebars of her bicycle and ride.

At first, she could not pedal fast enough to escape the voices in her head. Madear said it was "his high-chest attitude that signaled his mouth to put his butt in jail." Daddy Douglas said his "Iko" beating inside his chest would no longer let him "sit or stand silent in the background while colored men struggled just to live a simple life," the recitations repeated in her head as she sped, going down Gaines Street, and her parents' comments began to fade with the spinning of the pedals. Her "high-chest" taken from her Daddy's side of the family, emerged as the force behind her motion zipping down one of the seven hills of Tallahassee. Her uplifted breasts and entire body "AK" had developed in proportions that caused heads to turn. The girls at school whispered and the boys stared at the way her blouses hugged her "Iko." Unlike reality around her, when she rode her bicycle she was just a blurred vision.

The more she rode in the dark of night, the more she thought of Rowell. Sometimes she noticed him staring at her constantly folded arms and multiple layers. When their eyes met, she would look away and he acted unaware of the tension that drew them together. When he kissed her on the grassy hill above FAMU's band field, they fell back on the ground. Despite the ignition of passion, she became self-conscious and tried to fold her arms across her chest. Embarrassment of her "Iko" invaded their first kiss. When Rowell felt her arms move, he gently pulled them from their folded position and looked first in her eyes and then at her chest. She remembered his gentle gesture causing the lightness in her head to return just as the rest of the band moved like a herd down the hill. He had been her number-one prospect for a boyfriend.

"Now he is leaving too!" she thought to herself, pumping the bicycle pedals. "I'm not his girl," she continued to try to convince herself.

She saw two police officers sitting in a squad car at the Dixie Gas station where Gaines Street crossed Pensacola Street. A blue Ford Fairlane like the one that belonged to her family pulled out of the gas station in front of the police station. When she saw it, she got nervous because she thought it was her family's car. She relaxed when a long-haired white guy steering the car with one hand passed her and headed up to Pensacola Street. His other hand was across the shoulders of a woman sitting so close to him you could not see her face. The symbolism of partnership that came to her mind when she saw the police officers sitting there made her thoughts return to Rowell. They had been partners for what seemed like a lifetime, watching from the sideline. Now he was going in the game and she hadn't even seen him practicing, she reflected, half-sitting and half-standing, waiting for the traffic light to change.

The thought of Rowell not being around summoned her legs to pump the bicycle pedals faster and harder. She was blocks away from the intersection of Gaines and Tennessee Streets before she thought to look at her watch. She had pedaled the length of Gaines Street, separating FAMU from Florida State University, in twenty minutes. The thought of the distance she had traveled and the danger she faced if she did not return before her Aunt Sadie came across the street was exhilarating. Even more exhilarating was the crowd of people she saw standing down at the intersection of Gaines and Tennessee Streets. There must have been hundreds of people lined up and down the street with lights flashing on police cars everywhere. It reminded her of standing with Bethann "AK" the night Mr. Whittier's building exploded and her life changed forever. When she approached a point of entry in the gathering, she could see the crowd was made up of young whites primarily on one side and colored people mostly on the side of Tennessee Street that was nearest Frenchtown. There were some colored people interspersed in the crowd of whites. She figured they were college students too. Mostly she thought they were trying to get a closer look. She took her bicycle and blended in, watching the young whites just like the crowd of colored people across the street.

"Black people," she reflected and corrected herself mentally, thinking about her earlier conversation with Rowell.

She tried to push her way up near the front of the crowd to see. Police officers patrolled up and down the streets. Then, without warning, groups of young whites who looked not much older than she did took off their clothing and ran up and down Tennessee Street. White men and women. Big, little, in between, all sizes took off their clothing and ran as if they had just been set free. The blacks gawked and nervously laughed in disbelief. The police officers did their best to catch them but naked white people were running everywhere.

Indigo stood next to a stout white girl wearing black-rimmed glasses. She calculated the white girl could not have been more than two or three years older. Having Bethann constantly around made it easy for Indigo to strike up a conversation with a white person.

"Why are they taking off their clothes and running like that?"

"Because it's their bodies. They can do what they please with their bodies. Their bodies belong to them and they can express themselves any way they want to. It is their constitutional right! I'm Alicia," she spewed out, looking at Indigo for a reaction.

"Yeah, I know about the constitution. I studied that in my government class. But why they have to take off their clothes to express themselves? I'm Indigo."

"Liberation! The establishment is repressed. The government thinks they can make decisions that change our lives and silence us, Indigo. They are wrong! The one thing we have control over is our body. For that reason, we are streaking. Streaking to liberation! They cannot shackle our minds! We are rebelling in the natural. We must be free. We can free ourselves. Our bodies are beautiful and belong to us!" she declared, starting to take off her clothes, standing in front of Indigo on the back side of the crowd.

"Who is the establishment and what is repressed?" Indigo asked, noticing Alicia's beige-colored freckled exposed breasts sitting in a bra that was easily a "D" cup.

"Any group, organization or person that tries to indoctrinate you contrary to your reality," she rattled off as if she had rehearsed the definition many times, while zipping down her pants and pulling down both pants and panties in one motion.

She stood naked from the waist down to her shoes and socks. A beige bra with lace across the bra cups barely holding her large breasts was the only thing that kept her from being completely naked. She talked as she slid the bra straps down her arms and turned the fasteners to the front so that she could loosen them with ease. Indigo's inclination was to avert her gaze away from Alicia and her nakedness. But she was caught in the grip of the freedom Alicia spoke about. Her naked body captivated Indigo. She did not look like the women in Daddy Douglas's magazine of naked white women. Indigo did not want to gaze but Alicia's naked body was like a dead dog in the road. She knew the sight was something that would stay in her mind if she looked but she could not help herself. Her eyes were drawn to the statute of white nakedness that stood before her. She had never seen a woman or a girl her age completely naked. She had been taught to cover herself. When she had to put on her navy-blue gym suit for physical education classes, she mastered the art of doing it in the small bathroom stall.

"Girls who did take off their clothes in front of everyone in the gym class had a reputation of being 'fast and loose,'" she remembered.

"Some of the girls bodies were so out of proportion other girls gawked and made up stories about how their bodies came to be that way," she kept remembering.

Alicia stood brazenly naked without the tag of being fast and loose or strange. Her body structure was similar to bodies of black girls Indigo knew. Indigo strained to see where she kept her "gift" Madear suggested opened doors for girls of white lineage. In snatched glances, Indigo examined every visible inch of Alicia. She was busty and had skin darker than the color of her breast around her nipples, just like Indigo. The hair around her private was lush and thick, the way Indigo's was thick and bushy. The only difference Indigo could see was that Alicia's small waist extended to a wide flat behind and Indigo's proportioned waist led to a big round behind.

"Which probably came from my Momma more than anything else because I sure got the same big butt Madear got," Indigo concluded to herself.

"Are you going to just stand there and look?" Alicia challenged.

"I'm just trying to figure out what's it going to prove by taking off your clothes?" Indigo answered with budding curiosity.

"It proves I'm in charge of me. I am free. When the pigs cannot catch us or cannot find a law that we have broken for taking off our clothes, they come to understand we are free and will not be controlled. We will conquer the world one fascist establishment at a time. Then the only race that will matter is the human race," she proclaimed, beginning to take off her shoes and socks.

"My body is beautiful because it belongs to me. I am not some Madison Avenue definition of what beauty is! I am my own definition of beauty and tonight beauty is freedom." She danced around with her breasts hopping up and down in the air.

She and Indigo stood face to face. Alicia was fully naked now. She stood boldly without inhibition, in protest of a repression Indigo did not fully understand. Then she held out her hand and invited Indigo to join her.

"Come on and streak to liberation with me," she said, with the noise of the crowd increasing as more streakers jumped out in search of liberation and policeman ran after them.

Indigo's mind flashed back to her conversation with Madear earlier that evening. Madear's comments about her bust and contrast description of her daughter's lot in life cut deeply within Indigo's well of feelings. She thought of the way Magnolia looked when she flipped through the pages of naked white women in Daddy Douglas's magazine. She thought of her name Indigo, and her sister's name, Magnolia. She thought of Bethann. She thought of Martin Luther King and she thought of all these things her eyes had seen that surfaced "AK." She watched Alicia feeling comfortable in her own skin and something ached inside of her to feel the same.

She extended her hand and noticed the time on her watch. It was a quarter of ten. She clasped Alicia's hand and then she pulled it back. She began to loosen the buttons on her blouse and stepped forward. The "Iko" inside of her was commanding her feet to move. She wanted to answer the call.

"You got to go before it's too late," a little voice inside of her warned. She looked down at the dark fleshy part of her breast peeking above her bra through her opened white blouse.

"It's already too late," she thought to herself, turning to walk to find a safe place for her bicycle.

"Alicia, wait a minute, I got to put my bicycle up, I'll be right back."

"I'll wait for you, Indigo, if you're really coming back," Alicia said with a hint of suspicion.

"I am!" Indigo declared.

The crowd was getting bigger on both sides and the noise was deafening. It was not easy getting the bicycle through the swelling crowd. Indigo found some bushes beside the liquor store on the corner and put her bicycle up against the wall. When she finally got near the spot where she left Alicia, she could only see her looking from side to side. Indigo tried to walk around a group of black women onlookers who had come across the street to get a better look of the streakers but they blocked her path.

"This got to be one of the most craziest things white people or their children ever did," one of them said to the other one.

"Their Mommas and Daddies sending them up here to get an education and they running down the streets with their clothes off. What does taking your clothes off have to do with learning anything? In Frenchtown on this side of Tennessee Street, it could be a life lesson from the street, depending on who you with when you took your clothes off. But on that side of Tennnessee Street it's just plain crazy," the other one said, half-smiling and half-serious.

Indigo looked through the space that separated the women and watched Alicia fold her glasses in her hands and step to the front of the crowd to make her dash to liberation.

"It's got everything to do with everything," Indigo thought to herself. "Streak! Streak! Streak to Liberation!" Indigo chanted, trying to raise her voice above the pandemonium.

CHAPTER 23

"As a people"

January 1977

Dear Iko,

Yesterday I made love to Rowell,even if it was only in my mind. I spotted him by the Student Union building talking with two other dudes. They were standing on points of a broken circle of smoke puffs. He looked taller than he was in my imagination. When I walked up to him, he smiled that rat-tooth smile of his and the two dudes looked me up and down. One of the dudes asked me if he could go with me. Before I could answer, Rowell pushed his ultra-cool eyeglasses that changed colors in the sunlight up on his nose and stepped in front of me. The sun was not that bright because it was January. I was glad because I could see his eyes and they told me he liked what he saw. He put his arm around my shoulders and asked me, "What's up?" as if I belonged to him. He spoke his words very slowly and the puffs of smoke (that had to be reefer because it didn't smell like any cigarettes I ever smelled) came through his nose and made him sound like he had a head cold. His dude friends gave him a high-five and called him "Raw!" I knew then that he was deep inside the "cool" league. He and I walked off together but not before my nipples got hard and you could see them pointing clear through my new sheer Playtex Carefree bra behind my white blouse. I know he and the dudes saw them. I did not care. I wanted them to see. I especially wanted Rowell to see. I wanted him to know I did not need to cover myself the way I did when we kissed on the band field. I have liberated myself. At least that is what Alicia would probably say. I never saw her again but that night changed me. I stopped seeing my chest and the rest of me as something to hide. I have almost stopped worrying about what people say when they come up on these 36Ds. Yeah, I have liberated myself. Aunt Sadie tried to beat the black off me for riding my bicycle that time of night but it was worth it. If I had not met Alicia that night, freedom or liberation (it's all the same) would have left me behind. I did not want that. At least now I am on the path. Magnolia liberated herself and moved to Liberia. She even chose an African country with part of the word liberation in it. Madear liberated herself with a white boyfriend. Yeah, that is right. She got a white boyfriend. It took me a while to understand what she meant that night about her "happily ever after." Aunt Sadie always said what is done in darkness will come to light. The woman I saw sitting under a white man with a ponytail driving a blue Ford Fairlane at the gas station that night was Madear. He and Madear drove right up to the 400 block of Osceola Street and came in the house. That's Madear's story and I am still tripping over it. If the Black Muslims can let white women join them after they came in our neighborhoods full force "AK," warning us all whites were blue-eyed devils, what can I say. All this race and color stuff is too confusing. I cannot bear to think about it too much, much less write about it. I guess everybody is just taking their liberation when and where they can. Rowell did it when he took off and went to FAMU a whole year early. I guess he was getting his liberation thing down since I did not see much of him when I got there. When I did see him, he was always in a rush doing this or that. I felt like he and everybody else were leaving me behind. Now we are both college students. We are two people getting our liberation down. We will catch up with each other again and I will be ready for him. It is funny how my liberation started with my chest. Then everybody in the family says "Iko" is in my chest. These busty babies get me a lot of attention. Sometimes it is good and sometimes it is not good at all. People—mostly dudes—see my chest first and right away decide what kind of chick I am. Then when we start to groove they are surprised at what they find. It is kind of fun playing a "wild chick." I get a rush the way I did that night with Alicia. As long as things do not go too far it is right on. When things get out of hand, it can be a bad scene. Like that time I met this dude at a fraternity party. He said his name was Sam, which probably was a lie. We were two-stepping to Minnie Riperton's "Adventures in Paradise." It was as if she was singing right to me. She was cooing, making her voice do handsprings and back-flips. "I believe I am free. Let it free me." Her vocal exercises, summoned our bodies close. He was grinding me and I was grinding him back. Our hips were swaying to Minnie's music so close hot oil could not separate us. My 36Ds rested on his chest and he used his arms to squeeze them together like ripe melons. He felt hard as a rock up against my pelvis. My mind was going crazy trying to guess what he looked like down there. I knew I needed to put on the brakes but I was ignoring all my red flags. When Minnie stopped singing, I went outside for some air. He followed me. He was so fine in that moonlight. The Deejay put on Al Green's single, "Call Me." We started slow-dragging and grinding outside. I remember thinking about how Madear and Daddy Douglas looked dancing to Bobby Blue Bland music. I think I was feeling some of the same stuff they were. I just wished I had had the nerve to listen at the cedar closet crack when they closed the door to their bedroom after they stopped dancing. Maybe I would have put together a how-to guidebook and I would have been okay. Sam's body heat clouded my mind. The taste of his kiss was like rich chocolate you know you should not have. His smell saturated my skin when he hugged me and I wanted to lather my whole body in it. I felt like I was high. I could see myself but I could not stop. My head was spinning and my panties were dripping wet. He was so hot I could feel the wetness of his sweat-drenched shirt when he pressed his chest against mine to give me a deep-throat kiss. I was in the danger zone, caught up in a whirlwind of excitement and loving it to the max. We stopped our outdoor love frenzy long enough for him to offer me a ride home in his shiny red Impala.

It was just a short ride from the frat house to the 400 block of Osceola Street. It was long enough to convince myself if I went all the way with Sam it would be practice for Rowell. When we drove up near the band field, I knew it was no turning back. He turned off his headlights and asked for a kiss. I gave it up for the first time. It didn't feel the way I thought it would. The white clouds did not hover over me, the way they did when I kissed Rowell there. It was hard to get comfortable in the front seat of a two-door Impala with the steering wheel jabbing you in the ribcage every time you moved. He was rushing me like he had to be somewhere. He kept telling me to touch his "love rod." When he unzipped his pants, if I could have run I would have. I could not imagine how my vagina or "my source to reproduce the motherland," as Magnolia called it in one of her letters, was going to stretch to fit that monster Sam was calling a love rod inside his pants. To make matters worse, he bit me on the side of one of my

> 36Ds. I was ready to fight then. He could not have cared less about my pain or what I was feeling. So much for the peace and love movement. I guessed the brothers, or at least Sam, got other things on their minds. He snorted and grunted until his eyes went up in his head. At first, I thought he was having a seizure or something. I was taking a first aid class but we had not covered seizures yet. Then he and his "love rod" went limp and it was over. He leaned back against the car door, grinning like he had just had a good meal. I vomited. The next week when I saw him on campus, he acted as if he did not know me. Then I got a notice from the health department and learned he gave me the clap. That's when I made a rule. If Go-Go wants to get some, it is going to be with someone who is extra special. It is definitely going to be with somebody that I know will see to it I am enjoying it as much as he is. It's going to be with Rowell.
>
> Go-Go

Indigo put her pencil down and thought about her last sentence.

"We will have our time together," she said to herself, exhausted from an unfulfilled Saturday night and sleeping too long on a Sunday morning.

Nodding her head in assurance, she closed the writing tablet and put it in the bureau drawer for safekeeping. The mirror above the bureau caught her attention. She noticed her baby sister Blueberry peeking around the corner. She had on her Sunday dress. Indigo calculated right away that Blueberry had gone to Sunday school and probably skipped church since she was home before Aunt Sadie and Grandma Dovie. This marked a new flexibility in the Douglas mandatory church attendance rule since "AK."

Blueberry was almost as tall as Indigo was. Even though she had the bumps on her forehead that were a signal of adolescence in full force and the protruding bust line, Indigo's mental picture of her was stuck between the ages of five and six.

"What are you looking at, Blue?" she called out.

"Nothing, I mean I'm just looking, that's all."

"Did you go to church?"

"Just Sunday school and part of church. I stayed in church until time to put in the offering, then I left before the preaching started."

"Where is Davis Jr.?"

"He and some of his friends went to play ball after Sunday school. I didn't want to go with them so I walked home."

"Well then, why are you still standing there looking?"

"I said I ain't looking for nothing!"

"All right, don't get all uptight," Indigo spoke, looking at Blueberry, who was halfway in and halfway out the bedroom door.

Indigo stared at her, noticing the change in her body form. She was maturing. Indigo had not really paid that much attention to Blueberry over the "AK" years.

"She was the baby of the family. Now she is growing up and I hadn't even noticed," Indigo went over in her mind.

"Now what are you looking at?" Blueberry snapped.

"I'm looking at you, growing all up and out everywhere," Indigo smiled.

"I couldn't stay a baby forever. People change, you know!"

"Yes, I know. Just don't change too fast," Indigo admonished.

Blueberry turned her head toward the kitchen when the sound of Stevie Wonder singing "Living for the City" came on the radio. She left Indigo with her thoughts, bouncing down the hall, snapping her fingers to Stevie Wonder's music.

Blueberry's antics made Indigo smile because it reminded her of when sounds coming from the radio would make her and Magnolia's body parts jump into spurts of rhythms and bounces. She missed Magnolia. She wrote to her often to help her keep up with what was going on in the family and the United States. Next to what was going on in the Douglas family, the most important thing to write about was WTAL's Cousin's top ten list of soul songs. It took months for the letters and tapes to reach Magnolia. By the time Stevie Wonder's album with "Living for the City" on it reached Magnolia, it was not hot anymore. That did not stop Magnolia from writing back with a letter full of political commentary.

"My good sister Indigo, I listened to the tape of Brother Stevie Wonder's new songs," Magnolia wrote. "Please send more batteries. I listen to the music tapes each night under the twilight of the African skies. It brings me such pleasure. The manatees and hippopotamuses are learning the chorus. When I lie under the palm trees and play my recorder, they yelp in unison. When I reflect on the lyrics, my good sister, I am saddened that the racist grip on America has not loosened. Brother Stevie sings of America betraying the vision of the 60's. Slow the music down, sister, and listen to his lyrics in the song 'Village Ghetto Land.' He says the world for blacks has not changed: 'Now some folks say we should be/Glad for what we have./Tell me, would you be happy in Village Ghetto Land?' Liberia is the home of freed slaves. The good whites of the American Colonization Society over one hundred years ago made it so that freed slaves could settle in this beautiful part of our homeland. At first, I did not understand why the black Americans making Liberia their home had to live on the coast, but I have come to love the rain forest and all its jewels of paradise. It does not matter really. All sisters and brothers in Liberia live free and work toward freedom."

"Leave it to Magnolia," Indigo thought when she read the letter that arrived from Magnolia. "You can always count on her to take the 'j' out of joy. Only Magnolia could find a political message in 'bump to the funk' jams by Stevie Wonder."

Indigo believed Magnolia's letter was her usual peace-and-love motherland mantra, but the last line of her sentence about "where black Americans had to live" bothered her. "That sentence was the first time Magnolia, hinted if only slightly, that Liberia was not heaven on earth," Indigo thought aloud.

"I never really understood how or why Magnolia fell in love with Africa. I have never dreamed of Africa the way she has." She became distracted, looking at some of the FAMU students making their way up the hill leading to the band field. The sight of the group of students proved a brief distraction, then her thoughts continued.

"She says all black people came from Africa. How she knows that information I do not know, but Magnolia did always know everything. I do not know why but the Africa stuff just got all in her. Well, maybe I do. It started with that ugliness in the jailhouse visiting room with Madear and Daddy Douglas. It was so much dirty laundry being aired that day, even I wanted to do something to counteract it. It was such a mess. The Douglas family hasn't been right since," she reflected, walking to the back door, watching at Blueberry throwing rocks in the palmetto bushes, still wearing the dress she wore to Sunday school.

"Leaving college and everything you know behind to go Africa...A country you have only dreamed about, just does not make sense to me. I guess Magnolia just had to be in a place where she could feel comfortable in her own skin, like Madear said. You cannot get much closer to that than going to Africa, a whole continent of black folks. I have to give it to her. She is brave. A light-skinned sister has gotten a hard way to go since 'AK' and James Brown said say it loud, I'm black and I'm proud," Indigo mused, continuing to look out the back door.

Aunt Sadie and Grandma Dovie interrupted Indigo's thoughts as they came up the walkways with bags of groceries.

"Well, good afternoon, Miss Sleep-Until-Noon. I missed you in church this morning. Looks like it's going to rain this afternoon," Aunt Sadie greeted Indigo sarcastically.

"I didn't sleep till noon but I probably would have if I had gone to hear Rev. Hester preach," Indigo answered, reaching to help with the groceries.

"That's blasphemy. Don't blaspheme the Lord and his soldiers," Grandma Dovie interjected.

"No disrespect intended," Indigo added quickly to prevent an argument.

"You might not have intended it but you were disrespectful. The road to hell is paved with good intentions and with talk like that and lying up on your backside on Sunday mornings, that's the road you traveling on," Grandma Dovie spoke with one hand on her hip and the other making a point in the air with far more venom than the situation called for.

"Momma, the child was being fresh. She knows there was a time in this house she wouldn't have been allowed to lie on her butt on a Sunday no matter how old she was. The Lord says, 'Whosoever will, let them come.' Just let her keep on getting grown. she will become one of the whosoever will. Let's just not start a lot of fussing today," Aunt Sadie jumped in, trying to keep things under control.

"Humph!" Grandma Dovie grunted, rolling her eyes in Indigo's direction.

"Pastor Hester said in service that a special show about black people is coming on television tonight. Let's hurry and get our dinner on the table so we all can relax and watch it eating ice cream tonight," Aunt Sadie suggested, still trying to smooth things over.

"What's the show supposed to be about?" Blueberry asked, walking into the kitchen and reaching inside the grocery bags on the counter to see what was inside.

"All about us and how we came to be," Aunt Sadie answered, pulling pots from under the sink and turning on the hot water in the sink.

"Came to be what?" Indigo asked, looking toward her Aunt Sadie.

"Came to be as a people. How us black folks came to live in these United States. He said the name of it is 'Roots' and it's going to be on every night this week," Sadie answered, clarifying her words to be sure they were just as Rev. Hester said them.

"Oooh, too bad Magnolia isn't here. Sounds like it might be about Africans running around. She would love that!" Indigo giggled.

"I don't know. The Pastor said every black person in America should watch it and I know I am one black person who is going to," Sadie said, reaching for the ringing telephone.

"Well, right on. Power to the people, my sister!" Indigo teased just as her aunt picked up the ringing telephone.

Aunt Sadie laughed, waving the dishcloth at Indigo, and answered the telephone. "Douglas residence," she spoke in the receiver to the caller.

Madear's bedroom door opened and she walked out sleepily, clad in a short nightgown, trying to pull her long curly store-bought blond-color hair in order. It was all over her head, like she had been rolling from one edge of the bed to the other all night. When she opened her bedroom door, you could see the outline of a body lying in her bed.

"What's all this loud talking about so early in the morning?" she asked through a yawn.

"First of all, it's after two in the afternoon," Sadie began. "Second of all, you need to have the decency to close your bedroom door to your business," holding her hand over the receiver.

"Oh, it's just Drew in there sleeping," Madear sighed, fanning her hand across her face.

"Don't matter who it is, you ought to have some decency about yourself. You weren't raised like that," Grandma Dovie insisted.

"Everybody in this house knows Drew and I go together. If they don't know what that means behind closed doors, it's too doggone bad," Madear exclaimed, walking to the stove, reaching for the coffee pot.

"Bethann, everything is going to be all right. We can talk when I come in tomorrow. Stop upsetting yourself. Your Momma and Daddy are grown. They got to work out their own business. I'll talk to you tomorrow, okay?" Aunt Sadie was speaking into the phone, trying to end her conversation when she turned and more of Madear and Grandma Dovie's conversation caught her attention.

"Cree, the Daddy of these children lived in this house. How you think they feel about you displaying your man in their Daddy's bed? And Lord, what in the world you think Hiram would say?" Sadie interjected, having hung up the receiver.

"It is not Hiram's house. It is the rent man's house. These children know their Daddy's been in jail for ten years. More than half Blueberry and Davis Jr. lives here. That is what they should be upset about more than anything. Besides, Hiram and I stopped caring about what each other think a long time ago. Who was that on that phone? Little Bethann with one of her snotty-nose problems?" Madear spouted off, holding her coffee cup with two hands, expanding her loosely tied robe to reveal the lacy top of her nightgown.

"Still the same, Cree. You don't need to let these children see just how much you don't care about their Daddy. They got feelings too. You should respect the Daddy of your children."

"You got enough respect for both of us, Sadie. He gets enough respect from me for a man locked up for being stupid."

"You're right, I do respect Hiram. I do not know what you mean by what you're saying. Yeah, I respect him. Other people respect him too. Hiram and Mr. Benjamin being locked up for that explosion just been eating at Mr. Whittier for years. He was in a difficult situation with them partners of his. He had to go along with them. He never stopped questioning how things could have happened the way they did. When he visited Mrs. Whittier while she was in Shands Hospital in Gainesville, he started going over to Raeford to visit Hiram and Mr. Benjamin too. The minute she started improving, their relationship started breaking down from there. Raeford is not that far from Gainesville, just on the other side of Highway 95. He has been writing and visiting Hiram and Benjamin for years, trying to figure out some kind of way to help them."

"I don't see how he can help a person foolish enough to confess to doing something he didn't do. But then I bet Mrs. Trin Whittier is helping too and that's going to make everything all right," Madear said with a smirk.

"No, she isn't helping! That's one of her and Mr. Whittier's many problems, aside from him in some group organizing to build a Jewish syna...church here in Tallahassee and them mixing like oil and water."

"Synagogue, Aunt Sadie, not church," Indigo eased in.

"Yeah, that's it. Synagogue. I cannot keep all this straight, child. Now Mr. Whittier and Mrs. Whittier getting a divorce. Bethann is just beside herself. That was her on the phone. She is twenty but she still wants her Momma and Daddy to be together. Children are like that. Black or white, it don't matter."

"I haven't seen Bethann since that time she went with us to visit Daddy Douglas," Indigo pondered.

"She just needed room to grow past all the changes in her life the way you did, Go-Go, that's all. She's going to Florida State, living at home, pretty much the same as you except you are going to FAMU."

"Well, I haven't seen her and I don't want to see her. That goes for her no-good Momma too. Sadie, if you want to put your hope in Mr. Whittier helping Hiram and Benjamin locked up behind bars, that's your business, just leave me out of it," Madear emphasized, pouring the rest of her coffee down the drain.

"Cree, Hiram is my brother-in-law. I write to him and he writes me okay. He needs family to encourage him while he is locked up. You and him are going through whatever..."

"No, Hiram and I aren't going through anything. We are finished!" Madear corrected Aunt Sadie.

"Well, I ain't got nothing to do with all of that. I am just trying to be decent to the father of my nieces and nephews. If that upsets you, I do not know what to do about it. And his name ain't Hiram anymore. It's Hadif Ahmed," Aunt Sadie said seriously, then switching to a muffled giggle.

"Ha what?" Madear screeched.

"Hadif Ahmed," Sadie answered between laughs. "He is studying to become a Muslim so he changed his name."

"Well, if that don't beat all," Madear laughed.

Aunt Sadie looked over at the surprised expression on Indigo's face and rattled off, "Indigo, he's planning to call you and Davis Jr. and Blueberry as soon as he gets a telephone pass. Now act surprised when he does."

"I won't have to act," Indigo retorted, annoyed at hearing the news of her father's name change secondhand.

"Well, whatever makes him happy is all I have to say, because I'm going to do what makes me happy," Madear chirped.

"That much isn't a secret about you, Cree," Aunt Sadie acknowledged.

"Because I don't like secrets!" Madear protested, looking in Grandma Dovie's direction.

"Sometimes people need to keep some things secret," Grandma Dovie said without looking up from a pot of water she was running her hands through grains of rice in.

"But then it ought to be the people involved making the decision to keep the secret, not somebody making the decision because they just decided to make it just like they decide everything else," Cree hissed at Grandma Dovie.

"That doesn't make a bit of sense. If somebody makes a decision more than likely they got business making it or else they wouldn't be bothered with it all," Grandma said slowly and methodically while continuing to wash the white rice through her fingers.

"I'm beginning to get a headache in my eye just listening to you talk like that, Momma. Why don't you just say you made up your mind not to tell me my real Daddy was white because you wanted me to be tormented as a half-white, half-colored woman. You wanted me to be hated. Hated, Momma! You even wanted me to hate myself! That is what you were saying to me when you did not let me know who my real Daddy was. I got only one set of kin people when others got two. I am strange, Momma. Different from everybody else cause of you! Why don't you admit that, Momma? Because that is exactly the way it is," Cree blasted her.

"All right! All right now! We are not having any of that today. Today is Sunday. Let's just leave all of that stuff in the past where it belongs," Sadie jumped in, moving around the kitchen, starting to prepare Sunday dinner.

Cree gave a cutting glance in Grandma Dovie's direction and walked out of the kitchen.

Grandma Dovie never looked up from washing the white rice at the sink. Then she mumbled after Cree walked out the door, "Tain't gonna make no difference all the way around 'bout you being kin to them people."

CHAPTER 24

"Deeply rooted"

A roll of thunder followed by rain and a flash of lightning quieted the entire house. The one rule in the Douglas household, still active, covered thunder and lightning. When the "Lord was doing his work from the sky, everyone kept quiet." The Sunday dinner cooking on the stove was turned on low while family members retreated to their private corners of sanctuary.

Indigo's first inclination was to sit down and write Daddy Douglas a stinging letter about changing his name. Thunder and lightning or not. She could not decide if she was angrier because he did not tell her directly, or because he told Aunt Sadie and she announced it. She headed straight for her bedroom and opened the bureau drawer, pulling out her writing tablet. Grandma Dovie was making her way to her bedroom and saw Indigo with the tablet of paper in her hand, and the telephone rang.

"Paper draws lightning, I know you were raised to know that!" Grandma Dovie screamed.

Indigo jumped at the sound of her Grandma's voice, dropped the tablet of paper to the floor, and went in the hallway to answer the phone.

"Hello," she spoke, trying to hide her annoyance with Grandma Dovie.

"And get off that telephone before lightning comes through those wires!" Grandma Dovie continued to scream.

"Go, it's Rowell…"

"I can't talk to you now, it's lightning. Call me later," she spoke quickly, hanging up the telephone receiver.

"I wasn't thinking about the paper or the telephone! You do not have to get so upset about it. I forgot! It's just paper and a telephone, for goodness sakes!" she answered, startled and annoyed.

"Paper draws lightning and lightning can come through the phone wires. I'm eighty years old and if I got a mind to get upset, I will." Grandma Dovie leaned up against the doorway to Indigo's bedroom, folded her arms and stood firm, emphasizing her point.

"You're eighty? I didn't know that," Indigo gasped, showing her surprise.

"It wasn't for you to know. It wouldn't have made a difference if you did know, I'd still be eighty," Grandma Dovie spoke haughtily.

"I'm not trying to fight with you, I just didn't know you were that old. I mean eighty. No one ever said how old you were. Eighty is old, I mean, you've probably seen a lot of things," Indigo spoke fast and uneasily, trying to prevent an argument.

"I've seen plenty. Plenty good and plenty bad," Grandma Dovie responded, aware of Indigo's effort.

Grandma Dovie telling her age and Indigo hearing her tell it caused them both to stop and look at each other with new eyes. They paused and sat quiet, briefly. Indigo, not wanting the conversation to end, began talking with nervous laughter.

"You probably could have been on the show Rev. Hester wants everybody to watch tonight about how black folks got here."

"I could've added something to it. Probably couldn't carry the whole show, but I got pieces I could add," Grandma Dovie beamed.

"What kind of pieces?" Indigo prodded eagerly.

"The kind of pieces that hold eighty years together," Grandma Dovie answered, stepping in Indigo's bedroom and walking over near the bed where she was sitting.

Grandma Dovie started talking as if a traffic light had turned green, telling her to go. She told stories of her parents' travels in the Florida Panhandle. She spoke of the detours in their steps to avoid unpredictable disasters brought on by being colored and not white. She mapped out the difficult course her mother endured at the hand of white men who were determined to exercise what they believed was their right to release their procreative juices within the fertile caverns of colored women. When she talked of the pain of having been born in light-colored skin and having a child also born the same way in spite of marrying a deeply colored man, her eyes looked glassy and saliva trickled down the side of her mouth. She did not stop talking to wipe it away. Her words slurred slightly and she talked about herself as if she was talking about someone else.

Indigo was familiar with this kind of talk. Skin-color talk. She had heard it for the past ten years. Talk so hushed and powerful it bordered on what some black folks call roots or mojo. It saddened her to hear the same agony in the talk from her eighty-year-old grandmother's voice. Eighty years seemed a long time to still feel pain. Grandma Dovie fluttered her eyelids when she spoke as if she was reliving moments or wishing she could live it over when the drive back in time swerved to her child-bearing years. Fixed anger bordering on rage permeated the lines of her face and the glare in her eyes when she came upon the words of recollection, "Every dog got his day and some dogs got a longer day." Indigo had heard these words before. She remembered hearing them through the cedar closet as the last words Grandma Dovie uttered before her voice entered a season of silence. A season of silence that had lasted half Indigo's life.

"When your Grandaddy and I first got married in Port St. Joe, the steamboats were the biggest moneymaker in Port St. Joe. Your Grandaddy worked on the steamboat as a card dealer. His quick hands made him a good card shuffler. The owner of one of the finest steamboat companies in town was a white fellow by the name of Jack Booker. Mr. Jack recognized the talent in Nate's hands right away. When Nate and I got married, he wanted to quit working the steamboat and become a respectable married man. Mr. Jack lured him to continue working on his steamboat by hiring me as his chambermaid. He was cunning and enterprising but he was a drunk. He got drunk every night. He convinced Nate our working on the steamship together would give us a better life than most coloreds living in Port St. Joe. He was not interested in our lives and Nate and I knew that. He was interested in ensuring his profits. Mind you, his plan did work for us. We did have a better life than most colored people did on Port St. Joe. I took an interest in craft and jewelry making and he encouraged it. We had money, food and a place to stay. Life was good.

"People would come from all over Florida and beyond to ferry to Mississippi and New Orleans on his steamboat. The men came with plenty of money for card games and whatever else Mr. Jack had for sale on his steamboat. One of Mr. Jack's passengers taught me how to make glass beads out of arsenic compound on a ferry from Port St. Joe to New Orleans. Mrs. Jean-Claude was her name. She was a French woman traveling with her gambling husband. She made other jewelry too. I liked the glass beads the most. They could take your breath away they were so pretty. She spoke English pretty too. Her words came out as if they were flowers. She sure could make things sound pretty. She showed me how to measure and cure the arsenic to make glass. Now I liked that because it was all-natural. My kin people like using nature to make things. The steam engine room on the boat was my workshop when I made my glass beads. Some of the colored men working down there knew Nate and let me come down to work when Mr. Jack's foreman was not around. Mrs. Jean-Claude said the arsenic compound had deadly powers. It could kill a person fast or slow. She said it was hard to trace because it did not smell or it did not have a taste. I always kept a little bit of the compound up in my servant's quarters for my jewelry making. I knew one day I might have to use it for something else.

"Mr. Jack made sure his guests left with empty pockets when they stepped on ground in New Orleans or Biloxi. To be sure he got all the money he could, he got Nate and his swift card-shuffling hands to help him. He told Nate to play with two decks. One was marked and one was not. Whenever a player was winning too much at blackjack, Mr. Jack would give Nate a signal using a cigar in his mouth. Now, if he bit off the tip of the cigar, that meant to let him win until one pocket got full, then switch the deck. If he took the cigar out of his mouth, put it back, and crunched it with his teeth, that meant make the switch quick, fast and in a hurry. Nate became a master at reading Mr. Jack's cigar moves and Mr. Jack's pockets grew fatter and fatter. Things were fine for a while.

"Mr. Jack had a stable of white showgirls on the steamboat who entertained publicly and privately. When Mr. Jack got drunk, he would often take one or two of them to his private chambers. I knew the showgirls were robbing him blind but I was the colored chambermaid and that was not my business. I stayed in his chambers, making sure he or his Missus, when she took the trip, had everything they needed. Most times, she did not make the trip and I used the time to work on my jewelry making. Nate and I stayed in the servant's quarters right next to the private chambers, separated by a thick red curtain. Most of the times, I stayed by myself because Nate dealt cards all night. I was set up with all my jewelry-making materials and that occupied my mind when Nate was not there.

"One night a big gambler by the name of Schmidt asked Mr. Jack if there was a private card game he could take part in. Not one to miss an opportunity to swindle a gambler out of a dollar, Mr. Jack obliged him and took him to his private chambers. Soon as they got there, they went to work on emptying a gallon of Louisiana bourbon. Then Mr. Schmidt let Mr. Jack know he was on to his dealer's cheating ways and the income it provided him. He demanded a cut in the gambling profits or he was going to let the table know the colored dealer was dealing with two decks. This would have ruined Mr. Jack's steamboat business and somebody would surely have tried to kill my Nate. Mr. Jack called Mr. Schmidt a dog and everything but a child of God. Mr. Schmidt laughed in his face. They agreed to play a few hands of poker to settle the score. The winner would take all. Mr. Jack lost because he was too drunk to concentrate. Mr. Schmidt agreed to keep silent for twenty-four hours until Mr. Jack came up with a way to let those that needed to know his business had changed hands. Mr. Jack did not know whether to fall asleep or go blind hoping all his trouble would go away. You know they did not go away!

"Mr. Schmidt started getting comfortable right away in Mr. Jack's private chambers. He was pilfering through everything. I had not slept at all that night and Nate was upstairs shuffling cards. I heard the whole mess going on between him and Mr. Jack. I had a feeling there was not going to be too much good come of that night. When he yanked back the curtains to the servant's quarters he had a greedy look in his eye. He was looking for anything of Mr. Jack's that was worth having. He stood there for a minute laughing a deep belly laugh, looking at me. Then he wanted to know how widespread my duties were. He smelled like stale liquor and sweat dried over sweat. His brain should have been floating in alcohol with all that bourbon he drank. I figured he was too drunk to hurt me much and I had fought off men before, white and colored. I geared myself up to fight him off too. He was strong as an ox. He threw me on the small bed in the servant's quarters and dropped his solid sack body against my frame. He lay on top of me like a ton of lead. I knew I could not have moved if I tried with all my might. He was so heavy I thought my ribs were broken. When I tried to scream, he hit me in my face with his liquor-smelling fist. He busted my lip and ripped my clothes off. I just closed my eyes and wished I were somewhere else. He hit me a couple of times. I must have passed out because my mind took me to back to the bay during the moon festival season when I was a young woman. I just put myself in the midst of all those Indians celebrating in their finery and I felt powerful.

"After he finished his business, he made me get up and go get him a glass of water. I brought him two glasses of ice water laced with arsenic. Before he could finish drinking the second glass, Mr. Jack came back to the private chamber, talking fast, trying to make a deal to save his steamboat. He saw Mr. Schmidt drinking the water and yelled for me to bring him a glass of water too. Mr. Schmidt, feeling good with himself, offered Mr. Jack the second glass of water I had brought for him. Now I was not intending Mr. Jack no harm but harm came his way.

"They both died that night. I told the Missus, Mr. Jack and Mr. Schmidt had drunk bourbon all night. The town doctor thought the powerful Louisiana bourbon killed them after they drank it all night. Mr. Jack died in a chair in his private chambers and Mr. Schmidt died on his way to let the table know about my Nate's card dealing. He never made it to the card floor. The sheriff asked me to put a white sheet over Mr. Jack's face. When I did, I told Mr. Jack I was sorry for all that happened. I felt bad for him. He was good to Nate and me. Now, when I covered Mr. Schmidt's face, I whispered to him every dog got his day.

"Mr. Jack's Missus sold the steamboat right after the funeral. His son Joe took the money for the sale of the steamboat and opened a restaurant near where the steamboat used to dock. Joe knew his Daddy was fond of us so he let us put up a stand selling crafts and jewelry. Like any other halfway-enterprising colored person, we had to pay a stand fee to Mr. Jack's son Joe.

"He felt bad for the Schmidts losing their only money-earning relative. To help the family make ends meet, he hired one of them that called himself Smithee, to be a porter. Smithee hated Nate and me. He was on the card floor the night Mr. Schmidt died. Smithee earned a living helping passengers carry their luggage from the restaurant to the docks. I had Cree nine months later. Mr. Schmidt was a dog that had a longer day.

"Now it must look like your Grandma is some kind of killer, but it ain't so. I'm a survivor. Sometimes bad happens so the good can be appreciated. Now, hear me right, killing is wrong. The good 'Lawd' say so. There was nothing right about what Mr. Schmidt was going to do to my Nate or what he did to me. I hated him for it. I hated all white people for a long time. Afterwards, I started carrying a little arsenic compound in a sac around my waist just for protection. People thought I just carried my money strapped to my waist. I did not tell them anything different. It was not anyone's business anyway. I carried me a little jewelry knife too. It was little but it could cut anything that needed to be cut to a nub. That night the Klan beat my Nate and one came after me. I had my arsenic and my knife in my sac. When he came clawing after me in the woods, I used every ounce of my strength to get to my sac so I could kill him. Just before I was going to die trying to kill him, I heard the voice of Stud's wife singing down at the bay. Anacostia, Stud's wife, rescued me. She did not know whether I was white, black, blue or green out there in the dark. I was someone who needed help. My struggle became her struggle and we became people joined together out there in them woods."

Grandma Dovie looked exhausted. Her left hand twitched and flopped around on the bed as her talking slowed down. She could not control her hand's wanderings. Then she paused and the spasms of her body calmed down. She started again, invigorated, moving onto the next piece of family history that illuminated raising Cree and Sadie and their migration to Tallahassee.

Hours passed before she stopped talking and demanded they go in the kitchen to get something to eat so they could watch the television show Rev. Hester wanted them to watch. Indigo went with her but she was more preoccupied with trying to make her stories fit into the lane that led to the lives of the people in the Douglas home.

It was ten' clock and the promotions for the televsion show "Roots" was coming on. Grandma Dovie and Aunt Sadie sat in front of the television set in curious anticipation. Madear and Drew came in and out of the living room. Indigo, absorbed in her own reflections, stared at Grandma Dovie and Aunt Sadie more than the television set. She did not share their enthusiasm. She did not believe Rev. Hester's television show could add or subtract from the roots she had come to know that afternoon from Grandma Dovie's stories.

Drums began to beat a heart-pounding rhythm and a young African boy ran through the lush verdant thicket of what was to be the African bush on the television set. Indigo was trying to join in the obvious enthusiasm in everyone else's eyes but she could not. She was thinking about Grandma Dovie's stories. They breathed life into people she knew only vaguely from the cedar closet. She visited times and places that were foreign yet familiar. Her thoughts drifted to the night Cousin announced the death of Martin Luther King on the radio. It was the beginning of life changing, as she knew it.

She had told herself many times that Martin Luther King's dream was at the root of everything bad that ever happened to her family. After listening to Grandma Dovie that afternoon, she began to hear those old thoughts differently. The television set panned to rows and rows of Africans lying head to foot, sick and bleeding, chained together on a boat traveling across the ocean. The sight of them gripped her heart. She thought of the precise steps the agile drum major made leading FAMU's Marching 100 down Adam Street with the cheers of the crowd behind him. Then she thought of the newspaper headlines after Martin Luther King died. "Drum Major for Justice Slain." She stopped short of letting herself ponder the possibility that maybe somebody had to be a drum major for blacks and maybe that somebody had to be Martin Luther King and maybe Daddy Douglas, Madear and Magnolia had to follow his lead or at least try.

The more she contemplated, the more Grandma Dovie's story replayed in her ears and became deeply rooted in her mind. The "Roots" television series added to her newly insatiable taste for stories about "life before," as Grandma Dovie described. "Roots" captured her, spellbound, for the next eight episodes. The television networks said it had the same ripple effect across town and the whole nation. They reported blacks and whites watched the saga of "Roots." Everyone everywhere talked about the episodes. In the grocery store, at the shopping center, in the barbershop, on the bus stop, on college campuses and in church everybody was asking, "Did you see 'Roots' last night?"

The Tallahassee *Democrat* said on the front page, "'Roots' told the black story as an American story, stressing the power of the underdog and his or her struggle for freedom." From that point on black people you knew were talking about tracing their roots. Madear sent off for a book about tracing hers. One month she changed her blond store-bought hair color to a brown color similar to her natural color. Then she changed it back again.

Drew broke down and cried at the breakfast table after the fourth night of the "Roots" show. He apologized for all the generations of people in his family who owned slaves. Nobody knew what to say to him. Everybody listened and Aunt Sadie nodded her head but that was about as far as it went. The food was starting to get cold while he sat there "cleaning his conscience," as he put it.

Davis Jr. watched him closely from the minute he started his confession. He stared him up and down and said, "Are you going to put some butter on those grits and eat them or are you going to wait until they get cold?"

It took Drew a minute to comprehend what Davis Jr. was saying. He wiped at his eyes and said, "Excuse me?"

Davis Jr. said, "I said are you going to butter those grits while they're piping hot or are you going to let them sit there and get cold? There is only one thing worse than cold grits and that is warmed-up grits. We are about two minutes from having to warm up the grits again. Pass the food, man."

"Davis Jr., where are your manners?" Madear admonished.

"My manners are right here at the table. I just asked him to pass the grits. I did not say anything rude. I could have said we know you are saying all that 'sorry'crap because you are knocking boots with my—"

"Davis Jr., don't you speak that way! You're out of line," Madear shouted.

"No, Madear, *he's* out of line! He's way out of line. He's so far out of line he shouldn't be here," Davis Jr. shouted back.

"He's here because I want him to be here and he'll be here as long as I want him to," Madear said, standing up and walking over to Davis Jr. sitting at the head of the table.

Davis Jr. looked away as Madear spoke to him. Drew picked up the bowl of grits and handed them to Davis Jr. Davis Jr. pushed them away and got up from the table, declaring he wasn't hungry. Moment later, a rapid thud sound was vibrating through the open kitchen window. Davis Jr. was making powerful jump shots up against the light pole that he fashioned into a makeshift basketball stand behind the duplex.

Madear picked up her coffee cup, drank a swallow of coffee and opened the newspaper to the sales section. Aunt Sadie and Grandma Dovie sat speechless through the Drew, Davis Jr. and Madear exchange. After a few bites of toast, Aunt Sadie got up and walked out the back door. The thudding sound of the basketball hitting the side of the light pole stopped. Grandma Dovie ate only a small amount of food. Indigo noticed that she spilled a big glob of apple jelly on her housedress and didn't try to wipe it off. She also noticed Grandma Dovie was wearing a funny frown was on her face and her eyes looked distant. She dismissed her observations of Grandma Dovie as part of her rekindled interest in reconciling the Douglas family since she heard Grandma Dovie's story and watched the "Roots" series.

She had written Magnolia a letter after each "Roots" episode, excited to let her know of her new interest in Africa. She held back from telling her about the roots that Grandma Dovie shared with her. Even though she and Magnolia were adults now, she still relished having more information, especially if it pertained to the family. More importantly, she wanted to keep Grandma Dovie's information close to her. She needed to sit with it for a while. Aunt Sadie always said, "Sometimes you just got to sit with your mind before it comes to you what to do with what's on your mind." Getting her family back together like it was "BK" was what was on her mind.

She knew it was going to be hard. Even if she was able to somehow maneuver a family reunion, things were not the same. Daddy Douglas was in prison, Drew lived in the duplex with Madear, and Magnolia was in Africa. Despite what seemed like impossible odds, for the first time "AK" she was hopeful.

To please her Aunt Sadie and Grandma Dovie, that hope carried over to the next Sunday. She agreed to join them in church after the week of the "Roots" series broadcast. She sat in the same middle aisle in front of the pulpit. Aunt Sadie was a vision in pastels with matching hat and Grandma Dovie wore white from head to toe. Rev. Hester began posturing for his sermon by building on the enthusiasm of the scores of "Roots" watchers in the congregation.

"I say 'Roots' ushered in a good feeling about being black in America," he began with a gospel roll in his voice. "Say amen, somebody. As great as the 'Roots' series was, it can't take credit for this good feeling black people are experiencing today. This good feeling started when God gave Martin Luther King his dream."

"These people are just stuck on King," Indigo grumbled to herself.

"If it wasn't for King talking about his dream and taking a bullet, there would have never been a 'Roots' on television. His dream became a vision for America. His dream touched the hearts of all kinds of folks to tell the story of 'Roots.' Not only are we learning our history, others are learning our history and accepting us as people and other people as a people and so on. God's plan is working! This is the beginning of equality! This is the dream! You should be glad for Martin Luther King's dream today. Why don't you say amen, somebody!" Rev. Hester bellowed at his congregation.

Some of the members stood to their feet and raised their hands, shouting "Amen" in response to Rev. Hester's call. The sun glare coming through the stained-glass window warmed Indigo's eyes, causing her to turn toward her Grandma Dovie, adorned in white, standing with raised hands. The reflection of the sun glare beaming through the stained glass cast a multi-colored pattern against Grandma Dovie's extended white torso in praise of the 'Roots' series and absolving her own roots.

"Amen somebody!" Indigo said softly.

CHAPTER 25

"The coming"

March 1977

Dear Daddy Douglas,

Grandma Dovie had a stroke sometime last week. The "Roots" series had the entire house in such a trance we hardly noticed she was sick. Did you get to watch it? I know you have a television in the visiting room but I don't know what you have beyond those gray steel doors. I wrote to Magnolia after every episode. You should write to her sometimes. I'll send you her address. I know what you said in the visiting room that day but we are still family. I do not want to drag all of that up. It is a long letter or deep conversation for another time. I was really writing to tell you about Grandma Dovie. We probably did not notice she was sick because this is not the first time she has stopped talking. The twisted frown on her face and her left hand hanging limp by her side gave us a clue she might have had a stroke. The doctor said the stroke could have killed her. It did kill her voice. Again. Aunt Sadie has practically moved in, taking care of her day and night. She convinced the doctor she could take care of Grandma Dovie as good as any nurse in a hospital. You probably know as well as I do we do not have money for a big hospital bill. We're lucky to have Aunt Sadie. She's been good to us. I don't know what I would have done without her. She's been like a mother and a father all in one. I'm not trying to take anything away from you or Madear, and then maybe I am. I know

> you feel standing up for your "justice" was important for us but your being around would have been better. Speaking of things being better, I would have appreciated hearing from you that your new name was "Hanif." What's this about Mr. Whittier trying to help you and Mr. Benjamin with your appeal? How is Mr. Benjamin anyway? Aunt Sadie and I are planning to bring Blueberry and Davis Jr. to see you at the end of the month. You can tell me all the answers to my questions then. Hope you are well.
>
> Indigo

"How's she doing, Go?" Aunt Sadie asked, touching the top of Indigo's shoulder.

Indigo gently put her pencil on top of her writing tablet and lifted her body out of her Grandma Dovie's squeaking rocking chair to greet her Aunt Sadie.

"She's been sleeping for a long time. I was just writing a letter to Daddy Douglas. I told him we were going to come see him at the end of the month."

"We might go, it's a maybe. I have to make sure Momma is going to be okay while I'm gone."

"Maybe Madear can watch her while we're gone," Indigo suggested.

"In case you have not noticed, your Madear is busy tracing her family tree since she saw that 'Roots' television show. Drew is throwing in all kinds of money to help her. He has hired a private investigator to go back to Port St. Joe and help her find out who her real Daddy is. I guess she thinks it is going to change things. Drew is such a lovesick fool. Then most men are who hook up with your Madear. I don't think we can count on her to watch your Grandma," Aunt Sadie reported, trying to fluff Grandma Dovie's pillows without waking her.

"What is Madear hoping to find out?" Indigo insisted.

"Don't start me to lying, child, I don't know. Maybe it will make her feel better. Maybe she will come to realize she is good enough or just as good or both. I do not know. I don't begin to know what makes her feel the way she does when she looks at her skin," Aunt Sadie protested.

"Well, at least, since so many people saw 'Roots,' they can be comfortable in their own skin and start trying to find out how their skin got to be the color it is," Indigo conceded.

"Child, 'Roots' was a good show. I cannot say a bad thing about it. It gave a lesson to black and white people. Everybody, I mean all people have known for generations how their skin came to be in colors from alabaster to indigo. Nobody talked about it out in the open," Aunt Sadie instructed, busying herself around Grandma Dovie's bedroom.

"That's the problem! It has been the problem in this family. Everybody's so hung up on skin color and no one wants to talk about it. If we would have talked about more openly, Magnolia would still be here and Madear and Daddy Douglas would still be together," Indigo snapped, annoyed at the revelation.

"Not just the problem in this family, child. It is families all over, including black and white families across the United States. No one talked about it."

"Why not? It is always there. How can you expect a family to be a family if they can't talk about something always staring them in the face?" Indigo pleaded.

"Let's go into the kitchen. If she's resting good, I don't want to disturb her with all this kind of talk," Aunt Sadie prodded Indigo, tiptoeing out of Grandma Dovie's room.

"I'm not trying to make you mad or nothing, but sometimes I have to agree with your Madear. You are nearly grown but sometimes your dreaming seems like a story from one of those Dick and Jane books up in that box in your closet. That play-play stuff is stuck to you like glue. This world is nothing like Dick and Jane's world. It's a world ruled by power and fear."

"What is wrong with wanting a world like Dick and Jane? At least they talked about their problems. They were happy and loved each other," Indigo defended.

"Go-Go girl, Dick and Jane's biggest problem was their dog Spot running off somewhere or Puff their cat playing with their mother's ball of yarn. Your family's problems are one hundred times bigger than that," Aunt Sadie chuckled.

"Maybe the problems wouldn't be so big if we'd talked about them before everything got so out of hand," Indigo insisted.

"Things are not that simple. A man lost his life trying to get people not to judge by the color of the skin."

"Here we go with the wonders of Martin Luther King," Indigo mimicked

"For all those good grades you make in college, you don't know very much," Aunt Sadie chastised. "Martin Luther King shined the light on inequalities because of skin color. The more marches he led and speeches he gave, the more powerful he got. People who did not like what he was doing began to fear him. King put the whole topic of skin color out there for the world to hear. Then that show 'Roots' put it on television for the world to see. Seeing is believing."

"So the drum major for justice led the band so the crowd could hear," Indigo reflected, more for herself than for the conversation with her Aunt Sadie.

"If that's how you see it. For a week, black folks were like any other foreign group who ever came to this land of the free. Whites saw us struggle for freedom on television. They saw us as the underdogs. Ain't no guarantee things going to change but it's a heck of start," Aunt Sadie went on to say.

"In Madear's case I just want her to change back to being the Momma I used to know."

"There you go again. She's still your Momma...your Madear! She just cannot focus on you right now. She's got to take care of herself first," Aunt Sadie insisted.

"So I'm supposed to stop needing a mother, and a father for that matter, because they're both preoccupied."

"I can't tell you what to need. You know what you need because you are old enough to know. You can see where your Madear's head is. Now your Daddy, maybe he can give you what you need," Aunt Sadie tried to soothe Indigo.

"Yeah, I heard they are making the bars on the cells at Raeford a little wider. Maybe his reach can stretch to Tallahassee," Indigo quipped.

"Maybe he will be able to reach out to you sooner than you think," Aunt Sadie offered with a glint in her eye.

"You mean when we go to Raeford to see him?" Indigo quizzed.

"Your Daddy might be out of jail soon if Mr. Whittier and his friend have their way," Aunt Sadie supplied cautiously.

"What do you mean by that? And why would Mr. Whittier want to help Daddy Douglas and Mr. Benjamin so bad?"

"You know I asked him that same question. Mrs. Whittier and Bethann blamed Hiram and Benjamin for starting the fire, so naturally, I thought it was some sort of set-up when he said he wanted to help them," Aunt Sadie reflected curiously.

"Why are you so sure it's not a set-up now?" Indigo interrogated.

"Because things are different now. Mr. Whittier done had a complete turn-around. He has come to speaking his mind more with Mrs. Whittier and standing firm. To add to that, he has left his partnership with Krass and Pepper. He is starting another business with some other men. He talks about his parents and his religion all the time. He took that little box Bethann gave you and nailed it over his front door. Mrs. Whittier had a fit but it stayed. He says he has a responsibility to repair the world. I believe if he and his friend can help your Daddy and Mr. Benjamin, he will."

"I'd rather wait and see before I go giving Mr. Whittier some badge of honor. He is just as responsible as Bethann and her

Momma for sending Daddy Douglas and Mr. Benjamin to jail. He's the one who told the police what they wanted to hear."

"Indigo, if you were under the kind of pressure Mr. Whittier was under, you would have probably said your Daddy and Benjamin started that fire too. His partners and the police were hounding him to no end! The man was scared out of his mind. Pressure, power and fear are deadly combinations."

"What does power and fear have to do with this? I thought that was just reserved for the King?"

"Everybody wants power and is trying to get it one way or the other. It's not just about Martin Luther King, child. It is man…human in general. The ones with power are afraid someone different from them is going to get power. So they do everything they can to prevent this from happening, even if it means lying, stealing, killing or whatever. The ones different from the ones in power are afraid they are never going to get power.

"So they either accept that they are going be treated different or they fight back. It does not matter whether you are black, white, green or blue, Gentile or Jew. It's all the same."

"So Mr. Whittier lied along with his daughter because he was scared his partners would put him out of their little power circle if he didn't?"

"That's just part of the truth. Bethann didn't lie on purpose."

"Aunt Sadie, how can you say that? Bethann didn't see Mr. Benjamin start that fire and you know it."

"I know Benjamin as well as you know him. I know he did not do it. I know Bethann too and she believes she saw him throw something right before that explosion. The truth is somewhere in between. It just has not come out yet. Now, Mr. Whittier is a Jew. He did not always own up to being a Jew because them partners of his would not have taken a liking to it. Plus, you know Mrs. Whittier was not going to have anything to do with it. Southern crackers hate Jews about as much as they hate nigg…I mean Blacks. Being a Jew has not been too popular down here in these parts. When 'the King,' as you call him, spoke against inequalities, he spoke for Jews too. But before that, Jews pretended not to be Jews so that they could get good jobs and raise their families decently."

"Well, my heart is bleeding for Bethann and Mr. Whittier and their good life while my Daddy is locked up in jail and been locked up for over ten years." Flustered and full of sarcasm, Indigo walked away from her conversation with her Aunt Sadie toward the screen of the back door.

"It's all going to come out, you'll see. Everything is going to work itself out. Your Momma, your Daddy and Magnolia are all going to come out just fine. You will see."

Indigo saw Rowell walking up the hill, heading in the direction of her back door.

"Make sure you let me know when 'the coming' gets here, Aunt Sadie. Because I cannot see it from where I am," Indigo spoke over her shoulder as she pushed the screen door open.

She was relieved to see Rowell making his way up the hill in a slow stride. The sight of him was a welcome diversion from all her Aunt Sadie's sage observations, interpretations and predictions. She yelled his name and started down the hill.

"Go, what's up?" he yelled back, stopping and looking up at her coming down the hill.

"You are what is up, or you are what I wanted to be up if you get my meaning." She tried to come off coy but she was breathing hard from running.

"Yeah, that's what I want to talk to you about," he told her with a serious look.

"Well, here I am, let's talk."

"Right here, right now? I have to go to the Student Union for a meeting right now. I can't do it right now," he resisted, looking at his watch and moving his feet from side to side.

"That was the problem in total, you couldn't do it then." She was curt with him and realized she should not have been.

"Why are you talking like that? What's with you?" he asked, puzzled by her tone.

"What's with me? All right, be that way then. But remember I'm not the one afraid to let my feelings show, Rowell." Her words cracked as they came out.

The voices of a group of female students coming down the hill made Indigo turn around. They were singing a song about the "pearls of an Alpha girl." They all were dressed in pink-and-green sorority paraphernalia. Rowell noticed them right away and began shifting his feet even more. Indigo sensed his agitation but wanted to continue their conversation.

"Listen, Go, we're tight. You know that…" his voice trailed off when a vision of pink and green fashioned in Greek letters and massive hair wiggled next to him.

"Hey, Raw baby," she cooed, standing so close they could've been slow-dragging without music.

"Desiree," he answered, rubbing the small of her back, easing his hand down to the top of her hips that spread to a perfect valentine. He gave her a quick kiss on the mouth.

"I know we said we'd meet at the Student Union but I got there early and I didn't want to wait. I knew I would probably see you on your way there. Some of my pledge sisters had to come this way so I walked with them, hoping to see the Raw."

"And you did, baby, in the flesh," he continued, nuzzling her like she was some exotic delicacy.

Desiree's pledge sisters stopped briefly, offering pleasantries to Rowell. When he and Desiree became entwined, they continued walking. They did not look in Indigo's direction and Rowell did not offer to introduce her. She was speechless. Her mouth hung open and her eyes felt misty. She could feel her heart inside her chest beating fast.

"He belongs to me. He has always belonged to me. What is she doing to him?" she asked herself, refusing to accept what she was seeing.

She had never imagined Rowell sharing his affections with someone else. The thought had just not occurred to her. At this point, she was not about to allow it to occur either.

"Excuse me, do you mind bringing this public display to a halt? Rowell and I were trying to have a conversation. One that does not require your presence, I might add," Indigo sassed.

"I don't hear Raw complaining," Desiree snapped with her eyes locked on Rowell.

"He is not the complaining type. He does not complain when he is kissing me either." Indigo slung her words like she was a boxer taking the first punch. She was trying to punish Desiree for calling Rowell "Raw."

"Hold up, Go! Where is this coming from? Desiree and I got a thing going on. It's not like that with us," Rowell interjected with decisiveness.

"What is it like then? We have always had a thing going on. Oh are we taking turns now Rowell?" She was fighting back tears, wondering how things had gotten to this point of demarcation.

Indigo's words set Rowell off in a begging sonnet to Desiree that could rival the vocals of begging baritone Barry White. That was hard to do, since Barry White was on every radio dial you turned to, singing one love ballad after the other. Desiree pushed him away and flung her hair from side to side.

"Baby, please, please, it's not like that. Go-Go and I have been friends for a long time. We grew up together. She is tripping. It's you, baby. You and me together," he pleaded with her.

"If it's you and me, then you better get rid of her quick, fast and in a hurry because I'm not down with this at all." Desiree pulled her arm from Rowell's grip and walked off.

"I'll handle this, baby. I will be up to your room in an hour, you will see. It's you, baby," he assured her, sending hard glances in Indigo's direction.

"I'm not jiving, Rowell," Desiree warned, walking farther down the hill.

"Go, I'm burnt with you. What kind of trip are you on, girl? We down but we are not like that. We are friends. Tight friends. But you cannot come out like that. You are messing me up, Go. What's with you?" Rowell vacillated from anger to curious concern.

"You've made your point. I misread. No big deal. You were just being friendly when you kissed me like you wanted me. You were just doing what a tight friend would do when you whisked me out of the eyesight of your hungry-looking partners coming on to me. I got it now, Raw. You were just doing your Max Daddy thing. It did not mean anything. So go on off to 'Miss Head of Hair' dressed in pink and green Greek letters before she changes her mind."

"You did misread me. I mean yeah, I am attracted to you. We got chemistry. I am a man. Those dudes are my friends but they are not good enough for you. I was just protecting you. I was high. Things got a little hot and heavy between us. Those things happen sometimes. That happened a long time ago. I've changed. You've changed. I care about you Go but things are different now."

"So you care so much about me you can't show me the way I need for you to. Is that it? It's funny how people can claim they care so much about you, then when you need them to show you they can't manage to make that happen." She was crying softly now.

"Go, for goodness sakes! What is all of this? This cannot all belong to me. It cannot. It's coming from somewhere else."

"It's coming from what I feel inside."

"From what you feel inside of where? You are bugging! It is coming from some fantasy you have decided you want to make real. It is not real, Go. It is not real. You can't just up and change our relationship without telling me first."

"I didn't just change it. It changed. Besides, everyone else in my life can change the way they feel in relationships when they want to," she blubbered, realizing she was taking their disagreement far beyond the two of them.

"And that's how I know this has nothing to do with me. You are fantasizing when you ought to be realizing. This ain't about what you feeling for me. You do not even know me. You do not know what I am feeling or why I feel that way. You do not know what I like or do not like in a woman. You are holding onto the Rowell who used to chase behind you in elementary school. You are holding onto the past too tight. I have changed. Everything has changed. The person you are holding onto is gone. Not because I *want* to leave you, because I *had* to. You want to hold on to me because you think it is safe. You think if you are with me, things will not change. Change got to come, Go!"

"Don't let all those psychology classes go to your head, Rowell, it's not that deep," she tried to minimize.

"It's deep enough for you to be out here trying to start something you dreamed up with my girl Desiree," he quipped.

"I don't dream. I have not dreamed in years."

"You need to! Maybe if you let yourself you would dream up something better than the confusion you are trying to start!"

"Well, now I've stopped trying to start something, so you can just leave now," she told him, trying to regain her composure.

"If that is what you want," he challenged her.

"That is what I want," she conceded.

He stomped up the hill heading in the direction of the Student Union, perplexed by the intensity of the conversation between him and Indigo. Indigo wiped her face with her hand and headed back up the hill to her duplex. This was the first argument they had ever had that Rowell did not suppress his position to accommodate Indigo's mood. Indigo walked up the hill missing him, even though she could have turned around and caught him if she wanted to. She wanted to but she was not sure he would wait.

"Maybe he was right," she thought to herself. "I've practiced in four long one-night-stand relationships since a night with Sam in his red Impala started the first one. I was trying to get some experience to prepare for Rowell. Guys took one look at me and decided either I was too serious or they wanted more than I was offering. If I got a date, I did not get a second. You doggone right, I wanted something familiar," she justified in her head. All of his words bothered her, but what Rowell said about "not wanting things to change" continued to spin a web of truth in her head.

"Go-Go, can you come sit with your Grandma while I go to the store and run some errands? I need to stop by Baker's Pharmacy to get her prescription filled. I shouldn't be too long," Aunt Sadie yelled down the hill.

"Okay," Indigo yelled back. "Go ahead and do what you have to do." Indigo was glad she would not have to explain her swollen red eyes to her Aunt Sadie. She came into the house and went into the bathroom to wash her face.

"Your Madear is in your Grandma Dovie's room but she's leaving shortly. Davis Jr. and Blueberry went to the movies," she yelled back, running to catch the bus.

"Peace and solitude," she thought to herself, heading to her Grandma Dovie's room with her writing tablet. When she came to the bedroom door, she could hear Madear talking.

"This not about you, Momma, I have a right to my—" Indigo could not hear the last word of her sentence because Drew's voice piped up, saying, "Cree, she seems to be getting upset. Maybe we should go now." His voice was more anxious than usual.

Indigo pushed the bedroom door open. Drew took Madear by the arm and started leading her toward the door. Madear stood firm and looked at Grandma Dovie with the hardness of a glass eye.

"I just wanted you to know, now I know, Momma, and I'm going to get what's due me if it's the last thing I do."

Then she let Drew lead her out of the bedroom without saying a word to Indigo.

Indigo dismissed the encounter and slipped into her Grandma's rocking chair. She fumbled in her pocket for her pen, then looked down, preparing to write in her tablet. The whites of Grandma Dovie's eyes caught her attention. The white matter was so brilliant it seemed to ooze out of the corner of her eyes. She was lying on her back, staring into space. She was flapping her good arm around on the bed. Saliva slid down her chin. Her facial muscles were pressing the wrinkles around the twisted part of her mouth. Indigo thought she smelled urine. She convinced herself to wait until she felt more relaxed before tackling changing her bed sheets.

Indigo wasn't alarmed by Grandma Dovie's condition because the doctor had told them stroke patients often stared aimlessly but were aware of their surroundings and capable of emotions, even if they couldn't communicate them. He told them to have one-sided conversations with Grandma Dovie to stimulate her. For a moment, she wondered what details were in Madear's conversation with Grandma Dovie. Then she began to say aloud the things roaming around in her head and pouncing upon her heart. Her reaction to Rowell's comments about change headed the list. In a not-so-distant second was her disappointment in the estrangement of the family she once knew. Next to that was her sadness for Grandma Dovie losing her voice again, just as they made a start in their relationship. Her one-sided conversation evolved into operatic sobs about the maladies of the Douglases, their King and their middle daughter.

Grandma Dovie turned in Indigo's direction. Her movement distracted Indigo from crying. She blinked her eyes incessantly and her mouth untwisted itself.

"It ain't no power in the change, honeychild," she said in a voice scratchy and hoarse.

"What? What did you say, Grandma?" Indigo asked, wiping the snot from running down the top of her lip.

"I say the power ain't in the change, it's in the coming. Changes are just the steps that bring the coming. Changes can start and stop just like the wind. When what is coming gets here, ain't no turning back. I am ready for the coming. The coming is the power," she explained through her fading voice.

Indigo sat spellbound, looking through the afternoon sunlight beaming through the window cascading against the silver strains of her grandmother's hair. A dark shadow moved slowly down beneath her hair and expanded across the fair skin of her forehead. Her words flowed smooth as silk out of her once-twisted mouth. Indigo wanted more silken words. She sat and leaned closer to her Grandma Dovie's bedside, keeping her eyes on her face. The dark shadow expanded to her eyes and began to cover her nose. She wondered again about the nature of Madear's conversation with Grandma Dovie. She tried to guess the last words of Madear's sentence. She had not been able to hear what Madear said clearly. The beauty of Grandma Dovie's face kept drawing her attention. The years of imposed silence between them lessened and they spoke without words. She stroked the back of her hand and the dark shadow completely covered her face. In a fleeting moment, her eyes turned upward and her pupils fixed on the ceiling. Indigo buried her head in the urine-soaked sheets covering her Grandma Dovie. She stifled her tears and prepared to embrace "the coming" because she knew Grandma Dovie was dead.

CHAPTER 26

"The mountaintop"

"I'm Officer Dupree, I'll need to ask you to answer some questions. I'm sorry for your loss, madam." The officer stood looking right in Indigo's face.

When Aunt Sadie came back from her errands, the Douglas household became a residence of wailing walls. She took one look at Grandma Dovie and fell to her kneels in a wail of screams and tears. Indigo did not remember moving from the Grandma Dovie's bedside. But when the police arrived, she and her Aunt Sadie were in the living room sitting on the sofa, consoling each other. Somebody in the 400 block of Osceola Street called the police and a crowd began to gather in the front yard. The police called the undertaker. When Davis Jr. and Blueberry came home from the movies, they had to tell the police that they lived there before they could come inside. Word of Grandma Dovie's passing spread quickly and those who knew her in the neighborhood came knocking on the door to express their condolences or stood in the yard sharing stories about meeting her during her wanderings.

The police officer spoke looking at both of them until Indigo told him she was home alone when Grandma Dovie died. In an official tone, he stated more than asked, "I will need to see the deceased now…ma'am." Indigo did not move at first because she did not realize he was talking about Grandma Dovie. Aunt Sadie nudged her and they went into Grandma Dovie's room. She was still lying in the bed with her eyes staring up at the ceiling. Aunt Sadie pressed her lips together and swallowed hard, then she dropped her shoulders and walked over to the bed. She reached in her pocket and took out two pennies. Then she put the pennies in the palm of her right hand and touched Grandma Dovie's forehead, gently rubbing the pennies down to her eyebrows until they sat atop her eyelids, closing her eyes. Then she pulled the white sheet all the way over her head.

Indigo told the police officer how she sat in the rocking chair talking to Grandma Dovie until her mouth untwisted and she spoke. The police officer took notes with a red ballpoint pen on a white pad encased with black leather. He nodded his head and offered a few unimpressed un-huhs. Most of his curiosity centered on the actual time of Indigo's conversation with Grandma Dovie and when everyone else left the house. Indigo provided the answers that filled in his blanks, offering the time she entered Grandma Dovie's bedroom until her Aunt Sadie returned. He did not ask and Indigo did not offer to tell him about the one-sided conversation she overheard Madear having with Grandma Dovie while Drew was in the room.

Madear came in with Drew around midnight. When Aunt Sadie gave her the news of Grandma Dovie's passing Madear had a fainting spell. Drew lifted her in his arms, carried her to the bedroom, and closed the door. No one else moved to revive her because the aura of grief surrounding Grandma Dovie's passing had engulfed the entire household and left it motionless.

By the time the police left and the undertaker left with Grandma Dovie's body, Aunt Sadie had put a black head scarf on her head, put on one of her long black house dresses, called Mr. Whittier and began making a to-do list. Indigo felt exhausted from repeating the chronology of Grandma Dovie's passing. She knew if she went to bed, she would not be able to sleep. Blueberry and Davis Jr. had fallen asleep lying across her bed. They talked for hours in memorial of Grandma Dovie. They also educated Indigo about themselves.

"She called me by my real name when we were alone. Blusette Marie," Blueberry boasted.

"She'd come on the back porch when I was polishing my shoes and tell me the walk of a man has many steps and to make sure my shoes could step to all of them. Then she would show me different ones. Mr. Somebody, Mr. Dap Daddy, Mr. Man in Charge, Mr. Sweetback, and Mr. I Ain't Gonna Do You Wrong," Davis Jr. confessed, grinning.

"Which one are you?" Blueberry teased.

"I'm still working on all of them but I got my mind on 'Mr. Somebody,'" he said in his seventeen-year-old voice cracking under the balance of emerging masculinity and emotions.

They wanted to know about the last minutes of Grandma Dovie's life.

"What did she talk about? Was she in any pain? Did she say something about either one of us? How did she look?" They bombarded her. Indigo tried her best to answer their questions before sleep overtook them. The bed was just a notch above comfortable when Indigo slept alone. She knew they would eventually find it uncomfortable and retreat to their own beds during the night. But for the moment, they needed the comfort that only siblings could offer.

When Indigo wandered into the kitchen, her Aunt Sadie began reading off her "to-do" list.

"We need to get in touch with Magnolia and your Daddy. Those are probably the hardest two things to do. I figured you could handle them since Cree and I have a mountain of things to do before we can get this funeral together."

"Yeah, I can do those two things. That is not a problem. Is there anything else I can do, Aunt Sadie?" Indigo pleaded.

"No, child, you done enough already," Aunt Sadie sighed.

"Are you mad at me, Aunt Sadie?" Indigo asked quietly.

"No, Go-Go. The Lord wanted to change your Grandma Dovie's residence so he sent his angels to come get her. You could not do anything about that kind of plan if you had known about it in advance. Now we got to focus on what we need to do here."

The headlights of a car shined through the kitchen window. Then there was a knock at the back door. The clock above the stove said it was after two o'clock in the morning. Aunt Sadie got up to go to the door, mumbling, "When death comes calling, so does everybody else.

"Come on in, Mr. Whittier. You and Bethann didn't have to come out here tonight. I appreciate your coming, though," Sadie thanked them and her eyes began to swell up again.

"I know you must have a lot to do and I wanted to know if we could be of assistance. We would have been here sooner but I had to travel to Port St. Joe to sign the final papers for—"

"Daddy, do you have to start with that?" Bethann interrupted.

"Well, Sadie, you know that Trin and I are divorcing. Of course you do. You are like one of the family, that's why I am here. What can I do to help you?" Mr. Whittier asserted.

Bethann looked embarrassed. Indigo's disdain for Bethann had grown over the years but her obvious pain softened her. She thought of the Saturday afternoon she and Bethann spent playing make-believe up in her attic. Everything seemed so perfect in Bethann's Dick and Jane world that day. She knew the Whittiers were getting a divorce because she overheard her Aunt Sadie talking about it. But seeing Bethann and watching her react to her world changing added a new dimension to her thoughts. In the attic, she felt Bethann's world was in a galaxy a million miles from her own. But in the kitchen that early morning, she realized there were parts of their worlds that were very close together.

"Well, sir, that's mighty kind of you. I just looked over the insurance policy Momma been paying the Penn Company every week for years and it only allows three thousand dollars for the burial. We think we're going to need a lot more than that. Course, I have not talked to Mr. Patterson from Eternal Rest Funeral Home. I do know a nice funeral costs more than three thousand dollars. I want my Momma to be laid out nice," Sadie said, letting the tears make a stream down her face and flow through her words.

Mr. Whittier reached over and embraced her. The wetness from her face saturated the hairs in his newly grown beard.

"We'll lay her out nice, Sadie. You and me together," Madear walked into the room and stood in front of Mr. Whittier and her sister.

"We can't do it by ourselves, Cree, we're stretching to make ends meet as it is. We have to pay for all Momma's medical bills, you know…there just is not enough money to go around. If Mr. Whittier wants to help us, this ain't no time to be holding a grudge," Sadie admonished.

"I'm not holding a grudge with him, I just want Momma's funeral to be dignified," Cree sneered.

"That's a switch for the better. It is what we all want, Cree. Let's just try to work together to make it happen," Sadie pointed out, extending her arm to Cree.

"Your Momma was a link to my mother. She helped me to understand her last days. My mother was so distant and sad when we came to this country. The memories of our abrupt leaving and constant hiding to stay alive tormented her. We had to hide to stay alive. The only other choice would have been to die. It was because of hiding that we lost my only brother. We left our homes to be at the mercy of strangers to hide us. We kept quiet until night, traveling long distances, giving up all our possessions that weighed us down. We bartered for food and gave up our Jewish ways to avoid persecution. We came to America hoping all of that was over. But it was not true. We had to hide our ways in this country too. It broke my mother's heart and no matter what my father or I did, we could not mend it. When the townspeople of Port St. Joe spoke of the Klan rides, it would remind her of our suffering in our old country. She spent hours down at the river collecting stones for the Jews who were not strong enough to make the hard journey with us to this country. She collected the stones and sang the songs to keep their memory alive. She had rows of stones lined up alongside the river as symbols of a life she loved and could not live.

"One night one of the town men came in the store and asked my father to come to a Klan meeting. There had been some trouble in town. A colored woman had castrated one of the Klan while they were on a raid. The colored woman had gotten away and they were determined to find her."

"Black woman, a black woman castrated one of the Klan," Indigo interjected.

"I know, but she was called colored back then, I meant no harm," Mr. Whittier apologized and continued his memorial to Grandma Dovie.

"They were signing up white men to help all over town.

"'It's a service to keep the community purified and the niggers in line,' the man told my father with my mother standing by his side and me watching from the back. He tried to convince them that it would help their business. My father nodded and declined the man's offer. 'Don't want to be so much out in the front, want to work behind the scenes, that's understandable. Everybody cannot be a leader,' the man spoke while spitting out tobacco.

"My mother was hysterical. It was like she was back in the old country preparing to run for her life. She lit candles in the back room of the store. She insisted to my father that she needed to go to the river to calm herself. She grabbed her wrap, running out into the night to collect stones at the river. She met your mother that night. Your mother was the colored woman who castrated one of the Klan. I did not know for sure until that day I drove you to the jail.

"Since that day, I have remembered everything about that night my mother left, running into the night. I remembered her face and the candles she lit every Friday night in the small room behind our store. I remembered the black clothing she wore to mark her sadness. I remembered the black cloth she draped over the mirror on the anniversary of my brother's birthday. I remembered her and my father speaking of being Jews in happier times. But nothing about being Jewish had been happy for me, so I abandoned that way of life. I wanted nothing to do with being Jewish. After my mother died, my father went north because he heard he would have to hide less. I wanted success. I changed my name to Whittier. I was prepared to continue to hide and I did. I was not prepared for the yearnings deep within to overpower my zeal for success to be true to my parents' teachings. It started out in small ways. I saw the decency in people who were different from myself, people like Benjamin. I came to know his struggle."

"You came to knew how Benjamin was and how he struggled. Then you rewarded him by making sure he stayed locked up with Hiram in jail for something he could not possibly have done...is that what you are saying?" Cree snapped.

"I realize how you feel. You think I was reacting out of malice, like my partners. It is true malice was part of my burning desire for success. But supporting what my daughter thinks she saw was one of the hardest things I ever had to do because I knew Benjamin. But it was the best thing that ever happened to me. It opened my eyes to my past and the voices of my parents. A man named Berns owns a title company in my office building. He helped me to see and hear differently. He is Jewish and lives in Levy County in a community of Jews. The first time I went to his office, I noticed the mezzuzah nailed to the frame of his office door. I stared at it because it reminded me of my parents and the life they yearned for. He did not say anything then but days later he asked me why did I pretend not to know. I did not answer him. His question haunted me until I went to see him again. We have become partners in business and in the struggle to eliminate the discrimination of Jews and other oppressed people."

"So now you got religion and Hiram and Benjamin are still doing time," Cree pouted.

"Yes, I have embraced my religion at all cost. I know now it is who I am. Levy owns a title company. He has been doing some research studies on the property where the explosion happened. The title was very difficult to get but we got it. It turns out the property was owned by a gas company more than sixty years ago. The gas company had underground pipes. We believe the surveyor hit one of the pipes and caused the explosion. We have a network of Jewish friends who are lawyers, doctors and any other professionals we might need. They are working with us so Jews can be Jews openly without discrimination. One of the lawyers is working with us now. He, Berns and I have met with Hiram and Benjamin to prepare an appeal. If the courts will hear our evidence, Hiram and Benjamin could get out of prison," Mr. Whittier beamed.

"You're going to need more magic than finding titles to some property to get two men out of prison who have already gone to court and confessed to a crime," Cree smirked.

"She's right, Mr. Whittier, Hiram and Benjamin did confess to causing that explosion," Sadie added.

"Sure they confessed, and they had some help from the deputies' nightsticks too. They were not given due process, which America has promised all Americans. I would not have pursued any of this if I did not believe it was right. One of the things my father said to me on the night that the Klansman tried to recruit him was, 'You have the responsibility to repair the world.' This is my chance to repair all the hurt that my corroboration with malice has caused. We have added to the appeal brief that Hiram and Benjamin were coerced into confessing. It could take a while but we believe the evidence is so strong it cannot be ignored," Mr. Whittier insisted.

"That's a wonderful fairy tale but it's too late. You see, I have gone on with my life. I have not waited around all these years for Hiram to get out of prison. I got plans too. As soon as Momma is put away, I am going to Port St. Joe to see about Mr. Schmidt and get what's rightfully mine, whatever it is."

"Momma ain't off her cooling board yet and you're trying to pick the pennies off her eyes. When will you ever stop, Cree?" Sadie tearfully demanded.

"They're not her pennies, Sadie. I told Momma that this afternoon before I went out. I am going after my real Daddy's pennies. Maybe he can pay for Madear's funeral. He added to the misery in her life," Cree tried to explain.

"You told Momma about this. Cree, what is wrong with you? What is inside of that chest of yours? Did it ever occur to you that maybe Momma wanted to let her past stay where it is? And if you were going to do it, why did you have to tell her about it in her condition? You're the only living relative I got left but you are also the meanest one too," Sadie said tearfully, walking to the kitchen window.

"You say your real Daddy's name is Schmidt, living in Port St. Joe?" Mr. Whittier queried.

"Yes, why?" Cree growled at him.

"There are a number of Schmidt families living in that area. It is probably a coincidence but my wife's maiden name is Schmidt. On the Port St. Joe side of the Apalachicola River, people pronounce it Smithee. On the Apalachicola side of the river, it is pronounced Schmidt. But they are all related."

"Why are we talking about all of this when Momma has just died? This is Cree's mess and frankly, I do not care to be hearing about it right now. Let her go see about her Daddy in Port St. Joe after Momma is buried," Sadie demanded.

"You're right, Sadie, I'm sorry. We can talk about this later. There is so much we have to do. We have to find Magnolia and get her here. I don't know how to began to get her here from Africa," Cree spoke, trying to take the focus off Mr. Whittier's comments.

"I have friends working in Washington, D.C. who can help you with that," Mr. Whittier added softly.

Indigo had heard enough. The changes in her family were still going on. Now she had learned there were changes in the Whittier family even though she thought it was almost perfect. She guessed the coming Grandma Dovie talked about on her deathbed had not come yet. It was almost four o'clock in the morning. The air and conversation in the kitchen were stifling in equal proportions. She just knew she needed to leave and get some air.

When she walked out the back door, the conversation between Mr. Whittier, her Madear and her Aunt Sadie was still going strong without resolution.

She almost tripped over Bethann sitting on the steps of the back porch. She inhaled the early-morning air and it filled up her lungs. She exhaled and sat down next to Bethann.

"What are you doing out here?" Indigo charged.

"Sitting," she sighed rolling three stones in her hands.

"Whatever happened to happily ever after? Is it too much to ask for a family to stay together?" she lamented.

"You're one to be asking that question. Your claim to have witnessed a crime is what started my family to break up," Indigo charged.

"As it turns out, that same eyewitness account has also played a part in my family breaking up, so I guess we're even," Bethann pointed out.

"It is not about winning or losing, it is about changes and dealing with what they bring," Indigo began to explain, to her own surprise.

"What if you cannot deal because you don't know how to deal? Who should I ask? My choices are my beloved mother who is stuck in the past along with all its prejudices or my newly Jewish father who is determined to repair the world. I am being pulled and forced to choose to walk two different ways. I need two legs to walk and the legs need to go in the same direction," Bethann said, standing to stretch her legs continuing to roll the stones in her hand.

"I know what you mean," Indigo added, following her around to the clothesline. "That's all I've been trying to do since everything blew up. I just wanted my family to be together like you want yours to walk together".

They stood looking at each other in silence for a moment recognizing the similarities in their sentiments. Bethann broke the silence first by walking away from the clothesline. She stumbled over a Budweiser can and fell on her behind just beyond the clothesline approaching a pile of trash.

"What the heck was that?" she chuckled, leaning back on her hands.

"It's the Molotov cocktail you saw Benjamin throw that night," Indigo told her, still laughing.

"What do you mean?" Bethann asked seriously now.

"I was too embarrassed back then. It wasn't any of your business anyway. People got a right to do what they want to when they are home. You were just too nosey!" Indigo espoused, reliving her sentiments of the past.

"What were you too embarrassed to tell me, Indigo?" Bethann demanded.

"Mr. Benjamin drank cans of Budweiser like that one you tripped on every night. I am sure he was drinking one that night. He even rode around in his car with Budweiser cans. If anything, he threw a can of beer. It was not a Molotov cocktail. That was beer oozing out of that can," Indigo finally told her.

"How do you know it was a beer can?" Bethann questioned.

"Because he told me it was," Mrs. Benjamin spoke up from her opened window near the trash pile between the duplexes.

"My Benjamin may be a lot of things, but a murderer he is not. He was just trying to stand up and be a man. He threw a beer can. A can that could in no way cause an explosion. He was so tired of trying to climb that mountaintop to success at that firm. Each time he got an inch, he was pushed back down. When they accused him of starting that explosion, that was most favor he had ever gotten, even if it was negative. The Black Panthers said he was a freedom fighter. He was just trying to get somebody to listen to him on his job. Now he's been in prison all this time wasting his talent," she expressed, looking through the screen at Bethann and Indigo before taking another swig of Budweiser in a can.

"I know what I saw," Bethann said firmly.

"You know what you think you saw because of what you saw on television. You weren't close enough to be sure that was not a beer can in Benjamin's hand. Think about what your father's title company friend said. There were gas tanks underneath the land they were surveying. The surveyor was hitting stakes in the ground. He could have punctured one of the tanks and caused an explosion. Think about it, Bethann! Can you really be sure?" Indigo pressed.

"No! I can't be sure now that I know all of this about the gas tanks being underground, but I was sure when I said it back then. It is hard and it has been hard for me to understand why my father is helping Benjamin and your father. My mother almost died in that explosion. He is the one with the newfound power to repair the world. I never said I found that power," Bethann defended her position.

"You got more power inside you than you think. What do you think made you keep coming over here to the duplex with and without Aunt Sadie? I made it clear I didn't want you around," Indigo challenged her.

"I kept coming because of Sadie. She is like a mother to me. Sadie is my power source. She has a way of making things all right. And I also came because I didn't have anyplace else to go," Bethann relented.

"If Sadie is your power source, then you must know that she is that and more to me and my family. You cannot separate Sadie from us. We are part of the same fabric. I am not saying I am all right with being connected to you. I'm not even saying I like you and I'm for sure not saying I forgive you for all the trouble what you think you saw caused. What I am saying is changes in both our families just keep coming. I cannot do anything about them coming but I am ready to use everything in my power to deal with them instead of letting the changes deal with me," Indigo proposed.

"Would that be the 'Iko' power you carry in that high chest of yours?" Bethann teased.

"I did say you try to know too much, didn't I? How did you know about 'Iko'?" Indigo insisted, partly astonished and partly chuckling at Bethann's familiarity.

"You said yourself Sadie was part of the same fabric that you're connected to and I'm connected to Sadie," Bethann giggled.

The sun rose with the two of them sitting on the steps leading to the back porch exchanging familiarities about their families in hoarse voices and bloodshot eyes too tired to sleep or rest. When Mr. Whittier came out of the back door proclaiming the goodness of the morning, they stood up and walked down the steps and made way for him to pass. Mr. Whittier beckoned Bethann to get in the front seat of the car and promised to return. Bethann stood to comply leaving the three stones she juggled in her hand throughout their conversation. Indigo stared at the stones and drifted back to the afternoon she played with Bethann in her attic.

Indigo waved good-bye to them as they drove out of the dirt-filled circular driveway behind the duplex. Bethann looked back through the back window before they turned to go up Osceola Street and their eyes locked again together again in a budding friendship.

With everything that had happened yesterday, she doubted if anyone had brought the mail in. She thought of her Aunt Sadie's "to-do" list. She needed to start figuring out a way to get in touch with Magnolia. She considered taking Mr. Whittier up on his offer to help. It had been months since she heard from her, even though she had written her every night in January after each episode of "Roots" went off. She dug her hand deep inside the black regulation mailbox and pulled out a letter from Magnolia and letters for Madear. She tore the letter open and began reading it on the front porch.

Dear Go-Go,

I know you and all the Douglases are wondering why you have not heard from me. I have been moving around a lot. I love Africa. I really do. It is the motherland. I believe that within my soul. Unfortunately, not all the Africans in Liberia believe American blacks are a part of the motherland. This is why I was living on the coast of Liberia. The coast is where Americo-Liberians live. It's funny, Liberia was set up to be a republic for freed American slaves. It was supposed to honor our independence. But Go-Go, this is far from true. There has always been tension between the tribes and the government. Our President, who was an Americo-Liberian, died in 1971 and everything has gone downhill from there. His vice president took over and within months, he was assassinated in Liberia's first military coup. The coup is being led by an army sergeant called Samuel K. Doe. He is a member of the Krahn tribe and is vying for power. There is so much fighting going on because of who and what everyone is or is not, it makes me sick to my stomach. I had big dreams, Go. Dreams that Africa would hug me until I stopped thinking about Madear and my white father, whoever he is. Dreams that Africa was so black a white speck like me would blend into the darkness. I have a deep tan but let's face it, sister, we both know, I am nearly white.

I proved it to myself the other day. I was traveling with my friend Ebo up the mountains along the Liberian-Guinea border. Some of Doe's rebels approached us with machetes and guns. They began to harass Ebo, threatening to kill him because he was not from their tribe. I was so scared my knees were shaking. They thought I was one of the white missionaries and I let them. I let them think I was white. The very identity I have been resisting for half my life. When they asked me if he was my "man servant" I said yes. Go-Go, Ebo is my lover. He is a strong African man but that day on the mountaintop, he needed my whiteness to save his life. And you know when they let us go and I stood on the top of that mountain, I was glad for my whiteness. Right now, I am living in the mountains with Ebo but it is not safe. We will be moving once the rainy season begins. I got some of your letters about

"Roots." They were more than a month old when I got them. I think the whole idea behind "Roots" is fascinating. It has increased commerce in Senegal. Ebo and I are considering moving there. Many Americans are traveling to Senegal, trying to find their roots and bringing their US dollars. I am glad. Finally, it is known our seed began in Africa. But Africa is not utopia. There are still things like skin color, tribe membership and hyphen status that create fear, gain power and try to destroy the love affair with the motherland. But then you know these things because they are in America too. I will write as much as I can. Do not write to me because we are moving around. Doe's rebels will only take any packages that you send. I love all of you.

Magnolia

Indigo read the letter from Magnolia repeatedly. She looked at the date and it was more than two months old. The thousands of miles that separated Africa from Tallahassee seemed to multiply. Each mile seemed like a mountain too high to climb. Then she pressed her lips together, swallowed hard, exhaled and walked inside, holding her chest up high.

CHAPTER 27

"Promised"

April 1977

It took two days for Mr. Whittier's friend in Washington to get an answer from the Liberian consulate about Magnolia's whereabouts. It was another two days before they could arrange for her to fly home. Madear insisted the funeral service not be held until Magnolia arrived. She did not care if it did mean Grandma Dovie's funeral was going to be a week after she died. Aunt Sadie threw up her hands and gave into Madear's wishes. She said she did not care what Madear did as long as her Momma was buried decent and in order. The neighbors from the 400 block to the 800 block of Osceola Street were talking about how long we kept Grandma Dovie laid out on her cooling board. Rowell told me it was the talk of his Daddy's mail route. I barely spoke to Rowell when he called to offer his condolences. I think it was nice of him to call, considering how we ended our last conversation. I was not in the mood for any kind of nice talk with him. Aunt Sadie overheard her landlady, Mrs. Jenkins, talking on the telephone to Mrs. Wallace down in the 600 block. She was speculating the reason we kept Grandma Dovie on her cooling board so long was because she was part Indian. She was just about to go into detail with her version of Indian beliefs when Aunt Sadie walked in. The woman would not know an Indian if one walked up and knocked on her door. They were just sitting on the telephone gossiping, making up stuff where they did not have answers. Grandma Dovie never had anything to do with either of them. Madear and Aunt Sadie finished the obituary. It said, "Sunset service for Bright Star Dove Weatherspoon." All I ever knew was Grandma Dovie. I wished she would have told me more about her Indian ways. Her real name is beautiful, just like she was. I do not care about all the stuff the neighbors are talking about. Maybe I will later or maybe I will not ever again. Right now, my Grandma is gone and I miss her. I miss all the time I am not going to get to know her. Mr. Whittier called the Prison Board and got them to let Daddy Douglas to come to the funeral. Mr. Whittier did what he promised. He was wrong about Daddy Douglas and Mr. Benjamin's appeal though. The courts denied the appeal. Mr. Whittier says he will not stop though. He says he is going to write the Governor after the funeral. I got to give him an "A" for effort. Daddy Douglas will not be wearing his black suit. He is going to have to wear his prison uniform. It does not matter. Everybody in my family is going to be together for the first time since everything changed.

Indigo

At ten o'clock a blue hearse was parked in the circular dirt-filled driveway near the back porch of the duplex on the morning of Grandma Dovie's funeral. The sweet smell of crate myrtle buds blossoming in the air and the backdrop of fuchsia and white azaleas bursting until their yellow pistils peaked confirmed spring was in the air. The Springtime Tallahassee parade was scheduled to celebrate spring in a few hours.

"Grandma Dovie never lost her ways of celebrating the seasons. She loved the Tallahassee Springtime parade so much she would wander all day up and down the parade route. She just wanted to be a part of it. She told me one year she was going to stop the parade just long enough to get in," Aunt Sadie remembered. So when Cree insisted the funeral wait until Saturday, the same day as the parade, Aunt Sadie said she was inclined to go along with it. Grandma Dovie would walk out on the back porch every morning after breakfast. Look up at the bright sky full of puffy white clouds and head out for one of her walking wanderings. Grandma Dovie's body rested in the hearse inside the white coffin with silver handles on the side, but maybe Aunt Sadie thought to herself when she looked out at the hearse, "Her spirit has already started walking." Aunt Sadie instructed the undertaker to bring her body as close to the back porch as he could get her.

"She spent a lot of nights sitting on that back porch just looking at the sky. She always told me when you look at the sky, you can see all that you can have. Once you see it, then it is up to you to go after it," Aunt Sadie sobbed. "I just want her to be near her favorite place once more before she leaves us," she told the undertaker.

The phone rang nearly a dozen times before everyone could get dressed for the funeral. First Magnolia announcing her plane had been delayed in New York. She fretted about making it to Tallahassee in time enough for the funeral. Then she called back saying the real reason for the delay was because she changed her flight arrangements. She downgraded her ticket for a cheaper flight because she wanted Ebo to travel with her. She was calling back because she did not want anyone to be upset about Ebo being with her. The only way he could travel with her was if they took a cargo flight. The cargo flight left later than the flight she was scheduled to travel on. "It was bumpy but no more turbulent than life in Liberia since Doe and his rebels had been ravaging the countryside," she explained in way too much detail, considering the circumstances. She insisted Ebo had to come with her because "I have been with him nearly ten years and he is part of me!" Aunt Sadie announced Magnolia's conversation from the telephone in the hallway. Aunt Sadie nodded and assured Magnolia, "I promised my Momma I would bury her decent and in order. It wouldn't be decent and in order if you weren't here, so hurry up and get here."

Magnolia had been gone more than ten years, but she was pulling the rank of being the "oldest" like it had been ten minutes, Indigo thought to herself while brushing her teeth in the mirror. "It's beginning to feel like old times 'BK,'" she mused.

The correctional officer who would be escorting Daddy Douglas to the funeral called for directions. He told Aunt Sadie he had gotten the approval for Daddy Douglas to come by the duplex before going to the church service for the funeral. Daddy Douglas had a five-hour pass from the prison. The correctional officer said he didn't care how he used those hours, just as long as he and his family knew he would be carrying his gun in his hand. He warned, "If anything the slightest bit out of the ordinary occurs, I will not hesitate to use deadly force." She assured him deadly force would not be necessary. Her Momma's funeral was going to be decent and in order. "Momma would not want her sunset service to have a hand in any kind of deadly force."

Madear answered the phone when Rev. Hester called. He was speaking loudly, like he was in the pulpit. Madear held the receiver away from her ear as he spoke. He said he was calling just to make sure everything was moving along in timely fashion. He had scheduled another funeral in Wacissa later that afternoon. He wanted to complete Grandma Dovie's funeral by two o'clock in order to get to Wacissa by three-thirty. Madear put her hand over the telephone receiver and called out to Aunt Sadie

"Rev. Hester wants to know if Momma's funeral is going to start at twelve and be over by two, or is it going to be operating on colored people time? He's got somebody else to bury."

"Cree, did he really say that?" Aunt Sadie asked curiously.

"No, not exactly, but that's what he meant," Madear called back.

Aunt Sadie picked up the extension and assured Rev. Hester Grandma Dovie's funeral was going to be decent and in order.

Mr. Whittier drove up and parked his big Mercury on the side of the duplex so that he would not interfere with the funeral procession of the family cars. Bethann sat quietly on the passenger side. Albert Whittier had been up since dawn. His newly ex-wife Trin had called him four times from Port St. Joe before nine o'clock. She called demanding additional items out of the Killearn house she had given up in the divorce settlement in lieu of cash. She had already moved a truckload of furniture and other things to Port St. Joe that were stipulated in the divorce decree she could have. Mr. Whittier told the Judge his "interest was not into holding onto the things of my marriage life but rather letting go of them so that I can begin to live my life."

Trin Whittier was insisting Albert Whittier allow Bethann bring her the things she wanted. She claimed she needed all of the furnishings from her Killearn home to continue the lifestyle she had grown accustomed to. It seems she had grown accustomed to the name "Whittier" also. She ,opted not to return to her maiden name, "Schmidt." Only a few people knew her real name anyway, she claimed. In Port St. Joe they called her by called her uncle's name, "Smithee." "Schmidt" or "Smithee" were not names she intended to use when she re-entered the social circles of Port St. Joe.

Another reason she was determined to get as much out of the house as she could was because she knew Albert Whittier was putting the house on the real estate market on Monday. She also knew Albert Whittier planned to sell the house with everything in it. She stopped ranting about the furnishing she was leaving behind long enough to listen to Albert Whittier's off-handed remark about Sadie's sister Cree's real Daddy being a white man named Schmidt in Port St. Joe. She did not have anything else to say to Albert Whittier after that. "

She revisited her lineage in her mind. Her real Daddy was dead before she ever got to know him. "He never bothered to marry Momma. She was just one of his port stops while in between a game of playing fast-hand poker. Momma always talked about him having had a good hand at poker and lavished his winning on her. But he stopped making port stops at her house when she told him she was pregnant. Momma kept up with his whereabouts through his brother in Port St. Joe. She married the neighbor's 'good-for-nothing-but-drinking son' after I was born. When Momma died and he drank himself to death I went to find my Uncle Smithee. Some of

Momma's letters led me to him, even though he was not that glad to see me. My real Daddy cannot be the same 'Schmidt' Momma loved so much and the father of that nigger Cree. What white man didn't have some 'little nigger' children somewhere? That is what happened back then. It does not mean anything. Just because coloreds have decided they want to know more about their roots, does that mean the whole world is supposed to help them? I am not about to give up all I have gained because of some notion a Hollywood movie planted in the small minds of colored people. If niggers want to go to the trouble of finding their roots, they better be ready to accept where they lead and leave well enough alone for everybody's sake," she pondered to herself, scanning over her furniture list.

She quickly dismissed her thoughts and stopped her demanding about the furnishings and ordered Albert Whittier to let her speak to her daughter. She told Bethann to make sure she let Sadie know when she went to the funeral that she would "push up daisies before I let that 'nigger woman Cree' have any of my things in that duplex of hers." When Bethann tried to tell her mother she did not want to be involved in a fight between her and her father about the furnishings in the house, Trin Whittier tried to soften her approach.

She said, "Bethann, I'm as fond of Sadie as you are. She took good care of you while I was in the hospital and she is a good cleaning woman too. But the fact remains her sister Cree sat watching me die before help came and saved my life."

Suddenly, Bethann remembered the night of the explosion. She visualized her mother lying on the stretcher as clear as it happened. She could hear the ambulance attendants saying, "The colored woman helped saved her life." Her mother did not hear the words the ambulance attendants said that night. Bethann had tried not to hear them. Now the words rang in her head drowning out her mother's voice.

Bethann repeated her telephone conversation with her mother verbatim to her father. Afterwards he forbade her from using the word "nigger" in his presence. Bethann tried to tell him that she was only repeating what her mother said to her. He said, "Hatred spreads through the power of one," and refused to discuss the matter any further.

A portion of their trip from Killearn to the 400 block of Osceola Street was silent. Bethann periodically glanced at her father driving his big Mercury across town. She wondered if his calling to repair the world would one day call her. He occasionally returned her glance, speculating how he could make sure she got the call.

Davis Jr. sat next to Madear, wearing a starched white shirt with a black tie and perfectly pressed black suit, in the stretch limousine waiting in front of the 400 block of Osceola Street. He held Madear's white-gloved hand in his own big muscular vein-popping hand in a protective sort of way. He announced last night he would help carry Grandma Dovie's casket because he felt a "man" in the family should. Madear looked at him with understanding eyes, realizing the way he saw himself.

Drew opted not to ride in the limousine because of Daddy Douglas's anticipated arrival. Madear leaned against Davis Jr.'s broad shoulders, sucking up the mucous in her nose and wiping away dabs of water that sprang from her eyes. Periodically he looked down at his reflection in his shiny black polished shoes and nodded his head up and down, flinching emotion in his face. The back-porch course in man training that Daddy Douglas gave him and Grandma Dovie reinforced had paid off in dividends.

Drew came to the family limousine and stroked Cree's hair through the car window. He stroked her hair and just stood there as if he was trying to decide if he should get in or stay out. Cree argued with Sadie that Drew had just as much right as anybody to ride in the limousine with the family to the funeral, but Sadie would not hear it. She insisted that it would not be decent and she was bound and determined her Momma's funeral was going to be decent and in order. She declared Grandma Dovie's spirit would just linger around the 400 block of Osceola Street and not be able to take its rightful resting place if Drew, Daddy Douglas and the correctional officer rode together to the funeral service. Cree did not want to but she acquiesced to Sadie's wishes.

Drew had been her white knight in shining armor when Hiram went to prison. He was the first to pursue her after she actualized her whiteness. When her Momma said her Daddy was white in the visiting room of the jail, it gave her power. Power to be one or the other. Before that, she had lived a life of in-between. That afternoon was one of legitimacy propelling her out of the dark depth of one status to the echelons of another. She was angry with her Momma for taking so long to acknowledge her birthright. "Momma just didn't know my pain. If she would have just told me sooner, it would have made everything different," she thought to herself. Now she felt legitimacy had escalated her to the circle she wanted to be in and she was not looking back, even if she had to bury her Momma to fully enjoy it.

As much as she did not want to admit it, she knew in small towns like Port St. Joe and Apalachicola Schmidt and Smithee families could be from the same family tree. She also knew the real possibility her nemesis Trina could be a branch from one of those trees. "

"It didn't matter today," she told herself.

She contemplated where the search for her roots had taken her. From the moment she learned her roots extended beyond what she knew, it had changed her life. She wanted acceptance. When she learned her father was white, the news was the legitimacy she craved. It gave her permission to belong somewhere. The contradictions didn't matter, she told herself again. Life was full of contradictions. For starters, she was a part of Martin Luther King's dream that Hiram went to jail in protest of. She laughed to herself at the irony. She knew Hiram never dreamed his standing up was going to make his world change like this. But she was a part of that dream all the same, she vowed to herself. She looked down at her arms and legs and thought, "And that dream has made me comfortable in my own skin."

Blueberry walked with Aunt Sadie down the back-porch steps. Blueberry had cheerfully tolerated Aunt Sadie's fussing over the folding of the funeral service programs. Aunt Sadie wanted them "just right." Blueberry tried to fold them "just right" because when she told Madear and Aunt Sadie she wanted her real name printed in the program, they did not object. Madear told her "it was such a small thing to ask." To Blueberry, it was the biggest thing she ever asked for. When she got to the last porch step, she handed the undertaker the box of programs. The undertaker took one of the programs out of the box and flipped it open.

"They came out real nice, didn't they?" he asked, looking over his glasses.

"Yes, sir!" Blueberry answered.

"Which one of the grandchildren are you?" he asked, smiling.

"I'm Bluesette Marie," she answered, enjoying the sound of her own name. "See, there it is, right under the list of grandchildren, 'Bluesette Marie Douglas.'"

They both smiled. Indigo stood watching them, continuing to be amused by her baby sister's increasing maturity. Indigo heard the screeching of wheels and continued her walk down the steps. Blueberry walked toward her. The undertaker took his seat under the steering wheel inside the hearse.

The taxicab driver was driving so fast he stopped the cab with two of the wheels resting on the curb. A black man and a fair-skinned woman emerged from the green taxicab with "Quick Service" written in white lettering on the side. The man wore sandals and a gold embroidered long tunic top with matching pants. He had a small hat on his head that matched his outfit. The woman was graceful as a swan. She was dressed in a beautiful white long dress with intricate patterns of threading. Her white head wrap was piled so high on her head it looked like a hat. She wore a matching shawl draped across her shoulders. She stood outside the cab for a moment, looking around. Then she knelt and kissed the ground. The man stood beside her and helped her to stand when she lifted her lips from the dirt. After the woman stood, Indigo recognized her sister. But all the eyes of Osceola Street that could see were on the pageantry that stepped out of that taxicab. Indigo ran toward her with outstretched arms, signaling the rest of the Douglas clan to come running to welcome Magnolia in a family huddle. Madear came first, slowly making her way up to her first-born, Magnolia. She looked curiously at the daughter whom she created as one to bypass life's pain of standing in between. She looked, admiring her beauty, searching for some kind of evidence Magnolia to mark the time Magnolia had been gone. Magnolia stepped back when Madear approached her at first and Indigo, her siblings and Aunt Sadie stepped back to allow Madear to get closer.

Magnolia extended her arms in a grand gesture to Madear. "Mother," she said in a dialect tinged with her Southern upbringing and the years she spent in Africa. Madear had only to hug Magnolia and to look at Ebo at her side to see Magnolia's confidence and pride

After the Douglas reunion had gone on in the circular dirt-filled driveway for twenty minutes, the undertaker walked up to the family and said in a controlled bereaved tone, "Sister Weatherstone, Sister Douglas, we really need to be moving along. We are running about a half-hour behind schedule and I've been keeping the car running so the air conditioning could keep your Momma's body comfortable in this eighty-degree weather."

"We can't leave until Hiram gets here! He is on his way. The correctional officer called to get directions," Aunt Sadie exclaimed, fanning her neck with her hands.

"We're paying you good money, Mr. Patterson, so you should wait until we're ready," Madear glared.

Albert Whittier watched the huddled conversational antics of Mr. Patterson, Sadie and Madear from a distant. He could not see Sadie's face, which he could read like a book, but he could see Mr. Patterson's face. He recognized Mr. Patterson from their brief meeting when he took Sadie to his funeral home to make the additional deposit needed for Grandma Dovie's funeral service. Mr. Patterson had initially said he would not take a check. But when Albert Whittier pulled out his checkbook to pay the deposit, he quickly changed his mind. Albert Whittier began walking in the direction of Mr. Patterson's conversation with Sadie and Madear to see if he was needed to change his mind again.

"It's not about the money, Mrs. Douglas, it's about my being able to provide you good service. I have been burning a lot of gas just sitting in your driveway. There is a gas shortage going on, you know! If we do not hurry up and leave, we are going to be stuck in this driveway because of the floats passing. The floats for the Springtime Tallahassee parade are coming up Osceola Street to begin their route at Adams Street. Once they start making their way up this street, we will not be able to get out of this yard for a good hour. By then it will not matter because we will be out of gas and cannot move anyway," Mr. Patterson replied, clasping his hand together to make his point.

"You just can't leave now, it's been months since the children have seen their father, and this is a family occasion. Please work with us, Mr. Patterson," Aunt Sadie pleaded.

"I'll work with you until my gas runs out and then you will have to replace it," Mr. Patterson demanded, looking at Albert Whittier.

"All right, you got a deal," Aunt Sadie said hastily, turning away to look at the blue government-looking car coming up the driveway.

Hiram Douglas sat in a dark-brown khaki uniform on the passenger side of the dark-blue government official four-door sedan. The correctional officer was sweating in his hair and he was frustrated because he knew he was late. He brought the car to an abrupt stop right at the beginning of the dirt-filled circle. He got out of the car, wiping his head with a white handkerchief, and walked around to the passenger side. He opened the door and helped lift Hiram out of the car. Hiram's hands were handcuffed together with a chain leading to shackles around his feet. His face broke into a broad smile when he recognized his children. His smile shrank when his eyes fell on the tanned white woman dressed in African garb. Magnolia watched him, tentatively reaching for the hand of her companion, Ebo, as she did when they ran from Doe's militia in Liberia. Indigo, Blueberry and Davis Jr. raced to him. They tried to grab on to him but his cuffed hands could not move to return their affection. The correctional officer walked over to Aunt Sadie and Madear, who both stood staring at Hiram and began grumbling about his late arrival. He said there was an uprising at the prison in Raeford right before they were scheduled to get on the road. The inmates were rioting because of the overcrowded conditions. Albert Whittier stood listening to the correctional officer's report of the inmate uprising and blurted out, "The prison wouldn't have a problem if they would let the innocent go." Then he walked over to Hiram and embraced him, made a pivot, turning him around, and talked in private.

The correctional officer turned to Aunt Sadie and Madear. Then he asked, "Am I going to have a problem?" He pulled back the right side of his jacket, exposing his gun to emphasize his preparation for any answer that could be offered.

"Everything is going to be fine. Just fine," Aunt Sadie assured him.

Mr. Paterson jumped out of the hearse and walked hard, kicking a dusty cloud going up the dirt-filled circular driveway. He warned Aunt Sadie and Madear again that he was about to run out of gas. Now he added the threat of not making it to the cemetery if they didn't leave now.

Aunt Sadie and Madear didn't pay much attention to Mr. Patterson's threat because their eyes were on the long line of colorfully decorated flatbed trucks making their way up the hill of Osceola Street. They looked at each other.

Madear said to Aunt Sadie, "Maybe if we hurry, our funeral car processional can get out of the driveway before the floats completely stop the traffic." Madear's words were barely out of her mouth before Mr. Patterson jumped in the hearse and put it in drive. He pressed the gas pedal as hard as he could. He was determined to drive the hearse out of the driveway before the parade came up the hill. The minute the hearse touched the asphalt of Osceola Street, the engine made a "chugging" sound and sputtered. He pressed the pedal harder, trying to make a wide turn. The engine made the chugging sound again, then stopped completely. The hearse straddled across the median of Osceola Street. Mr. Patterson turned the key in the ignition three times and patted the gas pedal with his foot. The hearse would not move. It was out of gas. He got out of the hearse and stood with his arms folded, rolling his eyes at Madear and Aunt Sadie standing in the yard.

Aunt Sadie in her usual take-charge manner squinted her eyes with determination and replied, "Let's start Momma's funeral."

Madear stretched her eyes in disbelief. "Sadie, what are you doing?

"Having Momma's funeral decent and in order. We are going to have Momma's funeral on the four hundred block if we have to," she answered, walking over to the crowd of neighbors and funeral watchers gathered in the yard.

Albert Whittier convinced the correctional officer Hiram would not pose a threat if he removed the handcuffs off his hands so he could help lift Grandma Dovie out of the hearse. The correctional officer stopped short of unshackling his feet. When Hiram told the correctional officer he wanted to be a pallbearer, the correctional officer laughed.

"If you think you can carry a casket on your shoulders and walk in shackles without falling, I want to see it."

Hiram motioned for Davis Jr. to stand behind him as Albert Whittier and the other pallbearers lined up to lift Grandma Dovie out of the hearse. Davis Jr. watched his father order his steps in the chains around his feet and brace his shoulders to carry his share of the casket. Davis Jr. walked behind him, eyes and ears opened to a manhood training lesson. They sat Grandma Dovie at the base of the front porch steps with the front of the casket facing Osceola Street and the stalled Springtime Tallahassee parade. One of the pallbearers misjudged a step and caused the casket to plop down hard on the concrete landing. The casket popped opened and Grandma Dovie's hand fell out. Mr. Patterson quickly tucked the hand back in but not before some of the funeral watchers of the 400 block of Osceola Street saw it.

One of them said, "Grandma Dovie is speaking from the grave."

Albert Whittier stooped down and placed three stones on top of Grandma Dovie's casket. His mother's nightly chant began to play in his head, echoing softly through his lips.

"Heavenu Shalom aleheu."

Bethann watched her father repeating the chant. She could see in his face the words enthralled him. She hesitated at first but then she tried mouthing the words until she felt comfortable to give them sound.

Magnolia began dancing around Grandma Dovie's casket. She danced possessed of a rhythm beating deep within her soul, losing her head wrap and exposing her long sun-drenched brown silk hair. Her movements told a story flowing rapidly out into the crowd through her raised hands and lifted feet until they embraced her tempo. Daddy Douglas grinned with the kind of pride a father shows when watching a daughter.

When she finished dancing, Ebo looked at the sky, checking the direction of the sun. Then he placed his hands to his ears and began singing:

"Allah u Akabar Allah u Akbar."

Hiram walked over beside him and began singing the same song. Madear nudged Aunt Sadie and asked, "Who are they calling and what are they saying?"

Aunt Sadie turned toward the Springtime Tallahassee floats stalled in procession on Osceola Street.

"I don't know and it doesn't matter what it means to them. To me it means Momma got what was promised."

Epilogue

November 2, 1977

Dear Iko,

I promised that I would write to you until my Daddy came home. Looks like that time has come. Daddy Douglas is coming home. Daddy Douglas and Mr. Benjamin are to be released from prison in one day. They will come out together just the way they went in. A dream changed my family and my life and I resented that. I vowed never to dream again. When Daddy Douglas comes home, it will be a dream come true for everybody even if the pieces are different than expected. What a day that is going to be. Mr. Whittier helped them get on the early release program because of the overcrowding in the jails. They will still have to be on probation for two years but at least they will be home. Mrs. Benjamin has already packed her bags to move. She says she and her husband need a new beginning to start over. Mr. Benjamin is going to Levy County to work with Mr. Berns. I have not felt so excited since the whole family came home for Grandma Dovie's funeral. I thought my heart was going to just beat itself right out of my chest. My whole family was on the 400 block of Osceola Street the way it used to be. It was not the funeral that Aunt Sadie and Madear had in mind. But we all will never forget it. Mr. Patterson's hearse gave out of gas in the middle of Osceola Street and the Springtime Tallahassee floats could not make their way to the beginning of the parade route on Adams Street. The floats were lined up so tight they could not turn around. The floats stood lined up behind Mr. Patterson's hearse straddling Osceola Street while we had

Grandma Dovie's funeral in the front yard. Grandma Dovie finally got in her parade. It made the front page of the Tallahassee *Democrat.* The headline said, "Funeral Service Delays Springtime Parade." It was only delayed an hour. Some city official sent Madear and Aunt Sadie a letter threatening to fine them a fee because the parade was delayed. Aunt Sadie showed the letter to Mr. Whittier and Rev. Hester. They went to city hall and had a meeting with some town officials. It seems like those city officials are busier trying to answer Rev. Hester and Mr. Whittier's questions about why it took the sunset service of an eighty-year-old black woman who wandered all over Tallahassee to draw attention to the fact that the lives of white folk are the only ones re-enacted in the pageantry of Tallahassee's history. Maybe the Springtime Tallahassee parade is going to look a little different from now on. And now Daddy Douglas is coming home.

Magnolia is leaving for Senegal with Ebo tomorrow. They have plans to open a tour company on the Goree Island. They are going to capitalize on the bustling African tour business, now that blacks are going to Africa by the droves. Magnolia spent the last two years in the States finishing her degree in political science while Ebo worked and saved money for their business. Magnolia says it is her second call to the motherland. The first call she learned to love herself. Now when she goes back she will help others in their quest for identity and acceptance. Leave it to Magnolia to make a resume out of her beliefs. I am going to really miss her. I am not worried about my family being all split up the way I used to. Even though Madear and Drew left on a two-week exploratory trip to Arizona last week. Drew's family owns some land out there. If Madear likes it, she says they will stay. She said she needed a vacation after her two-year court battle with Trin Whittier ended in declaring them "half-sisters without an inheritance." The only thing they both got was a relationship with someone they despised. I went with Aunt Sadie over to Mr. Whittier's new house last spring. The house is near the new Jewish synagogue he helped build on Miccouskee Road. Bethann was there. We still disagree about what happened that night. The more we talk, the more we find our differences are similar. Aunt Sadie and I did this Seder dinner with her and Mr. Whittier. Mr. Whittier said it was a part of Jewish custom and was a dinner for healing and forgiveness. The wine was real sweet going down but it gave me a bad headache afterwards. And the food was nothing to write home about. Bethann and I laughed about it afterwards. She said she is studying to become a Jew. She tried to tease, saying she already knew what it was like to have blacks in her family. I know she was trying to make nice of Madear and her mother's relationship. Aunt Sadie said Bethann had been in the "family" for years and her mother's court case just made it legitimate. In a way, Aunt Sadie was right. I guess we got to get used to each other if we are going to "repair the world" like Mr. Whittier said over dinner, because Madear and her half-sister Trin are not about to.

Davis Jr. is living in a dormitory at Florida State. He got a baseball scholarship. I guess he may become another Satchel Paige after all. Bluesette and Aunt Sadie are going to be the only ones living in the duplex of Osceola Street until Daddy Douglas comes home. I am going to graduate from FAMU in December. I am one of the fall 1979 graduating class facing the world for the new decade. I accepted a job in a medical research lab in a small town in Connecticut. I start work at the end of January. After I got the job, I saw Rowell's father delivering the mail on the 400 block of Osceola Street. I told him about it and he gave me Rowell's phone number in New York. I had heard he was going away to law school but I did not know where he was going. We lost touch after that "Desiree" blow-up. I wonder is he still with her? I was just going through a lot of things back then. Some of the things he said to me were true, even if I could not admit them then. I did not want things to change and I spent every waking minute trying to keep them the same. I missed out on a lot in the process. I promised his father I would call him but I do not know if I will or not.

Indigo sighed, holding her pen to her chin, and looked at the picturesque Southern autumn sky of reds and oranges. She sat on the back-porch steps, trying to think of what else to write in her last "AK" entry to her Iko before Daddy Douglas came home, until Magnolia came down the steps in a flowing African dress, she called a bobo.

"Jumbo, Go-Go!" she greeted Indigo

"Jum what?" Indigo giggled.

"Greetings, sister!" Magnolia continued, dismissing Indigo's teasing.

"How come you never took an African name when you went to Africa, Magnolia?" Indigo asked curiously.

"Well, where did that come from? If you must know, I want to always be able to embrace those things that are intended to keep me enslaved. Then they have no power over me," Magnolia explained in a serious tone.

"Did Africa teach you that?" Indigo asked, half-teasing again.

"No, dreaming of freedom taught me that!"

"It taught you to change the whole way you look at things so that it can't upset you? Like your name refers to a white flower and Madear's...whatever," Indigo started to say but thought better of it.

"That's what dreams will do for you," Magnolia added, putting her arms around her sister's shoulder.

"I used to blame Martin Luther King and his dream for everything bad that happened to the family," Indigo confessed, half-smiling.

"It wasn't him really I was blaming. It was just the way people reacted to his dreams and his death, changing and turning their lives inside-out. It was like that dream of his had some kind of power over people that made them do things," Indigo tried to explain.

"It wasn't King's dream that gave the people the power. They had the power all along. Everyone has it. It swells up inside of you until it has to come out or burst. King's dream was just the catalyst that unleashed the power. It was the fuel that ignited the change. You got it in your chest, remember? Iko. Everybody knows when that chest of yours swells up, you are determined to make a move. When King died, masses rose and the world changed. Even the Douglas world changed. It had to or we wouldn't have survived to be the people we are today," Magnolia explained, kissing her sister on the forehead.

"Come to think of it, King's dream and my Iko started worrying me about the same time," Indigo reflected.

" The fuel unleashing the power," Magnolia reiterated.

The paperboy came barreling around the dirt-filled circular driveway on his bicycle, interrupting their conversation. The evening Tallahassee *Democrat* landed in the middle of Magnolia and Indigo's shoulders.

"That paperboy doesn't care where he throws the newspaper," Indigo complained.

"It doesn't matter, at least we get the news. In parts of the motherland the written word doesn't come for weeks," Magnolia offered, grabbing the newspaper, pulling the green rubber band off the rolled paper and putting it on her hair hanging down her back.

She unrolled the newspaper and looked at the front page. She pointed to the leading headline and nudged her sister, saying, "More fuel, Sister Go-Go!"

The headline read:

"President Carter calls for a National King Holiday."

Indigo read the headline and took a long deep breath. She felt her "Iko" rising in her chest. They nodded and placed their arms around each other's shoulders, walking up the back porch steps together, knowing their world would be changing.

Author's Notes

Much of the motivation for writing "Panhandle Dreams" came from Martin Luther King's powerful " I have a Dream" and "I have been to the Mountaintop" speeches and how people particularly in the Florida Panhandle reacted to hearing them. The names of the all chapters in "Panhandle Dreams" are paraphrased from those two speeches.

Chapters 1 and 4 through 11, 16 through 23 and 25 through 27 are paraphrased from Martin Luther King's "I've been to the Mountaintop speech.

Chapters 2,3, 12 through 15 and 24 are paraphrased from Martin Luther King's "I have a Dream" speech.

Chapter 3 Page 27 "And we just went on before the dogs and we would look at them; and we'd go on before the water hoses and we would look at it and we'd just go on singing, "Over my head, I see freedom in the air." is an excerpt from Martin Luther King's "I 've been to the Mountaintop" speech.

"Hevenu shalom alechem" in Chapter 5 page 47 is an excerpt of a Hebrew song that translates: "O God, we beacon you to send your peace upon all of us." The author is unknown.

About the Author

Gwen Parker Ames is a native of Tallahassee, Florida. She holds a doctorate in education from Columbia University, Teachers College. She lives in New Jersey with her husband and son.

0-595-23473-9

Printed in the United States
707800005B